OVER**EXPOSURE**

Kane gasped, losing consciousness briefly. Blood poured profusely from his wound. A noise sounded to his right—he scrabbled desperately away from it over the concrete floor. There was no time to use his own weapon. Again he heard the silenced shot just before he felt the white-hot barb of the bullet tear through his thigh. He grunted and jerked backwards as another spasm of pain rocketed through him. He was now fully exposed to his attacker.

THE HOLTZMANN PLAGUE

A Novel by
GARETH HARVEY

HarperPaperbacks
A Division of HarperCollinsPublishers

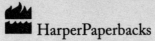

HarperPaperbacks
A Division of HarperCollins*Publishers*
10 East 53rd Street, New York, N.Y. 10022-5299

Copyright © 1996 by Gareth Harvey
All rights reserved. No part of this book may be used or
reproduced in any manner whatsoever without written
permission of the publisher, except in the case of brief
quotations embodied in critical articles and reviews.
For information address HarperCollins*Publishers*,
25 Ryde Road, Pymble, Sydney, NSW 2073, Australia

ISBN 0-06-101201-7

HarperCollins®, ®, and HarperPaperbacks™
are trademarks of HarperCollins*Publishers* Inc.

A paperback edition of this book was published in 1996
by HarperCollins*Publishers* Pty Limited (Australia)

Cover illustration by Ben Perini

First HarperPaperbacks printing: June 1997

Printed in the United States of America

Visit HarperPaperbacks on the World Wide Web at
http://www.harpercollins.com/paperbacks

10 9 8 7 6 5 4 3 2 1

For Lena

ACKNOWLEDGMENTS

I would like to thank three people, all women. My wife, Leanne. My friend, Kim Anderson. My editor, Louise Thurtell. Without them this book would not have been written.

But there are two lifelong companions who bear the lion's share of responsibility for all this—my parents, Dawn and John Harvey.

*". . . at Majdanek the living envied the dead.
Death is the natural condition of the Jew—
der unmenschliche Jude!"*

Statement from the dock by Jurgen Adolf Holtzmann, Commandant, Majdanek Extermination Camp, 1940–1944. Executed for crimes against humanity, 5 August 1965, Israel.

BOOK**ONE**

CHAPTER**ONE**

Inside the commercial Boeing 727, Colombian Air Force Captain Rodríguez Calvo stared out at the armoured personnel carriers parked by the runway and the soldiers lolling nearby. He knew most of the men were poor *campesinos* drafted into the army and not averse to bribes from the *narcoterroristas*. In Colombia, he thought sadly, we fight the enemy within.

He glanced back at his fellow passengers, their faces set in stern expressions as Avianca Flight 87 taxied along the grey tarmac of El Dorado airport. In a few minutes the city of Bogotá would fall away beneath them as they flew north towards Medellín over the Andes. Calvo plotted the flight plan in his mind, north-west over the lush valley of the Magdelena River.

In more peaceful times Calvo had taken his wife and children to the Magdelena Valley to visit his brother's *hacienda*. He recalled driving past Pablo Escobar's huge ranch and private zoo—*Hacienda Napoli*—its massive entrance gates topped by a single-engine Cessna that had supposedly smuggled *El Padrino's* first cocaine load to the *norte-americanos*. Odd, thought Calvo, remembering how he too had peered in excitement with the children; Colombians had no judgement on cocaine then. As his mind drifted further back, he remembered Escobar even being one of Medellín's parliamentary representatives. Back when Jorge Holtzmann and the *Brigada Fascista* had been just an itch in Colombia's rump, he thought grimly.

Calvo and his superior officer in *Operación Narcotraficante*, Colonel Alberto Tivera, had requisitioned the entire first-class section. Calvo looked at his bodyguards. They were nervous. Probably more afraid of flying than being shot! He smiled. He too hated others doing his flying, but it was more a matter of *machismo* than anything else; nearly all Avianca pilots had flown first with the Colombian Air Force.

He sighed and peered out of the window again, thinking of his children. What sort of life had he given them—they could not go to school, could not play, could not even visit their mama's grave without a squad of soldiers to escort them. All because their papa led search-and-destroy missions against the *narcoterroristas*. As the aircraft inched towards its take-off position he was washed by a wave of misery. The Andes loomed before him, as did his life and his struggle. This war will go on forever or be lost, he thought, staring blankly out, wishing that the flight and his corrosive inactivity would soon be over. At least now, he reminded himself, the Americans are fighting with us.

"Chief bad guy? Jorge Holtzmann, aka *El Jefe*, or, closer to the truth, *El Monstruo*—The Monster," thundered General Marlon Stone.

Kane paused outside the briefing room as the big Marine commander he had known since Vietnam delivered his initiation speech to the latest batch of Operation White Storm recruits. Although President Kirkland's anti-trafficking task force had been set up with much haste and little thought—apart from political expediency—Stone was determined to gather the best and brightest from all participating federal agencies and departments, then make them better and brighter. Some of his audience were military; the rest were CIA, DEA, FBI or Justice Department. Didn't matter where they came from, mused Kane, as far as the General was concerned they were freshmen.

"Holtzmann runs the cocaine show in Colombia the same way our dear departed amigo Pablo Escobar did in the eighties and the Cali boys did up till a few years ago. But Holtzmann is bigger, smarter, and much, much richer. First we knew of him was in the seventies as a would-be revolutionary. Called himself *El Jefe*—The Leader. His organisation, the *Brigada Fascista,* was modelled along Nazi lines. Hardly surprising—"

A few chuckles sounded through the room. CIA probably, thought Kane, filing their faces for future reference.

"You should all know just what a serious, grade-A fuckup our man Holtzmann is. But I'll remind you anyway," said Stone after a pause. "His father? Jurgen Adolf Holtzmann—Nazi war criminal. He ran the Majdanek concentration camp in Poland. Israelis tracked him down to Medellín in the sixties, a few years after they nabbed Eichmann. He was executed in Jerusalem in '65. Our man is the son of that sonofabitch."

A buzz started up amongst the audience.

"In the seventies, and eighties, Holtzmann Jr. was running protection for the Medellín Cartel as well as blowing up his fair share of government installations. Then—we figure—when Escobar and his boys bought the farm, the *Brigada Fascista* started in on cocaine themselves. The Cali Cartel had the marketing structure for a while into the early nineties, but Holtzmann had the brute strength. By 1995 we saw the first indications that we were dealing with a new supercartel in Colombia. Today the Sobrecartel controls most of the cocaine coming out of the South American subcontinent, and Holtzmann is sitting on top of the heap. We're up against a forty billion dollar a year industry—"

Stone caught sight of Kane at the door.

"Kane!" He exclaimed, too late for Kane to duck away.

"Ladies and gentlemen, Colonel Tom Kane, your superior on all field operations and interrogations." Stone eyed the room.

"Colonel Kane is currently responsible for our one piece of good luck in this bad-luck outfit."

Kane knew it was his cue to speak, and he battled the fatigue of a long day to do so. "Three weeks ago we captured Carlos Guela," he began. There was an intake of breath amongst those in the know. Guela was a big fish, a senior member of the Sobrecartel.

"He was holed up in Rio. He got careless and we got a tip off. Picked him up and brought him to Miami—"

Stone broke in. "Sounds simple doesn't it?" he laughed. "You should all be aware that the Argentinians do not know of this operation, nor will they. When and if Guela comes to trial he will have been tracked to Miami and arrested on US soil."

Kane nodded and finished. "Yeah, that was three weeks ago. So far it's taken two weeks for Guela to go cold turkey—yes, he is a user—and a week for him to bore the bejesus out of anyone who comes within earshot. Our problem is that Guela is on the out with the Sobrecartel, he's a loose canon. I don't realistically expect him to lead us directly to Holtzmann. We're trying for Ernesto Cortez, who used to run Guela's operation in the US before switching to Holtzmann and disappearing. We're trying," he repeated and looked at Stone.

And getting nowhere, his expression said.

"Thanks, Kane," said Stone, "now go get some sleep."

Kane raised his hand wearily to his forehead and left.

The huge plane finally reached its take-off position, wings flapping slightly in the stiff cross-wind. At the rear of the cabin a mother calmed her young daughter. The massive jets began to scream.

Anxious faces pressed against the terminal window in Avianca Hall. Those crowded at the glass were mainly peasants, to whom Flight 87 was not merely the evening commuter shuttle between Colombia's two largest cities, but a major journey, a farewell to family and loved ones. Many waved vainly at dots in distant windows they imagined to be their fathers or husbands, sons or daughters. None of them paid any heed to the lone figure on the tarmac below.

Slowly the aircraft began its run down the steel grey strip. Those watching forgot their apprehension, staring in awe at the magnificence of the sight as the Boeing's nose lifted and it soared skyward, effortlessly meeting and conquering the buffeting winds.

From the tarmac, Avianca supervisor Juan-Carlos López glanced up at the terminal window, then wished he had not. He thrust his hands deep into his overalls and walked away disconsolately. He had done the job he had known he would one day be asked to do. He'd always hoped he would die beforehand. Now his children would look upon a different father. He trudged across the tarmac and his eyes could not tear themselves away from Flight 87's rise into the setting sky.

The plane was over the *barrios,* turning sharply to the left to avoid the city proper, when López reached his office. Entering, he was too downcast to notice his secretary was missing. He did not even see his killer as his head was split apart by the burst of automatic gunfire.

The young *sicario,* his job done, walked calmly outside and jumped onto the back of a waiting motorcycle.

"*Esta bien?*" asked his partner. The killer nodded and lit a cigarette. It was the way. They sped off, looking like a pair of schoolboys on a joyride.

Above the city, Flight 87 droned on towards the north. Heads were turning from the observation window in the terminal building when the glinting aircraft tore apart with a soundless flash. Amidst the first rolling echoes of the explosion, those who had come to say farewell were spared nothing of the manner of their loved ones' deaths.

The 140 men, women, and children on board the aircraft had no chance as the Semtex plastic explosive detonated deep within the nose of the giant jet, shredding the cockpit and those in it.

Some passengers, like Captain Rodríguez Calvo and his men, died mercifully from the force of the explosion. For those further back in the aircraft there were scant seconds of conscious horror as the plane cartwheeled through the sky. Many were torn to pieces by the maelstrom within the cabin or sucked to their deaths through the ripped fuselage. But some, strapped to their seats as they had been instructed to do, endured the terrible plunge and died only when their section of the aircraft finally slammed into the distant Andean mountainside.

Pandemonium broke out inside the terminal building as black smoke spiralled into the sky.

Kane braked as the car in front swerved wildly. "Asshole!" he swore under his breath, watching it disappear into the blinding rain. Sheets of water billowed towards him. The lights of downtown Miami were all but invisible as Hurricane Marcy ripped up the Florida peninsula. Kane slowed the car as he neared his exit. It was not the fastest way home but it took him through the Row; his daily judgement on the world and how little he had paid it back.

The day had been futile. Guela had been at his arrogant worst. He pictured the rat face that had once been handsome and the frustration it was causing him. As he turned into Breaker Street, the main thoroughfare of the Row, he saw the first of its inhabitants huddled under a shop awning, a blanket only slightly obscuring the telltale glow of a crack pipe. He drove on slowly. The addicts knew his car, had long ago assumed he was a cop, but he had never picked them up and they had stopped being scared of him. There were fewer out this evening. The rain had driven most into the flophouses they called home. That any were out at all was a testament to the power of cocaine. Utterly degraded by their addiction, they did not care about anything else.

He gazed in pity at the few who glanced at him with their flared, dying eyes. *What's your excuse, man?* they asked him silently, seeing through the armour of his position. His hatred grew, as it always did. *I'm losing.*

Ahead, a girl tottered onto the street and stood unsteadily for a moment. As his headlight beams fell upon her she raised her face and looked at him, water streaming from her hair. Kane inhaled sharply. *Damn!* He hadn't seen her for a month and she'd been dying. Her face stared at him in hopelessness. Her spirit had gone; all that burned behind her eyes was need. The girl broke from the light and stumbled away.

Kane swung the car away from the Row and towards civilisation. Palm trees signalled the end of no-man's-land, silhouettes in the storm, their dark mop-tops shaking crazily in the wind like giant dandelions. Pulling his remote control from the glove compartment, he pushed the button. The steel gate swung open and he inched the car into its allotted space. He cast his eyes around the garage; his Beretta chafed beneath his coat as he walked towards the elevators. One night the Sobrecartel might come for him, so he endured and obeyed the "procedure", but it annoyed him. Reaching his floor, he scrutinised the corridor and then his apartment. Nothing. When he was finally able to fall onto the sofa, his relief was profound—not because he was still alive, but simply because another day had ended. He flicked the television on and a WorldNet anchor smiled falsely as she appeared out of the grey. It was too late for Lena; she was on prime-time now; a star. He thought about her as he stared dully at the news—an update on Hurricane Marcy.

Outside the clouds split with thunderous ferocity while inside he watched the pictures of their destruction. He felt like a drink.

The bottle was almost finished. *Elysian Grande Annee* cognac; one of only a thousand bottles distilled each year. Jorge Holtzmann swallowed another generous mouthful as he listened to the evening broadcast. Bogotá's main radio station was routed through to his mountain bunker above Medellín by powerful antennae hidden around his compound.

A smile crept across his face as he noted the time. He took another draught of cognac and stroked his dark beard as the alcohol slunk into his body. His anticipation was fuelled by the burn of the brandy in his chest. Sighing deeply, he reached forward to dribble more cognac into his glass, then checked his watch again. Soon his reply would be complete. *To your foolishness, President Vargo!* He raised his glass to the lamp and waited in the solitude of his bunker.

The radio music was finally interrupted by the announcement. "Avianca Flight 87, *en route* to Medellín from Bogotá has just crashed, apparently killing all on board. The cause of the accident is unknown but witnesses report hearing an explosion and authorities have not ruled out sabotage. There will be more news . . ."

He reached for his SatCom digital telephone and punched the number.

"Radio RCN," came the answer.

"Flight 87?" said Holtzmann slowly.

"*Si?*"

"Responsibility is claimed by *Brigada Fascista.* You will receive a full statement in due course. This is Holtzmann!" He cut off the call. A few minutes later, a nation and its people realized that the Sobrecartel had given its brutal answer to Colombia's latest treaty with the USA. The country was convulsed by a fear it had not felt since the darkest days of Escobar nearly a decade before. It was a declaration of total war.

Holtzmann warmed the carved crystal glass resting in his hand. Briefly exultant, the stare of his father's portrait jagged his consciousness. There were greater matters to consider. He stood and walked briskly into his communications room. *What have you to report, Kumarov?*

"Tom?" It was "Hog" Collins on the phone, one of the few involved in Operation White Storm who knew Kane well enough to use his first name.

"Yeah?" Kane mumbled. The TV was still on, flickering painfully before his sleep-stained eyes.

"Sorry, m'boy, but you'd better haul ass—the nasties have knocked an Avianca jet out of the sky." Collins' voice was controlled, but only just. "Stone's ballistic. Wants to work on Guela some more. Correction, friend, wants *you* to work on Guela some more. Tonight. He's in a deal or drop mode."

"Hell," mumbled Kane, dragging himself to his feet, thinking groggily. "Hog—keep Stone away, might be able to use his flameout. I'll be there soon."

"You piece of shit!"

Stone was white-hot, but on-cue. His voice erupted into the interrogation room at the time appointed.

Three A.M. Kane gave it passing thought as, for a bloodshot second, his eyes met those of Carlos Jesús Guela.

"One hundred and forty people!" the big general's voice boomed through the speaker. "*Your* miserable fucking friends have blown a hundred and forty fucking people out of the sky!"

"So what, motherfucker?" Guela's sneer split his thin face. "*Gringo* motherfucker!"

Kane smiled. Guela had no idea what Stone looked like.

"Hey? *Gringo* asshole!" the one-time king of Medellín taunted again.

There was a long pause, and Kane breathed deeply.

"Guela!" Stone exploded through the intercom again. "It's over! You and the murdering scum you're still protecting can go to hell and I'll write the fucking ticket!"

There was no reason in his voice. It was unfettered middle-American fuck you finality. It was a voice that had plagued the remnants of the Medellín Cartel—the Ochoa brothers, Rodríguez Gacha, and Pablo Escobar—to their ignominious deaths. It was a voice, Kane hoped, that would ring in Jorge Holtzmann's nightmares and those of his cronies in the Sobrecartel as they sat out consecutive life terms.

But Guela was unmoved by it. Some fragment of his mind beneath the cocaine destruction was still convinced that he was beyond the law, beyond justice. He shook his head slowly, arrogantly.

Suddenly the door was flung open and Stone launched into the room. Angered, he looked even more intimidating. In the split-second before his massive hand crashed into Guela's face, the Colombian looked in shock at Kane.

Yes, Stone is loco. Kane stared back impassively. *But he is our loco.*

Guela raised his head from the blow and sat very still as Stone's fury continued to wash over him.

"One hundred and forty *human beings!*"

Kane watched Guela's expression carefully. Watched the tics of fear and rage beneath the arrogance. The confusion. Even though Guela would probably end his life as a convict, he was used to respect. And as Stone's wrath ebbed, Guela's own grew. His lips tightened angrily as he spoke, almost hissing.

"Nothin' from me, motherfucker!"

Kane's eyes met Stone's. *Enough,* they said. His superior dropped his head slightly, glaring at Guela. A final low growl escaped his throat and he turned and left the room. For several minutes afterwards there was silence. Guela looked away from Kane, his eyes twitching and his tongue flicking over dry lips.

"I tol' you about Holtzmann!" he muttered finally. "You just din't listen! That fuckin' . . . ! If you really hearin' me you know is true. Holtzmann is me—he tryin' to be me! Know me, you goin' know him! Man, I was startin' with cocaine and then, you know, some kinda revolution. While him . . ."

Kane shrugged and stared at him without expression. *Reality time, Guela.* They were finished with him. One way or the other.

"Guela!" The speaker barked and Guela's head jolted up. It was Stone again—a chilling waver in his voice. "This is the end, Guela. You will help us get to Cortez!"

Guela looked around slowly. This time he was shaking as he squinted into the glass of the one-way mirror to face the disembodied voice.

"If you do not help us get to Cortez before Holtzmann throws him a lifeline," Stone's voice rang out, "you will be the first offender to be tried under President Kirkland's new federal trafficking laws. That means a certain death penalty, Guela."

"You lyin'," said Guela unconvincingly. He'd been locked away from the outside world for three weeks. "What this fuckin' law?"

"A lot of folk in this country want to see people like you fry, Guela. You and your friends just gave the President the best reason he could have. The new law will be announced tomorrow; America's response to the bombing of the Avianca flight," Stone said. "In States which allow it—and you really picked well in that department—there will be a mandatory death penalty for anything over one hundred keys.

So far we have you stone-cold in Texas for five hundred keys; South Carolina, two hundred; Florida? New Orleans? You've got a lot of dying to do, Guela."

The Colombian slumped back in his chair, looking to Kane for some sort of reassurance. There was none in the ice-blue eyes which gazed steadily back at him. Instead, Kane withdrew two sheets of paper from his coat and handed them to Guela. Both bore the same unmistakeable letterhead. Both were written in Spanish. The Colombian stiffened as he read them. The first confirmed the new federal legislation. The second was signed President Warren C. Kirkland and addressed to Guela personally. When he finished he stared fearfully at Kane, holding a document in each hand. One promised death, the other—reprieve in exchange for cooperation.

"In other words, Guela," Stone's voice growled suddenly through the speaker, "deal or die."

"*Señors,*" mumbled Guela, gasping for breath. "I need an attorney." He peered at the glass, then at Kane.

"Sure, Guela," said Kane after a moment's pause. "And the minute an attorney gets a hold of you, you're public. We won't be able to do a thing for you. Nor will the President." He reached over and took the papers from Guela's shaking hands.

"You want an attorney, you got one," Kane's eyes bored into him. "We keep these and you take your chances. But then you like to gamble, don't you?"

"They jus' papers, man." Guela's voice was thin. "Jus' damn . . ." The speaker hummed ominously, heightening the sense of a man deciding whether to bargain for his life, with his life. Kane was silent. Guela sighed deeply and closed his eyes. When he opened them he was trapped by Kane's unwavering stare.

"Oh, man . . ." Slowly he extended his manacled hands and took the papers back from Kane.

"I can think of only one place you can find Cortez," he

muttered. "An' if you do find him at this place he goin' to know for sure and for certain that it is me who tol' you. An' when they find me, whenever that might be, you won' need no laws to kill me. I will die the death of a—"

He drew breath sharply, crushed by his now utter dependency on the man who had captured him. The one-time drug lord and member of the Sobrecartel, whose rat cunning had deserted him only when he had become addicted to his product, knew he had no choice.

"But I will tell you . . ."

He got off the chair, his manacles jangling, and bowed as if in prayer. Resting his head in his hands, he gripped his hair, once long but now cropped short.

And from that strange crouched position he began to speak slowly and deliberately.

"Strike one!" Kane punched the air as he joined Stone behind the glass. Guela had finished and had delivered as promised. "So the President signed?" he grinned.

"Son," Stone turned slowly in the dim light of the observation room. "You're good, but I bet even you haven't got a full enough imagination to figure out what I'd do to see Holtzmann in that room."

"Try me," Kane chuckled.

"It was like you said, you crazy sonofabitch," Stone replied. "Not hard to get a signature on that piece of gilt-edged bullshit! Federal death penalty, my ass—from a *Democrat*?"

Both men laughed. Through the mirror, Carlos Guela rocked slowly on his chair.

CHAPTER**TWO**

It was midmorning in Moscow and Gyorgy Kumarov worked feverishly, his pale hands trembling as he checked and re-checked the cultures in the petri dishes. His eyes scanned the flickering monitor of the electron microscope.

"Da," he whispered, his entrancement so complete that he failed to hear the repeated plea in his ear.

"Comrade Gyorgy," the assistant tried again. "Telephone. It is *him!*"

At this, the slightly built Russian rose angrily, strode to the telephone and snatched the receiver.

"Yes?" he answered, his shrill voice piercing the hushed silence of the lab. The usual tirade began in his ear; always threatening, always demanding. Kumarov barely listened as he stared out at the gloomy streetscape of Kutusavsky Prospekt.

"Yes, *Señor,*" he said finally. "Soon, soon. I will send you a report."

So many interruptions! he growled to himself as he replaced the receiver and walked, not to his precious cultures, but to his computer and the tiresome job for his patron.

Plague cultures NW 23–50, he began typing. He begrudged every second that took him away from his real work.

Kane was woken by the silence. The hurricane had moved on and the quiet was chilling. He sat up, rubbed his eyes and glanced at the clock. *Five-thirty!* He'd had a scant two hours' sleep but knew it was all he would get. Exhausted, he lay back and faced the day to come. The name Ernesto Cortez throbbed in his head. He flexed his hand in the dimness; its muscled silhouette, testimony to the hours he spent on the range.

The glowing numbers on the clock were insistent, sunrise smudged the horizon. His nights had become nothing more than punctuation marks between endless days—too brief for any respite, but long enough to haunt him with nightmares. Rising, he dragged on a pair of swimming trunks and padded to the elevator. There was no one at the pool. He switched on the flow and dipped gingerly into the water. The sky was still dark above the perspex roof and, as he swam against the rush of water, he had the feeling of a vast weight on his back. He stroked methodically in the flow, trying to work unwilling muscles and a tired mind. Then he dressed, showered and was back in his car.

Today we come for you, Cortez. His hands gripped the wheel as if to crush it and his knuckles whitened.

The final page of the facsimile, scrambled at its source and sent via the secure SatCom digital satellite network, fell from the machine. Holtzmann flicked through the sheets of paper, snorting as he saw it was just a routine report from one of his "bankers."

In the shadows stood his bodyguard unit from the *Brigada Fascista*. Apart from them he was alone in his bunker. His needs had always been spartan, his vast wealth had not changed that.

Holtzmann's Sobrecartel was a highly feudal organisation

bound by fear. At each level, mules, traffickers, street dealers and money launderers skimmed as much as they dared. The rule for these underlings was simple; take too much and die. Those at the higher levels of the cartel were also beholden by fear to Holtzmann. They shared in the torrent of money flowing upwards, but Holtzmann took the most—and had amassed a fortune greater than that of many Third World nations.

He tossed the papers onto his desk. The figures before him would have been unimaginable to most, but to him they were incremental additions to the ledger. "Where are you, Kumarov?" he said, glaring at the fax machine.

Then, as if answering his command, the machine chirped. Holtzmann's eyes glinted as he saw the typeface. It was him. He snatched the first page and began reading as a further two pages rolled gently from the machine.

"Good," he muttered after a time, forcing himself to take the most optimistic view of the report. But his teeth ground at how slowly Kumarov's work was proceeding. It had taken so long to reach this point, so much planning, and now the entry of the Americans on the side of Colombia's *Operación Narcotraficante* was threatening everything. Kumarov would need to be pushed. He laughed aloud, and his bodyguards straightened in fear. Too often when *El Monstruo* laughed, other men screamed.

Again his eyes were drawn to his father and the photograph which as a younger man he had spared no expense in tracking down, restoring and enlarging. Draped on either side of the gilded frame were the banners that had once adorned the entrance to the Majdanek Extermination Camp.

His father had been proud of his service to the Reich. And he had been proud of his son. Holtzmann's eyes glistened with the past, and—perched on the edge of his ultimate purpose—his childhood opened to him. Their life in

Antioquia with its tin shacks and dusty soccer fields; his father's stories about the Reich.

He had grown up as determined to play a role in the future as his father had played in the past. Holtzmann met his father's eyes with steely resolve. *You will have your vengeance!* The certainty washed through him and his eyes narrowed as his hatred grew; the hatred that had been born when they killed his father. The hatred that had grown when he deserted his *mestizo* mother and ran with the street gangs; when he became one of the youngest *sicarios* in Medellín. When he forged the *Brigada Fascista,* then the Sobrecartel.

When he became *El Monstruo.*

He turned away from the photograph, his mind seething with what remained to be done, and how little time there was.

Fifteen hundred miles away in Miami, the man responsible for the Sobrecartel's entire North American operation was making love.

Ernesto Cortez looked down at the girl; her face was furrowed with pleasure and she gasped as he increased his tempo. Squealing, her hands reached for his buttocks, pulling him further into her. He held her face to his and watched as she came—watched her convulsing with ecstasy, biting her lip, and driving herself against him. Her back arched as a final spasm seized her then they fell together on the bed.

Outside, the summer noises of street musicians and pedestrians on the promenade drifted up to them on the balmy breeze and they slipped into sensual morning daydreams.

Cortez lived life high in the Sunshine State. Boats, cars, a penthouse—it was far from Envigado where he and Carlos Guela had partied with cheap beer as kids. But Carlos had gone *loco* in the end, and to work for him had become too great a risk. It had not been the money that had convinced Cortez to switch to Jorge Holtzmann, it was the legitimacy. It was a year since he'd left Guela and he did not regret a day of it. No dealing, no fencing, no laundering—just sitting in judgement. He was no longer Ernesto Cortez of course, but what was a name? He had so much power now—the Sobrecartel's main man in the USA, and an American citizen as well. He chuckled within the invincibility of his daydream, before daydream turned to comfortable sleep.

A noise sounded outside and he awoke with a start—a hangover from his days as a dealer. Always paranoid. He shook his head, smiled, and relaxed, falling back beside the girl's perfect body. Her breasts had goose bumps from the sea breeze blowing softly over them. She stirred and rolled towards him. Cortez felt himself harden and moved his hand between her legs. She grinned wickedly but kept her eyes closed, running her fingers along his stomach and then softly downwards. They would make love again, and then sleep. *Such a life!* Cortez thought with satisfaction as he felt her hot breath follow the trail of her hand.

"Cómo me gustas," he whispered, looking down at her. She knew what he expected. The sounds of ordinary people outside reached his ears as the girl's lips engulfed him.

Then the heavy steel door exploded inwards and somewhere behind him a window shattered. Blood welled from multiple cuts on his skin as glass showered over him. He looked up and saw the uniforms.

"Out! Out!" shouted one, brandishing a submachine-gun.

"What the fuck?" yelled Cortez.

"Ernesto Cortez?" came a stern voice from behind the storm-troopers.

"Who?" Cortez screamed. "You crazy motherfuckers!" His brain reeled with shock and indignity. Then, as his eyes flew around the room, he realised his predicament and reined in his fury.

"Who you looking for?" He forced the words through tight lips. "My name is Enrique Altoa."

"Ernesto Cortez," the voice repeated, deadpan.

"I am Enrique Altoa!" Cortez insisted. "You made a mistake here, someone has—"

"Enough, Cortez!" The voice came closer, its authority matching the size of the body from which it emanated. "Colonel Tom Kane, Operation White Storm." The man's eyes glinted with command.

"Man!" Cortez pretended surprise. "You some drug squad or something, right? I deal in cars, man. Enrique Altoa's Classic Lowriders. That's all . . ." He realised how unconvincing he sounded. *Carlos you motherfucker!* his mind screamed. He wiped away the blood trickling down his forehead and winced as he drove the shards of glass deeper into his flesh. "Man," he gasped, "this is . . ."

"Enrique . . . ?" whimpered the girl. She was in shock, oblivious to her nudity and the effect it was having on her captors.

"Get dressed, ma'am," barked Kane. "McVaney—escort her out."

"*Sir!*" the response snapped out.

Kane's icy-blue eyes flashed. "Did you hear me, ma'am?" he said impatiently. "Get dressed."

She mumbled in Spanish and scrabbled for her clothing.

Cortez swung around. "I got an attorney, he—"

"No attorneys," Kane said, looming over him. "No attorneys, no Miranda Rights. Your young friend will be kept for a few days while we explain the situation—your situation—to her. Cortez, this is not happening, never will have happened."

Cortez stared up at him, unable to speak. *Guela!* His heart damned his childhood friend to the devil. Kane smiled as he watched Cortez's anger grow.

* * *

Holtzmann knew it was a measure of the foreboding he had inspired in Kumarov that he had sent a messenger in his place.

"So, Galitsky," he growled at the unfortunate Russian standing before him in his bunker. "You come alone?"

"*Señor* Holtzmann," gasped the man, fearful and utterly exhausted by his thirty-six hour journey from Moscow. "Comrade Gyorgy wished to be here but he has reached a critical stage in his research."

Comrade? Holtzmann rolled the distasteful word in his mind as the man Galitsky continued.

"He also wishes me to inform you that he is very close to your goal. *Very* close!"

"As his report claims," replied Holtzmann slowly. "I also see his new demands." Kumarov was playing a dangerous game.

"*Señor* Holtzmann—in Russia today . . . everything costs so much, everyone . . . they are—"

"Be silent!" Holtzmann's command rang through the bunker. "Does your master understand how much he bleeds my efforts here? I am fighting a war in my country and he would aid my enemy by bankrupting me! He has been *very close* for nearly a year now and still he asks for more." He stood inches from the pudgy Russian, his face sweating with anger, Galitsky's with fear.

Kumarov's man made no attempt to speak but nodded his head vigorously.

"Come," shouted Holtzmann. "Let us speak to *Comrade* Gyorgy. You can inform him of my impatience."

Galitsky scuttled after him into a room containing a variety of radio and telephone equipment arranged in a large horseshoe. The Colombian gestured Galitsky to the single seat within the cluster of electronics, then reached over his shoulder and punched in his SatCom access number, handing the receiver to the Russian. "You have two minutes," he said.

Galitsky shuddered as the brief static gave way to a distant buzz. He prayed Kumarov was at home.

"*Da?*" The voice, heavy with sleep, leapt not only from the receiver but from a small speaker behind it.

"*Veenavat!* It is Misha."

"*Da. Chto za khernya tam u tebya?*" Kumarov responded angrily. Galitsky spoke in rapid-fire Russian but it did not concern Holtzmann. He smiled as Galitsky's ever-more pleading tone battled Kumarov's repeated "*Nyet!*" The man meant nothing to him, Holtzmann thought maliciously, but he soon would.

The Colombian raised his pistol as there was a final, furious "*Nyet!*" from Kumarov and Galitsky fell silent, turning around slowly with the receiver in his hand. Holtzmann stepped forward. Galitsky's downcast eyes glanced up and bulged with sudden terror. His mouth opened to scream but the noise was eclipsed by a roar as a hollow-point bullet tore most of his head from his shoulders.

Holtzmann's guards rushed into the room. Calmly he ordered them to dispose of Galitsky and thoroughly scrub the floor and walls. *Your reply, Kumarov.* Then he strode to the communications desk and grabbed the dangling receiver.

"The money will be transferred in the usual way, Kumarov. But this is the end. And you will visit me personally, with results, or you will meet *comrade* Galitsky again!"

"I will try," the distant Russian replied breathlessly.

"You *will*," said Holtzmann with icy finality.

"I will," responded Kumarov immediately. "And, *Señor?* What of Alexander Simenovich—the test community?"

"As planned," said Holtzmann. "Be swift. And remember," he added, "death is the same, in Moscow or Medellín. There *will* be a result."

He pushed the receiver back into its recess, and walked

out of the room, past the cleaning detail waiting at the door and into the open air. He looked around him, at the weaponry, the *sicarios,* and beyond, across the deep green jungle to the place where he had so briefly enjoyed happiness with his father.

His men looked at him and then quickly away.

Kane stared angrily at Cortez's flashing eyes; eyes that refused to admit their powerlessness, even after four days of interrogation.

"You listening?" he growled, but Cortez remained sullenly silent. After the initial shock of his capture, his self-possession had returned. He had not risen so far by giving in to threats, empty or otherwise. And he knew they were bluffing. This was America. He knew the game. He would endure his captivity until they allowed him an attorney. The lawyers he employed were the best and he had seen how deftly they could play the US legal system. Then? He would find out where this *gringo* lived.

Kane sighed as Stone entered the room. Both men felt the pressure of time passing. Neither had slept more than a few hours since the seizure of Cortez. The Avianca crash had changed the game—and their responsibility within it—not only by its magnitude but its timing. Holtzmann's strike had come so swiftly after the US treaty with Colombia had been signed, so soon after their first joint action with *Operación Narcotraficante*—a raid on one of Holtzmann's jungle laboratories. The treaty and the raid had taken so much diplomacy and investigation, so much planning, so much official permission, so much time—and Holtzmann had hit back with such impunity.

Is the whole country corrupt? Kane wondered bitterly. His weariness made Cortez's insolence doubly mocking. Time to play hard.

"General?" Stone's red-rimmed stare broke from the Colombian as Kane motioned him out of the room. Kane outlined his plan in the heavily guarded corridor, and Stone's massive features slowly creased.

"That's a high degree of difficulty," he breathed when Kane had finished. But he was hooked, Kane knew the signs.

"Lieutenant Marcus!" Stone barked to his adjutant. "White House, secure line."

Marcus snapped to attention and briskly trailed Stone's echoing boots.

Kane walked back into the interrogation room to wait. Finally Lieutenant Marcus returned.

"Sir," he addressed Kane breathlessly. "General Stone wants you."

Scarcely fifteen hours later, Kane and Cortez sat aloft in a Pave Hawk combat helicopter thundering over the vast rainforest east of Bogotá. They were flying low—five hundred feet—for maximum speed. On each side were two identical choppers—the latest in the Sikorsky S–70 series—part of Operation White Storm's contribution to its Colombian counterpart. Each of these air cavalry gunships bristled with air-to-ground weaponry and all carried napalm.

The shading of the endless green below varied but it was not coca plantations they were searching for. "A fine view, Cortez," shouted Kane against the drumming roar, his face set. Holtzmann's deputy could not speak. He had been close to catatonic since earlier in the morning when he had been roused and driven to the Jackson Air Force Base in Miami. From there, two F–25 USAF fighters had flown him and Kane to Bogotá, where the Pave Hawks and a detachment of Colombian Special Forces Marines had been waiting.

Cortez had lost his cool completely when he stepped out onto the tarmac of the military section of El Dorado airport and discovered where he was. Now, an hour into the helicopter journey, he stared down at the familiar territory still trying to refuse what his eyes told him.

It was a risky operation with their best asset, Kane realised, but time had run out; he had to crack Cortez before Holtzmann realised he had been taken. The Colombian turned around, shivering. His eyes met with Kane's, glittering behind dark sunglasses.

As they neared the target, the fear that his enemy might have been warned rose in Kane. If Holtzmann was expecting them, they were flying to their deaths. Security on the operation had been extraordinarily tight. *But this was Colombia,* thought Kane, grinding his teeth.

Stone had told him how grudging the President's authorisation had been, knowing the firestorm Congress would ignite if Kane's plan went wrong. Not to mention the affront to Colombian national pride if word leaked out that a *gringo* had played fast and loose with international law in their country. It would tear the nascent US–Colombian cooperation asunder.

Kane suddenly felt very alone, even surrounded by the crack squad of Colombian Marines. He thought bleakly about other failures. "Desert One"—President Carter's botched rescue of the Iran hostages—loomed high in his mind. Colombian raids on processing labs were usually carried out by fighter jets that could swoop to drop their napalm and soar out of danger in an instant. A hovering Pave Hawk was like a deadly insect, poisonous enough, but also a sitting target for weapons like the new generation shoulder-launched Stinger surface-to-air missiles. The intelligence that White Storm had received left Kane in no doubt that the Sobrecartel had SAMs and the men to use them. But the choppers were critical to his plan.

He stared out, past the quivering form of Cortez, towards the east. They would reach their target in less than fifteen minutes.

* * *

The air hummed with the sound of electric motors and the more distant throb of the generators that ran them. This "mother" laboratory was a village on its own, a loose collection of long low buildings, each housing a process vital to the large-scale production of cocaine. A load of raw coca paste was due and, in the centre of the camouflaged complex, a small wall of the sacked, purified drug was ready to ship out. Each sack was marked with the eagle crest of Holtzmann so it could be distinguished by the buyer and payments split accordingly. Each member of the Sobrecartel had his own such brand.

Chemist Dima Kylushin checked the main solvent bath and directed one of his staff to add more ether to the brew. Despite air-conditioning, the fumes were hideous and Kylushin hurried from the building as soon as he was satisfied that all was in order. He glanced at the massive quantity of cocaine stacked outside the next building. The trucks had better come soon or they'd have to move it in, he thought, looking doubtfully at the sky and the gathering clouds.

Like many of his compatriots, Kylushin was being paid more than he had ever dreamed of in his native Russia. He worked on a week-on, week-off basis, and spent his free time in a remarkable Medellín apartment with a succession of mistresses, champagne, and the best food. It was the life of his fantasies. His wife in Moscow praised him for the hard currency he sent to his family. All she required from him was a yearly visit. The remainder of his time he spent in Colombia.

Two days! he thought, slapping a mosquito. Two days and he would once again be in Medellín, awash in its pleasures. The girls there did anything for money. He felt his fifty-year-old penis harden and reached into his trouser pocket to grasp it, closing his eyes for a moment and visualising what would be done with it when he returned to Medellín.

Then the attack began.

"Colonel Kane, AA gun."

"Take it out!" shouted Kane. The Colombian pilots zeroed in on the danger; 81-millimetre SURA rockets whooshed from their pods.

"Yes!" Kane swore as he saw the Mauser anti-aircraft gun hanging uselessly from its twisted mount below. He did not even notice the absence of a figure which had—moments before—been standing near it. Chemist Dima Kylushin had been all but vaporised.

The surprise of their strike had scored them the Mauser but now the alarm was fully raised in the camp. Men were streaming from everywhere. It was not their number that concerned Kane, it was the precision with which they were manning their posts. Already heavy calibre machine-gun bullets were zinging through the air around them. *Please no SAMs,* he prayed, as the five Pave Hawks maintained formation and returned fire. In the lead chopper, the commander of the Colombian Special Forces unit, Colonel Miguel Vanquero, watched the scene with ferocious intensity and a measure of fear. *What would Holtzmann's response be?* he wondered. This raid was very different—because of the American colonel's presence and that of his prisoner.

"SAM!" Kane snapped. Coolly the Colombian gunner next to him lined up the small figure raising the deadly Stinger missile tube to his shoulder. Within a second the target was blown to pieces by the chopper's 30mm chain gun. Seconds later the Pave Hawks released their napalm and the camp was engulfed in an inferno.

"Okay, Vanquero, get us down," Kane shouted into the radio as the last of the napalm hit the ground.

The Pave Hawks dropped at the outskirts of the camp. Vanquero's men poured out but there were no defenders left. They had either been killed or fled. None had the stomach to fight these regular army troops, the helicopters, and the napalm, despite knowing they faced death for desertion if Holtzmann caught them. Vanquero secured the area. Time was short. Holtzmann operated his own attack helicopters—nowhere near as sophisticated as the Pave Hawks, but equally deadly if they were caught on the ground. Because of the length of their flight they could not afford the fuel to keep a watching chopper in the air, so they moved quickly. Flame-throwers and hand-grenades made short work of what remained of the laboratory complex. A stack of 44-gallon drums of ether, the electrical generators and every piece of capital machinery were dynamited. The machine-gun nests, even the toilets, were destroyed. Then Kane helped the Colombian Marines toss sack after sack of cocaine into the blaze. Nearly a billion dollars' worth of powder was transformed into an evil smelling cloud which rose above the destroyed lab.

Fuck you, Holtzmann, Kane thought as he strode towards his chopper.

Cortez twisted hysterically in his manacles, wailing in Spanish. The attack had unnerved him completely. The four other Pave Hawks began to lift off. Cortez looked up tearfully, comforted by the noise of departure.

Not you, Kane's eyes narrowed pitilessly. It was the moment. He pulled keys from his pocket, and unlocked Cortez's shackles.

"Out!" he yelled above the gathering roar.

Cortez let loose an animal scream.

"You're no use to us, Cortez," Kane bellowed back over the racket of the helicopters. "You've refused to cooperate. Your citizenship is fake. You are a Colombian in Colombia. Stay here!" Already the other Pave Hawks were aloft and his tone was final.

"No!" Cortez shrieked. Terror had taken over completely.

Terror of what Holtzmann would do to him when he found him.

Kane watched the fear peak, then moved forward and jerked Cortez out of the Pave Hawk. Like a terrified beast, the drug boss writhed on the ground, screaming and clawing the earth. Kane leapt aboard and gestured the pilot to fire the engines. The sound of his final hope departing sent the single thought of survival searing through Cortez's blinding panic.

"I will tell you. Please! *Anything!*"

"Cortez!" Kane shouted over the din, as the rotor swung faster and faster. "You've got thirty seconds. That's how much fuel I can spare!"

Cortez grasped Kane's trousers, as though trying to hold him and the chopper to the ground. *Come on,* Kane willed him, *speak or we've all lost.* Breathlessly, but with the precision of a man who knew he had only one chance, Cortez gave up a gem he knew was valuable enough to save his life; Jorge Holtzmann's SatCom digital code number.

Kane stared at him impassively—the Colombian had crossed the line irretrievably. Seconds ticked by. Kane was jubilant but gave no sign of it. The chaos around them magnified the effect of his nonchalance.

"Please!" screamed the desperate man. "There is more, I promise. I promise you."

Kane nodded curtly and Cortez was pulled into the belly of the Pave Hawk by two Marines. As they took off he pushed his head towards the gun-mount to watch the earth and its dreadful carnage disappear below him—the smoking memory of his past life. Then he felt Kane's hands wrap around his shoulders and found himself face to face with his personal monster.

"You were saying?" said Kane.

Holtzmann watched his men stonily as they witnessed the horrible scene. The deserter was still babbling for his life, even though his left shoulder spouted blood. Now the chainsaw was applied to his kneecap, severing his leg. Several men retched, but Holtzmann was immobile with total and absolute fury.

"Such is your loyalty to the *Brigada Fascista*," he spat as the deserter was finally decapitated. His men snapped their arms out in salute and he strode past them, looking each directly in the eyes.

As he entered his quarters even he could not help glancing at the sky. *Soon*, he swore—*soon you will know what manner of war you have started.*

CHAPTER**THREE**

Agent Angela Furness looked at her naked body in the mirror. The training demanded by General Stone for Operation White Storm had sharpened more than her reflexes.

She moved over to the pile of clothes she had bought with government money an hour before. Undercover was the part of the job she most enjoyed. Her clandestine tasks with the FBI before coming to Miami had been limited. Some of her new colleagues were CIA and she'd already determined that when her stint at White Storm was over she was going straight to the "Company" for re-training as a covert agent.

If they'd have her. She sighed as she pulled on her underwear. After fastening the bra around her tanned breasts, she changed her mind and dropped it to the floor, instead putting on the simple halter top without it. This was a career chance and she was going to shine. She swivelled before the mirror, pushing her chest out to test the effect. *Perfect,* she thought. *Perfect dealer's girl.*

She loosened her long hair and it fell across her shoulders to frame her face. Her mouth was large, her lips full and glistening as she pouted into the mirror. "Angie, you shoulda come from California!" her mother had often joked. She stood with her unclad legs apart, hands on hips. Her smile broadened. Quickly she pulled on the scrap of a skirt and positioned it carefully. Her eyes glittered as she saw how little of her was covered. She was shocked by the illicitness she felt. *Like a housewife stripping,* she thought. She knew the role she might have to play and already she was becoming that person. Feeling *her* thrills, *her* turn-ons. Her eyes flickered over the mirror a final time before she slipped on her white sandals and left the change room.

A wolf-whistle greeted her exit.

"Well, Furness!" came the crack. "Who's getting lucky?"

"Not you!" she snapped, not even bothering to turn towards the voice. Pete Dunne had been transferred with her from the Bureau in Atlanta. *He'd been a jumped-up asshole there too,* she thought with distaste, feeling his eyes on her as she walked down the long corridor towards Tom Kane's office.

Cortez! Holtzmann swore again. *Where are you?*

There had been no contact for days now and he needed to talk to him. Holtzmann forced reason into his mind, knowing well why Cortez might be incommunicado—arbitrating a dispute between cartel chieftains who didn't want their arguments to reach Medellín, or judging the fate of some regional boss whose greed had grown too great. And he would no doubt be preoccupied with the arrangements for the massive shipment of cocaine due to arrive in the US in the coming days.

Holtzmann knew the real cause of his frustration at Cortez's silence, and his mind grated with the unpalatable truth. The threat of *Operación Narcotraficante* had driven him deeper underground than he had been in years, and his window out of his mountain bunker—his eyes and ears in the US—was Cortez. He *needed* Cortez more these days and he hated such dependence. His mood darkened even further.

Finally the SatCom receiver squawked in the communications room.

"*Señor?*" came the crackling voice.

"*Están los ángeles contentos?*" Holtzmann replied quickly.

"*Lejos del diablo,*" said Cortez.

But despite the coded reassurance, Holtzmann's paranoia gripped him. It was an instinct he respected—it had served him well and he listened to it as he listened to Cortez.

"Do we have trouble?" he broke in abruptly.

The crackle increased, swamping Cortez's reply.

"*Si . . .*" his voice finally cleared. "Carlos is singing."

Holtzmann shrugged—he'd suspected Carlos Guela would turn traitor.

"They have you?" he snapped.

"No—but they have Salava," said Cortez haltingly.

Holtzmann shrugged again. Roberto Salava was a minor cartel front man, easily replaceable and too far removed from the hierarchy for his capture to be of concern, so Cortez's evident nervousness was disturbing. Holtzmann had a view of those he entrusted to conduct his business in the US—that sooner or later all fell victim to its corruption. Cortez had lived there almost seven years.

"Do you wish to be brought out, Ernesto?" he asked deliberately but without enthusiasm.

"What is your wish, *Señor?*" came the reply. "It may be difficult."

Holtzmann grunted in agreement. "I may have an alternative haven," he said after a pause. "I will advise you. Be careful, keep me informed."

"*Si, Señor,*" came the reply. Their time was up and Holtzmann broke the connection.

He left his bunker and paced through his compound, still troubled by the tone in Cortez's voice. He passed a squad of *Brigada Fascista* men being trained on the new missile battery he had smuggled from China, secure beneath its camouflage netting. He saw that work had finished on his final defence against any ground attack by *Operación Narcotraficante* troops. If they ever got this close, he chuckled maliciously. *Se acabó!*

He kicked the earth impatiently as he turned his mind to the previous day's raid on his laboratory. It was the second within a month. His spies within the government had been unable to warn him, but had at least provided him with the identity of the *yanqui* who led the mission. Thomas John Kane would be dealt with.

Ernesto Cortez was awash with sweat when he replaced the receiver.

Kane gripped his shoulders. "Okay, Cortez, calm down. Just think about what he said. What did he mean by an 'alternative haven'?"

Cortez made an effort to swallow and as Kane watched him, Holtzmann's raspy voice echoed through his mind. "I do not know," gulped the Colombian. "Spain maybe, the Sobrecartel is strong there."

Kane nodded, voicing his thoughts. "He's suspicious."

At this, Cortez looked up and shook his head disbelievingly. "Kane—Holtzmann is *always* suspicious."

Kane stared at him, preoccupied. "Think about it," he said finally, then strode off towards Hog Collins' office.

"Any luck?" he asked as he entered. The CIA man, whose nickname had been with him so long that few remembered when he had been slimmer and plain Steven Collins, was shaking with anger.

"Rules have fucking changed again," he swore in disgust. "The boffins at the NSA just called to tell me they traced the *outgoing* call to us—"

"And?" Kane interrupted.

"*And*, my friend," Collins pushed his chair back, "that's it! Can't trace the other end of a SatCom communication unless Holtzmann makes the call. Even SatCom themselves can't—or won't—tell us."

"Damn," breathed Kane. He'd hoped Cortez's call would turn up Holtzmann's precise location.

"NSA's got every computer this side of kingdom-come searching the ether," said Collins. "It's not going to be easy." He rubbed his forehead. "If you want my opinion, Tom—I think Cortez is shitting us. Surely he knows where his fucking boss lives?"

Kane shook his head dispiritedly. "I don't honestly think so, Hog. He says he hasn't set foot in the country for seven years, and even when he was there he claims to have only ever met Holtzmann once or twice. He was Guela's man, remember. He's given us some addresses in Medellín, but nothing we haven't got already from the local DEA—"

Collins snorted. "Threaten him with another trip home."

"I have," Kane gripped the edge of the desk and sighed deeply. Cortez would have to stay in circulation and Angie Furness would have to be out there with him. Dangerous for both of them and a difficult juggling act with the multitude of law-enforcement authorities also chasing Cortez.

"No option," he said softly.

"You watch out for Angie," Collins replied steadily, reading his mind. "I don't know if she's ready for this."

"I know, Hog," said Kane in exasperation. "And you put the torch to the damn NSA!"

"Will do, chief," growled Collins. He watched as Kane walked away, then reached for his half-eaten hamburger.

Cortez was dwelling on his misfortune at being trapped between two such madmen as Kane and Holtzmann when Angie Furness entered the room. He rose and promptly sat down again, mouth agape. Kane watched him with as much amusement as he'd felt for a while.

Angie smiled; her sheer blue miniskirt hugged her tanned legs. Her midriff was bare, her top tied loosely around her breasts. Her blue eyes and flowing brunette hair completed the effect.

"Agent Angela Furness—Ernesto Cortez," Kane introduced them. "Agent Furness is your cover and you are hers, Cortez. You know what you have to do; go about your business, and as far as we can we'll be clearing the path for you with other law-enforcement agencies. But don't push your luck, Cortez, with us or with the cartel. Be as discreet as you possibly can and do *nothing* you would not ordinarily do. Your calls to Holtzmann will be monitored by us and you will also give Agent Furness a reading on your situation as you feel it. Any sign of danger—to you or to Agent Furness—and we're pulling you out, is that clear?"

Cortez nodded his head.

"You are one of us now, not one of them," Kane continued. "I don't want you getting yourself killed, I don't want *anyone* getting killed. Try to double-cross us and I'll have no compunction whispering the right things in the wrong ears, got it?"

The Colombian nodded again.

"Okay," said Kane softly. "Go!"

Cortez rose and was led from the room by his guards.

"Furness," Kane said gently.

"Sir?" she replied.

"I mean it," he said. "No risks. He's a double-dealing dirtbag, remember. Play the game but stay aware. What I'm asking for here is caution, not heroics, okay?"

"Okay, sir." She smiled. "I know it's not a walk in the park."

Kane stared into her eyes for a minute. She was a good agent and perfect for the job with Cortez. But he sensed her ambition and the vulnerability that came with it, and that worried him.

"Take it slow, Angie," he said finally. "Real slow."

"I will," she replied, then turned and left his office.

It was now a waiting game, he knew. Watching and waiting for Holtzmann.

The torment continues, thought Cortez, driving back to his penthouse with Angie Furness. He looked at her legs cross and uncross, her skirt riding higher and higher, and wondered how he could spend time with this woman and not touch her. He looked away and ran over his cover story in his mind. He had met Furness in Fort Lauderdale and taken her to Hotel Paraiso—a complex of expensive private bungalows. Kane had provided the hotel accounts, complete with room service, dry cleaning and bar bills—all charged to Cortez's American Express card. An involuntary shudder of fear passed through him as he considered the days ahead. He glanced at Furness.

She was smiling.

Early morning. Another night's sleep cut short. The Row shimmered with filthy dew as Kane cruised along it, looking at the sleeping junkies left on the sidewalk by their addiction. The buildings along the Row closed over him and became a tunnel through which he was sucked. Even as he rejoined the freeway, he knew the tunnel would never end—only the nature of its darkness would change. Finally the concrete slab of the building which housed Operation White Storm opened its metal jaw to him and his contemplation was left on the other side of the armour-plated door.

"Sir," a voice rang out, "Saw you on the security cam."

"Dunne," he grunted as Pete Dunne approached his car. "Any word?"

"No problems anywhere, sir," grinned the other. "Angie called in last night. We've been taking good care of her, you needn't have come in so early."

"I'll come in when I damn well feel like it, Dunne," said Kane, walking to the elevator. "Wake Guela."

"Yes, sir," replied Dunne, chastened and trailing behind. "But he's probably up already. Think he's still on his product, the way he sleeps, the motherfucker."

Kane rolled his eyes; Dunne swore a lot and every time sounded like the first.

"Bring him to I-9," Kane said, punching the elevator button.

"Will do, sir, with coffee!"

"Yeah," muttered Kane as the elevator door closed the tiresome Dunne out. He refocused his mind on the nagging question that had awoken him.

Five minutes later he entered the interrogation room as Guela arrived from his cell.

"Fuckin' early, man. What's hap'ning?" mumbled the Colombian, sipping his coffee.

"Holtzmann," Kane replied steadily, lifting his cup to his lips. He swigged a mouthful before continuing.

"A hunch," he said. "What would he consider a safe haven outside Colombia?"

"Haven?" Guela shook his head. "I don't know?"

"Carlos," tried Kane gently. "Think. You travelled—Argentina, Bolivia, Paraguay?"

"Yeah," chuckled the other brokenly, raising his manacles. "An' look where it got me."

Kane laughed too. "You knew him when you had Parson's Cay, before the Sobrecartel. Who were his associates, his friends, back then?"

"*Holtzmann*—friends? He don' have none 'cept the devil," Guela sneered. "Let me think 'bout the Cay . . ."

Kane watched the Colombian carefully as he drank his coffee. Guela—following the example of Carlos Lehder—had at one time leased an island from Haiti during the rule of the military junta and used it as a paramilitary training camp and drugs trans-shipment point. Stories about its visitors were legend.

"Think," Kane urged.

"You think he's plannin' to go somewhere?" asked Guela, his forehead furrowing with concentration. "Think he's tryin' to escape you?"

"Maybe," tried Kane, but Guela laughed.

"You crazy," he exclaimed. "Holtzmann try to *escape* you? That's crazy! An' he's not crazy. In Colombia, everyone work for him—why go some other place?"

"Okay," muttered Kane. "What about one of his men? If Holtzmann wanted to get him out of the heat, away from us?"

Guela's eyes flared. "*Cortez!*" he swore. "You didn'?"

"Relax, Carlos," soothed Kane. "We got him. Just do me a favour and think about what I asked you, okay? If Holtzmann had a reason to send someone somewhere, where would he consider?"

"Nowhere else in South America," Guela replied. "His friends there are his worst enemies. Spain, maybe?"

Kane shook his head. "Yeah, I've heard that. Where else?"

"Germany," said Guela flippantly. "At Parson's Cay he used to talk about Germany all the time, man. His old man you know—we all used to drink to his respec'—he was *some* sonofabitch Nazi! And Holtzmann, he hated the Jews for what they did."

He rubbed his face and swallowed another gulp of coffee. Kane sighed and stood to leave. His waking hunch meant nothing; he knew it was just a way of filling in the wasted hours as he waited for Holtzmann to move.

"Hey, why not Russia?" Guela said suddenly. "Who knows? We all used Russians for the production. We dealt with the mafia there too. Yeah, man, we sold a lot of fuckin' cocaine to the Russians."

Kane looked at him from the doorway. "Take it easy, Carlos," he grinned lopsidedly. "You're thinking, that's good. Anything you come up with will raise your chances at the end of this."

Guela nodded. He knew he was expected to pay his way. "Yeah man, I will try," he said to the closing door.

"The boffins are getting better, Tom." Hog Collins lowered his bulky frame carefully into a chair. "Told me with pride they *can* give us some idea where SatCom calls end up. Traced our last one to the general vicinity of Colombia."

Kane winced as he sipped his coffee, his fourth so far that morning.

"But Holtzmann *has* been calling out," Collins said. Kane sat forward suddenly. "Trouble is," the other continued, "he appears to do all his work by fax. The calls are too short, ten, fifteen seconds at most—NSA says he's using one of the new 86.4K machines."

Kane's brow furrowed.

"Baud rate, Tom—VFF." Collins smiled. "Very fucking fast! What it means is we're still waiting for an old-fashioned phone call. But there *is* something curious about the NSA's traces so far."

"What?" asked Kane.

"Seems a bunch of these faxes are going somewhere in Russia," replied Collins.

"Russia?" said Kane abruptly.

"Don't get excited, Tom," said Collins. "We can't read them—digital and encrypted. Same'll probably go for the phone calls—if he ever makes one. Anyway, thought you'd like to know the latest and the brightest."

"By the way, Tom," he rose to leave, "you do know you look like a piece of shit?"

Kane chuckled. "Get out, Hog. Come back and tell me something I don't know."

"Yes, *sir!*" the other gave an exaggerated salute and departed.

Kane gave his mind over to considering what Holtzmann could want in Russia. It could be the regular bad business of the Sobrecartel. These days the Russians wanted to be more American than the Americans—and that included what they snorted up their noses as much as it did Big Macs.

Or it could be worse, Kane shivered. If Holtzmann was buying as well as selling.

Angie Furness grabbed the phone on its second buzz.

"Yeah?" she mumbled, her eyes focusing on the dim digital display of her watch.

"Kane here. You asleep, Furness?"

"No sir," she sat upright, the sheets spilling from her. *Jesus Christ, nine-thirty!*

"I need to talk to Cortez," he said quickly.

"Yes sir," she replied, still befuddled. "When?"

"Now!" he said.

"Sure, sir." She heard a noise and spun around. Her bedroom door creaked open. Cortez stepped in, grinning. Her eyes narrowed as she slid back beneath the sheets.

"It's Kane, you sonofabitch!" she whispered, with her hand over the receiver. His grin grew wider, and he slowly took the phone. The conversation was mainly on Kane's end. Cortez nodded as he listened.

"I understand," he said finally. He handed the phone back to Angie Furness and padded out.

Angie leapt out of bed and dragged a long T-shirt over her head. Cortez was in the kitchen.

"Coffee, *mi amor?*" he smiled as she appeared.

"Cortez!" she said through clenched teeth. "Bedroom— off-limits, got it!"

"Of course, *Angie,*" he replied. She snorted and stormed back to her room, as angry with herself as she was with him. Half an hour later she rejoined him.

"What was that about anyway?" she asked gruffly.

"Your boss." He handed her a coffee. "He had some more crazy questions."

Angie grunted, annoyed that Kane had chosen to speak directly to Cortez. Her head throbbed from oversleeping.

"You got an alarm clock in this damn apartment?" she asked after a while.

CHAPTER**FOUR**

Pulling away from Miami Airport, the man removed his hat and checked the local time with the cab driver. His passport, marked with the crest of The Netherlands, stated his name as Jan Hoegstardt. The occupation noted on his entry visa was "Businessman." He was neither, though he sounded foreign to the driver, who came from Paraguay.

"Four-thirty," the driver replied cheerfully. "How long you staying in Miami?"

"Two weeks," came the passenger's accented rasp.

"You working?" asked the driver politely.

"Yes," Hoegstardt said.

"Too bad, plenty parties here!" The cab driver replied.

The brute shifted beneath his Italian suit and grunted. Eventually they pulled into a hotel, a moderately priced establishment on Miami Beach and, though his fare came without tip, the driver nevertheless upheld the code of the Yellow & Black Cab Company. "Have a nice day in the Dade County area, sir."

Hoegstardt did not answer, but walked curtly into the small foyer carrying his suitcase.

"Asshole," mumbled the cab driver, screeching his tires

as he exited the hotel's circular driveway to hit the streets in seach of more generous quarry.

"Hoegstardt, Jan D." The nineteen-year-old blonde at the reception desk read aloud from the confirmation slip, smiling as she found a corresponding piece of paper in her registration files. It was the Festival of the Americas, and every arriving guest brought with them the threat of a booking gone wrong and no chance of being put right. She processed the credit card handed to her by the man, noting with passing interest the exotic name of the issuing bank. Then she led Hoegstardt through the ritual of filling his name and address on the registration card, before handing him a room key attached to an ostentatiously large brass replica of the Crown Hotel's emblem.

"There is a parcel for me," he said, his voice no more than a low growl.

"I'm sorry, sir," the receptionist replied, shivering inside as she met his cold stare. "There would have been a note of it on your—"

"There *is* a parcel!" His accent magnified his intimidating tone.

"One moment . . ." she backed into the office behind the reception desk.

The man withdrew a filterless cigarette from his jacket and lit it, exhaling a dense cloud which obscured the plastic "No Smoking" sign in front of him. The cigarette was almost finished by the time the girl returned, smiling with relief.

"Sir." She handed him the large padded envelope. "It was too big for the—" But he had taken it and turned towards the elevators without a word.

Carol-Lee Harris flicked her hair and sighed as she watched Mr Hoegstardt disappear. Then she remade her smile for an elderly couple approaching her with worried expressions on their faces. *Go away!* she willed them.

"Good afternoon sir, ma'am—can I help you in any way?" she asked brightly.

"Yeah, honey, we ordered a *twin* . . ."

Jan D. Hoegstardt grimaced as he entered his room. Tossing his hat and briefcase on the bed, he looked out at the beach below. His real name was Hermann Blucher. He had been born not in Rotterdam as his passport claimed, but in Prenzlau, near the Polish border of his beloved *Deutsche Demokratische Republik*.

When the malevolent East German secret police—the STASI—had fallen with the Berlin Wall, men like Blucher had been released upon the world, becoming part of an invisible army of mercenaries which included former comrades from other Eastern European and Soviet intelligence agencies. For surveillance and murder, former STASI officers were considered the elite. Most had been snapped up by criminal organisations and regimes—Blucher wasn't sure which category described Holtzmann, so total was his power in Colombia. All he knew was that the Latin and South American *mafia* needed Europeans for work in the US and Europe—where their own *sicarios* were too obvious—and that allowed Blucher and his former colleagues to name their price. The lesser cartels in Bolivia, Peru, and Ecuador paid well, but the goldmine was the Colombian Sobrecartel and it used him often.

Blucher pondered the names of his two targets as he paced. Kane and Cortez. Though the Colombian of the pair was technically only a surveillance job, he knew Holtzmann's operation well enough to know that once he doubted the loyalty of one of his own, death was the result. That suited Blucher. His view of the world, and of those who passed through it, was brutally simple and impregnable. For him, killing meant the satisfaction of the two needs he had lost with the downfall of the Party. Money and power.

His eyes drifted back into focus, and fell upon the envelope. Swiftly he tore it open and grinned as he viewed its contents. The Glock 17 pistol and suppressor lay side by side, deadly partners swathed in grease. He lifted the gun reverently from its plastic bag and began to clean it.

Ernesto Cortez lay on the beach, fifty yards from the yellow plastic ediface which greeted those arriving at the Crown Hotel. He peered at Angie Furness through sun-squinted eyes as she lay on her back next to him, smoking and reading a novel. The sun warmed him, enhancing his illicit daydream. He watched her slowly turn the pages, sweat glistening on her oiled body. Beckoning her, he gestured towards the suntan cream. Without demur, Angie placed the book aside and rolled towards him.

Cortez felt himself harden into the warm sand as her hands slid across his back and over his ribs. The muscles in her stomach moved with perfect symmetry and her breasts moved with her arms as she knelt before him. Her hands slid behind his neck and around his shoulders. Impulsively he grabbed her, rolling over as he did, so she was sitting across his thighs. Again she did not hesitate to follow his action and daubed her hands to rub his heaving chest. Grasping her lower back, he slid her further up, until the slips of their swimming costumes met. He pushed into her rhythmically and softly scraped the tips of his fingers beneath her bikini as her perfect breasts moved above his face.

She leant down to him as a lover might and pushed her lips into his neck. Then she hissed into his ear. "Enough!"

He smiled, knowing she would not break from him until he allowed it, and kissed her, pushing his tongue into her mouth. To any observer she appeared to respond, but he could feel the muscles tighten in her thighs and her teeth close on his tongue. He laughed as she squirmed out of his grasp. It had seemed playful but from behind the pages of her retrieved book her eyes flashed at him. With deliberate slowness he rolled over to conceal his erection.

Blucher stared at the beach directly below his room, his eyes drawn to the woman curled on her over-large beach towel, reading. He went to his mini-bar, uncapped a Heineken, then finally opened his briefcase and Cortez's file, withdrawing a single printed sheet and two grainy photographs. Holding them, and a pair of binoculars from his briefcase, he returned to the window. The woman's legs were now apart, joined by a strip of blue bikini. He grunted and filled his mouth with foaming beer. It was an effort to redirect his eyes away from the woman and onto the apartment block where Cortez supposedly lived. He brought the binoculars up and scrutinised the corner penthouse. The drapes were open. His eyes travelled from window to window. Satisfied that it was deserted, he returned his gaze to the beach. The woman had rolled onto her stomach and his telescopic stare ran the length of her sublime body. He sipped his beer slowly and chain-smoked, keeping one eye on the entrance to Cortez's apartment block while in his mind he violated the woman below.

She stayed until the dusk had driven all but her and her companion from the beach. Between glances at the apartment block, Blucher watched them leave. They walked slowly. The woman had thrown a colourful wrap around her body and as she crossed the boulevard with her companion, Blucher saw her face more clearly. Very American, he thought, but still magnificent. The pair walked beneath him and out of his sight, and he returned to his surveillance of Cortez's block. Suddenly they reappeared on the sidewalk, and he glimpsed the man's face as they ducked into the building.

Verdammt! He grabbed his binoculars and trained them on the penthouse, watching as Cortez and the woman entered and passed by the main window, then out of sight. He felt a surge of hatred for the Colombian. It was his common reaction on first identifying a condemned man—but was heightened in this case because Cortez now had something he wanted. Blucher scowled as the pair re-entered the living room and embraced. The woman pulled Cortez by the hands to the rear of the apartment where they stayed out of his sight for several minutes. *Fucking,* thought Blucher angrily. They reappeared, Cortez trailing the woman. She stood at the window.

Damn you! Blucher's eyes narrowed. She drew the drapes, and left him imagining what Cortez was doing to her, and she to him, until he could stand it no longer.

"How many times do I have to tell you, *I* run the show, *okay* Cortez!" Angie Furness shouted, her lips drawn tight in anger. "Any more shit like that on the beach and I'll rip your balls off!"

Cortez flopped back in the leather couch. His braggadocio had returned—Kane seemed a million miles away, and he knew, whatever she said, that Angie Furness was his to play with as he liked, in public. He stood and walked to his bar.

"Drink?"

She glared at him, furious. But another sensation was also there, she could not deny it. A taboo feeling of being out of control, being a man's to do with as he wished—like a whore. She gripped her thighs together. It was deeply illicit and ran counter to her adamant professionalism. But as she stared at his dark-tanned body falling into tight briefs she allowed herself the harmless perversity of thought.

"To our future," proposed Cortez, coming towards her with two drinks.

"May it be mercifully short," she replied, a little less harshly than before.

* * *

Blucher punched the number into his mobile phone. The private digital network which would carry his message was as secure as any used by America's secret agencies.

"*Señor?*" he barked.

"Are you in place?" came the reply.

"Yes."

"Watch Cortez closely. Deal with Kane," Holtzmann's voice was full of menace, a man used to ordering murder.

"Understood," said Blucher.

Thousands of miles away Holtzmann hung up.

Kane reviewed the day, and his scraps of evidence, against his will. The NSA had continued to monitor Holtzmann's faxes but the traces were tantalisingly vague. While unable to detect the exact location with any certainty, the NSA had again confirmed that a substantial number of the communications had been to Russia. The news troubled him. He did not know what it pointed to. Was the Sobrecartel operating in Russia? Was Holtzmann shopping for arms or matériel? The first possibility was the obvious one and the second scared Kane more than he cared to admit. Too much alarmingly sophisticated Soviet weaponry was turning up on the black market.

And then there was the latest trace to consider—an NSA capture on an incoming call to Holtzmann. The boffins were almost certain the call had been routed via the Miami cell of the Southern Digicom network. Kane shifted in his chair uncomfortably—Furness was sure Cortez hadn't made the call and Cortez insisted that there was no other person in the Sobrecartel senior enough to deal with Holtzmann directly. What did it mean? Kane's overworked mind refused to stop.

He hated waiting for Holtzmann to make his next move. He felt cornered. Had his quarry already sensed that there was something wrong? Kane sighed, knowing how tenous his link to Holtzmann was. If the drug lord cut Cortez adrift, the game was lost.

He massaged his temples and stared out at the glittering night. Holtzmann had him guessing, and he knew the answers he sought would not be the obvious ones. Guesses were not enough to act on. He replayed Holtzmann's voice in his mind, visualising him, not with any features, not even as human, but as an evil, opposing force.

His private line buzzed.

"Hi!"

It was her.

"Oh God!" he exclaimed, "Lena . . ." He sank back into his chair. "Where the hell are you?"

"Guess," came her exuberant reply. He looked at his smiling reflection in the office window and imagined her face. Such a serious face. Such a beautiful, serious face. Green eyes framed by a tangle of dark hair. Like a gypsy.

"Miami!" she laughed. "The airport."

"What?" he spluttered, launching forwards.

"Yep!" she replied. "Have to interview the Governor tomorrow morning and back to New York in the afternoon. So how are you, my dear? And are you *officially* here?"

"Yes," chuckled Kane, awash in her wonderful voice. "Believe it or not."

"*Great,*" she said. "I'm amazed to even find you in town. You haven't changed the locks have you?"

"Hasn't been that long, Lena."

"See ya there!" she giggled. "Love you!" He grinned as he put down the phone and pushed back his chair, but the familiar form of Hog Collins suddenly blotted out the doorway.

"Stone wants to brainstorm the NSA data," he said, his rotund face drawn with lines of fatigue. "Now."

"Damn!" Kane growled.

Together they walked wearily towards their commander's office.

* * *

Galena Chagall queued for a cab outside the American Airlines terminal, dealing with the inevitable public recognition as gracefully as she could. As the WorldNet cable network's star anchorwoman, she had learned to tolerate it with good humour. She'd scrawled five autographs by the time it was her turn for a cab. Settling into it, she stared out at the faces staring in. Sometimes it seemed like she *lived* through a TV screen, a roving lens. Her small-town childhood, her Russian emigre parents—the past seemed more real, in many ways, than the present.

The cab pulled onto the freeway and she sighed with pleasure at the prospect of seeing Kane.

Half an hour later, the taxi jerked to a stop in front of his apartment block and she dragged her dangerously overstuffed suitcase to the security door. Opening it with her key, she pushed through to the elevator. Three, four, five . . . the numbers glowed softly, a cool cocoon rising from the tropical heat outside. Swallowing her anticipation, she arrived at his floor. She hadn't seen him for what seemed like ages and thanked fate that they now had twelve hours together.

She turned the key in the lock and sighed with disappointment as she walked into darkness.

"Tom Kane!" she swore softly. Reaching around the door for the light switch, she stepped in over the scattered items of his life, dropping her suitcase and padding around his apartment like a cat, smelling his presence, revelling in the masculine disorder. She left the drapes closed, not wanting reality to confound her enveloping, evolving fantasy. Breathing quickly, she felt like she had when their affair began in Israel four years before. She had been WorldNet's correspondent there and hadn't known who or what he was, only that his ice-blue eyes and deep voice had captivated her from the instant she met him. The sensual, shared nights in her apartment in the Old City had gone on for a year. Then he had disappeared for almost as long, calling her when she had been shifted to New York to host WorldNet's prime-time bulletin. She remembered how instantaneously her passion for him had rekindled. She saw other men occasionally, but none excited her like Kane. He was powerful; he knew her soul.

She pulled her suitcase into the bedroom and unpacked it on the floor. Then she undressed wantonly and stepped into the shower, letting the water run hot and fast onto her body, sluicing in and out of her mouth, cascading down her. She looked down with satisfaction. Her skin was still smooth despite her thirty-seven years, her breasts firm. She ran her fingers over them and down to her thighs, closing her eyes as she moved her hands with the flow of the water. Her legs splayed out and she felt the water rush down each, and between, then she dried herself quickly with his rough towel and pulled a silk camisole and panties from her case. Walking into his living room, water dripping from her hair, she looked around for the makings of a martini. Ten minutes later she realised the futility of her quest, poured an iced water and returned to the bedroom. She switched on the bedside lamp and opened her file on Florida's controversial governor, George Brown. But she could not concentrate. After five minutes she closed the file, lay back on the bed and willed Kane to her.

Outside, Hermann Blucher looked at his watch with annoyance. It was eleven P.M. He had been watching for two hours and no one matching the description of Thomas Kane had entered the building. He grunted. This was going to be a difficult hit, and one in which he would have to take whatever chance presented itself. Static surveillance was a risk he could not afford. With a snort, he started the car and drove slowly away.

* * *

Lena was asleep when Kane finally arrived home. She looked unspeakably beautiful and he resisted the urge to wake her immediately. Instead he showered, washing the accumulated grime of the day from his body and noting with annoyance that he had gained a few pounds over the previous weeks. He stepped out of the bathroom in time to catch Lena's first drowsy glance.

"Evening," she murmured.

The joy of her presence rushed through him. They spoke no words—there was no chance to—as they scrambled into a frenzied kiss. He tore the silk slip from her body as they embraced. She gasped and bit his lip as she felt his flesh against her. They rose on the bed, her eyes staring steadily into his. Then their lips crushed together again. It was almost violent, so fiercely did they want each other. She flung her head back and he pressed his face into her perfumed neck, half-kissing, half-biting her as his hands slid down her back and lifted her onto him.

"Ahhh." Her body thrilled with anticipation as they kissed again and their bodies ground together. "Please," she whispered wildly. "Now!" He entered her suddenly and fully. "Oh God, Kane!" she screamed, bucking against him. There was nothing but the two of them. No sense but the one driving them onwards. Their bodies crashed together with a glorious impact, hurling them into the higher reaches of ecstasy until they tore apart inside and remade themselves as one.

They lay side by side for a time, and her heavy-lidded gaze did not leave his face.

"Hello heaven," she chuckled finally, resting her hands between his legs.

"You have no idea how good your timing is," he murmured, gently stroking the hair out of her eyes and kissing her. She was his immunity from the circling fatigue which waited to repossess him.

"Life rough, Kane?" she smiled, her hand slowly closing on him. "What's new?"

"Rougher than normal, Lena," he said huskily. "I . . ."

She pushed her face into the warm hollow of his neck. "It's okay, Kane. I've still got my security clearance." She felt a ripple of laughter pass through him.

"Should've stayed where you belonged," he said after a time. "You were too good to lose."

"Never regretted leaving," she whispered back. "Only not knowing you when I was there."

Kane grinned in the darkness. Fate was a fickle mistress, he had long ago decided.

"And so what?" he said. "You traded up, or down?"

"Don't know," she relied softly. "TV is crap. All of it. Except my little corner."

Kane let out a mock guffaw. "Your *little* corner?"

"Still little," she replied. "Just looks big to some people."

She kissed him lightly and lay against his chest. "Glad I know you," she said after a while. "You keep me insane. That's why I like war zones. They're like you. Crazy, illogical—"

"And a long way away," said Kane. "Like us."

"When's it ever been different, Kane?" smiled Lena. "We'll never be regular people, and you know what?"

"What?"

"Never want it to be that way," she said. "After Israel? Seeing you again was like nothing I've ever known."

He nodded in the dimness.

"Yeah," he muttered. "For me too."

The thought cast a net of memories over them and Lena stirred against him, her hands massaging him gently. "Mmmm, Kane. Too much talk, m'dear." She rolled fully towards him and he embraced her, kissing her deeply as his own hands began their sensual exploration of her body. His free hand entangled her hair and he felt her breasts against his chest.

"We're always saying goodbye," she whispered, strad-dling his body.

And for how long? Kane wondered, his head spinning with exhaustion and desire.

She rocked back on him, need eclipsing every thought, every question. The air hummed with anticipation and a midnight squall hissed against the window. Their eyes met across the heavy, humid space as she undulated upon his body. His breath came in jagged gulps, pinned in glorious purgatory between desire and its fulfilment. Her eyes re-flected the abandonment he felt. He breathed slowly; time had lost its meaning.

"I love you," she said huskily, and let her tongue linger on her lips.

She watched him watching her as the air arced around them, their only reference the storm intensifying. Her hair fell across her face and shrouded her expression as she moved her legs apart, slipping across him. Her nipples were like open nerves, thrilling at their exposure and the reason for it. Sweat ran in rivulets down her lean body, glistening on her skin, across her breasts, and further down. Her lips fluttered down to his bare torso, her tongue snake-dancing across his stomach. She felt his hands drag down her naked back and curve around her. She moaned as her body was shot through with electric intensity. She glanced up at him as he stroked her, her eyes losing focus.

"Lena," his soft voice surrounded her name. She rose, euphoric, one leg on either side of his pulsing body. The sight of him—revealed—was intoxicating. Her hips began to rock in a ritual of preparation and she felt control drift-ing from her.

"Yes!" she shouted aloud, tossing her head back as she slid upon him. Her back arched as his hands held her breasts and he thrust deep inside her. They spoke harsh-tender words as their sex became more frantic and the storm outside louder. She bit her lip as she rode him, her body joined to his with slippery lips while the rumble of his growl joined the din surrounding them.

She imagined him inside, her muscles gripping him like soft tongues as he plunged through them. He felt the grip of her lips around him as they slid along the length of him, and where they could go no further the heat was like a tunnel through which he hurtled, his body seeking release. But the tunnel was endless, her flesh engulfing his—and the drumbeat of sex boomed through them both. She kissed him with a ferocity which matched his own; pain and pleasure knew no difference. Their bodies writhed together and his lips moved across her face, her ears, her neck, devouring her as she gasped out the rhythm of his body between her legs. She opened herself to him as he entered her again. Her gasps became grunts pushed out of her by the force of him inside her. A barbaric chant. *Living. Dying.* Fighting against the flood of ecstasy as it washed over them. *Living. Dying.* Now it was as if she fought against him, but he was the stronger and she wanted him the more for it as he pulled her down with a violence born of desire and took her breast into his mouth. His arms encircled her tightly and she rode him as she would ride a wild animal into a hurricane, head down, cheek to cheek.

"Aaaahhh!" she growled between clenched teeth as she felt him flow through her and it seemed she was full of him, not just between her legs and the dark caverns beyond, but her whole being. Shuddering, he kissed her, the ricocheting agony-ecstasy still in possession of his body and mind— refreshed by her, reborn in her arms—as they drifted upwards through the lightening layers of sensation, until the first drifting currents of time caught them again, and transported them back into the room in which they lay.

After, as he stared at her gorgeous face, he experienced a moment of pure, adrenalin-driven optimism—a torrid concoction of hope, desire, and love.

He rolled over to her and his hand ran along the length of her.

"Lena—"

"No, Kane," she replied. "No words."

They lay in the thrall of passion until they slipped across the borderline of sleep.

CHAPTER**FIVE**

Papers were scattered around the bunker; the night had nourished him. Kumarov's latest report was good. Very good. Holtzmann had read it as he watched news reports of the protests in Bogotá and Medellín, heaping blame upon the *yanquis* for bringing their war to Colombia. Those he was paying to agitate against America were doing well. The Avianca bomb had shown the depth of his resolve, and Colombia was already losing stomach for the fight. He considered the fate of Colombia's current President: when he was forgotten, he too would die.

Walking to the far side of the room, he pulled a much-used video cassette from the cabinet and slipped it into the machine. He depressed a button and onto the screen flashed images of Majdanek. The pitiful wretches filed before his voyeur's eye, the grainy pictures showing the grandeur of the vision his father had embraced.

"Jurgen Adolf Holtzmann, commandant of the Majdanek Extermination Camp in which nearly one million men, women, and children were murdered . . ." the narrator's voice proclaimed, then his father's own words rang out as he scorned his captors from within the glass cell in the courtroom.

"You cannot judge me—you can only kill me, like a pack of beasts kills a man alone. But my will is the greater. Mine is the will of the *Übermensch*! And it will be again as it was at Majdanek, where the living envied the dead. Death is the natural condition of the Jew—*der unmenschliche Jude!* And death will find all of you—as one!"

Holtzmann rose. He clenched his hands and shut his eyes tightly. The time of his final vengeance drew closer. He stood for a moment in the darkness, in a place where thoughts alone could destroy. "And death will find all of you!" the oath hissed from his lips and spun around him, binding him to the vow he had made decades before, when they had come for his father.

In a daze he crossed the room, stopping before his communications console and dialling Kumarov's Moscow number.

"*Da?*" came the distant response after the second ring.

"Kumarov," Holtzmann rasped. "This is good. I am very pleased."

"Good," replied the Russian. "It has proceeded more swiftly than even I could have imagined."

"You see the value of encouragement," chuckled Holtzmann expansively. "When will you be here?"

"Two days," answered Kumarov.

"You will be met," said Holtzmann. "I am much looking forward to seeing you, finally."

"Yes," Kumarov replied enthusiastically. "And me also. I hope to have more to tell you, but time is—"

"Yes, yes," Holtzmann cut in. "Return to your work, we shall speak soon, face to face."

"Yes, *Señor*. This will be good!"

Holtzmann replaced the receiver gently. 'Soon *Judíos!*' he swore. 'You will wish you had killed me too.'

In a distant corner of the National Security Agency headquarters in Fort George C. Meade, Maryland, an infinitesimally short computer message ordered one of a bank of digital recorders to turn its attentions to another captured satellite feed. The intercepted SatCom call, which had alerted the computer by its access number, was duly logged by the computer, and an electronic memo advising its intercept was sent to the NSA Inter-Bureau Liaison. The authority code for the trace was that of Presidential Task Force Operation White Storm. Within milliseconds a parcel of information was received by a mainframe in Miami, together with an automatic alert order for the relevant White Storm Agent, Steven John Collins.

Lena woke early and watched Kane as he slept, wondering how it would be to do it every day. She smiled at the thought and pushed her body into his. Her warmth roused him and soon the clattering noises of the day beginning outside were eclipsed by the gasps of their morning passion. Their sex was always on arrival or departure. Now it was farewell and from their bodies sprang incoherent sounds of ecstasy. As Lena kissed him afterwards, she wondered, as she always did, whether it would be a month or more, and what Kane would be doing in the meantime.

"You never did get around to telling me why life is rough," she grinned wickedly.

"Holtzmann," the name escaped his lips involuntarily. He looked at her and was seized by the imminence of her leaving.

"Fuck him up, Kane," she said.

"If only," he chuckled. "Like to come back and help me?"

"Not this TV bimbo," she laughed, pulling the sheets from him. "Never was much good at that side of things anyway."

Kane stared at her and suddenly thought of Angie Furness. How much better Lena must have been.

"I bet," he smiled. "The offer's open . . ."

"It would have its distinct up-side," she said, kissing his cheek. "But right now I'm due to interview a bad guy of lesser dimensions, then . . ." She looked away for a second.

"What," he asked, holding her face gently and turning it towards him. "What's next?"

"Armestan, Kane," she replied, eyes down. "I hope."

"Oh, shit, Lena," he exclaimed. "Come on. That's a fuck-ing—"

"Yes it is," she said. "So better me than—"

"Jesus," he moaned, staring at the ceiling as the thought of her amidst what was currently the world's dirtiest war descended on him. "That place has no rules."

"And no reporters either, Kane. *You* lecturing *me* about wars?" Lena laughed under her breath. "And anyway, we may not get in. Might even have time for another visit."

Kane was silent.

"Goodbye again," she whispered, then rose.

Thirty minutes later they were standing on the sidewalk beside a waiting cab. Kane tossed her suitcase into the trunk then turned to her.

"Lena—"

"Please don't worry about me," she whispered, hugging him tightly. "I know about bullets remember."

She kissed him a final time.

"I love you, Kane."

"I love you," he said softly. "Good luck, Lena."

She was gone.

Staring back at him through the grubby cab window, Lena felt tears dampen her eyes. "Goodbye . . ." she whispered.

She tried to concentrate on the man she would be inter-viewing in less than an hour. Florida's Governor was a no-torious braggart and difficult to pin down. That was why she had been sent from New York. Her eyes flicked over her notes. The emotions coursing within her were not what was required. New York expected a tough, incisive interview. She was expected to perform.

"Goddamn you," she swore, her eyes chancing upon a photo of Governor George Brown in the file. She stared at it angrily until it, and he, were her mind's focus.

"Okay," she whispered to no one.

Kane stood for several minutes within the vaccum of Lena's departure, his mind spinning reluctantly back to earth.

Then he noticed the car—a blue Oldsmobile pulled out at the end of the street and drove slowly towards him. Too slowly. An alarm rang in his mind. A truck was approaching from the opposite direction. He backed quickly towards the apartment block. He could not see the driver of the Olds but his eyes took in the registration plate. The car was accelerating. Instinctively he reached inside his coat. "Damn," he hissed. His gun was in the apartment. He looked around swiftly for cover. The truck geared down and crossed the path of the Olds as it began to draw level with him. He did not wait for it to reappear, but spun inside the security door, his neck prickling. From within the building he watched the car drive off. He jogged up the fire stairs, his suspicion hardening that the war had come to him.

A pager call and a blinking E-mail message were the early links in a chain of events that ended in the massive frame of Hog Collins whooping for joy.

"You got it with a ten-second trace? Son of a bitch, Barney," he shouted into the phone. "Son, you have just entered the Hog Hall of Fame! You sure now?"

With a final bellow, Collins slammed the receiver down and immediately punched Kane's mobile phone number.

"Wait for this, Tom!" he exclaimed.

* * *

Kane scanned the street as he pulled out of the garage. There was no sign of the Oldsmobile. His car phone buzzed.

"Yes?" he snapped.

"Holtzmann made the call!" Collins' voice was barely controlled. "Just talked to the boffins. We know where he lives! The wolf's lair, old buddy. The fucking cave of the coke bear."

"Calm down, Hog." Kane's eyes continued to range the street ahead. "Line up Colombian liaison. Tell Samaraz I want to talk to him. I'll be there in ten."

"Will do!" said the other.

"And Hog," Kane said as his foot jabbed the accelerator pedal. "I think our friends just paid me a visit. Check out a Florida plate for me—"

"Sure thing," said Collins, suddenly worried, as he took down the registration number. "Still with you?"

Kane glanced into the rear-vision mirror.

"I don't think so."

"Get your ass in here, and fast!" Collins signed off.

Blucher wiped the interior of the car a final time before exiting the carpark for the short drive to the rental company.

"Thank you, Mr Lipman," purred the overly made-up woman as she checked his paperwork. "I'm sorry your stay in Miami was cut short."

Blucher nodded, his eyes blinking impatiently behind his sunglasses.

"That's fine, Mr Lipman," she said finally. "You have a nice trip now." He nodded again and strode out with another of his aliases consigned to history. He swore again at the missed opportunity; the American was proving a difficult hit. At least he now knew what Kane looked like.

He walked on past the offices of other rental car companies. It was what he liked about working in America, he thought, as he entered a set of glass doors at random; it was so convenient.

"Yes sir?" came the voice that sounded just like the one he had left. "Can I help you?"

"My name is Schmidt," he said. "I wish to rent a car."

"Hog!" Kane strode in, briefly winded by his sprint from the carpark.

"Can't raise General Samaraz! Bogotá's got the shutters down," Collins reacted immediately. Kane scowled; the Avianca crash and subsequent public outburst of anti-American sentiment had spooked the Colombian government and White Storm's liaison officer at *Operación Narcotraficante* was becoming more and more difficult to get hold of.

"Keep trying," he swore. "And I'll talk to Stone about contingency plans. I'll be damned if we're going to let them get cold feet."

"Why don't we go in after the fucker ourselves!" growled Collins. "Talk to *Narco* in this climate and all we're doing is warning him."

Kane shook his head with frustration. "Okay, Hog, fill me in."

Collins drew breath. "Holtzmann made the call at around 03:00 local time. To Russia. NSA couldn't track the downlink but vectored Holtzmann here." He stabbed his pen at a map of Colombia adorning his wall; it showed the SatCom call had been made from a location approximately forty miles south-east of Medellín.

"It's tough country," Collins summed up.

Kane studied the map intently, tracing contour lines with his eyes. Holtzmann had chosen his HQ well. "We'll talk to Samaraz, when we find him," he muttered. "But my guess is it's going to be difficult to surprise Holtzmann. He's sure to have early warning all through those mountains."

Collins nodded. "Air strike?"

Kane frowned. "Only with close ground support. If he's well-bunkered it'll just scare him off, make him angry. If we let him get away we might as well kiss goodbye to the Colombians!"

"Yeah," growled Collins. "Don't want to make Holtzmann angry do we?"

"The best would be a Special Forces ground incursion," said Kane thinking aloud. Then he snorted. "I'll ask Samaraz but he'll say no. He'll want maximum bang, minimum risk."

"How 'bout a fucking nuke," answered Collins. "Maximum bang!"

Kane grinned ruefully and rubbed his chin. "I'll be with Stone," he said. "Keep trying Samaraz. I'll fly down there myself if we can't raise him within the hour."

"Want to know about your tail?" asked Collins as Kane went to leave. "One Joshua Lipman, returned his car an hour after you spotted him. Hertz girl gave us a description."

A chill passed through Kane.

"American?" he asked.

"Nope," replied Collins. "Sounded 'European' according to the Hertz girl."

"That narrows it down," sighed Kane. "What else?"

"Not much," said Collins. "Big guy, mid-forties, well built, receding grey hair. We'd better assign a watch to you," he added. "This could be our mystery Miami caller, Tom."

"Could be," said Kane. "Warn Angie Furness and her team. And let me tell Stone."

"Got it," replied Collins, but Kane had already walked out.

"Yes, *Señor*," Blucher grunted uncomfortably into the phone. Cortez and the woman had suddenly decided to leave the beach for the bar opposite his position. He considered breaking the connection, then Holtzmann spoke again.

"Who is the woman?"

"I do not know." Cortez was now only fifteen feet from him, at one of the window tables. The woman turned and Blucher looked away quickly.

"I will not ask Cortez," came the reply. "Keep watching. You may need to deal with both of them."

"I understand," mumbled Blucher. "I will report back tomorrow. And Kane, I—"

"Finish him," barked Holtzmann and disconnected the call. As he turned around, Blucher burned with sudden anger at his primary target. *Thomas Kane, you are a dead man.* He shuffled towards the darkened rear section of the bar, ordered a beer, and lit a cigarette. The fire inside his mind grew stronger and Blucher withdrew a small bottle from his coat. He shook out two pills, raised spit, and swallowed them. Then he settled into his chair and, through a shroud of smoke, studied a television screen which was blaring out baseball scores. The barman brought his Heineken, and he sipped it as he monitored Cortez and his woman by their reflections in the TV screen. The woman had just received another drink. That Holtzmann might make her a hit pleased him. Men would do many things when faced with death, women even more. As he considered it, Blucher grunted impatiently. He was tiring of the wait. Thomas Kane would be killed that evening; Cortez and the woman the instant Holtzmann gave the order. His hatred for all three grew more intense in preparation and his eyes narrowed. Through a screen full of statistics about the Atlanta Braves he failed to see Angie Furness lift the drink-coaster beneath her cocktail and read the message printed on it. He missed her glance towards him. And even if he had seen her lean forward to speak to Cortez he would have mistaken it as a lover's kiss.

* * *

"He is not one of mine," said Cortez as they entered his apartment. Angie shivered, walking to the window and staring out. The Colombian seemed strangely untroubled.

"Would Holtzmann—?" she began.

"Of course," he said, walking behind her and holding her shoulders. "If he thinks I am becoming a *gringo,* he might set a jackal to watch the fox. Or he may be watching for your agents." He chuckled. "Or he may be watching *you!*"

"Don't!" Angie shook free of his grip.

"Mi amor," soothed Cortez. "I will ask Holtzmann about it. He will tell me."

Angie did not answer but flopped onto the sofa and stared ahead. She was scared, and annoyed because of it. Finally she stood and walked to the telephone.

"Hog?" she said when it was answered. "He's an unknown."

"Good work," said Stone as Kane informed him of the NSA trace on Holtzmann. "So what's the problem?"

"I think the Colombians have gone cold," Kane replied.

"Not much we can do about it," said Stone after a moment's thought. "Want me to talk to the President?"

Kane shook his head. "The more noise we make, the more likely Holtzmann will hear it."

"So what?" asked Stone.

"I want to go in with the Colombians," answered Kane. "See if I can't get an incursion team to snatch Holtzmann before the fireworks start. Their men are good—like that special forces colonel, Vanquero. It's the generals that stink."

Stone chuckled. "Careful, Kane, or I might just take that personally. Okay, get down there. Anything else?"

"We're tracking a massive consignment of cartel cocaine. Two tons," said Kane. "Cortez told us about it, came into Louisiana this morning."

Stone smiled broadly. "Two tons? Holy shit, your catch is starting to pay his way."

"Yeah," scowled Kane. "Let's hope they don't move the stuff too quickly, can't let it out of our sight."

"What's your man say?" asked Stone.

"Can't tell me right now, thinks some is bound for Canada. We're trying to set up an agent on the inside, but until we know . . ." His voice faded.

"Until we know *what*?" Stone was instantly suspicious.

"We've got another player," replied Kane reluctantly. "Think I was buzzed this morning. Cortez doesn't know him."

"I should order you in," said Stone, frowning.

"Too close to the endgame for that," responded Kane quickly.

"Yeah," said the big general. "All the same—"

"I'll keep you informed," Kane cut him off.

Stone shot him a stern glance. "You do that," he said. "And keep your damn head down in Colombia. You're getting too old for this!"

Kane chuckled. "General, if *I'm* old."

"Yeah, yeah," muttered Stone. "Get the hell out of here."

Gyorgy Kumarov sat alone in the Avianca First Class lounge at John F. Kennedy Airport in New York. The flight from Moscow had been long, especially for a man who travelled so little, and Kumarov shivered at the thought of what lay ahead. It would be another eight hours before he reached Bogotá and he had been unable to sleep since leaving Russia and the sanctuary of the Dom Chumy. He hated the unfamiliar. It laid raw his greatest fear: that he would be prevented from completing his life's work. He sipped a glass of juice nervously, refusing the ever-present attendant's offer of more. From time to time he tapped the keyboard of his laptop computer, more for distraction than anything else.

He disliked the United States intensely. So much activity

for so little effect; so much choice about matters of such little importance; so much noise and so little sense. He had visited once before, for a conference on microbiology during the eighties. His mouth pursed into a tight smile as he remembered the only pleasurable experience of that trip: the awkward and primitive theories on virology advanced by his American contemporaries.

He closed his eyes to shut out the presence of the attendant and her jug of juice. In the peaceful dimness he imagined himself sitting alone in the centre of a vast plain; as he drifted deeper into his daydream two figures approached him and he knew they were the sole survivors. Sasha and Holtzmann, with him between them.

"Your flight, sir." The voice scratched his consciousness like fingernails across a blackboard. He spiralled upwards from what had briefly become sleep and groggily opened his eyes.

"*Chto?*" he croaked.

"Your flight," the attendant repeated. "They're boarding first class now, sir."

"*Da,*" he said, waking and rising in the same instant.

"It's been my—" began the attendant, but her sole charge gave no sign of caring how much of a pleasure it had been serving him. She closed her mouth and briskly cleared his glass from the table.

"General Samaraz!" Kane's voice was tinged with both relief and frustration as the top man at *Operación Narcotraficante* finally came on line from Bogotá.

"Yes, Colonel Kane?" came the reply in perfect, accented English.

"Our people have pinpointed Holtzmann's location," said Kane. "We have to move on this urgently."

It was all Kane could do to stop himself from shouting. The Colombian had kept them waiting three hours.

"I understand your impatience, Colonel Kane," said

Samaraz. "But in these days I am not my own man. What do you propose, so that I can seek approval?"

Kane shot a glance at Hog Collins, pausing before trusting himself to answer civilly.

"General Samaraz," he said. "Special Forces must go in first, take Holtzmann and secure the compound. Air power and a larger ground force should be held in reserve."

"I see, Colonel," replied the Colombian. "You do not think an air strike followed by a ground attack would be the wiser choice?"

Kane rolled his eyes. "General, with respect, we have no information about Holtzmann's ability to withstand an air strike. At the very least, an incursion team could determine that. At best they could capture Holtzmann alive."

"And," snapped the other, "at worst they could be ambushed!"

"Sir," Kane tried. "I would like to be with the incursion team."

"Kane," replied Samaraz, dropping all pretext of formality. "There is only one of you to die. My men may only be Colombians, but I must consider their lives."

Kane sighed. It was going as badly as he'd feared. "General," he said finally. "I have great respect for your men in the field. I would not endanger them unnecessarily. But surely we must be certain that Holtzmann is taken. I don't think that is guaranteed by an air attack. If, somehow, he escapes, it will reflect badly on both of our operations, and on both of our governments."

There was a long pause at the other end as Samaraz digested this.

"Kane," he said finally. "You will send me precise details of Holtzmann's location; I will consider your request overnight. But even if I am persuaded of it, those to whom I answer may not be. I would suggest that you travel to Bogotá tomorrow—"

"I will come tonight, General," Kane broke in.

"No," Samaraz replied. "From the moment you are in this country, you present me with a security problem. Come tomorrow—it will give me time to consider our options. I must check what we have available for this."

"I will be in Bogotá by noon," said Kane, defeated.

"Until tomorrow, Kane," Samaraz concluded.

"Son of a bitch," swore Collins quietly as Kane hung up. "Fuckin' armchair generals!"

Hermann Blucher stared at his quarry from behind his companion. It was evening and he had hired a hooker for cover, telling her he was an insurance investigator. For the money she was getting she asked no further questions.

Cortez and his woman were deep in conversation, sitting at a sidewalk table in the adjoining restaurant. Blucher glanced impatiently at his watch. Monique, the hooker, smiled at him from across the table. Despite what she had grudgingly let him do to her in his room earlier, "Willi" was a good job. Her hourly rate doubled for as long as she was with him.

The couple he was so interested in got up from their table and walked away.

"Come," Blucher said gruffly, grabbing his hat.

Monique rose quickly to follow him, taking his arm and window shopping, as he had told her to do. Blucher's eyes narrowed as the pair ahead disappeared into Cortez's apartment block.

"Stop," he snapped at the hooker. She needed no encouragement, gazing longingly at a jewellery display. "We will go to my room."

"Sure, Willi," she said and began walking with him again. A man strolled towards them and neither she nor Blucher heard the faint whirring of a high-speed camera as it shot off twenty frames of high-resolution film in less than a second.

They sat in Blucher's room for nearly an hour before he

grew bored with his surveillance and took her. Even as he began pawing at her naked back and she ground her teeth to deal with the pain, a tiny cartridge of film was awash with chemicals.

"Bingo!" said Kane's voice in the orange-tinged darkness minutes later, as he was shown the photographs.

"They got shots of the guy," Angie told Cortez as she replaced the receiver. "They're worried!"

He shrugged. "It is not so strange as you and Kane think. I told you, I will ask Holtzmann what is hap'nin'."

Angie snorted at his nonchalance, wondering if it was genuine, or *machismo* for her benefit.

"Well I hope whatever it is happens soon."

"*Mi amor,*" Cortez said softly. "Is it so bad?"

"Yes," she snapped. She slumped into the sofa and picked up a magazine. "When do you have to call him?"

"Fifteen minutes," Cortez replied. "He will want to know about the Louisiana shipment."

"Okay," she said, without raising her head.

The silence was intense as they waited. Angie did not read the magazine but flipped through photographs and headlines to mark time. Finally Cortez moved across to the telephone. He breathed deeply, revealing the nervousness he had brushed off so shortly before, and with his left hand dialled the number. The connection made, he mumbled his code phrases. *Too quickly!* Angie thought. She listened, hearing only his side of the conversation, though she knew that somewhere at Operation White Storm HQ the call was being recorded.

"He is so obvious—I think he is watching me," Cortez was saying. Holtzmann stifled a growl of annoyance. Blucher was finished.

"Ernesto," he replied slowly. "Deal with him."

"Yes," said Cortez. "I will."

"Has the shipment arrived?" asked Holtzmann, to dispense with the topic of Blucher. He had a map of Louisiana spread before him in his bunker, marked with the landing point. Two tons; it was his largest and most audacious smuggling operation this year.

"This morning," came the distant reply. "All is safe."

"Good," Holtzmann said. "Any more trouble for you?"

"No."

Cortez replaced the receiver with a wry smile on his face.

"What? What?" clamoured Angie.

"There is no doubt our friend was sent by Holtzmann," said Cortez. "But I have just been ordered to kill him."

He laughed out loud, and in her relief, so did Angie—until the realisation of what she was laughing at struck her.

"We can't," she said.

"We have to," Cortez snapped viciously. "This is my world, not Kane's."

"No it isn't!" said Angie. Kane confirmed it as the phone rang for her a few moments later.

"We're going to bring him in," said Angie to Cortez. "But Kane said 'well done'!"

"Motherfucker," growled the Colombian, and Angie slapped his back good-naturedly. "C'mon, Cortez, lighten up!" She was buoyed by the threat removed.

"Let me buy you a drink!"

"This is it," said Agent Jerry Gonzalez as he climbed back into the car. "Receptionist recognised the pic. Registered under Jan D. Hoegstardt. Changed cars this morning. Checks out."

"Good work, Gonzalez," said Pete Dunne officiously. "Call the back-up."

Gonzalez reached for the radio. *Why had he drawn the short straw?* he asked himself for the fifteenth time that evening. Sharing a shift with Dunne meant enduring a non-stop flow of bullshit about his heroic life at the FBI. Gonzalez was older, wiser and from a different era of law enforcement.

"Target identified," he reported. "Crown Hotel, licence RHT657WZ."

"Roger," came the twin and immediate responses from the other White Storm surveillance cars. Gonzalez replaced the handset and idled the car towards the hotel's carpark, pulling up opposite. It was nine p.m.—they had been searching for the man they knew only as Joshua Lipman for seven hours.

"Let's go," grunted Gonzalez, pulling open his door.

"We wait for the others," said Dunne tersely, staring straight ahead.

"Chickenshit!" snorted Gonzalez. "Room 901, let's fucking go, Dunne."

"Listen Gonzalez!" Dunne whirled on him. "I am shift commander, got it?"

"Oh, man," Gonzalez sighed, trying and failing to control his anger.

One of Blucher's hands gripped the back of the hooker's head as it bobbed before him, the other held the binoculars to his eyes. His attention was so focused on the closed drapes of Cortez's apartment that his orgasm surprised him. Monique moaned as he came, doing her professional best to intensify the experience, but it was not enough.

"Dreck!" he shouted, pulling her from him. She swore at him but Blucher ignored her and again raised the binoculars to his eyes. There had been no sign of movement at the apartment for two hours. He checked his watch; a quarter after nine. It was time to deal with Kane.

"Come," he ordered Monique. Though her eyes flashed hatefully at him, she nodded; the bonus he had given her would keep her off her back for a month. Retrieving his hat and his briefcase containing the assembled pistol and silencer, he led Monique to the door.

Gonzalez stewed as the minutes passed, his eyes fixed on the poorly-lit entrance to the Crown Hotel's carpark. A set of headlights suddenly beamed out. He switched on the ignition and brought the revs up. The other car exited with a squeal of tires, jolting out of the hotel's driveway and onto the street. Gonzalez caught a glimpse of its registration plates and saw their target's distinctive hat silhouetted in the windscreen.

"There! There!" said Dunne even as Gonzalez was pulling out from the curb. Lipman was moving fast.

"Target mobile!" Dunne snapped, snatching the radio. "Come on, come on!"

Gonzalez swore at his partner's frantic outburst as he tucked their vehicle into the traffic, five cars behind their man. Dunne blabbered instructions into the handset for the two other chase cars. The lights on Lipman's vehicle wove in and out of the traffic ahead of them as the White Storm squad checked in.

"We pick him up at the first possible opportunity!" Dunne shouted into the radio. Gonzalez looked at him sideways.

"I'd say that's now," he said.

"On my command!" replied Dunne shortly.

Yes sir! mouthed Gonzalez. *Asshole!*

"Get out of here, Tom." Collins' bulk filled his office doorway. "You gotta be bright for Samaraz, remember?"

Kane nodded wearily.

"Until tomorrow, Hog," he said, mimicking the Colombian general.

Collins chuckled. "Boy, do I not envy you, *amigo!*"

* * *

Blucher parked the cab opposite Kane's apartment block. He was wearing the dead driver's baseball cap and glasses, his gun holstered inside his coat.

A woman was leading a tiny dog towards the building. He alighted from the cab and walked ahead of her to the security door intercom, as if checking the names for his fare. She smiled as she passed him, and pushed her key into the lock. Then she felt his steel grip on her shoulder.

"Take me to the garage," he ordered, opening the door with his free hand and thrusting her through it. She tried to scream but he slammed his hand over her mouth. "Make a noise and you die," he growled.

She nodded, feeling the cold barrel of his pistol against her neck. He walked her quickly to the steps leading down to the garage. The dog was dragged behind. Blucher saw Kane's car space was empty and in the neon-lit dimness he pushed his terrified hostage to a corner of the garage where a large dumpster loomed out of the shadows. He tightened his grip on her windpipe until she died. Her dog whimpered. Blucher broke its neck, lifting both it and the woman's body into the dumpster. He looked around for an ambush position, finding it behind a concrete column near the stairs. Then he checked his pistol in the light before slipping into the darkness.

Kane listened to Pete Dunne's voice on the radio with a growing frown. Dunne's transfer out of White Storm would be brought forward to the following day, he decided. He reached for the handset.

"All cars," he said matter-of-factly. "This is Storm One. Take Lipman ASAP!"

That done, and having the satisfaction of hearing Dunne's patter dry up, Kane checked the road ahead and behind as he neared his apartment building. He knew that at least two sets of lights out there belonged to his guard detail. He heard Dunne issue a final order as he turned into his garage. The two White Storm escort cars took up positions on either side of the street. Lipman would be theirs within minutes, he thought, as he watched the steel door rise slowly in his lights.

"Take him now," yelled Dunne again.

"Think Kane was mad?" he asked in an undertone with the radio off for a second. Gonzalez glanced at him contemptuously as he accelerated. Two other White Storm cars were ahead.

"Take him!" Dunne repeated for Kane's benefit.

"With target . . . slowing," reported the first squad as their car pulled alongside its quarry. There was a pause, then "Oh, shit!"

"What?" shouted Dunne. *"What?"*

Gonzalez floored their vehicle, drawing up to Lipman's car in a second. Behind the wheel, confused and staring around in terror, tears streaming from her eyes, was a woman wearing Lipman's hat. Guns were levelled at her as she slowed down.

Holy shit! Gonzalez swore to himself. "Kane!" he shouted, grabbing the handset from the hands of the catatonic Dunne.

"Kane. It's a decoy. Lipman is out there. *Kane!"*

Kane glided into the dim interior of the garage and sighed as his radio reception became white-noise. Outside his security detail took up guard.

He jumped from his car and began striding towards the stairs. The garage door was closing fast and it confused the movement he suddenly saw in front of him. He heard the barely discernible *pssht* as he dived to his left and a bullet seared into his shoulder. Tumbling over the floor in pain, he grabbed his gun from his coat and fired two shots to warn his escort. Then, growing dizzy, he crawled towards the dumpster for cover.

There was a screech of tires outside and a resounding crash against the garage door. Then another. His men were trying to ram their way in. Kane gasped, losing consciousness briefly. Blood poured profusely from his wound. A noise sounded to his right—he scrabbled desperately away from it over the concrete floor. There was no time to use his own weapon. Again he heard the silenced shot just before he felt the white-hot barb of the bullet tear through his thigh. He grunted and jerked backwards as another spasm of pain rocketed through him. He was now fully exposed to his attacker. Another bullet ripped into his stomach and, looking down, he saw blood pumping from the wound. It was a bad one, the thought spun through his mind, a very bad one. Now the ramming of the garage door was the one constant that kept him conscious. Every particle of him wanted to lie very still and stop the hurt. He felt his gun in his hand and brought it up, slowly, too slowly. His finger squeezed the trigger but the bullets sprayed above the approaching man. The ghostly image of his killer danced before his eyes and he pulled the trigger again. Blucher ducked and fired twice more at Kane.

The first shot shattered Kane's elbow. His gun clattered to the floor as Blucher's second bullet slammed through his ear. Kane heard himself scream out and was conscious long enough to see his attacker advancing again, racing the blackness of his approaching death. As everything was eclipsed, he saw a blinding white light and his ears rang with a noise too painful to be earthly. Then there was pitch darkness; nothing. Kane's heart, unable to endure the grievous destruction of his body, stopped.

CHAPTER **SIX**

Oh God! Oh God!" the hooker screamed again and again as she was led through the twisted remnants of the garage door and past the bloody mess inside. She stared at the body, blue-uniformed paramedics swarming around it like flies. Then she looked over at Willi, his face badly beaten.

"He just told me to drive!" she shrieked. "I swear. He said it was an insurance scam." She collapsed against Agent Matt Michaels, who let her drop to the concrete floor of the garage.

"What's your name?" Pete Dunne shouted at Blucher again. The German shrugged sullenly, though his body was pumping with adrenaline. He had been caught. He looked down at the man he had killed without sympathy, knowing he would receive none from his captors. Then he glanced up at his enraged interrogator in time to see the pistol barrel strike his face.

"Mother . . . fucker!" screamed Dunne.

"Agent Dunne," came the bellow across the garage. Stone had arrived. "You're not going to get out of this shitfight of your creation by pistol-whipping anybody. What the *fuck* did they teach you at the goddamned Bureau!"

"Sir?" stammered Dunne.

"Pulse!" came the shout from a paramedic. "Where's the chopper?"

Stone ran forward to where Kane lay.

"How—?" he asked.

The paramedic looked grim. "Bad," he replied. "We've gotten a pulse back, but that doesn't mean anything at this stage. I doubt he'll make it to the trauma ward; we're pumping plasma into him, but he's got a serious abdominal wound and possibly brain injury. Can't say." His voice trailed off and he turned away; his was a thankless job and he didn't much like providing a commentary to it.

"Save his ass, mister," growled Stone. "Goddammit, save him!"

The call for the chopper brought with it a vulture pack of media. Television crews swarmed outside the apartment block and around the taxi with its grisly cargo. Stone was standing immobile in the centre of the garage, quaking with rage at his impotence, when he saw the first of the TV cameramen reach Kane's stretcher, and momentarily slow its progress towards the descending helicopter.

"Out!" he howled, thundering towards the camera and its luckless operator. He gripped the camera in two huge hands and tossed it into the street where it shattered. Striding outside, Stone and his phalanx of agents cleared the area.

"They've got Kane's name, sir," one of his men reported breathlessly. "They've talked to the medicos and are reporting it as a murder."

"Jesus Christ," swore Stone. "Dunne!" The shell-shocked agent appeared before him immediately.

"You," said Stone, his voice wavering. "You and I will have our discussion about this fuck-up tomorrow. If you want that discussion to lead anywhere other than you never working for *any* law enforcement organisation again, you do what it takes to get a national security advisory out to every media outlet in this damn country. I want them to know that anyone who so much as whispers Kane's name publicly will be up on treason charges. It's their asses and your's, Dunne. *Got it?*"

"Yes sir," breathed Dunne and scurried off.

Stone noticed Hog Collins pulling up in his vehicle. "Kane's in bad shape," he told the CIA man bluntly. "Real bad."

"Hell," Collins sighed, shaking his head in disbelief. "I'll be at the hospital," he said finally and sped away.

The Avianca jet disgorged Gyorgy Kumarov as dawn broke over Bogotá. He was more fatigued than he could remember being in his life, and felt swamped by the babble surrounding him as he entered the arrivals hall at El Dorado Airport. He walked aimlessly, buffeted by the crowd, until there was a tug at his arm. Before him stood two young Colombian men perfectly attired in suits.

"Comrade Gyorgy?" the first asked in English.

Kumarov regarded him carefully. "You are from—?"

"Come," broke in the second. "We will not talk here."

Dazed, Kumarov allowed himself to be led through the bustling terminal to a black Mercedes waiting outside. He climbed into its air-conditioned interior. "You are from Holtzmann?" he blurted out.

His two escorts and the driver laughed. "And if we are not?" said one.

Kumarov angered suddenly. "If you *are*," he shrilled, "he will know of my displeasure!"

The laughter stopped abruptly and what had been a game ended.

"I am sorry," said the first, with a respectful tone. "Yes, we are from *Señor* Holtzmann."

After offering him a pastry and a whisky from a small bar secreted in the Mercedes—Kumarov declined the first and gratefully accepted the second—the leader introduced himself as Romero.

"You are tired?" he asked. Kumarov merely nodded, swilling the whisky in his mouth. Tree-lined suburbs gave way to skyscrapers as they drove towards the central business district of Bogotá. All around them, whirling in and out of the traffic with abandon, were scores and scores of motorcycles, each carrying a pillion passenger. Kumarov realised why assassins in Colombia most commonly struck from motorcycles. Romero noticed his interest.

"Some are ours—*Brigada Fascista*," he smiled. "You are indeed an important visitor."

Kumarov nodded again and accepted more whisky.

Presently they came to a grand structure built on a square overlooking the centre of the city. "Hotel Tequendama," said Romero. "You will rest here today. This evening we will travel further. It is a long journey."

Alighting outside the impressive hotel, Romero left his companions in the Mercedes and walked Kumarov through the high-ceilinged foyer to the elevators and then his room. Once there, the Colombian made a show of checking it with his pistol drawn, making Kumarov nervous. Then Romero opened the doors to the two adjoining suites. In each was a team of three men armed with automatic weapons.

"We take no chances," said Romero. "You are registered as Popov. Do not leave the room."

"I understand," replied Kumarov, heavy-lidded. "I have no intention of leaving." The whisky, together with the promise of a shower and sleep suffused him with pleasure. Romero shut the doors to the guards' rooms and left. Moments later, the Russian stepped beneath the warm gush of a shower. Then he crawled between fresh sheets and fell into the sleep that had been denied him since leaving Moscow nearly a full day before.

* * *

Collins waited alone at first, then was joined by Stone. Anxiety and countless cups of coffee churned their guts. Both men dreaded hearing the news they refused to admit was possible. Every figure in a white coat who approached them seemed ready to tell them the worst. The outside world was on hold.

Inside the emergency room at Miami General, specialists mustered from across the city worked furiously on Kane. They had no idea who he was, only that the entire working of the hospital seemed to be centred on their operating theatre. At four A.M. they began the last but most critical phase of their work, removing the bullet that had lodged near his medulla. A fraction of a millimetre more and his respiratory system would have lost its general command source. Three times Kane died on the operating table as the jagged bullet tore delicate tissue, cell-deep but critical. Three times he was revived with seconds to spare before permanent brain damage resulted from lack of oxygen. Three times Collins and Stone heard the emergency bell and saw a small army of white coats pour past them down the corridor.

Finally the last stitches were put into Kane's scalp. Trembling with exhaustion, the surgeon watched the man wheeled out towards the recovery ward. He peeled off his bloodied gloves and shook hands with his colleagues.

"Lucky, very fucking lucky," he murmured.

The theatre team talked vigorously as they scrubbed, speculating about the patient's identity. The anaesthetist, who had tended to Kane throughout the night and who as much as any of his medical comrades deserved the credit for his survival, listened to his colleagues, then finally—as they strode out into their corner of the carpark—said pithily, "Had to be military. Tough son of a bitch."

The others nodded as they walked towards their Porsches and Mercedes.

* * *

Kumarov woke slowly. The persistent buzzing had worked its way into his dream, and for some time he allowed it to stay there.

His eyes regarded the telephone warily from beneath his pillow. Then he stretched out a hand and pulled the receiver towards him.

"*Da?*" he answered sleepily. His tongue tried to raise spit within his parched mouth.

"You have thirty minutes," said Romero. "Please be ready."

Kumarov grunted and hung up. He lay still for a few minutes more, then dragged himself upright. Padding to the window he saw that it was night. By the time Romero arrived, Kumarov had washed and dressed, but his eyes were still half-closed and he felt incapable of anything but the most basic of tasks.

Romero led him down the long musty hotel corridor, and smiled as the neon brilliance inside the elevator seared into Kumarov's bloodshot eyes.

"You can sleep in the car," he said, "we'll be travelling all night."

Kumarov rubbed his face, the news failing to cheer him.

Outside the hotel, two Mercedes were waiting, their windows impenetrably dark. As he climbed into the second car, Kumarov guessed that the first was occupied by his guards from the hotel.

They set off and a silence descended on the group within his Mercedes, heightening Kumarov's uneasiness. Beside the driver sat a man who smoked constantly and made no attempt to introduce himself. From Romero's occasional glances, the Russian guessed he was one of Holtzmann's inner circle. Kumarov wondered what he had done to get there. Used as he was to the chaos and commonplace violence of Moscow, he could not help shivering at what faced him. Driving through one of the world's most murderous countries to finally meet one of the world's most wanted men, Kumarov remembered the noises of Galitsky's death.

"You will pass on my personal sympathies to Colonel Kane when he recovers," General Samaraz's voice oozed out of the speaker. Hog Collins grimaced. Opposite him, Stone sat stony-faced. Without Kane in Colombia, both knew that the taking of Holtzmann was beyond their control. Samaraz's tone confirmed it as much as his words.

"I had given serious consideration to Kane's proposal," he said. "But the choice has been taken from us."

"But General," Collins tried to protest. "Surely Kane's presence was not the only factor?"

"It was the *decisive* factor," replied the Colombian smoothly. "I'm afraid my decision has been made."

Stone allowed him to finish, then spoke. "General Samaraz, this is General Stone. If you are talking about a straight-out air strike, please allow me one last chance to counsel against it. I have to be blunt—if we lose our man we might as well throw our joint operation out the god-damn window."

There was a low chuckle from the speaker.

"You have not lost any of your directness, General," said Samaraz. "And I understand your concern. But, with respect, you do not know the terrain first-hand. The President is simply not willing to risk a ground assault without an initial air attack on Holtzmann's base. If I sacrifice Colombian troops needlessly, our joint operation will be even more quickly out of the window than you suggest. I will send you all details of our planning, your input will be most graciously received, but I will not alter the basic strategy."

Defeated, Stone reeled back into his chair and shook his head. "I understand, General," he said slowly. There was no point in aggravating the Colombian further. "When exactly are you planning to move?"

"Within forty-eight hours," replied Samaraz. "As soon as I am assured that we are ready."

Stone stared disbelievingly at Collins. *Forty-eight hours?*

"Well we'd certainly appreciate it if you could bring it forward," Collins said diplomatically, staving off an explosion from his superior.

"We will be doing all we can," said Samaraz. His voice had an edge of annoyance.

Stone breathed out. "General Samaraz," he said, as calmly as he could manage. "Would you have any problems if I came down to Colombia to *observe* the operation?"

There was a long pause, then Samaraz answered. "No objections, General Stone," he said.

The big Marine's eyes brightened for an instant. Then Samaraz continued, "You may join me at Army HQ in Medellín. Old soldiers such as us are beyond the rigours of the field, wouldn't you agree?"

Stone closed his eyes and ground his teeth.

"That'll be fine, General," said Collins hastily. "I will advise you of General Stone's arrival time directly."

"That is all?" asked the Colombian.

"Yes," said Collins. "Thank you . . . and good luck."

"Piece of goddamned shit!" roared Stone after Collins had hung up. They stared at each other across the desk.

"Get me a ticket to the circus, Hog," said Stone, rising wearily to his feet. "I'll go pack my clown suit."

Angie sat on the terrace of Cortez's apartment, staring out. Inside, the Colombian was relaying news of Lipman's "death" to Holtzmann. Angie no longer cared about Holtzmann; she was consumed by guilt and rage over Kane. Guilt that the team had let him down, rage at Kane's would-be assassin. She wished the man dead and, in thinking it, opened her mind to the possibility that Cortez's way may have been preferable.

"He spoke for only a moment," Cortez's voice interrupted her vengeful daydream.

"Oh, yeah?" she replied, standing up. "You're still his favourite boy then?"

Cortez looked at her quizzically. She stared at him; around them she felt the vacuum of the day close in. She felt alone, angry, and desolate. Nothing would happen, the hours would creep on; there was no hunt, no chase. Nothing. Just her and Cortez. Something suddenly snapped inside her and she reached out, taking him by the hand. Without a word she led him into the apartment and through it. When she reached the sanctuary of the bedroom she turned to him, eyes flashing. He launched himself towards her and she grasped him. Without reason, without an understanding of why, she clawed his back as she kissed him with bruising force, driving him back towards the bed. Then her hand thrust between his legs, rubbing him, grabbing him, wanting him inside her with a manic urgency. His arms were around her, pulling at the flimsy material keeping her skin from him. He was atop her now. Her fingers slipped into his jeans and gripped his erection in her hand. She fell into sensual madness. Their time together worked its effect. Carved by dangers shared with him, her false life seemed suddenly real. She closed her eyes, euphoric, as he lifted her down onto the carpet. Illicit sensation spun through her as she fell into the soft pile.

He straddled her, stroking her body which snaked with pleasure on the carpet beneath. Unbuttoning her blouse, he sighed as her breasts spilled from it. Slowly now she began to undress him, unzipping his jeans. Her eyes half opened and from her lips escaped sounds of pleasure as she saw what was revealed. She kissed his smooth belly and then traced her tongue between his legs, taking him in her mouth as she kicked off her slip of a skirt. *"Mi amor!"* he whispered. She moaned and shook her head in response, plunging forward onto him. And then he dragged her slowly up to him, kissing her lips, her damp face, feeling the length of her naked body against his. It was inevitable, unstoppable.

They rolled together, legs entwined, fingers touching glorious places. Then she lay back and stared into his eyes. He understood, and she watched his face as he entered her. Whispering wildly between clenched teeth, she felt him swell within her and widened her legs with a laugh that was swallowed. She arched towards him and felt his hands behind her, pulling her ever closer. Her body burned with increasing ferocity until finally the pleasure demanded release and she screamed, holding him as she twisted beneath; screamed again as she felt his muscles tighten and he came deep within her, juddering, rocking them both, her thighs gripping him to keep him inside her as they whirled into ecstasy together.

They lay together for what seemed an age until finally Angie spoke. "C'mon," she urged him huskily, pushing the damp hair from her face, utterly confused about what she had done. "Get dressed."

He groaned and rolled onto his stomach. She rubbed his back gently but without passion, trying to think. The same dark conviction that had plagued her for so many years settled upon her again.

"Oh, Kane," Lena murmured, deciding not to leave another message. She replaced the phone and looked blankly at the mess her apartment was in. Central to it was her suitcase, always either half-opened and half-unpacked or, as now, half-closed and half-packed.

The early evening twinkle of Manhattan was framed by her window. It seemed much longer than a day since she had seen Kane, and the thought that it would be so many more before she did again drove her to her cupboard, to pull from it the last things for her next trip.

Sitting on her suitcase to force it shut, she glanced at her watch. The WorldNet limo was ten minutes away. Idly she picked up the phone again, dialled and heard her mother's ever-formal answer.

Lena smiled, *"Mamochka,"* she said, slipping into Russian easily and for a short time at least deflecting her need for Kane with love of a much older variety.

Then the schedule of her life dragged her away again—to another aeroplane, another hotel, another country.

CHAPTER**SEVEN**

Deep beneath the jungle, bleary-eyed and exhausted from his journey, Kumarov finally met his master.

"Comrade Gyorgy," beamed Holtzmann. The Russian looked far younger than his years. Black eyes set in a pale, baby-smooth face stared back at him.

"*Señor* Holtzmann, your servant." Kumarov's high-pitched voice whistled through almost motionless lips.

Both men stared at each other for a moment with respect; Kumarov because he was now in the other's world; Holtzmann because on Kumarov's shoulders rode his ultimate ambition.

Kumarov spoke again, his voice echoing eerily within the bunker. "The costs have been greater than even I imagined," he murmured, dealing with the least palatable subject first. "I could not have predicted the avarice of my people after the Union collapsed. The materials I have required, and the equipment, have all had to come from sensitive Soviet research centres. It is true that you can buy anything in Russia today, but only at a price."

Holtzmann stared into the cold dark eyes. "Do not concern yourself," he said to the Russian, gesturing to a seat. "Vodka?"

Kumarov nodded. The liquor was brought and the scientist grunted appreciatively as he saw the label, then continued. He had rehearsed his speech during the long, silent hours of his journey through the Andes.

"However, the equipment has been but a fraction of the cost. Originally the total work of the Dom Chumy—the work I am now completing—was under the central authority of the Biopreparat, spread between laboratories in Moscow, Leningrad, and the testing facilities in Sverdlovsk and Vozrozhdonyiye Island. After the Union collapsed I had to bring those I wanted to the Dom Chumy so they could be under my direct control. More importantly I had to make our project invisible within the bureaucracy. Gorbachev, then Yeltsin, now Firyubin have all claimed to the West that the Biopreparat has been abolished, and it has. Apart from the Dom Chumy."

Holtzmann nodded at the term. *Dom Chumy*—House of the Plague. Kumarov's whistle-voice went on.

"Though we operate not five blocks from where the disgraced Mikhail Sergeyevich still maintains his reactionary 'Institute,' and less than four miles from the Kremlin and Krasnaya-ploshchad itself, we have surrounded the Dom Chumy with impenetrable walls of silence. But to keep those walls intact has not been . . . inexpensive."

"So I have seen," said Holtzmann.

Kumarov continued—he'd wanted to draw Holtzmann out and bury the matter that had killed Galitsky.

"One whisper of this, one word beyond the walls and the Dom Chumy would have been, could still be, dismantled forever. Its work—unique in the scientific world since the Americans abolished their New Mexico research facility in 1989—everything, would be lost. I am years beyond what was last known of this project and, with your assistance, my progress has been exponential.

"*Señor* Holtzmann, without your intervention and your continued support, all would have been discarded by the quislings who fill the Chamber of People's Deputies. If even one of those idle tongues let it be known that our work continues, the Dom Chumy would be razed. Even after such disasters as Chechnya, where my expertise would have been most . . . useful."

"I understand," said Holtzmann. He comprehended the scale of what Kumarov had achieved. It was mirrored in much of what Holtzmann himself had done in Colombia. The topic of its cost, having been raised and dealt with, was now finished; neither man had said a word about the messenger Galitsky—whose task it had been to deliver the very same apologia.

"So, begin," Holtzmann requested after a time. He dismissed his bodyguards to the ante-chamber and waited for the heavy door to click shut. In the dim light of the bunker Kumarov gave his progress report. Holtzmann's smile grew as he listened.

"I have developed a number of test procedures," intoned the Russian. "Tests which are superior to anything available in the world today. With these procedures I have been able to recognise and sort viruses at a much greater rate than was previously thought possible."

"Viruses only?" queried Holtzmann, interrupting him. "Are you not looking at bacteria as well?"

He is sharp, Kumarov remembered.

"Perhaps if I chronicle what has brought us to this point?" he said, correctly guessing that Holtzmann would take pleasure from such an account.

The Colombian nodded, and sat back in his chair.

"Mankind," Kumarov's words came slowly, "has regularly been afflicted by epidemics, some more destructive than others; the bubonic plague, smallpox and nearer our own time, influenza. Some of these plagues have been due to a bacterium, some a virus. In each plague episode, the responsible virus or bacteria was a commonly occurring chemical structure which became an epidemic disease in one of two ways. The first by leaping species. For example from primates to humans. What was dormant or endemic in one species became virulent, or epidemic, in Man. Most often a minor mutation in the virus or bacteria allowed this leap of species to occur and trigger a human plague.

"Or," Kumarov drew breath, "some social shift allowed a plague virus or bacteria which had become endemic in one civilisation to become epidemic in another. You see, when a plague has done its worst within a closed community, and enough time passes, the surviving generations build an immunity to the disease. The illness is still carried by them but its effect is only as a 'background' or childhood disease, like chickenpox, measles, or mumps. But if this host community then comes into contact with a culture that has never been exposed to such diseases, the latter will experience a plague. Witness the European invasion of the New World in the sixteenth century. Nearly sixty percent of the indigenous populations of the Americas succumbed to what were merely childhood complaints in the Old World."

Kumarov paused for a moment.

"And, when a virus or bacteria operates on *both* levels—that is, leaping species into a human community made vulnerable by social shifts—no one is immune. The first transferral of *Pasteurella pestis*—bubonic plague, the most destructive disease in history—was from rats to humans in isolated herding communities in Mongolia. The mortality rate in the individual communities was great, but over decades they evolved rituals of hygiene which offered them some protection. Then the Mongol empire shaped itself and in time set its sights on Western conquest. The Mongols were the first mass horse-borne army in history; they moved across the European continent with astonishing speed, and with them bore *Pasteurella pestis*. Like a river of poison, the Black Death flowed into the densely populated countries of the West, decimating their cities, travelling on ships to further shores—through the Mediterranean region and finally Britain. When it was over, this single strain of bacteria had accounted for over fifty percent of the population of the known world."

The Russian sighed. "Perhaps out of respect for history—for *Pasteurella pestis*—and perhaps because the technology was more in place for such a search, I *did* originally consider that a truly antibiotic-proof strain of bacteria was our goal. But now? *Now* I believe we will be better served by a virus."

Holtzmann listened with rapt attention.

"Two recent epidemics illustrate my thinking on this," Kumarov went on, perfectly in control of his subject. And in control—however briefly—of Holtzmann.

"A little over a hundred years ago it is believed that the forerunner of HIV-1, the virus primarily responsible for the Acquired Immune Deficiency Syndrome—AIDS, was endemic in a species of primates in Central Africa, occasionally infecting nomadic human tribes with whom it came into contact. However, because those infected with the primate HIV lived in small tribal communities, when the virus did strike humans it quickly died off with the deaths of its hosts. It was not sustainable. And—as with the bubonic plague in Mongolia—strict tribal taboos on sex may also have contained it.

"As we know," Kumarov strode slowly around the bunker, "until the early 1980s no one even knew what HIV-1 *looked* like. From preserved tissue we know, retrospectively, that the first Western case of AIDS occurred in 1954, but it was still a very slow-spreading disease. Then two social events occurred at roughly the same time which allowed HIV-1 and AIDS to move into epidemic proportions; the sexual revolution among the West's male homosexual communities and the burgeoning use of intravenous drugs. Add to this the existence of huge cities, as opposed to the small African villages that HIV-1 had previously visited, and the resultant effect is the current epidemic of

AIDS. While its means of transmission remains viable, the size of the communities it now inhabits makes it impossible for the virus to kill *itself* off by killing *all* potential hosts, especially given the extended time AIDS takes to dispose of those it infects. Thus, it is a sustainable, if moderate, epidemic.

"But widespread though it is, and even though there is no cure yet, AIDS *is* containable. Unfortunately for it, the HIV-1 virus has chosen an immensely restrictive method of transmission. It can only be transferred through an actual interchange of bodily fluids. In short, AIDS is deadly only because there is no cure, not because of its mode of transmission. Though its victims would undoubtedly disagree— it is not, and will not become, a true plague. The same, incidentally, was true of the short-lived Ebola outbreak in 1995."

Holtzmann, straining to follow Kumarov's strange dissertation, poured the Russian another tumbler of vodka.

Swallowing quickly, Kumarov continued.

"But, *Señor,* let us look at another epidemic—again a virus; influenza. Influenza has been a remarkably successful viral plague. While never having had the effect in one episode as *Pasteurella pestis,* it has, through the ages, killed upwards of five hundred million people. Its first major plague effect was in 1610, its most recent in 1918, when it killed over twenty million people. But still it has returned through this century again and again. Influenza is important to our project as a model, because it is an *infinitely adaptable* virus, which—even though we have vaccines— will surface year after year in slightly different forms and take many lives. Why? Because of its mode of transmission. It is carried through the air. The virus has mastered mass transmission, and kills in the short space of time between a new strain appearing and a new vaccine being developed."

Kumarov's eyes were shining in admiration for this remarkable genetic rogue. Holtzmann was also transfixed—he guessed what was coming next.

"My task," Kumarov said slowly, "was to find within an animal community, or deliberately mutate, a virus as deadly and obscure as HIV-1, but which has a mode of mass transmission and swiftness of mortality equal to influenza."

Kumarov paused and stared directly at Holtzmann, eyes narrowing now as he spoke his final words—quietly and without drama, for there was enough in the words themselves. "I believe I have found such a virus, *Señor.*"

Holtzmann rose from his seat. Kumarov poured the remaining vodka into his mouth, dribbling some through his smile.

"You—?" the Colombian stuttered, his steel-edged boots rapping the stone floor as he paced.

"Yes," said the Russian triumphantly. "Because my new test procedures allowed me to *isolate* viruses—a development on the furthest borders of imagination for the rest of the world's research community. Because of *your* commitment to this work, *Señor* Holtzmann, I can now look at viruses as I might look at fruit in a grocer's shop. As I say, historically this has been in the realm of fantasy. Viruses have been virtually undetectable; they alter cells to suit their own genetic mold and render themselves indistinguishable from the cell mass. But now I can see them. And so I have found the one."

Holtzmann grabbed his shoulders and shook him. Suddenly the millions he had spent meant nothing; the search for Kumarov, the cost of his research and his "walls of silence." Finally it had crystallised as power. The power to strike back—his breathing quickened—the power of the plague.

Kumarov's grin distorted his face as he read the other's mind. "The Holtzmann Plague," he said slowly. His words hung in the air.

"Yes," hissed Holtzmann.

"When released," Kumarov continued after a time. "I have no doubt that the virus I have isolated will be more virulent, more deadly, than any the world has seen. You will find it well worth your investment."

Holtzmann did not speak for several minutes, his eyes fixed on the portrait of his father.

"And you?" he asked quietly as he finally turned to face Kumarov again. "What is your pleasure in this?"

"Me?" replied the Russian, forcing his own gaze away from the old photograph on the wall. "I have three masters. The first is my science. That has now been served; this discovery is a pinnacle I could once never have hoped to reach. The second is my brother. To him I have a debt of honour—without him I would have perished as a child on the streets; now my discovery can help him as it helps you."

"And you," he said simply. "You are my third master."

"Are you then as pitiless as me?" said Holtzmann.

Kumarov regarded him for a time, thinking. It was difficult to remove Holtzmann from what he knew of him. "Perhaps," he said carefully. "And perhaps I am more so. Apart from Sasha there is no one I care about, no one whose life I feel sufficiently strongly about saving, no one whose death I would move to avert. There is Sasha and there is—"

"No, do not include me," Holtzmann stopped him with a chuckle, "that would be overly generous."

Kumarov shrugged. "You have done what my brother did, *Señor,* you have allowed me to continue. I should care about your life."

Holtzmann laughed again; a low, disturbing sound. "I think you are happiest peering at these worlds within our fingertips, rather than the world as it is?"

The Russian nodded. "It is true, you need only come to my country now to see it. The mass is not a pleasant thing; rapacious for pleasure, gorging on whimsy and producing nothing apart from that which sates other appetites. Is mankind so worthy? I do not think so."

Holtzmann came close to him. "My power, Kumarov, comes from the mass. I feed its pleasure. Do you see the irony?"

Kumarov's thin lips split in a grin and he nodded.

"But I am curious," Holtzmann went on. "How you will feel when you see the effect of your creation?"

"I too am curious," replied Kumarov slowly.

The USAF fighter-trainer Hog Collins had rustled up at such short notice taxied across the tarmac towards the waiting motorcade at Medellín's José María Córdova Airport. Impressive, thought Stone, staring out from the cockpit, though he could see no sign of General Samaraz. The pilot shut down the T-38 and Stone clambered out of the tight-fitting seat, gratefully stretching his cramped muscles. A smartly uniformed Colombian Army officer stood at the bottom of the steps.

"General Stone." He saluted crisply. "I am Major Márquez. General Samaraz is waiting for you at HQ."

Stone returned his salute and stepped into the armour-plated limousine, sandwiched between the army convoy. In all, he was being protected by nearly two companies of heavily armed soldiers. Samaraz was obviously trying to impress him, but his efforts were serving only to advertise his presence, thought Stone, wincing at the overkill of his Colombian colleague and feeling even more concerned about the operation he was about to witness. They drove out through a guarded exit, then roared into the narrow streets of Medellín.

Fifteen minutes later, with a great grinding of gears and screeching of brakes, the motorcade pulled up outside a large building in the centre of the city.

"This way, sir." Major Márquez opened the limo door. Stone stepped out and, still in his flight suit, was led past an honour guard lining the building's front steps. By the time he reached what he assumed was Samaraz's operations room, Stone's pessimism was complete.

"General Stone!" the familiar voice boomed out. "You look very well!"

"General Samaraz," replied Stone, forcing a smile onto his face. "You also look well."

"Polo," Samaraz smoothed his jacket, which fell from broad shoulders to an enviable waist. "The sport of kings. Or in Colombia," he laughed, "of generals."

"So when does it start?" asked Stone, barely concealing his anxiety.

"Come, come!" replied Samaraz. "I think you will be pleased. There have been some changes." He waved his hand over a huge relief map in the middle of the room and swiftly outlined the details of the attack on Holtzmann's base. Stone listened with great interest and growing good humour. Despite his earlier truculence, Samaraz had modified his strategy, and it was a critical change of plan. A Colombian Special Forces brigade was to be choppered into the target area directly after the air strike by two fighter squadrons of the Colombian Air Force.

After Samaraz's explanation, Stone's smile was genuine. He slapped his Colombian counterpart on the shoulder, then unclipped his briefcase. "They're late but they're here," he said, opening the manila folder.

Now it was Samaraz's turn to smile as he saw the high-definition US spy satellite photographs.

"You'll see the target is well camouflaged, but these have to be SAM batteries," said Stone, jabbing his finger at the photographs. "And machine-gun nests on the perimeter."

Samaraz nodded enthusiastically and pressed an intercom button. Within seconds he was joined by the men who would lead the air and ground assault on Holtzmann's base.

"Colonel Vanquero, Captain Gomez," he introduced them quickly and informally. Vanquero saluted, then gripped Stone's hand.

"I was sorry to hear about Colonel Kane," he said. "I met him when he was here."

"He's bad but he'll pull through, Colonel," replied Stone. "He's sorry he couldn't be back for this."

"Here!" Samaraz impatiently directed their attention to the photographs. Both Vanquero and Gomez nodded appreciatively as their eyes flitted between the satellite photographs and their maps and flight plans.

"Definitely SAMs," grunted Gomez.

"We will not be using napalm," said Samaraz abruptly, his tone changing. "Missiles, cluster, and anti-personnel bombs. We must be able to distinguish Holtzmann's remains." Stone looked up, wondering who Samaraz was talking to like a kindergarten teacher, and came face to face with Colombia's president, Juan Vargo.

"President Vargo," said Samaraz. "General Marlon Stone, US Marines."

Stone saluted the older man. "Mr. President."

"General Stone," answered Vargo in a soft voice. "We are hoping for a victory today."

"We are that, sir," replied Stone.

"Then let us begin," announced Samaraz.

Stone saluted the two field commanders as they left. "Kick ass!" he whispered into Vanquero's ear.

"And take names, sir," replied the Colombian Marine.

Stone offered a silent prayer as he watched the men depart. Then he followed General Samaraz and President Vargo into the adjoining communications room.

The picked-at remnants of lunch surrounded them in the dimness of the bunker. Neither man had an appetite, though Holtzmann's voracity for details about Kumarov's research was insatiable.

"So how will it kill?" the Colombian savoured his final question.

Kumarov inhaled deeply; his mind felt almost spent as

he struggled to find a mode of explanation that Holtzmann would understand.

"Each virus," he began, "possesses genetic *hooks* which it uses to attach itself to host cells. These hooks have been more difficult to detect than the viruses themselves, but they are as crucial to the production of a potential plague virus as its ability to survive in the atmosphere and its method of transmission. I was searching for a specific type of viral hook that would allow the organism to attach itself to, and then mutate, erythrocytes."

Holtzmann's eyes narrowed.

"Human red blood-cells," explained Kumarov. "The virus had to enter the lungs and seek out erythrocytes during the respiratory process—"

"But how will it kill?" Holtzmann interrupted.

The Russian coughed. "The primary mutative effect of the virus on red-blood cells is the disabling of their critical function in the respiratory process. In essence," his mind grasped for simplicity. "In essence, the red-blood cells will be robbed of their ability to absorb and transport oxygen through the body of the infected subject. The subject will therefore suffocate."

Holtzmann looked at him steadily, then comprehension dawned on him. "Tell me, will it be a painful death?"

"That I . . ." stammered Kumarov, but Holtzmann waved his hand.

"Enough," he laughed. "You have done well with your explanation."

Both men fell silent for several minutes. Then Holtzmann called for coffee and after it was delivered, spoke. "I have been in contact with your brother."

Immediately he saw that he had startled the Russian and drummed his fingers as he awaited the response.

"I . . . did not know," Kumarov faltered. Inside he seethed; this had not been agreed between them. "When, why—?"

"That is of no importance," said Holtzmann. "In any case, you will be pleased to know that I was able to be of great assistance to Alexander Simenovich."

Kumarov guessed he was being deliberately provocative, using his brother's patronymic. But he could not let the matter go unchallenged. His confidence, even within this bunker at the centre of Holtzmann's empire, had returned. He'd seen the Colombian's need for him.

"In the matter of my brother," he said slowly, "I understood that you would allow me to make the arrangements. Sasha is a volatile man, he—"

"I too am volatile!" Holtzmann shouted, rising to his feet and spilling the contents of the table. His bodyguards rushed in and levelled their weapons at Kumarov. The Russian stumbled back, terrified and confused. Holtzmann glared at him and Kumarov glimpsed what burned behind his eyes. Then a malicious glint came into them, and the Colombian extended a hand.

"You see, Kumarov," he smiled. "Perhaps your brother and I are well suited. He, like me, has one aim, a single ambition that knows no obstacle. Like you also?"

Still shaking, Kumarov nodded weakly.

Holtzmann continued. "I spoke to him because I intend to be present for your testing."

The Russian heard the words and knew he could do nothing to change them. The thought of Holtzmann looking over his shoulder brought him no joy at all.

"He did not tell me this," Kumarov said finally.

"Do not presume to know anyone, Kumarov," Holtzmann said. "We are together—the three of us—because our ambitions coincide."

"Yes," said Kumarov softly. "We begin testing within the month. Alexander Simenovich has arranged—"

"Yes, he told me. And so we shall see how your virus— *and you*—survive in the real world."

"There are a number of small-scale tests to be done, and

the delivery system to be prepared," Kumarov answered, trying to calm himself. "Do you really need—?"

"I have already made arrangements with your brother," Holtzmann broke in. "My temporary absence from Colombia will confuse Vargo and the Americans, as it will my rivals here. By the time of my return the country will have chewn itself apart. Vargo will suffer daily embarrassment as the campaign waged by my well-paid servants against him continues. My rivals will move to supplant me and will instead destroy themselves. None of them have the *Brigada,* which already I have ordered back to their homes with their bank accounts full, to await word of my need for them.

"You see, Kumarov," Holtzmann stroked his beard. "This is no whim on my part."

"But the Americans," persisted Kumarov. "If you are found to be—"

"Enough," Holtzmann growled. "I have a purpose that is not served by sitting in this pit!"

"I understand," said Kumarov simply.

There was no marking on the door which was guarded by two Marines. Inside, Kane's hospital file had only a numerical identification. His attending physician was also a Marine—Stone trusted no one else.

He lay face up, drifting through the fog. Dulled by painkillers, his brain juggled disparate dream-like glimpses of reality. The shapes surrounding him had gradually grown harder edged as the hours dragged on.

"Tom?" The whisper perforated the dream. Hog Collins was standing over him. Kane blinked and nodded, squinting at the familiar face. He tried to speak but found he could not, and only a sandpaper sound rasped from his throat.

"Steady, Kane. You've had a hell of a time."

As he stared, unblinking now, Kane remembered. He

made a feeble attempt to sit up, but felt a hand on his shoulder.

Collins spoke slowly, in an undertone. "We caught the guy. Stone's with Samaraz. Relax, the world's okay."

Kane nodded and fell back.

"Command squadron, in position," Captain Gomez's voice came crisply over the radio. Stone looked at the perspex map behind him as Samaraz's adjutant, Major Márquez, indicated where Gomez's aircraft were located.

"Holding thirty thousand," the leader of the second squadron of Kfir C 7 fighters reported.

Stone knew that there was an additional fighter squadron comprising slower but only marginally less deadly Cessna A-37B Dragonflies ready to attack Holtzmann's headquarters in a third wave if required. Colonel Vanquero's special forces men were aboard their Pave Hawks and Black Hawks, already airborne and circling in a hidden valley ten miles below the target. It was, by any standards, a major strike force, and testimony to how dangerous the Colombians considered Holtzmann to be.

"Preparing to attack," Gomez's voice again broke the stillness of the communications room. Stone tightened his fists, and imagined the fighters five miles above him, diving out of level flight for their attack run.

"*Please* kick ass!" he whispered.   .

Kane's body throbbed with dull pain as he drifted on the periphery of sleep. His awareness slowly gathered and he heard muted radio traffic. Opening his eyes he saw Hog Collins hunched over a radio set.

"Hog," he groaned. Collins looked at him, reaching forward to kill the sound.

"What is . . . ?" Kane whispered.

"It's going down," muttered Collins guiltily. His vigil had been constant but he had been loathe to miss the strike on

Holtzmann being relayed from Medellín to Fort Wright—the Department of Defence communications centre fifty miles from Miami.

"Let me hear it," Kane hissed through his fog.

Collins glanced towards the door. "Tom—"

"Let me . . ." repeated Kane slowly. Reluctantly, Collins stretched out his hand and turned the volume up. The perfectly controlled voice of the duty radio officer at Fort Wright filled the room.

"Better than HBO," Collins grinned nervously in the sudden radio silence preceding the first air attack.

Kane grimaced through his bandages.

"Colombians report the command air squadron is approximately thirty seconds from target," the dry monotone emanated from the radio.

Collins crossed himself.

"So," Holtzmann was saying. "You cannot stay here, but fortunately you have only to travel to Medellín—it is not far from here. Your flight leaves in six hours. Contact me on your return to Moscow."

"Immediately," replied the Russian.

Holtzmann shook the other's hand. "You have done well, Kumarov," he said gruffly.

"Fifteen seconds," Gomez announced. In the sky above the Andes six glinting jet fighters, the cutting edge of the *Fuerza Aerea Colombiana,* plunged down at an astonishing rate. Ten thousand feet above, the second squadron of FAC Kfirs commenced its dive. Slung beneath the Israeli-made fighter-bombers were heat-seeking missiles and laser-guided bombs, augmenting their cannons and machine-guns. In the lead bird, Captain Gomez's eyes focused on the patch of mountain jungle that he would soon turn into a fire zone.

"Five seconds." He glanced at his weapons systems, all were armed and ready. His fingers itched to loose them.

"Command one, commencing attack," he said smoothly, flicking his missile switches on.

"This is it, m'boy!" Collins could not restrain himself. Kane shifted in his bed.

"The attack has begun. Repeat, the attack has begun," came the deadpan voice from Fort Wright.

"*Señor* Holtzmann?" Kumarov turned as if having forgotten something.

"Yes?" Holtzmann asked.

But the answer didn't come. The first explosion shook the earth above and a whirling blizzard of debris tore through the underground chamber.

"No!" screamed Holtzman. "*No!*" but his shriek was lost in the maelstrom.

Stone whooped as the explosions sounded behind Gomez's crisp damage reports. Being a Marine, he always found this side of war breathtakingly clinical.

"SAMs destroyed," radioed Gomez. "Zero deployed."

"We caught him sleeping, Stone!" bellowed Samaraz.

"Let us be sure that he is there, General," replied President Vargo tensely.

"Colombians are really playing ball, Tom," said Collins. "We may just have the sonofabitch after all."

Kane looked up at Hog; the pain was closing in again but beyond it, a dark doubt gnawed at him.

"The Colombian Special Forces have surrounded the compound," came the report from Fort Wright. "Colonel Vanquero reports saturation damage to compound defences . . ."

Beneath his sheets, Kane's left hand clenched as the seconds passed.

"Moving to centre of compound," Vanquero's cool voice echoed through the communications room.

Stone gripped the desk. *Come on, come on,* he willed, *Find him!*

"No return fire from main building," Vanquero continued.

"Jeep—southwest corner of compound," one of the circling Black Hawk pilots reported excitedly. "Target destroyed," he added seconds later.

"Investigating," said Vanquero on the ground. The minutes ticked by. "Still searching for primary target," he radioed finally. In the communications room, Samaraz hit the table with frustration.

"Where are you, Holtzmann?"

Dead silence reigned in the room, broken only by the radio transmissions.

"Entering main building, no sign of enemy. Proceeding to—"

Then came a noise so deafening that it blew out many of the radio speakers ringing the communications room; a thunderclap report of a huge explosion.

Stone's face paled.

"Alert! Alert!" screamed one of the chopper pilots. "The compound has blown up. Colonel! Colonel!" But Vanquero did not reply.

No one from the fifty-man special forces brigade replied.

"How?" gasped Samaraz, collapsing into a seat. His president stood, smoking a cigarette; his hands, his whole body, trembled.

Stone looked blankly at the map before him. "Someone detonated a booby trap," he said, as if talking to himself. "A self-destruct mechanism. Couldn't have been automatic, missiles would have tripped it." He rubbed his forehead, pushing the balls of his hands into his eyes until they hurt.

"He has defeated the Colombian Army," said President Vargo with pitiful anguish in his voice. "He has won."

Collins reached forward glumly and lowered the volume. Reports were still coming in from Fort Wright, echoing the chaos in Colombia.

"Guess they'll use all the choppers to evacuate their wounded," he mutterd. "Can't imagine anyone would've blown the place without Holtzmann giving the order."

Kane's eyes closed and the nauseating darkness of pain and defeat gathered him in.

BOOK**TWO**

CHAPTER**EIGHT**

Kalin was not a reasonable man. He was a man of God and had no need of reason.

"We will push on with our struggle, with divine righteousness and fury," he screamed into the microphone. "To drive the infidel back into the mountains from whence he sprang. *Vygnat arabov von!*"

Below, amidst the crowd, Galena Chagall shivered as she glanced around at the faces in the mob.

"This is fucking impossible!" swore her cameraman as the mass pushed forward.

"Calm down, Terry," Lena warned. "It's early days. Just get enough for cover but for God's sake make it look like we're recording every damn word."

"Yes boss," came the terse reply.

Lena swallowed her anger. Her working relationship with the cameraman recommended by her news editor, Jack Mahoney, had gone from bad to worse during the weeks they'd spent in Novominsk—capital of Kalin's self-declared republic of Danzanstan in former Soviet-Armestan. She looked at Harry Berg, her soundman, but his attention was fully taken up with providing Terry some measure of protection from the buffeting crowd.

As Kalin's speech continued, Lena translated his Russian in her head. He was railing against the *araby,* "arabs": native inhabitants of Armestan, now the enemy of the *danzany,* the "white" Armestanis. The response of his audience became more ferocious with every new exhortation.

That Kalin was mad, Lena had no doubt, even though she had yet to get close to the *danzan* leader. Pale and slight, he did not even physically resemble those he led— sun-darkened, third-generation ancestors of the first Soviet mass deportation, when Lenin had "relocated" nearly a million Belorussians to Soviet-Armestan. More than seventy years separated them in time from the plains of Belorussia—and now they numbered over three million. The *danzany* were claiming the land as their own, and under Kalin they had all but succeeded in taking it.

Lena guessed the crowd numbered in the hundreds of thousands. Virtually the entire able-bodied *danzan* population of Novominsk had turned out for the rally and Kalin's speech. Not that there were any ethnic Armestanis left in the city, she reminded herself, apart from the prisoners-of-war languishing in camps outside the city; away from the prying eyes of the few Red Cross personnel who had been allowed into Novominsk. *And away from us,* she thought with disgust.

"*Vygnat arabov von!*" the call was taken up now. "Drive the Arabs out!" The mass roared its approval of Kalin's message.

Lena wondered at the power of this small man, dwarfed by the huge bank of speakers, who had gathered the disparate strands the white *danzan* community into a battle-force.

Lena winced as Kalin's tame Russian Orthodox priest, Father Orkavich, blessed the crowd. Kalin himself was hustled off-stage, leaving the crowd to its chant and to the host of minor speakers planned for the day's rally. His body-guards huddled around him as they pushed through the ranks of the faithful at the rear of the stage and into a black Volga. Stumbling towards them, but prevented from getting too close by the density of the crowd, Lena and her camera crew watched as the three-car convoy revved away from them.

"Bloody great," swore Terry. He turned on their *danzan* minder, a junior member of Kalin's staff. "Thanks for the fucking warning, dipstick!"

Lena had had enough. She grabbed her cameraman by the shirt and dragged him away.

"Listen you asshole," she snapped when they were out of earshot. "I don't care how many fucking wars you've covered for Jack Mahoney, if you don't keep your mouth shut you're out of this one! Got it?"

"Suits me, love," drawled Terry.

Lena glared at him in fury, wondering whether he played up his Australian macho image just to rile her.

"We're the only crew here," she went on. "The *only* one! They're suspicious, they hate Americans—"

"Good on them," Terry came back. "Not that fond of Yanks myself." He was fed up with Lena and the whole "star" system she represented.

"Fuck you, Woods!" said Lena under her breath, as Sergei Pulkakov, their ever-present shadow, approached them, trailing an apologetic Harry Berg.

"Back to Chateau WorldNet, then?" cracked Terry. There was complete silence in the van as they bumped their way through the potholed streets of Novominsk to what remained of the old InterEurope Hotel.

As his convoy wound up the slopes of the Markesh mountain range towards the huge former monastery that was now his headquarters, Kalin glanced back at Novominsk and the enormous crowd spilling out from its central square. *The war was so-nearly won.* He let the thought, and the dream it described—Danzanstan—hang in his mind for a minute, before concentrating on more immediate concerns.

"Any word from Tumakoc?" he asked his adjutant.

"The siege holds, Kalin," replied the man immediately. "The *araby* again failed to break through this morning and suffered many casualties in the attempt."

"Good, Marco," said Kalin.

The besieged *arabski* city to the north was one of only a few Muslim enclaves still resisting his militia. But they would not survive long, thought Kalin, as the car swung through the steel gates of the Monastery. His face betrayed little, though the imminence of Tumakoc's destruction and the manner in which it would be destroyed brought a gleam to his deep-set eyes.

Inside his headquarters he went swiftly to the war-room, a capacious basement beneath the Monastery complex.

"Kalin!" snapped Boris Rodionov as he entered.

Rodionov, Kalin's chief-of-staff, had been a Major-General in the Red Army before the Soviet Union disintegrated. Now he brought his military experience to the fight against the *araby*—and so far the army he directed had proved to be an almost irresistible force. Though a canny enough field commander, Rodionov knew he had a large measure of luck on his side; the Armestani division he had commanded for the Soviets had been almost exclusively composed of white Russians—*danzany*. It had been a central tenet of the former Soviet Defence Department that "native" conscripts and regulars be spread thinly through the Red Army to avert their possible support for nationalistic uprisings in their homelands. Rodionov's division had been based in Novominsk, fully equipped with latest-generation Soviet armour and weaponry, together with four squadrons of fighter aircraft and fighter-bombers stationed at the nearby Shaklin airbase. Indeed, for three years—until 1994—Rodionov had been the ranking Russian Army officer in Armestan. Then Kalin's call to arms had come and

Rodionov had switched his allegiance, bringing nearly ten thousand regular soldiers with him. This force had since been swelled by irregular *danzany* militiamen, while his enemy, the *araby*—or *Kadashi* as they called themselves—had struggled back to Armestan from their far-flung Russian Army divisions to defend their people.

From his height of well over six feet, Rodionov stared down at Kalin and their eyes locked. The other occupants of the room were silent. Rodionov was like a great shaggy beast, slightly stooped, his hair a brown clump parted on the left by a vicious scar; his "Afghani badge" as he called it. His blue eyes peered from beneath eyebrows also made sparse by injuries of war. Next to him, Kalin looked almost a midget though his eyes were fiercer than most men's.

"We have reports of a column of refugee *araby* on Mount Barkusk—the Tumakoc road," Rodionov said. "Around three hundred."

"Stop them," replied Kalin curtly.

Rodionov nodded. While both men knew the refugees would be mainly women and children, there was no pity in their expressions or in their minds. The massive general gestured to one of the junior officers in the room.

"Advise Ranovich to proceed with his attack against the *araby* on Barkusk," he growled. "He will be expecting the order."

The *danzan* officer snapped a salute and rushed out.

"Any other general business?" Kalin asked quickly, his eyes sweeping the room. There was no answer.

"Then leave us," he commanded. All but Rodionov disappeared. "Boris Nikolaevich," Kalin said sternly when the room had cleared. "There is a matter I must inform you of." The two fell into a discussion conducted in such hushed tones that even had there been listeners beyond the heavy oak door, nothing would have been heard.

* * *

Outside, Lieutenant Vasily Moroz walked into the gathering mountain breeze towards the communications building, smiling. He was pleased that Kalin had issued the order he was about to pass on. Though he was barely twenty, it was as though Moroz had lived his life for this struggle against the *araby* he so despised, and had despised from his childhood. Now another blow was about to be struck in the cleansing of Danzanstan. The pug-faced youth was jubilant. *Araby* would again be dying in the face of *danzan* bullets.

"Hoxa." His shout echoed through the small room.

One of its occupants turned around and gazed at him, annoyed by the disrespect of the younger man. "*Sergeant* Hoxa," he replied, but Moroz paid no attention.

"Hoxa—contact Barkusk," Moroz snapped self-importantly. "Orders from Kalin himself. Ranovich's men are to proceed with their attack."

The sergeant took the news with an internal wince, which became a scowl as Moroz left. Unlike the youth, Grigor Hoxa took no pleasure from the massacres which had become such a common part of this war. Not that he would contemplate making his opinions known. He had seen how dissenters were treated.

"Novominsk to Barkusk." He spoke slowly into the handset.

"Barko here, go ahead Novo!"

Hoxa communicated Kalin's order to a man he knew would relish discharging it.

"Where in the hell *is* Armestan anyway?" The question was delivered with utterly unnecessary but equally predictable volume. Jack Mahoney looked beyond Peterson to the sky-scrapers of lower Manhattan and withstood the "dumb-down" act of his superior as it crashed about him. As Eastern European News Editor for WorldNet he was used to it.

"Former Soviet Central Asia," he began slowly. "South Georgia, north-west corner of Armenia—"

"What I mean is why the fuck would anyone apart from you and the Princess care who lives or dies there?" roared Peterson.

Asshole! The single word echoed around Mahoney's mind as he struggled to contain his instant, Irish fury. His flared eyes took in the whole pitiful sight that was David Peterson, Executive Vice-President of News at WorldNet—a cloddish man who had risen to his position not by any knowledge of journalism or news-gathering, but by selling more advertising space than his competitors for the job.

Peterson liked to affect a boorish manner—but one which left his underlings in no doubt that it actually concealed a cunning managerial mind. He strode about his office throwing a baseball between his hands, then juggling it, another affectation which had spawned a running joke amongst the host of WorldNet journalists, editors, and anchors he had so far managed to alienate. To Peterson, went the line, integrity must look something like a baseball.

"It's showing all the signs of becoming the flashpoint for a showdown between the Christian and Islamic republics in the former Soviet Union—not just a minor civil skirmish but a full-scale war between Russia and the Central Asian republics," Mahoney answered. "The Islamic states won't allow another Chechnya or Bosnia. Moscow won't abandon its people there. It's a dangerous stand-off and a dirty war, as bad as Bosnia at its worst. The US is tut-tutting but won't step in, nor will Western Europe. It's the sort of story World Net is *supposed* to be about!" Mahoney took a deep breath. He knew his words had not penetrated a mind currently requiring all of its resources to keep a baseball aloft.

Peterson snatched the ball from the air, walked up to him and brought his face uncomfortably close to Mahoney's.

"The Princess comes home, Jack," he barked as the baseball clattered onto the marble floor.

At his sides, Mahoney's fists clenched and unclenched as he held them back from Peterson's arrogant leer. "*Lena* will say no," he finally countered.

"No?" spluttered Peterson. "*No!*" He snatched a sheaf of papers off his desk and waved them in Mahoney's face. "Do you have any fucking idea how much it's costing this network to have our prime-time anchor on fucking study leave?" he swore. "*I* won't wear it. *Caspar* won't wear it."

"Well let Caspar fucking tell her!" Mahoney finally exploded. He stood stock-still for a second, glaring at Peterson, then stormed out before the fury peaking inside led him to do worse.

"Only a little while," Shukhrata Mahmud whispered to the limp bundle she held so tightly to her. "Only a little while, *baboud.*" The phrase had become a mantra for her. She was just another desperate face amongst the crowd which surrounded her. Some were from her village of Kmurna, some were those they had picked up on the journey. She and her baby were all that remained of her family. Her resolution that the child who bore his butchered father's name would not die had sustained her during the march. So quickly and brutally had the *danzany* attacked, and so hopeless had their plight been from the outset, that she had fled only with the clothes she wore, and the tiny shape of Hamed still wrapped in his bedding.

"You will not die, *baboud!*" she hissed fiercely under her breath, as the afternoon sun fell behind the mountain and plunged them into chilly shade. Around her, Shukhrata could hear only the sounds of footfalls, and the massed whispering of other mothers willing their children on, or youths urging their mothers—there were few fathers among them—not to fall, urging them to go on. Urging them to live—just as she pleaded with Hamed, suffering the innocent pain of hunger, and not knowing why his body was racked with the shudders that herald death.

Shukhrata looked ahead at the bare slopes stretching before her then glanced again at Hamed's face. His dark eyes stared up at her constantly. Shukhrata forced back her tears and ground her teeth as she struck out on the trail with renewed determination.

Then, suddenly, she was scrabbling this way and that on the scree, covering Hamed as bullets seared into her body. Her screams of fear became howls of agony as bullets continued spraying through the air around her, vicious lumps of lead—penetrating faces, stomachs, hearts, and brains—like a cloud of white-hot locusts that had descended on them. Shukhrata shuddered as her pain escalated, hugging Hamed as the bitter darkness approached. The child began to cry as the life passed out of his mother, making pitiful noises which continued long after the rattle of automatic fire had given way to more methodical killing.

Now the *danzan* attackers moved in a line through the dead, seeking out those who had survived and finishing them with a single bullet to the head, or a bayonet thrust into the chest. An old man who had been faking death screamed as the knife entered him and his young executioner laughed, twisting the bayonet inside him until he was silenced. The attackers applauded their comrade's discovery and action. One of them stood over Shukhrata.

The youth who had killed the old man looked across as a baby was dragged out from beneath the dead woman. The militiaman swung it around, shouting in hatred and triumph, until the infant's screams of incomprehension reached a fearful pitch.

"*Blyadskiye araby!*" he screamed and hurled the five-month-old victim high into the air. Shots rang out as one or two of the men fired at the baby before it struck the ground. Then it glanced off a sharp rocky outcrop with a small explosion of blood and tumbled down the steep slope, out of sight. The men's eyes turned away and they resumed their task more quickly now; their bloodlust for the enemy had been sated, now they were just completing their orders to leave no *araby* alive.

Abdur Mohammed watched as they approached him, his eyes frozen open with fear. He forced them shut and clenched his fifteen-year-old jaws tightly closed so that he would not scream. In the stillness of a life so precious that it was now being measured in seconds Abdur promised Allah revenge for what he had seen. He heard footfalls; closer and closer. They stopped, and the sucking sound of a bayonet entering and withdrawing from a body, and the gasp of final pain which accompanied it, carried to his ears. Every nerve in his body readied itself for the shock of the knife, and in the madness of the moment his sole wish was that the *danzany* would kill him with a bullet. Then he felt a sudden blinding pain in his temple and all went black.

"Finished, Dimitri?" Ranovich, the squad leader, shouted. The militiaman looked at him across the bloody piles of slaughtered *araby,* then back down at the three at his feet. He dropped his rifle and circled the barrel over the bodies. Then he casually pulled the trigger. His bullet smashed into the old woman's skull, and its contents spattered the faces of the two who lay on either side of her, a teenage boy and girl. The militiaman kicked the boy's head again as he had done moments earlier, and turned to rejoin his squad.

"Finished!" he shouted.

As he re-entered the vast newsroom that also served as a backdrop for their news broadcasts, Mahoney watched Lena's replacement deliver the evening bulletin. He shook his head and walked on to his office. Mary Hutchins was good, but nothing separated her from the great mass of WorldNet anchors.

Reaching his office, Mahoney glanced up at the publicity

photo of Lena on his wall. He never failed to be transfixed by it. She was the best—a ferocious journalist with an intelligence so rare in television, but she was still, in all senses, a woman. He knew that just about every man who had ever met her felt the same instant desire for her as he had. As he still did, he thought disconsolately.

You know I adore you, Jack, she had said. He smiled brokenly and sat down. Over the years he had tried to convert his passion into a more paternal emotion. And she kept her privacy so intact that even he, her favourite news editor covering her favourite part of the world, had little idea how she spent her spare time and with whom. He sighed and looked away from her photo.

He had at least another two hours to wait before her latest report from Armestan came in; it was time he did not begrudge. The meeting with Peterson ebbed quickly from his mind. However management decided to resolve the situation it would not be by ordering Lena home. She was too valuable a star, with too many "outs" in her contract. And, like all stars, she could be as volatile and tempestuous as the occasion demanded—but not about the size of her dressing room, the placement of her publicity shots or having a personal hairdresser on the road, Mahoney grinned, thinking how other WorldNet anchors would react if told they were going to Armestan. Most would think it was a spread.

"Mary Hutchins, WorldNet." The sign-off stirred him into action, and he strode out again into the eerie hum of the newsroom, a chamber that was workplace for nearly three hundred WorldNet staffers, of which a scant twenty were his. By day they pumped out the same bulletin to the USA as to the rest of the world. By night, while the smaller WorldNet operation in Washington continued to deliver the domestic bulletins to insomniacs around America, Mahoney and his team beamed out WorldNet International, with a larger component of foreign news, for the European and Asian daylight hours.

"Slow news day, Jack," said Hutchins as he passed the anchor's desk.

"Yeah," he said. "The best for the world is the worst for us." Then he remembered that she was Peterson's current lay. He decided not to stop and chat; the image she would provoke, of Peterson in bed, was about as revolting a thought as his mind was capable of.

"Like it, Jack?"

Lena glanced at Harry Berg, sitting next to the portable transponder assembled at the hotel window. Both of them knew that the five minute backgrounder on Armestan they'd just sent to Mahoney was little more than wallpaper. Her anxious query bounced off a SatCom satellite over Turkey and down to New York.

"It doesn't set me on fire," came Mahoney's truthful reply via the same route.

"We're trying," said Lena. "I know what we need, but it's softly softly here. And if we get anything from the other side it'll have to be unattributed or we'll be thrown out."

"I understand, Lena," Mahoney replied down the line. "Just resist the temptation to do anything stupid, okay? Make your contacts and give me good analysis. You keeping up with the news outside?"

"Some of it," said Lena. "Is that UN convoy still blocked by Kalin's troops?"

"More than blocked," said Mahoney. "UN troops were Pakistani—real smart move. And I mean *were*."

"Oh dear," replied Lena. "Reaction?"

"Pissy as usual. Listen, Lena," he said abruptly. "Before we lose the link, I have to warn you that your friend and mine wants you home."

Lena laughed, tossing back her cascade of dark hair.

"Peterson?" she chuckled. "Is he there?"

"No," said Mahoney. "Want me to get him?"

"Just tell him I was asking after him," Lena winked at Berg.

"Anything else?" asked Mahoney.

"No, Jack. He's got my number if he wants to tell me anything. Lines are bad though."

"Yeah," Mahoney laughed. "Real bad, I hear. Anything else? How's Terry going?"

"Bye, Jack!" Lena said curtly.

"That good?" he said. "Work on him, Lena."

"Sure Jack, bye," she repeated.

"Bye," came the distant reply. "Same time tomorrow!"

Lena stood at the window staring out at the grey cityscape of Novominsk. *Out there somewhere,* she mulled, *a war was going on. Out there somewhere was something that might finally make the world take notice of the Armestan tragedy. Would she find it?* she asked herself disconsolately. Not for the first time since joining television did she wonder if she could have made any more of a difference by staying in uniform.

Beside her, Berg began the meticulous job of repacking the SatCase. She glanced down at it, still in awe at the technology it described. No larger than a suitcase, it was the latest word in satellite news-gathering; a solar-powered transponder which could beam back field reports from almost any spot on earth.

"What I need to do is get shot," she announced.

"True," Berg chuckled. "Terribly true."

"Buy you a drink?" she asked.

"You go down," Berg replied. "I'll be another half hour or so with this. Terry'll be down there."

"Terrific," said Lena. "Reason enough for a drink!"

As she walked past the non-operational elevators and down the five flights of stairs to the shattered hotel's only just operational bar, Lena felt Kane infiltrate her soul. She swallowed the concern that had dogged her for the past two months. His phone had been disconnected and his private office line was answered only by voices who refused to admit anything. And he hadn't called her. Why? She tried to convince herself that he was professionally incommunicado, but her heart nursed dark doubts. *It had happened before,* she told herself, but her yearning to talk to him swamped rationality. She needed Kane like she had needed no other man—more with each day of his absence from her life.

"What I would do with you if you were here," she whispered within the musty confines of the stairwell.

Half a world away, with Lena's story edited and slotted into WorldNet International rundown, Jack Mahoney nursed the remains of a beer. He was drinking alone at Nickels, a Greenwich Village bar that was the network haunt. The joke went that WorldNetters came to Nickels because it was all they were paid. Mahoney came every night, usually late—the lot of a man whose beat was eight time-zones ahead of where he lived.

"Mahoney," the voice was British and he recognised it; Craig Massey, the network's legal reporter.

"How's the Supreme Court?" grinned Mahoney. He liked Massey; the Englishman had a dark and twisted sense of humour.

"How's the Supreme Soviet?" laughed Massey. "Now why did those bastards have to go and ruin a good line!"

"Beer?" Mahoney asked, lighting another cigarette. WorldNet was a non-smoking building and he made up for it with a vengeance after-hours.

"Who says the English and the Irish can't settle their differences in a civilised manner!" said Massey. "Thank you, I will."

He pulled up a seat. "Had a fight with Peterson, I hear?"

Mahoney smiled ruefully. There were no secrets at WorldNet. "A full and frank exchange of views, Craig."

"About Galena?" asked Massey, as fresh beers arrived.

"Yeah," said Mahoney. "Wants her home."

"With all due respect," said the other, "and with none for the esteemed Peterson, I can't say that I blame him *that* much. Her stuff's been pretty dry. Hardly the sort of story to make your name on, I would've thought."

"She's already made her fucking name, Craig," Mahoney retorted. "Not that she cares about that kind of shit anyway."

"Sorry, old boy," quipped Massey, playing the part of Brit to the hilt. "Take no offence. Let me amuse you about Peterson."

"Wouldn't be hard," Mahoney cracked.

"Bastard nearly got himself charged with treason!" said Massey, dropping his voice conspiratorially.

"What?" Mahoney spluttered as beer went down his windpipe.

"Some fancy name for it anyway," grinned the Englishman. " 'Broadcasting counter to national security interests.' That sort of caper. I was called in on it."

Mahoney remembered how, true to its penny-pinching style, WorldNet also used Massey as a standby corporate attorney. "What was the story?" he laughed.

"Some shoot-out, a couple of months ago," replied Massey. "Came up the line from Miami. Our boy down there had the name of the victim, a spook or some such thing— one of ours. Evidently the local lad thought he was on to another Watergate, convinced his news editor, who convinced New York and so on, all the way to Peterson."

"And?" asked Mahoney, eyes watering as he took another deep swallow of beer.

"And," Massey continued. "The Feds had put out an all points bulletin that the victim's name was *verboten*. Publish and be fried. But dear old Peterson wanted to risk it!"

"So what happened?" Mahoney gasped.

"He very nearly broadcast it," squawked Massey triumphantly. "Seemed every WorldNet lawyer was away that day—my turn to play silk. It was Peterson versus the world! He had, I hasten to add, been to a *particularly* long boardroom lunch with the advertising department."

Massey winked and continued in a dramatic tone. "*So* at precisely ten to six I was summoned to the great man's chamber. I viewed the piece at five to six. By the time I had read the official gag order it was *two to six!*"

The Englishman paused and took a gulp of his beer. Mahoney was caught up in the story.

"And at precisely one minute before six," Massey swaggered deliberately, "I killed it."

Mahoney shook his head and laughed beneath his breath. "Stupid fucking idiot," he swore, "and what would have happened to him?"

"The law's the same as contempt, basically," said Massey. "No set term, but you can bet the Feds would have thrown the book at us. They hate the media, and what kind of figure would Peterson have cut in court?"

"You know, Massey," said Mahoney. "I quite liked you up to this point. Why couldn't you have left your worthy judgement until a minute *after* six and spared us Peterson forever?"

"Yes," grinned the other. "I know what you mean. Pity really, in retrospect. The lawyer in me, I suppose, one's duty to defend the defenceless—"

Mahoney snorted and they sat drinking silently.

"Who was the Miami reporter?" asked Mahoney after a time. "I'm surprised I didn't hear about it."

"That was part of the package," answered Massey. "Reporter was Little, Josh Little. Don't think he's still in our employ. Sounded like the sort of chap who thought the collapse of the Soviet Union was a clever Russian conspiracy to dupe us then nuke us."

"Uh huh, and Castro killed Marilyn," Mahoney grumbled. "One less of those won't matter. Who was the spook?"

"Can't say, old chap," chuckled Massey. Mahoney rolled his eyes as the other looked around in an exaggeratedly furtive fashion.

"C'mon," Mahoney jabbed him with his elbow. Massey straightened, and frowned as he tried to remember.

"Honestly, Jack," he said finally. "I've completely forgotten. Seriously! That's the booze for you."

"Yeah," said Mahoney. "Another?"

"Why not!" laughed Massey.

They drank past midnight, outlasting most of the passing WorldNet parade.

"Share a cab?" slurred Mahoney eventually, vaguely recollecting that Massey also lived uptown.

"My dear chap, how very kind," Massey responded, even more drunkenly. As they pulled up by Massey's apartment block on 51st Street, the Englishman bid Mahoney goodnight and tottered into the darkness.

"Oh, *Jack*." His yell broke the night as the cab pulled away.

"Stop," shouted Mahoney, chuckling as he watched Massey shuffle towards him, attempting to snap his fingers.

"I've got it," he exclaimed. "Kane!"

"What?" laughed Mahoney. "What the fuck have you got?"

"The name! The spook, you fool," Massey giggled. "Kane, Thomas John."

Mahoney shuddered, sobering instantly. He leapt from the cab and grasped Massey by his coat.

"What happened to him?" he asked. "What happened to the spook?"

The Englishman reeled back. "Oh, killed I believe. Not sure, why—think the Russians did it?" Cackling, he jerked himself free of Mahoney's grip. "Farewell until the morrow, dear boy!"

The cab jolted crazily up Park Avenue but Mahoney was oblivious, his stare fierce and unfocused. His mind was a mess as he remembered his bitter envy. He hadn't been supposed to know Kane's name but Lena had spilled it. She'd been like a girl with him. Mahoney chewed his lip as he recalled the night in Jerusalem—the longest and most painful in his life.

And now the man responsible was dead.

CHAPTER**NINE**

Kane flicked off the remote and rolled over in bed. The weeks had passed—or was it longer? he wondered disconsolately. His pain was a dull background throb. His wounds were largely healed, but the dissipation of his body and soul remained.

Hog Collins' daily visits, and Stone's less regular attendance at his bedside, had kept him in tune with White Storm's operation, but there had been little joy in any of the news. Holtzmann had disappeared and the Colombian *Operación Narcotraficante* had been all but wound up. President Vargo, facing an election, had agreed to reconsider his country's extradition treaty with the US, the centrepiece of his anti-drug offensive. The nation had been deeply shocked by the deaths of nearly fifty men in the attempt to take Holtzmann, and the main Colombian opposition party had forged ahead in the opinion polls by exhorting America to solve its domestic drug problem before asking Colombia to suffer the wrath of the Sobrecartel. Kane had seen news reports of the massive anti-US rallies in Medellín, Bogotá, and Cali. That evening he had even seen one of the most respected members of President Vargo's cabinet raise the possibility of legalising the cocaine trade.

He had also seen Lena. He grunted and pushed his head into his pillow. She was a constant soothing presence both in his troubled dreams and during his equally uncomfortable waking hours. But that she was in the middle of a war zone brought an ache to his soul to add to the greater ache. He wanted to talk to her, badly. Collins—the only one at White Storm who knew of their relationship—had made some discreet enquiries at WorldNet. "Sat link to the studio once a day—costs 'em twenty grand an hour," he'd reported back. "If you want to make friends in New York when you get out you can try—but that's it. No phones. No other way."

Kane stared at the ceiling. He had been wounded before but rarely had he lost his will to go on. Now he was hovering perilously close to that point.

"Fuck it," he grunted. He rose quickly and dressed, grimacing as he switched on the light and caught sight of himself in the mirror. His hair had grown back over his scalp wound as a clumpy crew-cut and while he no longer wore any bandages, there was an ugly scar where the lower half of his left ear had been. He turned from the mirror and threw his few belongings into a bag, opened the door and greeted the two Marines on duty outside.

"C'mon," he said. "I'm going home."

"Colonel Kane, sir!" jumped one. "No can do, sir. Orders are for you to remain here, sir."

"Orders just changed," he growled. "Now haul ass!"

"Yes, sir!" said the second Marine. The first looked momentarily confused then fell in behind.

"Do you men have transport?" asked Kane. "Or am I going to have to call a cab?"

"Yes, sir!" said the first. "I mean, the rest of the boys are at the main entrance, sir."

Kane grinned despite himself. It had been a while since he had endured the peculiarities of "grunt-speak." "Let's just cut the rank bullshit, okay?" he said as they reached the elevators. "Chrissake, I'll probably lose mine tonight. I'm Kane and you are Taylor and Wallensky, right? By the way, someone'll probably want to know what I'm doing. Tell 'em, will you?"

"Yes, sir!" came the chorused response.

Collins got the first call. "Kane, you sonofabitch," he swore quietly, checking the time. "Jesus Christ."

He put the phone down, sat up and then picked it up again. His fingers punched the number and he winced as Stone's sleep-addled voice came on.

"Hog?"

"General," Collins said quickly. "Kane's just checked himself out."

There was a momentary pause as Stone considered this. "Have the Marines gone with him?"

"Yeah," said Collins. "Got the call from their vehicle."

"Climb back in the cot, Hog," said Stone. "Can't say I blame him, myself."

Collins shook his head and smiled as he hung up. "Welcome back, Tom," he murmured before sleep overtook him again.

Kane looked out at the spectral world as the Humvee roared towards his apartment. Mist swirled before his eyes. It was the same fog that had enveloped his mind for the past weeks. They slowed, pulling up to his apartment block. An involuntary shudder went through his body as he saw it.

"Begging your pardon, sir, but we'll have to check whether the building is secure," announced the Marine called Wallensky.

Kane nodded, handing him the key. Wallensky gestured to his colleague and they dropped out of the Humvee.

An older Marine who was driving the Humvee laughed as he watched the pair.

"You'd think it was Saddam's goddamn bunker," he said. Kane smiled. The two returned and led him into his apartment.

"All clear," said Wallensky when they were inside.

"I'm thankful," replied Kane wryly. "You boys like a drink? I go as far as coffee or water."

"No thank you," said Wallensky. "We'll be on duty out here, sir!"

"C'mon," chuckled Kane. "Make yourselves at home."

"If it's all the same," replied the Marine. "It's kinda difficult. See, General Stone said—"

"Okay," said Kane. "I understand that one. Well thanks, I appreciate it, men."

Wallensky beamed, glad to finally be able to get back to his standing orders. "C'mon Taylor!"

The two marched smartly out. Kane knew it was unfair, but he could not help laughing at their zealousness. He poured himself a glass of water and breathed the stuffy air of his apartment with something approaching happiness. As he looked around, the strange unfamiliarity made him realise how long his convalescence had been. Then he noticed his answering machine, its light blinking softly. He touched a button and there was a momentary whir, then Lena's voice broke into the apartment.

"Hi Tom, it's Tuesday. Thinking about last night most pleasurably. The interview with Brown went as expected—watch it if you like, it'll be on tomorrow night. Bad news for me about Armestan, good news for you—it's going to be weeks before we stand a chance of getting in. I'm heading off to London tonight though, just a couple of days—call you when I get back, okay? That's all I guess. I love you."

She had left the message the day after he had been shot. There could have been no more, he realised as his eyes were drawn to the Post-it note stuck to his phone. White Storm had changed his number.

He rubbed his face and lifted his eyes to the window, staring numbly into the night.

"I love you," he whispered.

Dawn broke over the Colombian city of Cartagena. The high-security fence around the newly renovated house on *calle Assuncíon* attracted no attention. In this town such precaution was commonplace.

Dr. Alberto Morales edged his deep-blue Mercedes towards the curb, ensuring his eyes did not make contact with the occupants of the two cars outside. He had been coming to the house daily for the past two months and knew, in the realm of its owner, it was discretion or death.

He walked quickly to the front gate, which swung open immediately. The watchers inside were expecting him, having monitored his progress to Assuncíon Street. Reaching the front door, flanked by two men armed with automatic weapons and a pair of German Shepherds, Morales was ushered along the familiar corridor to the large bedroom. As always, he stared directly ahead during his journey, not wanting to see anything but what he had been called upon to see: his patient.

One of his escorts switched the lights on in the room and he moved swiftly to the bed. The patient was awake and grunted as Morales began his work. Today was his final examination. The wound had been septic when he'd first seen the man and he smiled proudly as he looked at it now. It was all but healed and so was the lesser injury to the patient's head. His examination took a little over half an hour during which the patient did nothing more than stare at Morales. He had not spoken during any visit.

Dr. Morales wondered about the identity of his patient. The man was European, of slight build and, from his pallor, probably rarely saw the sun. Because of the security and prestige he was being accorded, Morales guessed he was of great importance to the Sobrecartel. And now he was cured, he thought with satisfaction, already thinking of the amount by which his bank account would increase.

"He terminado," he informed the guards, washing his hands in the en-suite bathroom.

The men turned and Morales walked between them. But they did not retrace their steps to the front door as usual. Instead they climbed a flight of stairs and entered a huge living room. They motioned Morales to enter and, as he did, a figure turned from the far window and watched him approach. The doctor's mouth went instantly dry.

"Señor Holtzmann," he gasped, extending his hand even though he was half a room away.

"Morales," Holtzmann replied, unsmiling.

Morales stopped and lowere dhis hand. That the man he and all Colombia knew as *El Monstruo* was living, not dead or severely injured as the government was still claiming, came as no surprise. That he was actually standing before him in sleepy Cartagena was like an electric shock to his system. Holtzmann's eyes glittered behind his trademark dark glasses.

"It is my stomach, Morales," he said. "It is in torment. You will give me something to calm it."

There was no talk of diagnosis, it was simply an order given to an underling, and Morales obliged immediately. He bent to reach into his bag, his trembling hands finally finding the two medications he was looking for.

"Señor." The bottles lay in his outstretched palm. Holtzmann took them, and read the labels. Without raising his head he asked Morales. "The other man—how long?"

"There is no need for further treatment," Morales replied.

Holtzmann nodded thoughtfully.

"Go," he said and turned back towards the window. Morales scuttled from the room and was led back to his car. As he unlocked its door, his eyes met one of the watchers in the car adjacent. The Sobrecartel man held a finger to his lips then dragged it across his throat. The surgeon nodded and drove off as calmly as he could. Only when he neared his own beach-front *hacienda* did he allow himself the slightest smile at the absurdity of having treated *El Monstruo,* Colombia's, possibly the world's, most wanted man, for stomach-ache.

Later that afternoon, awash with the pleasure of another job for the Sobrecartel completed and the small fortune it had earned him, Morales drove to his country-club with his wife. They were to attend one of Cartagena's incessant cocktail parties. He approached a turn in a stretch of road bordered by thick jungle and slowed his Mercedes to make way for an oncoming lorry. Cursing as he struggled to control the car on the loose shoulder, he heard his wife scream. He looked up in the instant the lorry collided with their car, hurling him and his wife into the windscreen. Both were barely conscious as their killers reached into the car and looped garottes around their necks. When they were dead and the Mercedes well ablaze, their executors summoned the local *Policía Municipal* to the accident.

Holtzmann swallowed his third series of pills as he stared out over the city. Though he had dealt his enemy a terrible blow, it had almost been at the cost of his own life, and Kumarov's. *Brigada Fascista* assassins had been dealing with those he suspected of co-operating with the authorities, those who may have helped lead them to his bunker. Thoughts of his revenge had filled the time as Kumarov recovered from his injuries but now he was consumed by a sense of urgency.

He turned from the window, crossed the room to the telephone and sat by it, waiting while a highly placed official of the *Corporacion Telecomunicaciones Nacional* earned more money than he had ever dreamed of; the price of a secure line out of Colombia for thirty minutes a day. The official would come under suspicion when the computer logs were filed at year's end. But by the time the Cartagena safe house was raided Holtzmann would be gone. He stroked his beard thoughtfully. Using the national telephone system was a tactic of last resort, but one his enemies would least suspect. It suited him that the government in its election fervour was claiming his death. It suited him well.

He looked at his watch impatiently. The number was being dialled now, he thought. Minutes passed as the elaborate connections were made. Finally his telephone buzzed and a Spanish voice informed him his call had been successful. Waiting for this connection had been his ritual for a month. On many days he waited in vain.

"Condor?" came the distant subject of his thoughts, hardly decipherable through the static.

"Alexander Simenovich," he replied. "Your brother will be able to travel in the next two or three days."

"Good," said the voice. "We await you both."

"The airport?" asked Holtzmann.

"Is secure, but you must supply us with a precise flight plan."

"I understand," said Holtzmann, staring out at the glint of a police and ambulance convoy winding through Cartagena's outer suburbs.

"Your security is assured," repeated the voice, confused by the sudden silence. "When will you—?"

"That depends on your brother," Holtzmann responded sharply. "Within two weeks."

"Good. Give him my regards, Condor," the sombre voice concluded. "I have nothing more to report from here."

"Good," said Holtzman. "We shall speak again."

He hung up slowly and there was a soft knock at his door. It was Pablo Simón, the *sicario* he used on his most sensitive jobs.

"The boys took care of Morales," the chief-assassin reported, walking into the room with a swagger. Tall and powerfully built, Simón had done much for the Sobrecartel over the years. Holtzmann stared into his pitiless brown eyes, but did not speak for a time.

"You wanted to see me, *Señor*?" the other said, with a touch of nervousness. He knew it was foolish to presume anything with the man seated before him.

After an interminable wait, Holtzmann finally spoke. "We must bring Ernesto Cortez out of Miami before my departure."

"Alive, *Señor*?" Simón asked, failing to stop the corners of his mouth turning up. He did not like his contemporary who had risen so high within the cartel.

"Yes, Pablo, very much alive," growled Holtzmann. "For now," he added after a time. "He will not be expecting you. The *yanquis* may be watching him. I do not want them to know I have survived. Do you understand?"

"Yes," said Simón, "we will—"

"*You* will ensure that Ernesto does not look to have been taken by friends," snapped Holtzmann.

"I understand, *Señor*," said Simón, and Holtzmann was sure he did.

"Be prepared for the *yanquis,* Pablo," Holtzmann cautioned him. "They are hurting now. Let us make them hurt some more."

The *sicario* smiled broadly. "Yes, *Señor,* we will!"

"Go," said Holtzmann. "He must be here within the week."

Simón dropped his head and left. A few minutes later, another figure took his place.

"Ah!" exclaimed Holtzmann with genuine pleasure. "You walk, Kumarov."

Kane woke early, his body-clock used to the hospital routine. He stared around his dawn-lit bedroom for several seconds in confusion. He had slept more deeply than he could remember, unaided by drugs, untroubled by dreams.

Pounded by a headache he staggered towards his shower and stood beneath the warm flow, willing himself back into the world. The headache receded to a tolerable level and he dried himself briskly. A sense of purpose was finally re-invigorating him. He still hurt, there was no doubt about that, but it was real—something to overcome not passively endure.

His Marine escort ensured a lightning fast commute to Operation White Storm HQ, but as he walked into his office Kane saw that he'd still been beaten by Hog Collins.

"Palace coup, Tom," Collins looked up from Kane's desk, grinning broadly. He stood and swayed his bulk towards Kane.

"Planning on taking care of quantum mechanics, now that you've mastered medicine?" he laughed.

Kane slapped his shoulders. "So, *what,* Hog?" he asked. "What the hell are we doing?"

"Ernesto-fucking-Cortez for me, mostly," replied Collins as Kane eased himself into his chair. "Almost worth getting shot to avoid. Every damn agency you want to name has its hooks into him and guess who's playing quarterback? Right now we've got about twenty hours of video deposition and if there's anyone in this damn country *not* working for the Sobrecartel, I personally want to buy them dinner."

Kane chuckled. "When does Stone want to move on them?"

"It's called Operation Roundup," replied Collins. "Ready to go—multi-state, multi-agency, multi-jurisdictional. Stone wants to launch it ASAP. Just as soon as Holtzmann surfaces—if he's still alive."

"He is," said Kane shortly.

"Don't be so sure, partner. Hasn't been a peep out of his SatCom code since the Colombians went in."

Kane snorted. "Doesn't mean anything, Hog, and don't

start believing it. Has anyone from the cartel tried to contact Cortez?"

"No. Everything's frozen for now. Even the two tons that came into Louisiana. It's like they've just shut up shop. And Holtzmann—"

"Holtzmann hurt us, we hurt him," Kane interrupted. "Sonofabitch probably suspects Cortez is in our bed. And he has other means of communications, other bases of operation. It's called regrouping. He's out there somewhere."

A woman entered the office holding a mug of coffee. He nodded his thanks but she lingered.

"Oh," grinned Collins. "Meet Shari Smith, your personal assistant."

"*Secretary!*" she corrected.

Kane took his coffee gratefully. "Secretary?"

"Yes, Colonel Kane," Shari replied. "Glad to meet you." She smiled warmly and withdrew.

Kane watched her exit. "Why?"

"Stone's cracked. You're the son he never had—" It was as far as Collins got before a glare from the other side of the desk stopped him.

Kane took a swallow of coffee and gathered his thoughts. "Presuming Holtzmann is still with us, what we have to figure out is why he's not rubbing it in our face, in the Colombian government's face?" He paused. "If he's not doing business, what in God's name *is* he doing?"

Collins shrugged. "You've seen the news, seen what Vargo is saying? I mean, even our damn president's saying it. That it's the end of Holtzmann and the whole damn Sobrecartel."

"*Bullshit,*" said Kane softly. "That's dangerous thinking— even if it's true."

"Guess they've got to explain the casualties somehow," Collins sighed, "Vargo's fighting an election. He'll lose and that will be it, finito."

But Kane was not listening. "This time we get him on our own," he said, sipping his coffee. "Let's stop thinking like the DEA, Hog. Get our friends at the Company to start looking at other links. Where was he faxing when the NSA was tracking him? Russia. What did Guela and Cortez say? Russia. Get the Company boys to look there for starters. I want another way into him. This time we bypass the Colombians."

"I think the Colombians are gonna be real glad to hear that," chuckled Collins. "And by the way, the CIA Russia desk ain't a boy, remember?"

Kane smiled. "Susan Haywood. Good enough."

"If we can get her interested," cautioned Collins.

"I'll talk to her myself," said Kane.

"Fine by me," smiled Collins. "Meanwhile, on the subject of talking, I have one more day to endure with Cortez. How Angie's managing I don't know."

"How is she managing?" asked Kane quickly.

Collins paused at the door. "Doing a fine job, no complaints, no sign of burning out. She's just one of the bad guys now."

A frown played on Kane's face. "She was never meant to be in this long. If Holtzmann suspects Cortez—"

"I know, Tom," Collins broke in. "Security's been beefed up. We got half the outfit watching her."

"Good," Kane nodded.

"Oh yeah," Collins added as he left. "Forgot to tell you. Still no closer to who or what our Mr Lipman is. Holtzmann never did tell Cortez. I've been trying hard—asshole won't say a thing. Stone's been letting him stew, but you might want to ask bright-eyed Susie about him as well."

"Okay, Hog," said Kane. "Just might pay my respects to him myself."

"Sack of shit'll be a damn sight worse for seeing you,"

Collins chuckled. "But if you get a rational noise out of him I'll swap places with Angie."

"Go, Hog," laughed Kane. The rotund CIA man swung himself around and all but collected Stone who had appeared behind him.

"Kane," said the big general as Collins left. "You and I need to talk."

"Let's start with the subject of my secretary," Kane smiled.

The six men spread through the arriving crowd were all travelling as tourists. Six anonymous faces jostling with the horde towards Immigration Control at Miami International Airport.

"Length of stay?" Immigration Officer Joseph MacFarlane asked, studying the passport. His eyes flicked up briefly to its owner.

"About two weeks," came Pablo Simón's accented response.

"And what will you be doing in the US during your stay, Mr. Augusto?"

"Hopefully some relaxation," said Simón, with a smile.

"Thanks, sir," said Officer MacFarlane. "Have a nice stay in the Dade County area."

"Thank you," replied Simón and walked away. He paused inside the terminal only long enough to ensure that his companions had passed through as well, then turned and strode briskly into the Miami afternoon. His men split up; each had their separate tasks in the job that faced them.

"Now Kane," Stone warned. "If you're going to involve the Company directly, we'll need the President and the NSC to come in on it."

"I'll put a call in to Susie Haywood," said Kane. "Get the ball started. I'll throw her Lipman as bait. Nobody sits in front of Hog for that long and says nothing without being somebody."

"Okay," shrugged Stone. "We'll do this. I've got to be in Washington next week for a lunch with the President. You join me—you can see Haywood at the same time."

"She'll be at the lunch too?" asked Kane, his eyes twinkling. Word was that Stone and the firebrand head of the CIA's Russia desk had once been an item.

"Jam it, Kane," growled Stone.

It took the ferociously efficient Susan Haywood less than three hours from the time of Kane's call.

"Kane!" her strident voice rang out of the receiver. Kane held the phone away from his head as he listened to her.

"What these assholes so abundantly fail to realise is that the thing that put 'em on the open market in the first place put their files out there too. His name is Hermann Blucher, aka Hans Schmidt—now *that's* original—former STASI agent, badly wanted by German intelligence for some particularly not-nice things."

"How 'not-nice'?" asked Kane, suppressing a chuckle.

"Makes what happened to you look about as serious as a flossing," retorted Haywood. "Not that I'm not overjoyed at your recovery."

Kane shook his head. They just didn't make them like Susan Haywood any more, in fact he doubted whether there'd ever been another the same. In the treacherously difficult area of post-Soviet politics she had no earthly equal.

"Blucher used to have some heavyweight responsibilities," she continued. "And some heavyweight colleagues, both STASI and the rest, including our former friends in Moscow. This was no garden variety dirty rotten commie."

Kane laughed out loud.

"He must have cashed in his secrets a while back if he's stooped to trying to plug vermin like you, Kane," she went on. "But I gotta tell you, the Germans are real worried that he's working for the druggies. Not 'cause he's a good shot—which he clearly *isn't*—but because of the shit he apparently once had his hands on."

"What kind of shit, exactly?" asked Kane.

"Well they're a bit cagey on their side of the Siegfried Line, so I was kinda hoping you could tell me that. *Quid pro quo,* Kane . . ." Haywood paused to catch her breath. "I guess not."

"Susan!" Kane broke in. "This guy was a favour—"

"Ain't no fucking favours, Kane!" snapped the other. "Do you have any idea how many STASI, KGB . . . How many former Soviet and Warsaw Pact spies there are out there on the open market? Each one of these guys knows something. We need to know who's told what to who. From what the Germans *aren't* telling me, my guess is that your man has told a helluva lot to someone, and I want to know their names, ranks, and phone numbers."

Kane gripped his sides. "Susan, I'll be in Wash—"

"Yeah, I'll be waiting for you," she interrupted. "And if you amateurs manage to get this guy to talk in the meantime, could you just ask him for some of those phone numbers . . . as a favour?"

"Of course, Susan," Kane replied, exhausted by the conversation.

"By the way, you do have Marlon down there don't you—it's not just a *Stars and Stripes* myth?"

"Yeah," answered Kane cautiously.

"Embarrass him for me, Kane," laughed Haywood. "Tell him I want his body badly!"

"Thanks, Susan," Kane replied. "I needed that."

"See you," she said. "Washington, next Tuesday."

Minutes later, Haywood's file on Hermann Blucher was electronically transferred to White Storm's computer network. Kane called it up and studied it.

"Shari?" he depressed his intercom. "Who's with Lipman at the moment?"

"Michaels, Colonel Kane," she replied. "Matt Michaels."

"Tell him to get ready for a visit," he said. "And it's Tom."

CHAPTER**TEN**

America should understand our struggle more than any nation," Kalin paused, licking his lips as he formulated his English. "It has fought Iraq, Iran, Libya. These countries, all Islamic. Does your President wish my country to become another Islamic enemy?"

Lena shifted in her chair. "But reports of massacres, ethnic cleansing—"

Kalin interrupted again. *"Nyet!"* he spat, his eyes glinting. "As I have told you, this is all propaganda. This is enough for now."

And, scarcely five minutes after he had entered the room, Kalin left. Lena fumed as her cameraman and soundman re-packed their gear.

"He is a great man," murmured Sergei, their minder.

"Uh huh," replied Lena through gritted teeth.

"This afternoon we have permission to see the prisoners," Sergei continued.

"That's good, Sergei," Harry Berg piped up after a long pause during which neither Lena nor Terry made an effort to answer.

* * *

"*Why*, Kalin?" Rodionov asked after the TV crew left.

"They are our puppets, Boris Nikolaevich," said his leader. "They see only what we choose to allow them to see, and their view becomes that of the world's. If it were not them, it would be another. If we were not seen at all, the *arabski* propaganda would be the only view. We cannot allow that—it is the way of war in our time."

The big Red Army veteran snorted, unconvinced. "She may speak Russian," he growled. "But she sleeps with the *araby!*"

Kalin laughed; a brittle sound inside the close quarters of the bunker.

"She has beauty, Boris Nikolaevich! Surely that is in her favour?"

"Yes, Kalin," Rodionov leered in agreement, "there is that."

"And," Kalin gestured to the flickering TV in the corner of the room. "We can keep watch on her."

"Now," his face became stern. "Enough of this."

The two men strode from the war-room up into the clear light of the morning. Their Jeeps and escort awaited them. Half an hour later they pulled up in front of the sprawling Shaklin airbase outside Novominsk. The aircraft left by the Russians when Kalin had launched his war consisted of four squadrons of Su–17 "Fitter" interceptors and MiG–27 fighters, eight Mi–24 "Hind" helicopter gunships, and a handful of aging Tu–142 "Bear" prop bombers. Kalin growled under his breath as he looked at his fleet, knowing how quickly they could have sped his war to a conclusion if not for the UN-sponsored air-exclusion zone over northern Armestan. But it was not the aircraft that he and Rodionov had come to inspect this morning. Their interest lay inside the large hangar complex abutting the airbase.

Walking across the tarmac, Kalin's vexation at the impotence of his aircraft gave way to pleasure as the small door to the immense steel building swung open and there, beneath swaying neon lights and surrounded by heavily armed men, sat three SS–25 mobile launchers. Each SS–25 "Sickle" missile was capable of delivering a warhead to a target nearly six thousand miles away. He strode through the complex to join Mikhail Shevchuk, his lone *danzan* weapons engineer. That Kalin possessed three such awesome weapons was solely due to Shevchuk and his avarice. During the first rumblings of Kalin's uprising, the meek-mannered Red Army engineer had approached his commander, Boris Rodionov, with a deal; three SS–25s slated for destruction in return for fifty thousand US dollars. Rodionov had agreed.

Shevchuk was working on the payload bay of one of the SS–25s. Nearly fifty feet from nose to tail, the massive missile was mounted lengthwise on steel supports, a clutch of electric winches slung over it. The SS–25 was equipped with a complex warhead, comprising an independent propulsion and inertial guidance system. It was this that Shevchuk was in the process of meticulously removing.

"How goes your work, Misha?" asked Kalin softly. The bespectacled engineer looked up.

"Well, Kalin," he replied with the enforced tranquillity of a man who for thirty years had dealt day-in day-out with weapons of mass destruction. His slender fingers manipulated the tool on the shiny steel skin of the missile.

"This is the first, Kalin," he went on, his eyes flicking back down to follow the work of his hands. "By next week, all will be completed. Including the MIRV."

"Good—move them back to the mountain as you finish them," said Kalin. Shevchuk nodded.

Kalin watched him as he continued work. Minutes followed, the silence broken only by the tinkling sounds of Shevchuk's industry.

"All is in readiness then," smiled the *danzan* leader finally.

"You have great faith, Kalin," said Rodionov as they left the hangar.

"With good reason," the other gave a thin chuckle.

As he walked through the vastness of the WorldNet newsroom, Mahoney mulled over the dilemma he faced. The news community was a relatively small one and WorldNet was even more incestuous than most media organisations. Peterson's blundering with the national security order had ensured that, sooner or later, Lena would find out the truth about Kane. He scowled, his hangover failing to mask the deeper sensation troubling him—that he was not unhappy about Kane's death.

He checked his watch. It was early afternoon, Lena's next satellite feed would not be for three hours. He had until then to defeat the nagging voice inside him.

"Bullshit," Terry said in disbelief. Lena's heart sank. The ethnic Armestani "prisoners" numbered about forty and were immaculately presented.

"This is it?" she asked Sergei. She had known that their visit to the prisoner-of-war camp would be stage-managed but this was beyond the bounds of absurdity. The huge camp was twenty miles out of Novominsk, a sprawling complex that had once been the district's largest prison. The plumped-up, washed, and coiffed prisoners playing checkers and soccer were a sick joke in this most vicious of wars.

"Guess we have to shoot it," muttered Terry. For once he and Lena were united—by their mutual disgust at what they were being shown.

"I'll wait here," growled Lena and watched as her camera crew walked closer to the pathetic group, Sergei trailing dutifully. A group of *danzan* guards laughed uproariously as Terry and Harry set up and went to work. She walked over towards them slowly.

"Cigarette?" she asked in English.

The guards looked at her blankly. She gestured with her hands.

"Da, sigaryeta!" laughed one and flicked a packet from his pocket.

"Thank you," said Lena, taking one and waiting for a light. "Do any of you speak English?"

The young soldier who had given her the cigarette held out a lighted match. None of them gave any indication of having understood her. She laughed helplessly and threw her hands in the air. And in the awkward silence that accompanies such lack of communication, she looked towards the prisoners and gestured.

"Good," she said, indicating with her hands how well fed the men looked. The soldiers laughed at her mimicry and began to talk animatedly in Russian.

"She wants to fuck them, Dimitri," cracked one of the soldiers.

"Maybe she could also fuck the ones they left on Barkusk," another retorted. Lena's ears tingled and she dragged carefully at the rough Russian cigarette.

"She couldn't tell their cocks from maggots by now!"

The group laughed uproariously. Lena finished her cigarette, thanked the men and walked slowly towards Terry and the prisoners.

"How's it going?" she asked.

"What do you reckon," he muttered under his breath. "Looks like Club-fucking-Med."

"I know," she replied. "Let's wrap."

"Yeah," he said. "One more shot and I'm outta here. Any other joy-spots lined up today?"

"We'll see," she said.

They climbed back into the beaten-up Volkswagen that was serving as their camera vehicle and jolted back to the hotel. Lena glanced at Terry; his anger had subsided over the past three days, but his disinterest was palpable. She considered what they had to do and wondered whether the Australian cameraman would live up to Jack Mahoney's expectations.

Kumarov grimaced as the pain jagged his side again, but even the constant throbbing reminder of his injury could not dim the pleasure he felt at this moment. Machinery and equipment—the supplies that would sustain his final push to triumph—were piled before him, meticulously packaged and labelled. He glanced outside and saw the jostling, honking Moscow traffic on Kutusavsky Prospekt, banked up behind an unfortunate motorist whose ancient Zhiguli had broken down or run out of fuel. In disgust he turned away from the bedlam that had become so commonplace; back to the order of his laboratory. His eyes narrowed as he watched an assistant run final checks on cultures infected with the virus before placing them in the temperature-stabilised containers he had ordered specifically for the next phase.

Death had come too close. The thought haunted him now, as it had since his hellish escape from the Colombian jungle. And he knew the walls of silence he had erected in Moscow at such huge expense could crumble soon. Too many were now clamouring for his bribes. But despite the necessary compression of time, now that he was about to leave his motherland forever, Kumarov allowed himself the passing luxury of reflection.

During his career at the Dom Chumy, he had developed many virulent biological weapons for his masters at the Biopreparat. But since his escape from Holtzmann's bunker he had dreamed as he never had before; of stilling the rabble, silencing the cacophony—the din of the traffic outside, the gaggle of bureaucrats and parliaments, the soldiers, the criminals, the school-yards. He nodded soberly as he imagined the vast desolation—all Man's works remaining on an empty earth. The renewal of mankind by the few.

He tapped his finger impatiently on his chin. He would not know the plague's mortality and morbidity rates until he had conducted his tests on human subjects. His eyes glittered at the thought. The size of the promised test community would leave no doubt about the virus's efficacy. And then would come the last act, he mulled; an act not of the intellect, but of the soul. He sighed as he again imagined the silence and his fist clenched unconsciously.

His team bustled before him, and his fingers kept up their steady, tetchy rhythm against his chin. The ever-present threat of discovery hung over him. He knew it would take just a word—a word in anger, in guilt, or in greed. He ran over the names in his mind—those whose silence had cost so much. Their reluctance to disclose their treachery would shelter the conspiracy for a time, and by then it would no longer matter.

His fingers stopped tapping abruptly.

"Make haste!" his shrill voice rang through the laboratory.

"Motorbikes?" Terry looked dubiously at the man Lena had tracked down. "What route does he suggest?"

Lena put the question in Russian to the swarthy mechanic who, for five hundred US dollars, had agreed to take them to Mount Barkusk that evening.

"Through the east of Novominsk, to avoid the Moski Bridge," she translated his answer. "Then into the Markesh Range and Barkusk."

Terry rubbed his face thoughtfully.

"You stay here, Harry," he said. The soundman nodded as Terry continued. "I'll use the camera mike, and I'll need the sun-gun. If they come looking for us just say Lena and I are in the sack or something."

"Yes, Harry, lie unmercifully," Lena snorted, then added

in a more serious tone. "Feed today's material to Jack. Tell him what's up. If something happens they can raise hell from there."

"Fat lot of good that'll do with this mob," said Terry steadily. Then he held her shoulder. "Listen, truce—okay, Lena? Those soldiers were probably spinning you along, but if we do find anything up there . . ." His voice trailed off for a moment. "I mean I've got no worries about going with you, but just realise what we're walking into. That's assuming Ivan here doesn't shop us at the first checkpoint."

Lena looked at him. "Point taken, and thanks."

Dressed in the collection of ill-fitting clothes their guide had supplied, they crept silently along the dark hotel corridor and down the fire escape. As they entered the rear courtyard, Ivan gestured to a small shed on the far side. There was a full moon and their figures cast faint shadows on the crazed cobblestones as they crossed it. Inside the shed were two vintage motorcycles. After a quick lesson in their antiquated gearing, Terry helped Ivan pack the camera and portable light for the trip. Then they mounted up, Lena riding pillion on Terry's bike. No one spoke. The engines purred into life with a smoothness belying their age—their owner had tended them well—and they pushed the motorcycles slowly out into the yard.

They idled onto the road. There was still a loosely enforced curfew in Novominsk, but since the bulk of the fighting had moved away from the city few observed it. Still, in a country where gasoline was scarce and late-night joyrides an uncommon thing, they would be conspicuous. They turned south and rode past their first checkpoint. A sleepy soldier barely looked up as they passed and Lena's grip on Terry's coat loosened with relief.

They continued without incident until they began the climb up the winding road into the Markesh mountains. Then they saw them—a group of *danzan* irregulars lounging around a Jeep. One stepped onto the road and motioned them to pull over. Lena tensed. The militia units were largely composed of thugs for whom the civil war was little more than a chance to even old scores and profit as much as possible.

"No English—act drunk," Lena whispered into Terry's ear as the louts approached them. They surrounded Ivan's motorbike, prodding curiously at the crates fastened to it. Then they walked over to Terry and Lena, whistling as their torches played over her face. She bit her lip as they circled her.

"What kind of man is this?" one sneered at Terry, who was slouched over the handlebars.

"Please," she said, half-dismounting, half-pulled from the motorbike. "He is drunk."

"If he is drunk, why is he driving the bike, darling?" came a voice from the rear of the group.

"I cannot . . ." Lena averted her eyes.

"Where are you from?" said the same voice. Lena paused, she knew her Russian sounded foreign.

"Moscow," she replied. "We were visiting my uncle in Novo when the fighting began."

"Moscow," another sneered. "We are honoured."

"And where are you going?" the voice persisted.

Their guide broke in. "Harfa," he shouted. "We have a plot there! Enough of this!"

"Be quiet, old fool!" the leader of the thugs snarled, coming forward. "So, darling, what shall we do with you?"

Lena fixed him with her eyes. "It may be a long war," she said with deliberate wilfulness. "And people should look out for each other."

The thug smirked, but still his eyes did not break from her steady gaze.

"Would you say so?" he said, licking his lips. "And where would I look out for you?"

"You will find me, if you care to," smiled Lena. "I am often in Novo."

The man's face mottled with desire, and he reached forward and grasped her head. She went to cry out but his lips slobbered over her mouth. Terry stiffened, but it was over. The thug drew back and laughed.

"Go," he said, glancing at Terry, who slumped as he walked away. Shaken, Lena remounted the motorcycle. Terry raised himself and accelerated slowly away.

"Well done," said Terry when they were clear. "But it's a dangerous game."

"Did you have any other ideas?" she replied.

"No."

Thirty miles ahead of them, its peak capped with snow, Mount Barkusk was outlined by the moon. As the wind slapped her face, Lena felt afraid—the darkness surrounding them housed the enemy. After a time she shut her eyes but that made it worse. She opened them reluctantly, grinding her teeth against the fear.

It was almost midnight by the time they'd travelled the road which twisted through the lower ranges and joined the main westerly route across Mount Barkusk. The guide stopped his bike and advanced towards them, waving his hands.

"He doesn't want to go on," Lena translated. "He says it's as far as he agreed to come."

"Does he know what we're looking for?" asked Terry.

"No," replied Lena.

"Tell him to stay with the bikes," said Terry. "And tell him to give us an hour."

"What?" said Lena. "What are we going to do?"

"Go on foot," Terry explained quickly. "This road can't be more than five miles long. If something happened, the chances are it happened pretty close. And I don't think old Ivan should cop a guernsey at it, no matter how much you're paying him. Do you?"

Lena shook her head and spoke to the guide in Russian.

He gesticulated in anger as she argued with him. Finally the promise of another hundred US dollars calmed him and he went snorting away to his motorcycle to unpack Terry's gear.

"You strap the sun-gun on," said Terry.

Lena fastened the belt for the portable light round her waist as Terry slung the camera on his shoulder.

"Let's go. If there's been a massacre up here then you can bet we'll smell our way to the bloody thing."

Lena grimaced at his casualness. They moved off the road a distance of three or four hundred yards and began traversing the loose scree surface of the mountain. Terry was right. Within twenty minutes the stench hit them.

"Oh God," breathed Lena, pulling her coat across to cover her mouth.

Terry stopped. His face was pale. "Seems like you were right."

The putrescent smell led them further away from the road.

"Shit!" Terry was the first to see what faced them in a dry stream-bed, scattered between two lines of boulders. "Switch the light on, Lena," he said grimly.

She flashed on the light, almost screaming as she did. In mounds, lying together as they had fallen seeking final shelter from the rain of bullets, were the corpses.

"Two or three hundred," Lena said softly. The faces and bodies were rotting, and scavengers had obviously been rampant in the area. Most of the corpses had bones stripped clean, protruding at odd angles, but the mangled and rotting remains all bore some article of clothing, some pathetic remnant of what had once helped define them as human. The dead were obviously Armestani *kadashi*. And they were, in the main, women and children.

"What a mess," grunted Terry. "Let's get on with it." He flicked a filter switch on his camera. "I'll shoot it shaky and grainy, okay? Should keep us out of trouble with Kalin—

make it look like home movies from the other side." Both knew their footage could not be attributable to them and its origin would have to be disguised.

"Okay," it was all Lena could do not to gag.

"Close-ups first," said Terry. "Get the light in there, Lena."

For half an hour they worked methodically through the corpses. In the glare of Lena's light they saw faces eaten away and yet somehow not losing their final agonised expressions, skeletal hands clasped in death; babies, their tiny forms strewn from their mother's arms and whole sections of their bodies torn away by both scavengers and bullets. The light was beginning to dim when Terry called a halt.

"Can't do much better than that," he said. "We need to get a couple of wide shots. Let's hope that fucking light hasn't given us away." They clambered onto a large boulder overlooking the massacre. The light held out barely long enough to illuminate the largest group of bodies and allow Terry two shots showing the extent of the killing. Then it faded to nothing.

"C'mon," said the cameraman. "Let's scarper."

"Yes," said Lena. "I've had enough."

"You did well, Lena," Terry whispered. "Real well. I mean it."

"Thanks," she said softly. Then they quickly retraced their steps, dodging the loose rocks and boulders until they finally made the road. The moon shone off the mountain with a surreal glow and the utter silence was almost a physical weight upon them.

"Hope Ivan's still there," said Terry as they walked back. "It'd be a helluva place to spend the night."

"Even if he is we've still got to get home," replied Lena after a time. Their minds were working slowly, still circulating the images of what they had seen.

Their guide saw them approach and immediately began cursing, pointing at his watch. Terry ignored him, repacking the camera and handing their precious video-cassette to Lena, who pushed it beneath her clothes.

"Better keep clear of my friend on the way back," she tried to joke.

"The way you look, I wouldn't worry," replied Terry. They glanced at each other, their forced humour failing.

"Let's go." Terry kicked the motorcycle into life.

Lena closed her eyes to the wind. She had finally managed to do some real reporting in Armestan but the thought seemed somehow empty. Her fear had been replaced not by horror, or disgust, but wonder. A deep, dark wonder at man's monstrousness.

Three hours later, after a return journey which, if uneventful, also seemed to take in most of the Markesh Range, their guide finally led them into the rear courtyard of the hotel. Lena thanked and paid him. He smiled broadly, his earlier anger forgotten at the sight of the dollars in his hands.

"Next time," he said in Russian. "You call me, okay."

Lena nodded, then joined Terry as they raced up the stairs to Harry's room. Harry opened his door cautiously, his face creased with sleep.

"You're back," he said groggily.

"Dynamite," whispered Lena. "We've got to get this to Jack, pronto."

Harry nodded his head towards the SatCase, already set up from his earlier feed. "You want to cut it down?" he asked wearily. Lena shook her head.

"No," she said. "Feed it raw. Nothing we can say about it."

Harry's eyebrows raised.

"A fucking massacre," Terry explained. "Bodies everywhere."

Moving more swiftly now, Harry wired the camera to the SatCase to feed the material. It took less than five minutes, but it was another hour before they could patch into the satellite. Finally they were through and Jack Mahoney's voice suddenly echoed through the headphones.

"Lena, where the hell have you been?"

"Stay cool, Jack," she said quickly into the camera's microphone. "We've got half an hour of material. Massacre by Kalin's men on Mount Barkusk. That's B—A—R . . ." She gave Mahoney the facts as Harry fed their images through to New York.

"Got it," Mahoney was saying. "Holy shit!" he exclaimed as he began seeing what they had shot.

"It wasn't us, right Jack?" said Lena. "Terry's done what he can in the shooting, but it's got to look like something you got from the Armestanis, okay?"

"Sure," he replied, agitated. "We'll take it down a few generations here. This is great stuff, Lena."

She glanced at the monitor and—terrible though the images were—she knew what he meant.

"Glad you like it Jack," she said. "We're going to have a lot of bullshitting to do tomorrow, so don't let *anyone* attribute this, okay?"

"Got it," he snapped back, and then there was silence as the remainder of the material was fed through.

"Check the tape, Jack," said Lena. "We're going to wipe our copy."

"Tape is good," replied Mahoney after a moment. Then he said, "Lena, are you alone online?"

"Yes, Jack." She gripped the headphones to her ears.

"I've got to tell you something. I'm sorry but it's bad news, Lena."

"Go ahead," she said, with a sense of foreboding.

There was a pause, then Mahoney's voice came back on. "It's your friend, Lena. The one I met in Israel. Kane. I don't know if you're still—"

"No!" she cried, his tone warning her. Then anguish blazed through her soul as Mahoney uttered the words. "He was killed. I'm sorry, Lena."

She rocked in distress, clutching her arms to fight the tears. "No, no, no."

"I'm sorry," Mahoney repeated, his voice cracking.

She did not—could not—answer him. She did not feel Harry's hand on her shoulder or hear Mahoney in her ears. Mute with shock, she dragged the headphones off and backed out of the room.

"Lena?" said Terry.

She glanced at him, her eyes shot through with grief. Her lips trembled uncontrollably and a strangled sound came from them. Terry stood and walked towards her.

"Lena, you okay?"

She turned and ran. Her wail echoed down the corridor outside.

"Jesus," said Terry, slipping the headphones on and speaking into the mike. "Jack—what was that about?"

"Friend of hers," Mahoney's voice came back. "More than a friend. Died. Take care of her, okay?"

"Yeah," muttered Terry. "Do what we can."

Lena fell onto her bed, burying her head into the pillow, her body racked by great shuddering sobs that seemed to explode within her and from her. His name became a mantra, part of the torment. His face came in the darkness and so tightly did she grip the pillow to her own that it was as if she was seeking to join him. She was suffocated by her grief but there was no release from it.

Her tears ebbed only as the night ended and she opened her stained eyes to the gathering dawn. Her hands were fists as she walked slowly to the window and stared bleakly out.

She had been abandoned.

CHAPTER**ELEVEN**

She opened the door and saw Terry lying in the corridor, tangled in blankets on the threadbare floor.

He groaned as he awoke. "Lena?"

"Yes, Terry," she said softly. "I'm—"

"Jack told me," blurted Terry as he sat up. "Want to talk?"

Lena looked at him. She wasn't sure whether she could.

"Helps, y'know," he said, standing, swathed in a blanket, and holding her by the shoulders.

"Oh, Terry!" It was more a gasp than a sob and he hugged her, feeling her face buried in his neck. Gently he walked her back into her room and closed the door.

"Tell me about him," he said. "And cry if you like."

"I've only known him four years," she whispered. "And one of those was lost. Nothing like him has ever happened to—" Tears dripped from her eyes and she sniffed as she wiped them away.

"His name is Kane. And the thing that hurts most is that we could've had so much more time together. He was a Marine. So was I—"

"You were what?" Terry broke in despite himself.

Lena looked away. "US Marine Corps," she murmured. "The best way out of where I grew up."

"Shit, I never knew," breathed Terry.

Lena went on, brokenly. "He was Special Forces, I finished up in media liaison after college. Knew his name, he was a Vietnam hero, but that was all. He had no idea I existed. I was twenty-one years old, I had to wait till I was thirty-three . . ."

Terry rubbed her neck softly as she wept. After a time she stopped and raised her head again.

"What happened?" he asked. "If you want—"

"He was shot," Lena replied sharply through clenched teeth. "I don't know any more. He was high up in Operation White Storm, the anti-drugs force. The bastards killed him."

She turned and stared deep into Terry's eyes for comfort. Minutes passed, then she shook herself free of his grip.

"C'mon," she said huskily. "We'd better get our shit together. Kalin's going to be on the warpath."

"You—?" began Terry.

"No," she croaked. "But that's not going to change anything."

She walked in a tight circle around the room, driving her mind into the reality of the day.

"Terry," she said finally. "I—"

"Just take it slow. Real slow," he said, his face marked with concern and sympathy. "I'm here if it helps."

"Thanks," she whispered.

Cortez looked carefully into the lens of the video camera, trying to avoid Hog Collins' eyes.

". . . and I have given this statement freely and voluntarily," he intoned.

Collins swilled a quick mouthful of coffee. "And you have told us everything you know about the operation of the criminal organisation known as the Sobrecartel—of which you admit your membership—in the full knowledge that this tape will now be used as evidence against Jorge Holtzmann and others you have named in future criminal prosecutions?"

"I have," said Cortez.

"And you further acknowledge that you will continue to advise the United States Federal Task Force Operation White Storm in its efforts to bring to justice other members of the Sobrecartel, including Jorge Holtzmann?"

"I do."

"Thank you, Mr. Cortez. For the record, this interview between Operation White Storm Agent Steven John Collins and Ernesto Velásquez Cortez, is now complete at 1:40 P.M. on the date previously indicated."

Collins rose and switched the camera off, removing the last of what had become a library of nearly a hundred evidence tapes; a comprehensive picture of the Sobrecartel's US operation.

He walked back towards the Colombian. "This'll keep you on our side for a while, Ernesto."

Cortez shrugged. He was beyond caring. Dog-tired from the weeks of interrogation, he wanted only to get it over with and return to the intermittent distractions of Angie Furness.

"You really think you will win this?" he said softly as Collins flopped into an armchair.

"Cortez—who the fuck knows?" Hog replied dispiritedly.

In a back hangar at Medellín's Olaya Herrera airport, José Mercado worked feverishly on the rush job, almost smudging the paint as he drew his brush along the final letter of the company's name—*Recursos Unidos*. Then he began on the second aircraft's call-sign. He glanced nervously at the two *matones* standing behind him, suits bulging ominously. Their faces were blank and as he turned back to his work he wondered if he would be killed when he was finished. He had never worked directly for the Sobrecartel before.

As the black paint slipped onto the white surface of the Gulfstream's tailplane, Mercado wondered at two such large jets being hangared at Olaya Herrera—by far the smaller of Medellín's two airports, and used only by domestic air traffic. He had done similar work on similar aircraft, but always at José María Córdova Internacional, where he had often chatted to the flight crews preparing them for journeys overseas. There was a service crew at work on these aircraft but they—like him—were toiling in absolute silence.

His work completed, he packed his tools slowly, not daring to look at the *matones*. Finally he walked towards them, head bowed.

"Terminó?" asked one gruffly. Mercado nodded, raising his head. The cartel man stared at him for a second, then flicked his head towards the hangar door. The signwriter needed no further encouragement, and bit his lip with relief as he slipped back out into the Medellín sunshine.

By the time the Gulfstreams lifted off from the short grey strip at Olaya Herrera two hours later—wearing their false livery and beginning their flights north—José Mercado was well drunk and getting drunker.

"Life is good," he announced to the only other occupant of the bar, who looked at him bemused.

"Si," he replied, raising his own glass to his lips.

"Verdammt!" gasped the prisoner as Kane entered his cell.

Kane stood before Blucher in silence. His presence—his existence—had a profound effect on the German, who dropped his head and began rocking slowly in his chair.

Then Kane spoke. "Hermann Blucher."

Blucher's head jerked up as he heard his name and he gazed at Kane, his face ashen. His mouth opened but no words could fight their way past his shock.

"You face serious charges in the United States." Kane

paused for a moment before continuing. "But our government has acceded to the wishes of your government for your extradition. It is to be hoped that when you have been tried for all relevant offences in Germany, and served whatever sentences the German courts set, you will be returned to this country to face charges of murder in the first degree and attempted murder." Kane spoke in the manner of a man disinterested in his words or their effect, then stood, and without even looking at Blucher, left.

"The master," chuckled Collins as he joined him in the observation room. "But why this tack?"

"Hunch," replied Kane simply. "Germans don't tell us much about what they do to ex-STASI agents, especially those they seem to want as badly as this guy."

Collins grinned. "Does Stone know?"

"Doesn't need to," said Kane. "Unless it works."

Behind the mirror, Blucher shifted backwards and forwards in his chair. Kane wondered what was going through his mind; wondered what he had done that might now be haunting him.

But what he could not know was that Hermann Blucher was a borderline paranoid-schizophrenic, whose disease, in the absence of his regular medication, had cycled through the weeks to its most destructive phase. For days now, unknown to his captors, he had been plagued by malevolent daydreams and delusions, delivering terrifying judgements on his predicament. The shock of seeing Kane and the ultimatum he had just delivered had edged his schizophrenia over the line. His thoughts clashed like cymbals, reminding him what he had done to others in his position; others like him, blurred and protected by falsehood until they literally ceased to exist. A dizziness descended upon him and the silence in the room became a buzz-saw that felt like it would split his skull. He gripped his hands in his hair and tried to wrench the noise from his mind. It was a moment that had been waiting to happen; the thin webbing of sanity was shredding and his madness boiled over.

"I will speak!" he shouted suddenly, thrashing about in the chair to which he was manacled, desperately seeking a response from his unseen captors.

Kane's eyes widened as he witnessed the man's torment.

"I can tell you," gasped Blucher, his eyes bulging towards the mirror. "We can deal—I have information about Jorge Holtzmann!"

"Okay," said Kane, as astonished as Collins. "Seems the man wants to talk."

"Jesus Christ," was Collins' only response.

Blucher's screams faded abruptly as Kane walked in. His eyes slowly cleared, set in an expression of hopelessness. Kane stared at him, trying to understand his motivation.

"So tell me," he said finally.

Blucher talked in the undertone of a man born to spying, punctuated by moments of manic babbling. He spoke for nearly an hour with hardly a pause for breath, outlining his history with Holtzmann, the assassinations he had carried out, methods of contact and payment. Valuable information, thought Kane, but not dramatic. He shook his head dismissively.

"What about Holtzmann in Russia?" he said instinctively. "We know about Russia, Blucher." The German's eyes flared in his bullish head.

"Yes, I have friends in Moscow," he said. He paused for several seconds before continuing. "There is a man I have heard of—Holtzmann's man in Russia."

He sighed and again fell silent for a moment. "A comrade of mine, Andrei Marcovich—Askenov is his family name, former KGB—we became very drunk together. He told me he was a *zwischenhandler*—bagman—for a high-level bribery ring within the Ministry of Defence run by a man he knew only as Comrade Gyorgy. Andrei did not believe the corruption was limited to that ministry, nor that he was the only bagman involved. But he was sure the money was coming from Holtzmann."

Blucher licked his lips. "He would meet Comrade Gyorgy always at the Filyovsky Park metro station where he was given the money. Great amounts of money. Very important people—"

"Comrade Gyorgy," Kane intruded. "What was he? Also former KGB?"

"No," replied Blucher. "A scientist."

A chill passed through Kane and the German nodded knowingly.

"How did your friend know Holtzmann was involved?" asked Kane through tight lips.

"Comrade Gyorgy ordered an assassination," replied Blucher. "Andrei was given the job. The target was a communications expert. Before he died he told Andrei he had set up encryption equipment and a secure satellite communication system for Comrade Gyorgy in Moscow. He was made to check the system to various sites in Colombia. That was why he was killed."

Kane breathed in deeply. "Comrade Gyorgy's full name—were you ever told it?"

"No. Even Andrei, I am sure, did not know it. It was not what he called himself when he was with Andrei."

Kane stared at him. "Then how? And how did he know he was a scientist?"

"The hit—the communications man," replied Blucher. "The equipment he set up was in a laboratory facility in Moscow. His staff called him Comrade Gyorgy."

"Address?" snapped Kane. Blucher shrugged. "Perhaps Andrei knew; he never told me."

"Blucher," Kane said quietly. "You will give us details about your friend Andrei. We will need to contact him."

"But he is dead," the German shook his head. The

confession had quietened the clamour in his skull. "Andrei . . ."

"We have to find this Comrade Gyorgy, ASAP, Hog," Kane snapped, reaching his office.

Collins' huge form collapsed into a chair. Kane clenched and unclenched his hands. Both men were flustered.

"Blucher is as mad as a jackass, but if he's right," Kane paused, "Holtzmann may be getting his hands onto some weaponry. *Fucking* serious weaponry!"

Neither man would allow himself to say the words, but both realised how possible the once unimaginable now was. The thought that an individual—a drug trafficker—could obtain a nuclear weapon would have been laughable such a short time ago. Now, Kane thought glumly, with chaos reigning in Russia, not only was it *not* inconceivable, but a most rational conclusion.

"You believe him, Tom?" Collins' voice broke the silence.

"Doesn't matter whether I do or not," Kane replied. "It needs to be checked out. Even the possibility scares the living shit out of me." He reached for his telephone and called Susan Haywood in Washington.

"Susan," he began the instant he heard her voice online. "I just talked to Hermann Blucher—"

Stone walked in and waved to Kane, and sat silently, head shaking as he listened to Kane lay out Blucher's information to Susan Haywood. The intercom buzzed. Stone snapped his finger on the button.

"What is it, Shari?" he said in an undertone.

"There's a Jack Mahoney on the line from WorldNet asking about Colonel Kane. Wanting to confirm—" she got no further.

"Tell him if he calls this number again I'll fucking lock him up," Stone barked. "And remind him it's still a federal offence to publish Kane's name." He snorted and lifted his finger from the intercom.

·

"Who else knows this?" Kane repeated Haywood's question to the others. "You, me, Hog Collins, and General Stone. I'll put you on speaker." A second later her distinctive voice invaded the office.

"Hi, y'all," Haywood announced. "Looks like you've got yourselves a live one. Comrade Gyorgy, hmm? Marlon, I'll have to take this to the DDO, it'll mean some tracking on the ground in Moscow, do you have a problem with that?"

"None, Susan," said Stone, unruffled by Haywood's familiarity. He, like Kane and Collins, knew and trusted Clark Mitford, the CIA's Deputy Director for Operations.

"Your *multi*-agency task force down there," cracked Haywood in closing, "just moved a whole lot closer to strictly Company business! You still coming up, Kane? Marlon?"

"Me and *General* Stone," replied Kane with a grin. "Day after tomorrow."

"Hope to have something for you by then," said Haywood. "G'bye!"

"It'll be a fucking pain in the ass when *she* goes!" Kane remarked.

"Yeah," said Stone gruffly. "For whoever she goes to."

"This is Josh Little, *TV Extra.*"

The man's voice and the name of the tabloid show he worked for grated in Mahoney's ear. "Little," he said. "Jack Mahoney, WorldNet."

"Well waddaya know!" exclaimed Little. "Head hunting?"

"Just want to ask you about the murder you covered for us in Miami a couple of mo—"

"The one WorldNet squashed?" Little's voice interrupted indignantly. "Well don't expect I'm gonna—"

"Little, this is not for air," reacted Mahoney.

"Don't particularly care," said Little. "You guys screwed me on that—rolled with the friggin' Feds."

"Little," sighed Mahoney, "just tell me what happened."

"Oh right, so *now* you wanna know!"

Mahoney chewed his lip. "Please," he said reluctantly.

There was silence at the other end. Then Little spoke. "First of all, there was—is—a government conspiracy to cover up a murder. This guy Kane was a Vietnam vet, a friggin' hero—and his death has never been made official. And what I want to know is: who the fuck killed him? No charges have been laid, nothin', but publish a friggin' word of it and you're dog meat. I had a source, a hooker who was there, saw it all, was willing to talk. Then she got leaned on. Nothing adds up. It's a friggin' conspiracy."

Mahoney listened to the drivel intently, hoping to glean a fact out of the bullshit.

"Furthermore, where's the body? Kane went to Miami General, must've been DOA. Where to from there? Even spooks get friggin' funerals. I just can't figure it."

Mahoney wasn't surprised Little couldn't figure it. "Can I just ask, Little—what would seem to be the salient question here: Are you sure he died? I mean, couldn't this be better explained if he—"

"Fuck you!" retorted the voice. "What do you think? I don't check my friggin' facts? Fuck you, and your chicken-shit network!" He hung up, leaving Mahoney holding the receiver with the barest hint of a smile creasing his face.

"Little by name," he mused as he started to dial another number. "Little by nature."

The man—by his incompetence—had set serious doubts rolling in Mahoney's mind about Kane's "death."

Angie Furness ran her fingers through her billowing hair and laughed. Laughed at herself; at the boundlessness of her self-delusion. Laughed at what she was doing with Ernesto Cortez. The weeks had dragged her through the familiar territory of depression and self-loathing until she had beaten them. Cortez was her lover now, it was simply a fact. And anything they wanted to do they could, on cartel business.

Beside her, driving, Cortez looked at her curiously, and laughed as well. He did not understand her outburst; he understood little about her at all. But he laughed at the pleasure of being with her and not in front of a video-camera answering questions, where each answer took him another step away from his past life.

Straggled behind and in front of their car, amidst the traffic, were three unmarked vehicles—their perennial White Storm escort which had grown so familiar that it was now as invisible to them as it was to the rest of the world.

"Oh, Cortez!" Angie said breathlessly above the roar of the wind. "I'm one fucked up piece of womanhood."

"You're one fuckable piece of womanhood, *mi amor,*" he laughed.

"So glad you think so," she replied, running her hand along his thigh, gripping it high up as it tensed to accelerate. It was madness, Angie thought, being with this man she had begun by despising. Sweet madness.

He winked at her and swung the wheel to exit the freeway. The country ahead was beautiful, littered with fall leaves, a visual cacophony of orange and red. Angie had said it was her favourite part of the world. They would pass through farmland and fields fallow with winter's approach. She gulped the country air greedily as it whistled around her.

"Cortez, this is gonna be *good!*" She grinned, contemplating the long weekend ahead, a million miles from Miami.

They were driving slowly as they came off the exit and joined the narrow country road. As the rules of the game required, the lead White Storm vehicle was far ahead, checking the route. The two remaining escort cars were spread out in the thin stream of traffic. Cortez's vehicle was behind a battered flatbed truck hauling a load of hay. Then they heard the ominous scream of motorbikes approaching fast.

The bikes appeared from behind the flatbed, two men on each. Angie reached for her weapon, a semi-automatic pistol, and fired. One of the men slumped and fell onto the road, but the remaining *sicarios* brought up their weapons, briefly and lethally.

"Cortez!" Angie screamed a terror-stricken second before her body was torn mercilessly by the bullets. Blood gushed from her and into a fast-growing pool on the floor, as the car slammed into an earth wall.

From ahead and behind, the two primary White Storm vehicles accelerated frantically towards them, agents appearing out of windows, guns levelled. As they did, two more of Pablo Simón's *sicarios* kneeled up in the rear of the flatbed truck with deadly cylinders balanced expertly on their shoulders.

Neither the White Storm cars nor their occupants had a chance. What faced them were Swedish AT–4 anti-tank weapons, designed to penetrate eleven inches of armour plate from three hundred yards. Bullets rattled from the guns of the doomed agents even as there were two flashes from the flatbed and two high explosive warheads buried themselves into their target vehicles and detonated. Twin fireballs careened off the road.

Alerted, three miles ahead, the third White Storm car spun around. Operating procedure gave the agents no choice. The car thundered back down the road, automatic weapons fire pouring from its windows as it neared the flatbed in the vain attempt to rescue Cortez and Furness. Again a man stood in the flatbed, levelled his weapon on the cab, and fired another AT–4 warhead. In a split-second four agents were torn apart within the exploding wreckage of their car.

In less than three minutes, Operation White Storm had lost twelve agents.

But Angie Furness was still alive.

"Oh God, Cortez," she gasped, her body jerking with pain. "Help me!"

Cortez bent and snatched her weapon. The three motorcycle assassins dismounted and walked towards them. Cortez went to depress the trigger.

"Ernesto, you are in enough shit already," said the muffled voice within the helmet of the leading *sicario*.

Cortez's finger froze. A leather-gloved hand pushed back the visor. It was Pablo Simón.

"You're dead, motherfucker," shrieked Cortez.

"Orders, Ernesto," smirked the other. "*El Monstruo* wants you home. An' I think the fact that you seem to have so many friends here is gonna make him real curious." There were chuckles from his companions.

"What's wrong, *amigo?*" Simón taunted as he faced Cortez down. "You in love?"

Cortez dropped the gun to his side slowly, rage giving way to cold fear. Holtzmann was alive. He shuddered as Pablo Simón's eyes bored into him.

"Worried, *amigo?*" he said. A groan from the fallen *sicario* distracted him. Simón looked back and saw the extent of his subordinate's injuries. He shook his head and motioned to one of the men at the flatbed, who walked over and finished him off with two shots.

"Now," Simón grinned unpleasantly as he gestured towards Angie. "Kill her."

Angie stared up hopelessly as Cortez inexorably raised his weapon.

"No . . ." she pleaded.

Cortez closed his eyes, pulled the trigger and fired. Then he turned away without looking at what he had done.

"Let us go," growled Simón, ". . . *amigo.*"

Kane brushed the police Polaroids to one side. Hog Collins sat opposite him, his steely expression cracked by welling tears. Their anguish was such that they could not speak. Angie Furness had been given a break and it had killed her. Killed her, and twelve other men and women. Outside Kane's office, a hush settled in the planning rooms and corridors of Operation White Storm. Some agents sobbed quietly, or dealt with their grief in the same shocked immobility as Kane. Most were in the main strategy area, shuffling papers and files disconsolately. None pretended indifference; they all cared.

They reached the Florida Keys by evening. During the journey, Cortez's mind had been racing faster than the screaming engines around him, engorged by fear. Angie was dead and Holtzmann knew of his treachery. The motorcycles pulled up beside a small jetty. Pablo Simón jumped off his machine and walked towards him with the same swagger and sneer Cortez remembered from their time together in Colombia.

"He wants you bad," laughed Simón evilly.

"Pablo," growled Cortez. "What is this?"

"I am only a humble *sicario* remember, Ernesto," said the other, walking past him towards a hut. "How could I know what is on *El Monstruo*'s mind?" Ahead, Cortez made out the shape of a large boat in the water, and a man standing in it. Behind him he heard Simón speaking on a telephone but could make out nothing of his conversation. He dismounted the motorcycle and sat on the ground, his stomach convulsing. Finally Simón came out of the hut and, with a brusque gesture, ordered Cortez to his feet.

"We go," Simón grunted.

Cortez walked between his captors to the boat and within seconds its captain fired the monstrous engines and they were propelled out to sea at high speed. The water on the Gulf of Mexico was mirror smooth, and the sleek craft hurtled across it unimpeded. Pablo Simón and his men reloaded their weapons and, as he watched them, Cortez had to remind himself that he was their master in another life.

They travelled in pitch darkness. The neon-green of the radar console illuminated the face of the *capitán* and in the absence of anything else to occupy his attention, Cortez stared at him—as if the man's expression might reveal his own fate. But there was nothing except a constant angry focus on the night ahead.

The hours passed with painful slowness, for although the physical reaction to his fear had calmed, his imagination continued to wreak havoc within. He tried to think about Angie—but he could find no pleasure in her memory sufficient to distract him from the terror that drenched his soul.

After leaving the Olaya Herrera airport in Medellín, the Gulfstreams flew at two hundred feet above the Atrato River towards the northern Colombian coast, cloaked from radar within valley walls. Passing Cartagena, one of the aircraft banked away from its companion and climbed abruptly, entering the jurisdiction of the Cartagena air-traffic control tower. A Sobrecartel employee was on duty, as planned, and made the appropriate false entries into his computer.

As its partner touched down in Cartagena, the lone Gulfstream continued to fly low across the Caribbean Sea, north-west towards the Gulf of Honduras and thence to its destination.

The sun spilled from the horizon—a stab-wound in the sea. Cortez made out the dark mass of land ahead.

"Progreso, Yucatan," the *capitán* announced to no one in particular. Cortez nodded. They approached the coast of Mexico cautiously. Within the hour those on board saw the approaching shape of a small vessel.

"Simón," the *capitán* pointed. Pablo Simón and his men trained their weapons on the nearing boat. The craft hove alongside and the man aboard waved to them.

"*Señor* Simón?" he shouted. "All clear." Moving quickly, Simón, then Cortez and the others, stepped between the gently pitching boats. There was the briefest *"adiós"* from Simón and the two vessels parted, one turning seawards at high speed, the second chugging towards land.

Their new beaming *capitán* chatted as they covered the final ten miles to Progreso, a small fishing port on the Yucatan coast. They docked in the busiest part of the port, where their anonymity was assured by the flock of identical craft surrounding it and the noisy labour of their crews preparing for the day ahead.

The *capitán* gestured to a car waiting by the wharf.

"Come!" said Simón, sharply.

The car drove ten miles inland, passing signs to a town called Merida. They turned off before the town itself, pulling up at a sleepy airstrip near which a few crop-dusters and other prop aircraft were parked, rusting in the heat. At the far end of the runway sat the Gulfstream, its sleek shape glinting in the morning sun. Simón bundled Cortez out of the car and jogged to the waiting aircraft. Within minutes they were airborne. Cortez's breath caught in his throat as he saw the man in the cockpit: Enrique "Diablo" Sánchez, Holtzmann's personal pilot.

"Ernesto," he roared over his shoulder as he swung his aircraft around steeply to begin its journey south. "How long has it been? You comin' home, *amigo*!" Cortez tried to smile but fear was eating him away.

Kane sat unhappily at the White House lunch. At the head of the table was President Kirkland, smiling genially at the powerbrokers arranged before him. The guest of honour, Caspar Norton, sat at the opposite end of the table. General Stone was next to him, his expression fixed and frigid, hardly glancing at his neighbour.

Caspar Norton. Kane recalled the man's extraordinary life. A multi-billionaire, some said the richest man in

America, who had made it all himself. Shipping had brought him his first fortune, when he'd invented the container ship. He'd only ever experienced one major scare during his seemingly irresistible rise: the '87 market crash had almost robbed him of everything. But he had survived, somehow.

Norton was known for his ability to pick a trend, having made billions since resurrecting his empire after 1987 with computer software and operating systems. He'd also turned to television, trying to outdo Ted Turner and Rupert Murdoch at their own game with WorldNet, a global satellite television network which pumped out twelve channels twenty-four hours per day, each in twenty different languages decoded by a simple and inexpensive device attached to, so far, about thirty million television sets worldwide.

Norton was also Lena's boss, Kane reminded himself with distaste.

"Yep, soon the only words that'll give CNN any meaning will be Caspar Norton's Network," he bellowed in his Arkansan drawl.

How could an Arkansan invent a container ship? thought Kane as he listened impatiently to this man who had to be listened to. Norton's home state had even put up a statue of him, to stare with bronze superiority at the black slums of North Little Rock. Kane shook his head; there was no justice in the type of people chosen to make vast quantities of money.

He let Norton's burly boasts wash over him as he again considered Cortez's disappearance. Holtzmann had taken back, or killed, their one tenuous link to him. Now their only signpost was towards the mysterious Comrade Gyorgy. And where did he fit in?

Kane's mind spun slowly around the problem for the hundredth time, then flashed, finally making a connection. He checked his watch to see how much longer he had to endure Norton, and how soon he could get to Susan Haywood.

"That gal in Armestan has beat CNN to the war," President Kirkland proffered in conversation. The muscles in Kane's neck suddenly tightened.

"Galena Chagall, Warren, our resident anchor bitch," Norton retorted. "She won't be in that damn-fool place for long. She's worth a million bucks a day to me sittin' pretty in New York. The advertisers love her, and can you blame 'em?" he chuckled lasciviously, and the other luncheon guests, all men, joined him.

"Cain't imagine what she'd be like in the sack," continued Norton. "Probably fuck you and then grill you on how it was."

The laughter was louder this time. Kane remembered Lena telling him of Norton's grotesque efforts to bed her. His eyes narrowed as he fixed them on the man at the end of the table, hatred coursing through his body.

"Ah guess it's just a matter of time before we put someone out of business," Norton returned to his familiar theme. "I s'pose it'll be NBC—they've never had a news division worth a pinch, and now their drama's gone belly up too. We give 'em everything."

Kane stood suddenly, gazing angrily at Norton. All eyes at the table turned to him and Stone scowled.

"I apologise, Mr. President," Kane said, trying to force his stare away from Norton. "I—I have to make a phone call."

Kirkland smiled—he always smiled—and waved him to the door. "Go get a bad guy, mister," he laughed.

An embarrassed chuckle spread around the table and Kane heard Caspar Norton start up again. He spent several minutes pacing the halls of the West Wing calming himself down.

Returning to the dining chamber's ante-room, he picked

up a telephone and dialled Susan Haywood's number. She answered almost immediately.

"Susan," he said tersely. "I want you to contact Mordy Elazar and bring him in on this, should have thought of it before."

"Shit, Kane," Haywood exclaimed. "Mitford's got his boys scouring the motherland for this motherfucker Comrade Gyorgy. He's ours! No one's gonna want to bring Mossad in at this stage."

"Do it, Susan," muttered Kane through clenched teeth. "Mordy may know something."

"And if he doesn't we'll just go ahead and tell him, right?" replied Haywood sarcastically.

"We're supposed to be friends," snapped Kane.

"Like I said before," she said. "No friends, no favours."

Kane sighed.

"I'll see what I can do," said Haywood after a moment. "There's only about a hundred possible contenders for our Comrade Gyorgy, I guess we have to narrow it down somehow. But no promises—and as soon as you're done there you'd better get over and formalise this thing. I'm not carrying the damn can for you."

"Sure, Susan," he finished, replacing the receiver and walking reluctantly back into the lunch.

". . . and so General Stone," Norton was saying. "Much as I respect you as a warrior and all, I have to say I think you're missing your calling with this current foolishness."

Kane's eyes glanced at Stone as he sat down. The General gripped the table, trying to release some of the fury rebounding within him. The room turned dead silent, but Norton—accustomed to an audience beholden to him, and not accustomed to diplomacy behind the closed doors of power—forged on.

"Seems to me instead of spendin' all these millions on fightin' the damn Colombians, if you legalised the damn dope and let all the freaks shove as much of it into their damn bodies as they want to, it'd not only be a great business but the rest of us could live in God-fearin' peace. If I was running the show . . . but that's hardly worth thinkin' about is it, Mr. President?"

A primal force erupted within Kane's body as Norton's unvarnished bigotry spewed forth, but the reality of who he was—and in what setting—dropped its boom-gate on him. All he could do was glare into Norton's pig eyes, and all he could think of was that this same man decided what tens of millions of people watched as "news."

Finally it was over. Kirkland stood and grasped Norton's shoulders.

"Caspar, I think this damn job would make you crazy in a month," he laughed. "But come and try it some time." His acolytes chuckled as genuinely as they could. Norton leaned back and beamed.

"Just like to let you know how the people think, Warren. My sworn duty to all you up here."

Kane dropped his head as the false camaraderie bloomed around him and the lunch petered out.

"Kane," Stone shook his head as they drove away from the White House. "If that asshole ever so much as looks like sitting in the Oval Office, I want you to remind me to kill the sonofabitch in the nastiest way I can think of."

"Yep," said Kane shortly, still quivering with rage.

Neither spoke as their car sped them to CIA Headquarters in Langley, Virginia. Then, as they were nearing the sprawling complex, Kane remembered.

"General," he said. "I told Haywood to get Mordy Elazar's help on our mysterious friend in Russia."

Stone nodded.

"Should have thought of it before, given that Holtzmann is the world's richest Nazi," Kane added.

"Apart from Caspar Norton," was Stone's only response.

* * *

Susan Haywood had not changed a scrap in five years. Same severe hairdo, same flashing eyes and make-up. She stood before Kane and Stone in a vivid red dress.

"Kane you sonofabitch," she laughed, grasping him in a bear hug. "Which bits did they shoot off?"

"Nothing you haven't already got on your wall, Susan," he chuckled.

"Marlon." She turned to Stone and embraced him as well. No mean feat, smiled Kane. Then he noticed the slight man behind her: CIA Deputy Director of Operations, Clark Mitford.

"Sir," said Kane.

"Been a while, Colonel Kane," said the other. "And you, General Stone."

Stone nodded.

"Let's get started," said Mitford crisply. "I'll tell you from the outset I'm not keen on the Israelis coming in on this, they're too interested in playing the man not the game. Convince me otherwise, Kane."

"I know what you mean," Kane began. "But I'm afraid Holtzmann is too far ahead of us in the game. Time has run out and I think we have to play the man. Holtzmann has billions of dollars behind him, more than any other individual or terrorist organisation has ever had. It's my firm belief, knowing Mordechai Elazar and his special reason to be interested, that he may have information vital to us bringing Holtzmann to justice."

"Come now, Colonel," smiled Mitford. "Let's dispense with the niceties. If we let Mossad in, the decision about Holtzmann is sealed. There won't be any trial with fancy lawyers, here or in Israel. But I'm still not convinced we should share intelligence on this. Run it all by me, Kane."

Kane did, outlining what White Storm had learned about Holtzmann: the *Brigada Fascista*, the estimated earnings of the Sobrecartel and the spread of its US-based operations. He laid particular emphasis on the evidence for

Holtzmann's interest in Russia; Guela and Cortez's testimony, the NSA-traced faxes to Russia via Holtzmann's SatCom code, and finally the information from Hermann Blucher about "Comrade Gyorgy."

"Why let Mossad in?" he summed up. "Because, since the formation of White Storm up until Blucher spilled his guts, we were looking for a very rich drug trafficker, and figuring how to stop him *earning* his money. But I'm certain that Mossad has been looking for a very rich Nazi, and trying to figure out how to stop him *spending* his money. They will have approached the whole thing from a different angle. I think that's vital in this. The faxes gave us a clue about Holtzmann in Russia, the German confirmed it. Has this agency looked at such a connection before?"

Mitford did not answer but glanced at Haywood.

"Nope!" she said. "I mean we dicked around between ourselves, but as far as a serious effort to spy him in the kaleidoscope, I can comprehensively own up to zip."

Kane smiled at her and continued.

"It would be negligent for us to work independently of Mossad," he said.

"I have to agree," Stone added his own voice to the fray.

Mitford looked at both men.

"Okay," he said simply. "Tell Elazar."

Alexander Krupchev settled into the seat of his delivery van, eating a quick evening snack. He had been combing the area around Filyovsky Park all day, inquiring at private hotels, even bars, about the scientist Gyorgy whom he had supposedly met while drunk and who had offered him employment. It was an excuse that most of those caught in the upheaval of the Russian economy could understand. He picked up his mobile phone and called his colleague, Dimitri Petrovich, who was working the telephones on this latest CIA goosechase.

"Dima," he said through a mouthful of pickle. "Any luck?"

"No," laughed the other. "Can you imagine the answers I'm getting? It's madness."

Krupchev agreed. "But it's their money. I'll call you tomorrow morning."

"You working tonight?" asked Petrovich.

"Yes," grumbled Krupchev, thinking of the addresses he still had to cover. "Until late."

"Tomorrow, Alexei," chuckled the other. "I am going home to pack my ears in ice."

Krupchev hung up and climbed out of his van, crossing the street quickly to the Gasteenitsa Gogol. His approach was followed by the eyes of a surly concierge. Krupchev stopped in front of him and began his story again.

CHAPTER **TWELVE**

This is outrageous!" Kalin's body shook and his Russian spewed out in staccato fury.

They had been summoned to the monastery an hour before and still Kalin's rage was undiminished. Exhausted from her sleepless night, Lena struggled to stay alert. Kalin was more than angry. He was dangerous.

"I allow you to come here," he shouted. "I allow you free access. It is as if you are in New York or London, and you betray me!"

"We had nothing to do with that footage," Lena said firmly. Behind her stood Terry and Harry, not needing to know Russian to understand what was being said.

Kalin stalked closer to Lena, bringing his face up to hers. "You are lying," he screamed. "Where else did that, that . . . *arabski* filth come from if not from you?"

"I have not seen the material but I understand it is amateur video," replied Lena, determined to keep her lie cohesive, hoping fervently that the irregulars who had stopped them the previous night had not reported their passing. "My network, along with several others I understand, received it directly from an Armestani source—"

"Acht," bellowed Rodionov, following the conversation with disgust. "There are no *araby* anywhere near Barkusk."

"You are lying," growled Kalin again, with greater malevolence in his eyes.

"That is not the case," said Lena. "But can I ask you for your explanation of what the footage shows?"

Rodionov stepped forward. "You dare—" but Kalin chopped him off with his hand.

"It was an attack by the *Asmani,*" he said. "That is the truth—will you report that?"

Lena looked at him, disgust welling inside. It was a lie; but one with a specific purpose—to test her. Kalin knew she could not possibly believe that the Asmani, a Sunni Moslem sect from Armenia, were responsible for an atrocity against the Armestanis. Both were fighting the *danzany*. His answer was also a threat.

"I will report that as your view, Kalin," she replied steadily. She would get Mahoney to run the story only on WorldNet International, and only for a few bulletins.

"Good," his smile became open now. "I shall expect it. And tomorrow you will be taken to Mount Barkusk, where we shall view this barbarism together."

Lena swallowed her rising bile. He was as wily as a rat and knew that by being seen at the site, he could further shift responsibility for the massacre to others. In two moves he had beaten her.

"Bastard!" she swore as they regrouped at the hotel.

"Like we're his personal little publicity machine," grunted Terry.

"We can't keep covering it this way," she said.

They both looked at her quizzically. "Far be it from me, Lena," said Terry, "a simple cameraman, but I fail to see what we can do about it, except leave the country."

"If he lets us leave," replied Lena. "Which I now very much doubt. He controls the airport, and the instant he

knows we're going he'll know for sure it was us who shot the footage."

"See what you mean," said Terry.

"So we go over to the other side?" asked Harry Berg with remarkable directness.

"Oh, shit," Terry began. "I—"

"That's exactly what I'm suggesting," said Lena firmly. "Look Terry, even if we did get out of Novominsk, that would be the end of it for me. New York wants me back in the studio like last week. This place *needs* to be reported on." Her determination to stay had—for the moment—replaced her grief over Kane.

"New York, eh?" mulled Terry. "Price of stardom."

Lena nodded. "Right now," she said, "a toad named David Peterson, whose knowledge of geography extends about as far as Ellis Island, would like to forget he'd ever heard of Armestan. I can't let WorldNet do that."

"So where and how?" asked Terry after a moment's reflection. "The border is three hundred miles away."

"It's not going to be easy," she said.

Terry chuckled despite himself. "Nope, I guess not," he said. "That's the kind of perception that makes you a star and me just a humble shooter."

Lena laughed for the first time since she'd heard the news about Kane. "Okay, what I mean is it'll take time, is that plain enough English for you?"

"I'll see how sensible it sounds after a beer," he replied.

The crisp Washington air steamed around Kane's face as he entered the CIA safehouse. The car that had brought him from Langley remained outside; the two agents assigned to watch him had a long night ahead of them. Kane closed the door, fumbled for a light switch and dropped onto the living room sofa.

Almost immediately the phone buzzed. He spent a moment locating it: an operator at Langley was on the line.

"Colonel Kane? Hold for Miss Haywood," said the voice. He shook his head.

"Kane," she said. "You undressed yet?"

"No," he chuckled. "I only just left you, Susan. What's up?"

"Taken us this long to track down Elazar," she answered.

"And?" he asked impatiently.

"Jackpot," came Haywood's reply. "You were right. They had to go to back-files, but Comrade Gyorgy is now one of only three possible men, and all of them will scare the bejesus out of you. One we've traced and he's clean, standby for two and three, both of whom Firyubin's people are denying all knowledge of."

"Shoot," said Kane.

"Gyorgy Fydorovich Pasternov," said Haywood slowly. "Specialist area—enhanced radiation warfare. Know what that is?"

"Neutron bomb?" Kane answered.

"You got it," said Haywood. "Just up Holtzmann's alley and within his budget. Ruskies say they're no longer making 'em, but can't tell us the whereabouts of the project's former chief scientist."

"Go on," said Kane, heart sinking.

"Gyorgy Alexandrovich Kumarov," she replied. "Less senior in the scheme of things than Pasternov. Used to be Moscow's bright boy in the Biopreperat—the Soviet chemical and biological warfare division. Russian denial is even stronger on that score.

"In any case, Elazar says his people have tracked godawful amounts of money being transferred from suspected Holtzmann accounts in Europe to Russian banks, and I mean *godawful!* If he's buying from either of these two we're all in deep shit."

"Right," muttered Kane.

"Mitford's got everyone and anyone we own in Moscow out on the hunt," Haywood's voice raced. "Mossad too—

seeing it was *our* German that turned up Comrade Gyorgy," she could not help adding.

Kane winced, knowing how indelicately she would have made the point to Elazar.

"The Israelis are even more shit-scared than we are, if it's any consolation, Kane," Haywood finished. "You don't need an IQ like mine to figure out who his first shot's gonna be at."

"No," said Kane. "I'll talk to Mordy when we're through."

"We're through," said the other succinctly. "Happy nightmares, Kane."

"You too," he breathed, his finger cutting the call off. He hit a button and the Langley operator came back online.

"Yes, Colonel Kane?" she asked.

"I need Mordechai Elazar, Mossad, Jerusalem," he said.

"Yes sir, connecting you."

The returning Gulfstream swooped in over the ocean to make its landing at Cartagena's Ernesto Cortiso airport as another fortune was earned in the control-tower.

Pablo Simón and Cortez stepped out of the jet once it was safely inside the hangar with its twin. Simón led Cortez into a waiting car and they drove quickly away. Cortez's terror was like electricity sparking in his body. The last time he had been in Colombia was with Kane, the turning point in his life. The question of whether Holtzmann knew screamed in his brain as the car wound its way through the seaside city. Simón made it worse, chuckling to himself as he watched Cortez sweat.

Finally the car turned into *calle Assunción* and drove through the high steel gates. Cortez stepped out gingerly and walked towards the house as though every step was agony. He dropped his head as he entered and went where he was led, until finally he heard the dreaded voice.

"Ernesto?" Holtzmann turned to face him. "You understand it had to be done this way."

Cortez's head spun and his body threatened to give way.

"*Señor,*" he said slowly through dry lips. "I understand."

"The woman," continued Holtzmann, walking nearer. "It seems you have been careless."

"She was nothing," replied Cortez.

"But she was with the *yanquis,*" said Holtzmann. It was a statement, not a question. "And it seems there were many *yanquis* with you."

"I . . ." stumbled Cortez. "I did not know."

Holtzmann was quiet for several seconds as he regarded his lieutenant. "So, Ernesto," he said finally. "You have betrayed me?"

"No, *Señor!*" replied Cortez emphatically, feeling the room close in on him.

Their eyes locked in the sudden, chilling silence.

"We shall see," Holtzmann breathed, turning away.

"Comrade-doctor?"

Kumarov paused on the stairs, annoyed. The ancient concierge stood below him.

"There was someone here this evening, looking for you, comrade-doctor," said the concierge, wheezing on his cigarette.

"What?" hissed Kumarov, his body tingling with premonition. "Who?"

"It will be a long winter, comrade-doctor," coughed the concierge, whose name Kumarov knew only as Mostovich. The scientist glared at him; his days and nights had been endless this past week. He shuffled down the stairs quickly and withdrew a wad of notes from his pocket.

"He said he was looking for a man named Gyorgy, but he described you," said the man. "He said you were drunk together and you offered him a job. He seemed like a cop, comrade-doctor."

Kumarov straightened. His mind whistled with fear.

"Mostovich," he said breathlessly. "I, I am . . . as it

happens, travelling to the north. I am leaving tonight." He pulled some more money from his pocket. "You will inform me if this man returns, *immediately,* is this clear?"

"Yes, comrade-doctor," snuffled Mostovich, bowing his head as he took the money. Kumarov turned quickly and scuttled up the stairs. The old concierge smiled a toothless grin as the comrade-doctor's money joined that already received from the earlier visitor. It had been a profitable night and was set to become even more so. He shuffled back to his post, picked up the bakelite telephone next to his seat, and dialled the number, waiting only an instant.

"It is Mostovich, comrade," he said softly. "He has returned. He is travelling tonight."

Five minutes later the dark blue mini-van pulled up a hundred yards from the Hotel Gogol and extinguished its lights. Mostovich glanced up and down the street, then shuffled across to it. He put his hand through the open window and withdrew it, clutching money.

"I will step onto the pavement when he leaves," he whispered, turning from the van.

Once inside the dingy foyer of the private hotel he made his coughing way up the stairs. Pausing outside Kumarov's apartment to collect himself, he knocked.

"Comrade-doctor," he said softly. "The man has returned."

"Where?" Kumarov gasped.

"The winter—" began Mostovich.

"Svoluch!" swore Kumarov, but seconds later opened his door fully and handed Mostovich another wad of notes.

"He is in a dark blue mini-van," said Mostovich. "Near the corner of Ytelovna Ulitsa."

"Good," muttered Kumarov. "I will have a car coming to meet me, Mostovich."

"Yes, comrade-doctor!" replied the old concierge and bowed again. In scarcely four hours he had made more than two months' wages.

* * *

Inside his apartment, Kumarov's mind worked feverishly. It was a threatening catastrophe, whoever his watcher was. He packed a few belongings then grabbed the telephone. Audacity would be his only saviour. He called the first number to prepare everything at the laboratory. Then he dialled a second number.

"*Da?*" came the befuddled answer.

"It is Comrade Gyorgy," Kumarov hissed.

"Gyorgy," the voice jolted. "What—"

"Be quiet," ordered Kumarov. "I have requirements." Swiftly he outlined what he needed.

"Comrade Gyorgy!" the voice responded. "It is impossible."

"*Nothing!*" Kumarov shrilled suddenly, "is impossible. It is only a question of price."

"Obviously I must call you back," said the voice.

"Tonight," snapped Kumarov. "Soon!"

"Yes, yes," replied the voice. "As soon as possible."

In the long hour that he sat by the telephone, Kumarov imagined the sounds of brakes screeching outside, of weapons being cocked; the noises of his imminent capture. The seconds became like the blows of a pick against his temple. Then the telephone clanged. He snatched it up.

"*Yes?*" he gasped.

"It can be done," the voice was much more business-like now. Kumarov crumpled forwards.

"*Klass!*" he breathed with relief.

"The cost is high. Very, very high."

"How much?" asked Kumarov, knowing he had no alternative.

"Twenty million," said the other. "US dollars."

"No," croaked Kumarov. "It is too—"

"It must be deposited in the following account before you leave," said the voice, not indicating it had heard

Kumarov. "If it is not there by nine o'clock, the deal is off. If it is you may proceed, here are all the details."

Kumarov scratched his pen across a torn notepad, his mind whirling. In a daze he replaced the receiver, then began the laborious process of contacting Holtzmann.

"There is no other way, *Señor*," he finally gasped, nearly two hours later. "I am sorry, there is no other way. I have been discovered."

"Mordy!" Kane's greeting was heartfelt.

"Good to hear your voice, Tom," said the old Israeli, his deep tones ringing out of the receiver as if he was in the next room. "We finally came together on Holtzmann."

"Yeah," said Kane. "Thanks for making my day." He imagined the Mossad chief at the other end of the line. Elazar's crowning achievement as a field agent had been to track down and capture Jurgen Holtzmann in 1965. Now he was hunting the son, thought Kane, shaking his head at the irony of life.

"The pair we gave you are the devil's alternatives," replied Mordechai Elazar. "Wouldn't have narrowed it down without your renegade STASI man and his Comrade Gyorgy, as Susie Haywood made abundantly clear."

Kane chuckled. "Figured she would, Mordy. What's your read?"

There was a cough at the other end of the line and Kane remembered that Elazar was approaching seventy these days.

"Hate to say it, Tom," he replied, "but my money's on Pasternov. The neutron weapon suits Holtzmann's needs."

"Which you regard as?" asked Kane. It was difficult to believe they were discussing such things.

"I've been watching Holtzmann for a long time, Tom," replied Elazar. "Call it an interest in the family if you like."

Kane smiled.

"It is clear to me," Elazar went on, "that Holtzmann has

purchased one or two of the lunatic fringe groups on the Arab side. The bombing of Yad Vashem last year bore his hallmark, as far as I am concerned. Should he come to possess a weapon of mass destruction, I have no doubt that his primary target would be a large population centre within the State of Israel. I believe, Tom, he might hit Jerusalem in revenge for his father."

Kane listened silently. The Israeli drew breath.

"It is not, I might add," he said, "a theory much in favour with my younger colleagues in the Knesset Security Committee, or the Defence Council. They have short memories, I am afraid to say."

"Surely though, they must be concerned that one of these groups you say are sponsored by Holtzmann, might . . . ?" Kane let the question hang.

"I have told my people that I do not believe Holtzmann would entrust any such major weapon to these groups," replied Elazar. "They may be effective in annoying and embarrassing us for a fee, but they are too unreliable and unsophisticated for the type of devices we are discussing. He may, after all, even in the worst case, acquire a maximum of one or two such weapons. He is unlikely to acquire an armoury. Therefore he will want to ensure their most efficacious deployment."

"So why not the other scientist, the biological weapons man?" asked Kane.

"Kumarov?" mused the Israeli. "We know little about him, and certainly at the point we lost track of him in 1989 I doubt he had the seniority to act as a provider for Holtzmann. I am not ruling him out, Tom, let us see what our combined resources can flush out. I simply tend to think that it is more likely for Holtzmann to be looking for a nuclear or enhanced radiation device that can be detonated *in situ* by a specialist team. Chemical and biological weapons are a much more complex item—Holtzmann would need either a sophisticated delivery system, or a chemical or biological agent unknown to Western intelligence. It is unlikely that—whatever else they have done—the Russians have squandered their roubles on such frippery. We have no indication that the Biopreperat—Kumarov's old employer—has been active at all since 1989. On that, at least, it seems the Russians kept their word."

"What I can tell you, Tom," Elazar continued. "Is that, whatever his grand design may be, Holtzmann has been incredibly busy in Russia. From chemists and small-scale equipment for his cocaine manufacturing enterprise, to a variety of confusing and contradictory 'purchases.' It is like joining dots without numbers, trying to guess his intent without ever glimpsing the larger picture."

"I know what you mean," replied Kane ruefully.

"And *now* comes your evidence, Tom. Massive government corruption to cover a conspiracy, possibly nuclear or biological weaponry."

"I guess it had to happen one day soon," said Kane. "Russia's become the biggest yard-sale in history and Holtzmann's got the money."

"Quite right," Elazar replied. "I engaged one of my staff in the singularly unrewarding task of calculating Holtzmann's income versus expenditures—in his Russian purchases, in fighting you and his own government. Our figures are shaky at best, and his complete involvement in Russia unknown. But even a cautious analysis leads to the conclusion that he is gambling if not everything, then a sizeable portion of his fortune. When a man does this," he concluded, "he has a mission to complete at any cost. You know what I believe it is, Tom."

There was a long period of dead silence as Kane considered Elazar's words.

"And we were after a simple drug-dealer," Kane said self-mockingly. "What the hell have you done to our little task force, Mordy?"

"You have done it yourself, Tom," chuckled the other.

* * *

Krupchev tried Petrovich's work number again. It was five A.M. and Krupchev was still parked outside the Hotel Gogol. He thought about calling Petrovich at home but decided to allow him an hour's more sleep. He rubbed his eyes, raw from cigarette smoke and fatigue. Then, suddenly, he saw a car pull up to the hotel, and a slight man walk out of the foyer. Behind him stood the concierge. It was Gyorgy Kumarov, thought Krupchev in triumph. He raised his binoculars to his eyes for a second to be sure he knew his target's face. Then the concierge backed into the hotel and the car roared away.

Krupchev started the van and tailed Kumarov's vehicle, jotting down the license plate for Petrovich to check. His fingers punched the mobile phone. It took five attempts to get through Moscow's still-rudimentary cellular network but finally his colleague answered groggily.

"Dima," Krupchev exclaimed. "Comrade Gyorgy Kumarov—" He got no further.

"Yes!" Petrovich yelled through the phone. "It is one of the names. I got the word last night."

"And you did not tell me?" snapped Krupchev.

"I am sorry," muttered Petrovich. "Natasha was—"

"I am following him," Krupchev broke in. "He lives at the Hotel Gogol, Zhukov Street. I am on Ryazansky Prospekt, heading east."

"Good, Alexei," said Petrovich. "I'll try to rouse someone to join you. I will call you back."

"Okay," replied Krupchev.

He followed the car along Ryazansky Prospekt for about five kilometres and slowed as he watched it pull into a warehouse complex on the eastern outskirts of Moscow. Krupchev found a location to park his van and wait. He wanted to get some photographs of the target as instructed, so he unpacked his camera, put on a lens, and checked its settings. He was about to call Petrovich when the gates of the complex swung open. Krupchev saw Kumarov walk out and look directly at his van. He dropped the camera and looked slowly away, checking his watch as if he was a courier waiting for a parcel. *Kchortu!* he swore to himself. From the corner of his eye he saw Kumarov gesture, and a truck appeared, obviously heavily laden. It rumbled slowly towards him.

A pistol was abruptly shoved through the window. Krupchev shouted and struggled for the gun, but he felt a pair of powerful hands grip his neck from the other side of the van. He was taken. His two captors dragged him out of the van. The truck stopped alongside them and Krupchev was pushed roughly through the canvas flaps into its rear. For a second he could see a huddle of men and some large boxes in the dimness—then a filthy bag was pulled over his body and a rope strung tightly around his legs. The vehicle squealed away. Panicking, he heard the sounds of heavy traffic. They were on a major road. Working through the shock of his capture, he guessed they were back on Ryazansky Prospekt, heading towards Moscow.

In the cabin of the truck Kumarov watched the outline of Sheremetevo Airport grow closer. *Now we will see, Marshal Gdlyan!* He could scarcely breathe. His heart was a wild drum-roll and he continually glanced into the mirror to check for the pursuers whose presence was terrifyingly tangible in his heightened state. The Americans? The CIA? His terror was complete. As was his unquenchable rage at his prisoner, the spy.

They reached the gates to the military entrance of Sheremetevo which were locked. An argument broke out between his driver and the guards. The event magnified in Kumarov's scared eyes, and he leant from the truck to add his angry shriek to the bedlam. Finally a Jeep tore up to the gates behind its surly defenders and an officer leapt out, shouting orders furiously. The gates swung open. Relief flooded Kumarov as the truck rumbled through onto the tarmac, following the jeep. Ahead of them he could see the other five trucks lined up before the huge Ilyushin Il–76 transport jet.

Twenty million dollars! thought Kumarov, hardly able to believe it. He grinned like a schoolboy in the brisk breeze as he observed the massive aircraft.

The noises of take-offs and landings alerted Krupchev to his location. He shouted for help, hoping he might be heard above the ebb and flow of the airport's roar.

Kumarov whirled around and snatched a spanner from the rear of the truck, bringing it down with his full force on the sack containing the prisoner, smashing it into the shifting, screaming lumps. He gestured to the driver, and the truck joined the convoy which rumbled up the Ilyushin's tail ramp and into the aircraft.

The officer who had cleared their entry to the tarmac came over. "Comrade-doctor Kumarov," he saluted. "Marshal Gdlyan wishes me to assure you that everything is in order. The arrangement you promised has been fulfilled. The crew? They are assured of safe passage after landing at the destination?"

"Yes," replied Kumarov.

"*Praschai!* Good luck then, comrade-doctor," said the other. "I will wait here until you have taken off. Then I too must become invisible."

The officer winked as he turned towards his jeep. Kumarov watched him walk away. The flight crew drove up in an open-roofed vehicle and climbed aboard. Kumarov glanced around again as his remaining men negotiated the ramp into the belly of the Ilyushin. *We will make it!* he rejoiced, as he too strode up the ramp. Standing at the top, he gathered spit in his mouth and hacked a gobbet towards the ground of his once-loved *Rodina*. He watched carefully as a crew member operated the controls to raise the aircraft's ramp, then he stared outwards until the country in which he had been born was blotted from his view. He strode into the aircraft's interior, giddy with disbelief.

"Kumarov!" Haywood's voice was hoarse. Kane had just walked back into his office in White Storm's Miami head-quarters in time to get her call.

"Comrade Gyorgy—it's fucking Kumarov," she repeated. "Mordy was wrong."

"What's happened?" asked Kane calmly.

"One of our gophers in Moscow tracked Kumarov, near Filyovsky Park, just like your German said," said Haywood. "Now we've lost him."

"Lost who?" Kane asked quickly. "Kumarov?"

"Kumarov and our man," said Haywood angrily. "The other 'Comrade Gyorgy' turned up as a visiting professor in France. Kumarov is it!"

"Keep me informed," said Kane quickly and hung up. His fingers were hovering above the intercom even as Shari's voice burst from it.

"Mordechai Elazar on line one, Colonel."

He snatched the phone. "Mordy," he began. "We've—"

"I know, Kane," said the other, his voice husky with the lateness of the hour in Israel. "We employ the same people in Moscow. So it would appear to be Kumarov. Let us hope his disappearance is only temporary. Since we spoke I have received a little more detail about him from our sources in Moscow. It doesn't please me, nor will it you."

"Go ahead," said Kane.

"We've obtained details of some of Kumarov's scientific work in the seventies," replied Elazar. "The files were ware-housed as part of the 1989 protocol—we just paid a hefty sum for them. Kumarov was a lot more important to the Soviets than we imagined. At the time of the supposed clo-sure of the Biopreparat he was running their germ warfare program. There was a particularly nasty series of experi-ments conducted in the mid-70s at Vozrozhdonyiye Island off Sakhalin. As a result, the Soviets had, ready to use, strains of anthrax, tularaemia, and antibiotic-resistant bacteria. In fact there's some circumstantial evidence that they may have been deployed in Afghanistan."

"Jesus," breathed Kane.

"Here's the clincher," Elazar continued. "The papers we obtained identified his research facility within the Biopreparat as being called Dom Chumy."

"What's that?" Kane snapped.

"House of the Plague, Tom," Elazar said slowly.

Kane was silent for a moment, then he sighed. "Thanks, Mordy. I hope to God we find him."

"Keep in touch," replied Elazar.

Holtzmann paced inside the cage that his Cartagena safehouse had become, then stood at the window and stared sightlessly out, his stomach churning as he contemplated what was beyond his control. He puffed slowly on a cigar which, when finished, would join the countless others cleared away by his men.

"*Señor?*" Pablo Simón offered him a coffee, but Holtzmann did not reply.

The giant transport jet shuddered down the runway and lifted off slowly. Inside it, Alexander Krupchev began to grasp the scale of the operation he had unwittingly been caught up in. He raged silently against the *Amerikantsy* for not warning him. A simple surveillance job? *Khernya!* He did not know exactly what was happening but his intelligence background told him that it was either an extremely sensitive official operation or it was illegal. He did not want to consider the latter; if an Ilyushin was being used in a criminal enterprise, it was bigger than he cared to imagine.

As he lay alone, his head resting on the sack he had managed to squirm out of, Krupchev made his decision. It was not a difficult one given that he knew his disappearance would not be reported by the Americans. He would cooperate with his captors completely. Even his limited knowledge of the CIA's operations in Moscow would be helpful to them—whoever they were. He shivered as he felt the Ilyushin bank steeply.

The door opened and he was suddenly jerked to his feet by two men. A third stood behind them.

"We are all comrades you know," Krupchev blurted out immediately. "We serve different masters, but to the same ends. My name is Alexander Vasilyevich . . ." His words tumbled out but his voice trailed off as he met the icy gaze of the central figure.

"Your *name* is of no concern to me," came the man's high-pitched voice.

KGB! thought Krupchev irrationally, his jangled mind throwing him back to another time.

"Please. It was simply a surveillance," he pleaded. The emotionless black eyes stared at him without reacting.

"You work for who?" asked the man. "The CIA?"

Krupchev nodded. He hung his head, then thrust it up with determination. "I tell you . . . I know nothing about you. My comrades and I were given a name . . . Gyorgy, that is all. It was low-level surveillance. The *Amerikantsy* were fishing . . . *tavarishch*. Comrade, I am telling you the truth!"

"Good," Kumarov smiled thinly. "Now you will leave, *tavarishch?*"

In the split-second before the two men lunged for him again, Krupchev read the dreadful intent behind the black eyes boring into him.

"No, you cannot," he began blubbering. "We are comrades. Please, *you cannot!*"

Kumarov's men dragged the shrieking man down a long corridor. Krupchev flailed his arms, and kicked futilely at them, but it did not slow his inexorable progress through the aircraft. Now they were in the cargo bay, and he realised beyond any doubt what they meant to do to him. He screamed even louder, and wept the name of his wife as he was thrown to the metal floor, fingers reaching instinctively for a hold—*for anything!* The man with the black eyes shrieked an order. One of his men stamped on Krupchev's seeking hands while the other operated the controls to lower the enormous cargo ramp. Slowly the giant maw of the Ilyushin opened, revealing a ten-thousand foot drop, increasing every second as the aircraft continued its ascent. Now the ramp was sloping down, its rippled surface frosting up as the icy wind whistled over it. Kumarov, braced against the wall, shouted against the din but his words were lost in the terrible roar.

One of the men kicked Krupchev in the face and he began to slide away, his smashed fingers disobeying their agony, still snatching at the surface across which he was now accelerating. His scream became that of an animal as he rolled down the ramp.

"Cargo ramp—what is going on?" shouted the Ilyushin's captain through the public-address system.

Krupchev's right hand jagged on a steel splinter spiking out of the ramp's sheer surface. He grasped onto it vainly, trying to push himself to safety with his feet until he realised that they now hung in the air. His flesh gave way on the splinter, and his eyes bulged with horror as he cast Kumarov and his men a last dreadful stare. Then, still screaming to be saved, he fell.

The ramp was almost closed by the time the flight engineer reached them.

"Blyad!" he shouted breathlessly. "What the hell is going on?"

Kumarov looked at him, unblinking. Echoes of the insane rage he had just satiated rebounded within him. The spy was dead, that was all that mattered. There would be no more attempts to confound his work, he swore; the attack in Colombia, his recovery; the agony of his last long night in Moscow, within sight of his escape, yet every second expecting to be taken by the authorities; the final panic of his drive to Sheremetevo. His madness in dealing with the spy had broken the chains of terror that were threatening to strangle him.

"What is going on?" screamed the flight engineer again.

"Research," Kumarov replied through tight lips curled in a smile. The ramp clamped shut. "For *Marshal Gdlyan!*"

The flight engineer stared back; Kumarov's eyes glittered. He knew there was not the slightest chance that the plane would turn back and its crew risk the wrath of such a senior officer. He snorted and brushed past the other as he walked away. The flight engineer growled with anger as he proceeded to disable the ramp's manual override switch. Five minutes later he passed the arrogant comrade-doctor and his men in the passenger compartment. Vodka was being opened and glasses circulated. *Duraki!* he swore silently and made his way back to the flight deck. Behind him he heard the toast raised.

"Za vashe zdoroviye!"

CHAPTER **THIRTEEN**

It is a dreadful chapter in this war," Kalin was saying seriously, as he and Lena walked through the piles of rotting corpses. In daylight the sight was even more stomach wrenching.

"If evidence is needed," Kalin continued, "of the nature of the enemy we face, if the world needs evidence of the barbarism against which we fight, this is it."

Lena looked around futilely. "Information that WorldNet has received suggests that this was done by your side."

"Would I be here?" Kalin laughed. "No," the *danzan* commander continued, "we are civilised Christian men, this is beyond us. Where is this *evidence?* I can tell you that my troops repelled a large force of Asmani *mudjahadeen* from Barkusk."

Lena shook her head in disbelief at Kalin's ploy. "But the Asmani have repeatedly stated that they are in support of the Armestani—" she countered.

"This is not true," he said abruptly. "And here is the evidence."

Lena stared steadily at him.

"Have you seen enough?" he asked, his face wrinkling as if with disgust.

"Yes," whispered Lena. There was nothing she could do. Kalin would expect to see her report on the massacre broadcast on WorldNet that night, and she had yet to find a way of leaving Novominsk.

They packed the camera gear and climbed into their van with Sergei, their minder. Even he was silent on the return trip; the sight had clearly unnerved him. Lena watched him carefully as they drove; he had told her many times that he believed the *danzan* struggle was one of Christianity against the evils of Islam—that it was a holy, honourable war. He was clearly a devout young man, blinded by Kalin's rhetoric. But somewhere within the believer's mind of Sergei Pulkakov there was a need to be absolved from what he had just witnessed. As they pulled up at the hotel, he took Lena aside, away from their *danzan* driver.

"This . . . Kalin," he whispered to her in his rudimentary English. "This . . . not true."

"I know," Lena replied quietly in Russian, and there was a tremendous sadness in his eyes as he climbed back into the van. His soul felt no lighter for having spoken to her. Lena watched him go, then turned to Terry and Harry.

"Poor kid," she muttered.

"Just another asshole," growled Terry. "So do we feed it to New York?"

Lena raised her hands hopelessly.

"Why don't we give Ivan the mechanic another try," suggested Terry. "Maybe he can get us out."

"I will," nodded Lena, without conviction. As she dragged herself up the stairs, memories of Kane infected her again, adding to her despair. She excused herself from her colleagues and walked to her room with its shattered view over Novominsk. She looked out until thinking of Kane's death in a place where death was so ordinary forced her to her bed, to cry.

* * *

"Susan Haywood on two," Shari's voice came through the intercom.

Kane reached for the switch automatically as Stone and Collins straightened themselves in their chairs. They had been gathered in Kane's office since earlier that day and had so far weathered three conference calls with Haywood and Clark Mitford.

"Kane," her voice sounded slightly calmer than it had on the previous call. "The DDO has brought the Russians in as well."

Kane raised his eyebrows as he stared at Stone and Collins. Mitford came online.

"It was our only option," he said. "If Kumarov is spooked we haven't got the resources to track him down on the ground in Moscow, or wherever he may be. We had to risk it."

"I follow you, sir," replied Kane.

"The Israelis are on high alert," the DDO continued. "In case Kumarov is heading their way. Elazar's fear is obviously that he's making for Lebanon or Syria."

An air of fantasy was gripping all of them, Kane thought as he listened. The game was moving fast and in directions which stretched everyone's thinking.

"Have the Russians come clean about Kumarov?" he asked Mitford.

"Still telling us what we already know," replied the DDO. "That he's been off the map since '89, along with his facility."

"What about Russian stockpiles of biological agents," asked Stone. "Anything missing, stolen?"

"Nothing to miss or steal," said Mitford. "Again, the Russians *claim* everything was junked right after the deal was done in Oslo."

"Do we trust 'em?" growled Hog Collins.

"No," said Mitford bluntly, "wait!"

The three in Kane's office heard the distant mumbling of a conversation at the Washington end.

"We just heard from Moscow," reported Mitford. "Susan's checking it out. They've found our man's car in some industrial site outside the city. Searching it now. Standby."

Mitford signed off and the line went dead.

"It's fucking cops and robbers," grunted Collins. "Found the man's car? Great, next they'll find his socks."

"Calm down, Hog," replied Kane, but he too was tired and dispirited. He felt Holtzmann's presence in the air, too ghostly to grasp, too frightening to ignore.

"We have cleared Russian airspace," the captain's voice droned over the Ilyushin's PA. "Currently over Georgia. Going to get bumpy here, strap in."

Kumarov's men fastened their seatbelts nervously as their beast of an aircraft ploughed into a storm front and began bucking. Kumarov clenched his fists, counting down the hours of their journey, and the hours left until their escape from Moscow was finally assured.

"Elazar on one," Shari Smith's voice was strained with fatigue. She had been at her desk for an unbroken stretch of fifteen hours.

"Tom," the Israeli's voice boomed through the room.

"Check," grunted Kane. "What's up, Mordy?"

"Have you heard?" Elazar began.

"Haywood on two," announced Shari through the intercom.

"No, Mordy, but I think I'm about to, Susan's on the other line," said Kane.

"Russians are missing an aircraft, a big one," said Elazar rapidly. "Call me back!"

"Will do," snapped Kane, flicking onto the call from Langley. Stone and Collins leaned forward in their chairs.

"Susan?" barked Kane.

"Kane! The Russians are in a fucking force-nine gale," her voice raced. "Eight hours ago a Russian Air Force Ilyushin transport jet took off from Sheremetevo Airport, supposedly bound for Volgograd on a routine flight. It never arrived. Moscow lost radio contact shortly after take-off, Volgograd control failed to pick it up on radar."

"Crashed?" asked Kane quickly.

"No distress call, no reports of an accident," she answered. "It gets worse, Kane."

His hands clenched as Haywood continued.

"The Russian Air-Vice Marshall in charge of the Volgograd district, one Vladimir Mikhalovich Gdlyan, has also disappeared, along with his family and members of his personal staff. We've got our sats looking for the plane but it's worse than useless—we don't know where to start."

"SatAir can't find him?" asked Kane sharply, breaking the stunned silence in his office. "They must have logged some kind of flight plan to get off the ground."

"Allow me to let you in on a little secret, Kane," retorted Haywood. "SatAir's catch-22. It only detects aircraft where few aircraft fly. Over Europe it's useless, can't tell one flight from another in that beehive!"

"What type of Ilyushin?" asked Stone.

"Standby, General," said Haywood. Kane noticed in passing that she addressed him by rank. Seconds later she replied, "Il–76 'Candid'."

Stone whistled. "Not too many places you can land one of those."

"No," Kane shook his head. The Russian transport was one of the largest aircraft in the world.

"Still no trace of Kumarov?" he asked.

"No," said Haywood. The conclusion was obvious.

"Shit!" snapped Stone.

"That's all, I'm afraid to say," said Haywood. "Standby."

"Yeah," grunted Kane. "Got to call Mordy." The cycle was beginning again, a noose drawing tighter. "Fuck this," he said suddenly. "General, do you still have your Lear on standby?"

"Sure," Stone replied. "Why?"

"Like to get myself up to Washington again," said Kane, standing. "With all respect, White Storm's a sideshow right now."

"Couldn't agree more, Kane," nodded Stone. "Go ahead, haul ass."

"Preparing to land," announced the PA. Kumarov's eyes glistened with sudden emotion.

"Yes!" he breathed as he heard the rumble of the under-carriage descending.

Lena was outside the hotel. Beside her, the guide who had taken them to Mount Barkusk was swearing softly as he considered her final offer. The first inkling of the noise reached her ears, a peculiar sound in a city attuned to those of a purely ground war. She stared up into the late after-noon glare. Then she saw it, and gasped as it banked high over the city. As she watched the immense aircraft descend towards Novominsk she became aware of another sound; closer, more familiar. She whirled around in time to see a convoy of *danzan* regulars approaching. Instantly the two events linked in her mind.

"*Padazhdi!*" she hissed to the man. She sprinted across the hotel's back courtyard and up the stairs to their floor. Careering into Terry's room, the booming roar of the jet overhead filling her ears, she gasped hoarsely to her sur-prised cameraman. Harry Berg was also there, tinkering with the SatCase.

"The jet. Get a shot!" she stammered. Terry bounded across the room and slung his camera on his shoulder, rais-ing it to the window a few seconds before the Ilyushin disappeared over the horizon to land at Shaklin airbase.

But it was enough time for her to glimpse the flag on its tailplane.

"Russian," she gasped. "They're helping *officially?* Terry," she said urgently. "Hide the tape—Kalin's men are coming!"

Terry whipped the video-cassette out of the camera and pushed it into a large crack in the floor near his bed. The sound of heavy footsteps echoed in the corridor outside. There was a pounding on their door. Terry opened it. Boris Rodionov stood before him, bristling with barely suppressed fury.

"You saw the aircraft!" he shouted at Lena in Russian. The sound of the jet still lingered in the air.

"You will stay here," Rodionov snapped. "Do not attempt to leave, there will be guards outside. Do you understand? This is a serious matter."

Lena nodded, her mouth dry with sudden fear. Rodionov fixed her with a final baleful look then stormed out. The threesome heard the clatter of weapons as his men took up their stations outside the door.

"Oh fuck," said Terry. "What's all this about?"

"The Russians are supplying Kalin," whispered Lena. "It's unbelievable. If it gets out, the Islamic republics will go ballistic!"

"Why didn't he ask for our tapes?" replied Terry.

"I don't think he's figured out the SatCase yet," said Harry quietly.

Lena gripped her hands together tightly. "Rodionov's going to want to do something serious to us."

"Shit," breathed Terry, his instincts confirming what Lena had said.

"How serious?" ventured Harry, his face ashen.

"Fucking serious, mate," Terry muttered, his cockiness gone.

Lena rubbed her forehead feverishly. "The only thing we can do is get the tape to New York."

"With the goons out there?" Terry shook his head.

"Terry," said Lena, trying to stay calm. "You know we're in danger—serious danger. Our only hope is to let Jack know—feed him the material. Any better ideas?"

Terry dropped his eyes.

"She's right," Harry agreed, turning to the SatCase.

"Hurry," Lena urged him.

Fifteen scared minutes passed. "Can't patch in," said the soundman, his voice broken by fear. "Circuits are busy."

"Shit!" Terry snorted. "Isn't there an emergency channel on that thing?"

"I'm scanning the range, Terry," Harry replied tersely.

Lena stared out of the window, trying to contain her own peaking anxiety. In the distance she saw the looming shape of the Monastery, and shuddered to think how their fate was being discussed.

"Come on, Harry!" she erupted after another fifteen minutes had passed. Her palms were sweating as she watched the vain attempts of the soundman to make contact with WorldNet headquarters in New York.

Harry Berg did not answer but his slowly shaking head and violently trembling hands said it all.

"Kalin, I *insist*. This risk we cannot take!" repeated Rodionov as a samovar was brought in for their arriving guests. "There is no way of explaining the aircraft's presence here. The television crew must be killed."

Kalin cupped his chin in his hand, furious with himself for the oversight. "It is best. So, an accident?"

"Of course," Rodionov replied. "And as soon as possible." He glared suddenly at the man setting cups around the samovar. "Leave us!" he barked.

The orderly scuttled from the room. Seconds later he was followed by Rodionov, bellowing orders.

* * *

Sergei Pulkakov watched Rodionov gather the men in the courtyard; a squad of crack regulars.

"They are going to kill the *telereporterov*," giggled the youth next to him.

"No, Vasily," Sergei replied, shocked.

"Yes, Sergei Petrovich," grinned the other. "They will join the *araby* on Barkusk and you will have no more work. You will have to fight for a living again."

Sergei stared at him for an instant. Vasily Moroz was a thug who dishonoured his *danzan* uniform. Sergei walked away slowly. The men standing around Rodionov—they were all like Vasily, he realised. At that moment, watching them, knowing the cruel mission they were laughing about, Sergei Pulkakov lost his faith in Kalin. Holding his hands together briefly, he made a silent prayer to his God. Then he slipped around to his quarters at the back of the Monastery, and retrieved his Kalashnikov. He walked the hundred metres to the sprawling carpark on the east side of the complex, climbed quickly into the familiar van, and started it, driving off in a daze.

"Sergei," the soldier manning the perimeter guardpost greeted him with a wave. "You are busy today."

Sergei tried to laugh but it caught in his dry throat. He waved as he passed and dared not look back. He could already hear the roar of heavy vehicles starting up behind him.

Harry swore aloud as the satellite orbiting overhead resolutely refused to accept their upcoming signal.

"Harry!" Lena turned from the window, her face drawn. "The Monastery. Something's coming!"

The soundman glanced at her then frantically scanned his available frequencies again.

Sergei looked behind and saw the dust cloud of the following vehicles. They were about two miles behind. He depressed his foot and the van jolted crazily over potholes, threatening to overturn. A voice grew louder and louder in his head, willing him to turn back, telling him he was dead if he drove on, but he did, all the time muttering prayers under his breath.

"Yes!" Harry exclaimed. They were through to New York. He swung around and hit the play button on Terry's camera, wired into the SatCase.

The WorldNet operations manager in New York came online in the headphones with a lazy drawl. "Wind back, Novominsk, just wait for us to—"

Lena launched forwards and snapped into the camera's microphone. "This is Galena Chagall. Record this and get Jack Mahoney or you're history!"

There was a startled noise and the sounds of shouting in the background.

"Recording, Miss Chagall! We're getting Jack."

"Voice record this," Lena broke in. "Play it to Jack."

"Recording audio two!" came the almost instantaneous response.

"Dust's getting closer, Lena," said Terry from the window, grim-faced and scared. "Definitely our friends."

Lena began, trying desperately to slow her frightened voice.

"Jack, follow this," she spoke slightly above a whisper.

Harry Berg leant forward and wound the audio level up. He nodded.

"This is Galena Chagall in Novominsk, Armestan. This afternoon at approximately 4:30 P.M. a Russian Air Force transport jet landed here in Novominsk, the first evidence of direct Russian involvement in this conflict. Shortly after cameraman Terry Woods shot the footage you are now seeing, our crew was placed under armed guard by rebel president Kalin's chief-of-staff, Boris Rodionov. It is now 5:15 P.M. and from our hotel we can see a contingent of troops moving from Kalin's headquarters towards the centre of Novominsk where we are situated. As of this time the Russian aircraft has not yet taken off, and we . . . *Oh, God!*"

There was a loud shout outside the door and Lena froze.

"Lena! Lena!" Jack Mahoney's voice rebounded through her headphones. "Lena, what the fuck—"

"We're about to be taken by Kalin's men," whispered Lena, terrified.

"Lena!"

The shouting in the corridor intensified and Terry leapt over to her, tearing the headphones off her head.

The door burst open.

Three *danzan* guards backed into the room, arms raised. In front of them stood Sergei with his Kalashnikov levelled. "Take their weapons," he screamed in Russian. "Take their weapons. Rodionov is coming. They are going to kill you!"

Lena grabbed one of the rifles; Terry and Harry followed her lead.

"Come, come!" stuttered Sergei.

Terry snatched his standby camera in its case with his free hand. "Take this," he shouted to Lena, tossing her his rifle. "You know how to use the fucking thing!"

"No, no!" shouted Sergei as Terry grabbed another case.

"Yes!" shrieked Terry, hustling the petrified youth into the corridor. "Let's get the fuck out of here!"

"Where?" gasped Lena, fumbling with the unfamiliar rifle.

"The back!" yelled Sergei and they sprinted down the corridor. As they entered the back courtyard they saw the van, its motor chugging. They bundled in as silently as they could manage in their desperate haste. Terry jumped behind the wheel.

"Where to, Sergei?" screamed Lena as Terry jammed the accelerator pedal to the floor and careered away. A deep-throated roar heralded the arrival of Rodionov's brigade at the front of the hotel.

Sergei was too terrified to speak; he pointed to the left and Terry hurled the van around the narrow corner, gunning it along the cobblestoned street.

"Sergei," Lena grabbed his shoulders and shook him. "You have to think clearly!"

"They are going to kill you," he stammered again. "Rodionov, Kalin . . . I could not!" Then he thrust his head out of the window and began vomiting. Lena shook her head, still holding him. The sound of automatic weapons fire started up behind them. She and Harry whirled around, but it was Sergei who saw their pursuers first.

"They are coming," he choked. His face was streaked with vomit and he was weeping with fear.

"Oh God," Lena gasped through teeth chattering with shock.

"Lena!" Terry yelled desperately. *"Use the fucking gun!"*

Whipping around, Lena thrust the barrel of the AK47 out of the window, fumbled for its safety, jammed the buttstock into her shoulder and looked down the sight. Seconds later, as a *danzan* Jeep tore ahead of its companions and closed on them, Lena squeezed the trigger. A spray of bullets erupted from the muzzle and ricocheted uselessly off cobblestones. Fighting the recoil, Lena brought the weapon up, its magazine almost empty.

But it was enough—her final burst of fire caught the driver of the Jeep in the throat, and as her gun fell silent she saw the vehicle spin crazily and slam into the first of those behind.

"We're not fucking dead yet!" screamed Terry, his hands gripping the wheel with crushing force.

"No," Jack Mahoney croaked as the din in Russian erupted through the studio. The camera microphone was still live, and Lena's final words were ringing in his head.

"Get Alex for a translation—*hurry!*" he yelled. "And keep recording! I want to know what the fuck is going on."

His orders were carried out by a studio crew numbed with shock. Then the sound of gunfire blasted through the studio.

"No, Jesus please," cried Mahoney, grasping his head in his hands. *"Lena!"*

At that moment the burly form of David Peterson lurched into the control room.

"What's happening?" he began.

Mahoney turned on him. "Lena and her crew," he yelled. "That's what, *asshole!*" He grabbed Peterson's coat by the lapels.

"Taken prisoner or murdered, I don't know what yet," he said, now with an icy edge to his voice. "What I do know is that we have footage of a fucking Russian jet helping those Nazis, and you had better raise hell in Washington about Lena or I will take you a-fucking-part!"

Peterson was stunned into silence.

"You hear me, Peterson?" Mahoney brought his face even closer. "The only chance Lena and our people there have is if this becomes an international incident. Make it happen, Peterson. Get Norton to call the President. *Make it happen!*"

WorldNet's Executive Vice-President of News backed out of the office slowly.

"Sure," he mumbled. "Take it easy, Jack, okay?"

The phone buzzed and Holtzmann walked slowly towards it, as if reluctant to pick it up. He had been waiting nearly eighteen hours.

"Yes?" he said softly. His back stiffened and his face cracked into a broad grin. "Excellent! *Excellent!*" Relief shuddered through his exhausted body and he swung around to stare out of the window at Cartagena. "Soon I will be with you," he said.

* * *

Cortez was awake, his dreams even more terrifying than his waking nightmare, when Pablo Simón pushed into his room.

"He wants to see you," grinned the *sicario* and led him out.

Cortez entered the upstairs room, saw Holtzmann, and heard the sound of Simón's weapon being cocked behind him.

"*Señor?*" Cortez asked, staying upright with difficulty. "You—?"

"These days I find sleep difficult," replied Holtzmann, rising slowly from his chair. "And you are one of the reasons."

Cortez went to speak but the sight of Pablo Simón moving to the far side of the room, his gun levelled, dried the words in his mouth.

"You should be concerned that Pablo did not kill you as he wished to," said Holtzmann, advancing towards him. "But I did not hire a fool, and you will not be permitted a common fool's death if you have betrayed me."

Holtzmann stopped a few feet from Cortez, his eyes glittering malevolently.

"This is a critical time for me, Ernesto." An ending, of sorts. But eventually I will have to begin again, and I must decide whether you will be there. You know the *yanquis,* you know them better than any man I have employed. My fear is that you are one of them. Are you?"

Cortez shook his head fervently. "No, *Señor,* I—"

"*This,*" snapped Holtzmann, "is your final chance. If you are a *traidor* you will tell me *now!*"

Cortez's mind was in turmoil, but he knew he could expect no mercy, whatever he said.

"I am not," he said, pushing out his chest in defiance.

Holtzmann regarded him for several seconds, circling him.

Cortez's body shook but he said nothing. Finally he

heard Holtzmann speak again, from behind him, and felt his breath in his ear.

"As I said, Ernesto," he rasped. *"We shall see."* He left his lieutenant standing, waiting, as he walked slowly across to the window overlooking Cartagena.

"Come here, Ernesto," Holtzmann grated. On weak legs, Cortez obeyed.

"Have you ever considered why I chose this path?" said Holtzmann, in an eerily calm voice.

"No, *Señor,*" Cortez replied.

"Vengeance, Ernesto," said Holtzmann. "And when my vengeance is achieved, I will use the *Brigada*—" he thrust his finger towards the window, "—to make *that* my dominion. And if you are still alive, I will need your help. The *yanquis,* having paid for one dream, will be made to pay for the next."

Cortez shuddered, not fully comprehending his words.

Holtzmann whirled on him. "If you die," he said, his face now only inches from Cortez's, "this will not concern you. If you have been loyal, you will be rewarded in a manner you cannot even imagine."

Cortez swallowed hard. *"Señor,"* he asked. "What is your vengeance?"

Holtzmann laughed and the sound echoed through the room. "The Jews," he said. "I will destroy them."

He stared into Cortez's eyes then motioned him to a chair. "I have a need to speak of it," he smiled. "Leave us, Pablo."

When the *sicario* was gone, Holtzmann began.

"We will be leaving here soon," he said. "I have purchased a weapon, a single weapon that will bring about my vengeance."

Cortez gulped. "You have a—"

Holtzmann cut Cortez off. "Not as you think, not *nuclear,*" he said. "Though I once thought it would be the way. No, Ernesto, my weapon is more powerful than even that, for its effects will spread through their mongrel country. And," he leaned forward. "It will make them suffer."

"Then—?" ventured Cortez, astonishment seeping through his fear.

"A plague!" whispered Holtzmann. "*A plague.*"

CHAPTER**FOURTEEN**

Caspar Norton sat in front of Mahoney. Behind him Peterson, swelling out of his blue suit like a tulip about to bloom.

"Galena Chagall is worth a million dollars to this network," Norton bellowed. "And I'll damn well pay that to get her back. I will *not* have the friggin' bureaucrats screwing this up. Find some way of making contact with this Kalin asshole."

"Mr Norton," Mahoney reacted. "Much as I want Lena back, we can't be paying ransoms for journalists. Lena wouldn't go for it anyway, I know her, and she knows it'd threaten everyone we have in the field."

"Wouldn't pay it for just anyone in the field," Norton grinned at Peterson. "Don't you be telling her that though, Mahoney."

Mahoney felt nauseous.

"Or what about the footage?" asked Peterson. "If they want it so badly, we'll swap it for Lena."

"*And* the crew," snapped Mahoney.

"Yeah, you can be sure of that," said Norton, but Mahoney wasn't.

"In any case," Mahoney tried, "offering the footage sets the same dangerous precedent—"

"Well damn it, Mahoney," Norton shouted. "What do you suggest? Should I chat to Ross Perot and hire some green berets to parachute in and rescue Chagall . . . and the crew?"

"Talk to the President!" said Mahoney straight.

"I'll tell you something, mister," Norton's face puffed up as he poked his finger at Mahoney, "I will not let some dumb-ass bimbo get this country involved in a part of the world it has no business being in. Understand me?"

Mahoney's face paled with fury, but Norton was not done.

"I'll pay money," he spat. "Shit, I'll pay this skunk *two* million but Chagall better be damn grateful when she comes out."

"That's enough, Mr Norton." Mahoney stood up. "I'm resigning and you can read about the reasons in the *New York Times.*"

Norton cast him a malignant glare. "Oh will you? You sonofabitch." His ample body trembled as he raged at Mahoney. "And just maybe you'll find yourself in a heap more trouble than Chagall, mister. Don't you threaten me!"

"Mr. Norton . . . ?" Peterson stumbled. "Jack?"

The proprietor of WorldNet was livid, veins bulging on his neck, but Mahoney stood his ground. "I have a job to do," he growled. "I'll do it until tomorrow morning." He turned and strode out.

"When this is over," snapped Norton as the door closed. "I want him sacked."

"Yes, Mr. Norton," whispered Peterson.

Mahoney walked back to his office. Lisa Mulcahey, the editor who had been with him during Lena's satellite feed, was waiting for him impatiently.

"Jack—!" she began as he entered, but one glance from him was enough to silence her.

"Don't!" he warned. "What did Alex have to say?"

"He didn't know. The soldiers in the room kept referring to their commander as 'General,' and his voice is apparently shouting 'Find them, find them!' "

"And the gunshots?" asked Mahoney.

Mulcahey shook her head. "Don't know. You heard 'em—they were damn close."

"Jesus Christ," whispered Mahoney to himself. The editor looked at him and a wave of sympathy passed through her. Everyone who worked with Jack Mahoney knew what he thought of Lena Chagall. His life orbited around her.

"Jack," she said softly. "They might have gotten out. We just can't tell."

He looked at her.

"Dub me the edited piece and a copy of the original tape," he said slowly. "This is between you and me, Lisa. Norton's vetoed us broadcasting the story or going to the government. I'm going to try to get it on the overnight out of Washington."

Mulcahey's eyes widened with disbelief. "Jack, you'll—"

"I'm gone already," he said. "I've got to fight this, Lisa."

Mulcahey nodded. "Think I'll make it two copies of everything," she said. "Just in case you lose in Washington."

Within a quarter of an hour she was back. Mahoney took the tapes and stuffed them into his tattered briefcase.

"Thanks," he said. "Put the others somewhere safe, okay?"

"Sure," she smiled. "And for what it's worth, I think Lena's worth the fight, Jack. We all do."

Mahoney grunted his farewell and raced out to the elevators and down to the sidewalk. Apologising to a waiting WorldNet night staffer, he took his cab.

"Marine Air Terminal," he gasped. "I need to make the last shuttle."

"What's the tip?" came the seasoned reply from the front.

"Fifty or nothing," shouted Mahoney.

"Deal!" Within ten minutes they were hurtling through patchy traffic on the Triboro Bridge at eighty miles per hour.

All it took were two passwords and five simple keystrokes into the computer terminal in the Cartagena control tower to change the records in the SatAir global air-traffic network. Two Gulfstream IIIs, call-signs Tango Delta Foxtrot and Charlie Hotel Victor, *en route* to La Paz, Bolivia for sale, had aborted their take-offs from Ernesto Cortiso airport. Flight plans for the Gulfstreams, logged into the SatAir network an hour earlier as required by international law, were automatically deleted. The corporate jets, supposedly owned by the Colombian prospecting company *Recursos Unidos,* were safely back in their hangars.

Except, of course, that they were not. In fact the two identical Gulfstreams were still in sight of the control tower, climbing steeply away from the runway in tandem. Such elaborate subterfuge was needed because the year-old SatAir network took an intense and unhealthy interest in all aircraft departing Colombia, no matter how legitimately. The mandatory SatAir flight plan gave the network's satellites a place to look, and if they found nothing—as would have been the case with the pair of Gulfstreams—a worldwide alert would have been raised.

"Adiós amigos!" shouted yet another air-traffic controller whose bank balance had been swollen by his complicity. But even he would not have believed who was on board one of the now-distant aircraft banking over the Gulf of Darien.

Holtzmann sat at the forward section of the leading long-range jet. Extra fuel tanks in the rear of the aircraft had reduced the main cabin seating to four. Next to Holtzmann sat Cortez. Behind sat Pablo Simón and another *sicario,* nursing their automatic weapons, unwilling to relax. For them this journey was a disturbing break with normalcy.

Through the thick windows of the jet, Cartagena was cloaked in twilight. Holtzmann shifted comfortably in his seat. He was confident and pleased.

"Tango Delta Foxtrot, Charlie Hotel Victor—climb to thirty-three thousand . . ." crackled the cockpit radio for the last time. Diablo Sánchez whooped as he pushed his aircraft into a climb. The second Gulfstream, occupied by Holtzmann's *Brigada Fascista* bodyguard unit, followed Sánchez's lead. Its pilot, Eddie Montana, waved as the two aircraft pulled alongside each other for the ascent.

"This is a motherfucker, Eddie!" whispered Sánchez to himself, turning his eyes from the other jet to the controls in front of him. They would first travel northeast, passing directly from Colombian to international airspace over the Caribbean, and then dead east, across the Atlantic to Tenerife in the Canary Islands. There, a member of the Sobrecartel's Spanish operation had arranged refuelling and transit facilities.

"Only four and a half thousand miles to go, *amigos!*" Sánchez shouted. Holtzmann smiled at the pilot's enthusiasm and settled into his seat as the jet reached its cruising altitude. Only then did Pablo Simón and his colleague, a wiry man nicknamed Pancho, place their weapons at their feet and open beers.

"Cognac, *Señor?*" Simón asked.

"Yes," replied Holtzmann.

Simón passed forward a glass and Holtzmann raised it in a silent toast, then savoured the burn of the cognac in his mouth. He stared out into the gathering gloom. Specks of light defined land as they passed into the night, but before long the impenetrable blackness of the Atlantic swallowed them. It was a curious sensation, Holtzmann realised, one he was not used to. His confinement was suddenly disturbing. His stomach knotted and an eerie fear of the future drenched his mind as the plane droned on, creeping incrementally across the vast expanse of white-flecked darkness.

He swallowed his cognac and called for more, taking increasing pleasure in its effect as it slowly calmed him.

"Zhora!" Kalin's voice rang through the chamber as the other was led through the door.

"Sasha!" Kumarov all but rushed across the room. The two men embraced heartily. Boris Rodionov shook his head at how eerily similar they looked. Both had exactly the same glittering black eyes.

"Your flight, *bratishka?*" asked Kalin.

"As they say, Sasha," chuckled Kumarov. "A flight is good when it is over."

"Especially a Russian flight. Come, come!" Kalin waved to the table. On it sat a steaming samovar and food.

"Boris Nikolaevich," ordered the *danzan* leader. "Show Gyorgy Alexandrovich's men to their quarters, then join us."

Rodionov nodded. "And the crew of the Ilyushin?" he asked.

Kalin looked at his brother, raising his eyebrows.

"They are a liability, but we may need them," said Kumarov.

"Keep them here," Kalin ordered with some reluctance. *"Under guard!"* he added.

"Kalin, the television—" began Rodionov.

"Enough!" snapped Kalin angrily.

"What?" began Kumarov.

"It is nothing, a minor disturbance," Kalin glared at his chief-of-staff. Rodionov dropped his head and withdrew.

The two men sat at the table and Kalin poured tea. It was many years since they had been in each other's presence and for several minutes they discussed the intervening time. Then Kalin turned the conversation to the present.

"I have advised Holtzmann of your arrival," he began. Kumarov nodded; the matter of his brother's parallel dealings with the Colombian still rankled with him and Kalin sensed it.

"We are a *troika* in one way, Zhora," he said slowly. "But I also have specific needs here. Holtzmann was able to assist me."

"Weaponry?" asked Kumarov curiously. "Surely not."

Kalin laughed. "Zhora, he comes to us for *weaponry*! No, he assisted in protecting our funds from the *yanki* freeze. He has some fine bankers in his employ."

Now Kumarov laughed as well. "Banking? It is a strange world, Sasha."

"Yes!" agreed the other. "He will be here tomorrow. How long will you need, before . . . ?" Kalin's eyes glinted, observing his younger brother carefully as he sipped his tea.

Kumarov replaced his cup. "It will take some days to set up the laboratory facility here," he answered. "The isolation rooms, particularly, will require at least a week's testing to ensure their seals are tight. The virus itself is ready. Are the missiles and warheads ready?"

Kalin swallowed his tea and licked his lips. "Soon," he said. "They are being made ready."

"Your targets?" Kumarov asked.

"The first," replied Kalin, "is Tumakoc. Population about 150,000. My men have it besieged."

"Fine," said Kumarov. "It will be a good test. I will need accurate weather maps of the area, daily."

"You will have them," said Kalin.

"And I warn you, Sasha," said Kumarov. "Holtzmann will want to—"

"Yes, I know," said Kalin. "And surely, if Tumakoc is a success, the final targets can be hit simultaneously?"

Kumarov nodded. "If . . ." he said quietly.

"Confidence, Zhora!" laughed Kalin. "Perhaps I should tell you that my primary objective is Kirkusk."

Kumarov gasped. The old capital of Armestan had been

the republic's biggest city before the war and the fighting had only swollen its population.

"Two million," Kalin confirmed, reading his brother's thoughts. "Two million *araby!* Vengeance is mine, sayeth the Lord—He will deliver the plague upon the infidel."

Both men were silent at the thought.

"Our destiny is joined again, *bratishka!*" Kalin said finally.

It was nearly midnight when Jack Mahoney stepped into the control room of WorldNet's Washington studio. It was tiny by comparison to the New York operation, and manned by fewer than ten people.

"Jack," came the shout from across the room. It was Frank Pluchowski, nominally the overnight news editor in Washington. In reality, Mahoney knew, the twenty-three-year-old was scarcely out of journalism school.

"Frank, buddy," he laughed and the younger man reddened at the vigour of his recognition.

"Still pumping it out down here," Mahoney said.

In the studio Holly Chang was nearing the end of her half-hour bulletin. In the corner of the control room Gerald King—one of WorldNet's few Afro-American anchormen—was reading his scripts for the next shift. Mahoney nodded to him. King was one of the network's real pros and ten years Mahoney's senior, but like most other minority newsreaders who Norton was forced by law to hire, he was stuck in Washington on the overnight beat.

"What's up, Jack?" he asked, putting his script down. Mahoney chewed his lip, looking bleakly at him. Did it have to be Gerald?

"Great story from Lena in Armestan," he held up the videocassette. Frank Pluchowski chose that minute to re-enter the control-room.

"What's that, Jack?" he asked brightly.

"Story from Lena Chagall in Armestan," repeated Jack.

"Great stuff, she got the first pictures of the Ruskies helping Kalin."

Pluchowski looked blankly at him for a moment.

"Armestan," laughed Gerald King, half-disgusted at the man's ignorance. "White supremacists, same old story!"

"Yeah, right, Gerald," Pluchowski grinned nervously. "So why didn't you feed it down the line, Jack?"

"Picture quality is bad enough as it is, didn't want to lose another generation," Mahoney replied. "And I have a few errands in DC tomorrow anyway, so," he waved the cassette in front of Pluchowski, "brought you your very own copy."

"I'd heard you took good care of Lena, Jack," said the younger man conspiratorially. King coughed and Mahoney let the comment pass.

"I've written the studio link," he added. "Can someone get it into the teleprompter?"

"Sure," replied Pluchowski eagerly, sensing that his crack about Lena Chagall had not gone down well. "Jack? This does . . ." he paused suddenly at the doorway. "I mean this *is* okay with Peterson is it? I'd normally check with him on a breaking story."

"Armestan's hardly a breaking story," replied Mahoney, allowing just an edge of annoyance to creep into his voice. "It's simply *late*."

King chuckled and Pluchowski nodded fervently. "Got it, Jack. Right!" he said, exiting.

Kane looked at King, wanting to warn him but knowing he could not. A minute later Pluchowski was back into the control room. "Okay, it's in the teleprompter," he said. "Gerald, you're on in five. Jack, where does it go in the rundown? What do we lose?"

"Lena's the lead," replied Mahoney. "What else have you got on domestic?"

Pluchowski handed him a rundown sheet, and he read it quickly.

"Kill the toads," he said with a chuckle and Pluchowski

drew a line through a feature piece on Australian cane toads which was to end the bulletin.

"Larry." He pressed the intercom. "I'm coming down with a new lead from Galena Chagall. We're killing the toads." He walked out of the room clutching Mahoney's cassette, not realising what he had said.

"An earnest young man," remarked King, with tears of laughter in his eyes.

The Gulfstreams purred thirty-three thousand feet above the desolate Atlantic, tiny specks in the night, four hours from the Canary Islands.

Holtzmann was asleep, dreaming; images of a vast dark army marching with him at its head on a white horse. His father marched with him; the horde scattered before the chant and roar of his men, surging on, vengeful, invincible. Banners of blood trailed their advance.

Unable to relax, Cortez watched Holtzmann's changing expressions in the dim light. There was no innocence in his master's face, even in sleep.

In the cockpit, Diablo Sánchez hummed happily. For all his years with the Colombian Air Force, then Avianca, then the Sobrecartel, Sánchez had yet to fall out of love with flying. He glanced at his co-pilot illuminated by the minimal cabin lights. Juan Ruiz was snatching an hour's sleep. Outside, the other Gulfstream floated alongside in the dark sky.

Suddenly the radio crackled to life. It was an emergency SatAir broadcast. Juan stirred beside him, but did not wake as a chart slipped from his knees to his feet.

"Attention—this is SatAir Atlantic! Aircraft currently at North 120 degrees, West 95 degrees please identify yourself. Your course is not consistent with any logged flight plan."

"*Joder!*" swore Sánchez as the speaker repeated the message. He glanced out at the companion jet on his port side.

Its pilot, Eddie Montana, dipped the wings of his aircraft to indicate that he had heard the SatAir transmission. *"Joder!"* Sánchez swore again, looking skywards through the cockpit windscreen. Their course and bearing would appear no-where in the global air-traffic computer network. Techni-cally the two Gulfstreams did not exist, which was why the roving eye of the satellite had picked them up. But Sánchez knew they could have done nothing else except chance it; had they logged in with SatAir, no bribe on earth would have prevented them being monitored closely in flight and searched on their landfall in Tenerife. In the international war against the Sobrecartel, every flight out of Colombia suffered the same fate. Once they left the Canary Islands it would be a different story, but for now Sánchez knew that he and Eddie Montana had only one choice—fly the way they did on their smuggling runs into the States; the way he had flown to collect Cortez from Mexico.

At one hundred and fifty feet above sea-level.

Beside him, Juan Ruiz awoke in time to hear the third repetition of the SatAir message.

"I told you," he observed sleepily. "Now they will track us all the way in. We're fucked."

Sánchez growled at his co-pilot's laconic wit. They were not fucked, he knew, but the option was a sonofabitch. He calculated his fuel supply and the miles they still had left to cover.

"Take it down, Diablo," slurred Ruiz, closing his eyes again. "What's your alternative?"

"You fly the fucking thing, *hijo de puta!*" Sánchez swore, but he knew he had no choice.

"Son of a whore," he shouted, but Ruiz did not respond.

Four fucking hours! he thought, carefully pushing the air-craft into a dive, checking to see that Eddie Montana was following him down. After passing through five-thousand feet, he brought the Gulfstream into a shallower descent. At a thousand feet he switched on the powerful noselights of the jet, specially modified for this type of flying. He allowed himself a tight smile as he imagined his passengers' shock when they woke and saw the ocean before their eyes.

Still the plane descended, and Sánchez's hands tightened on the controls. The dive became shallower and shallower. Now the altimeter read three hundred feet, but his eyes never deviated from the pitch darkness ahead. He knew some of the monster Atlantic waves could account for nearly a hundred feet by themselves between crest and trough. The surface of the ocean loomed before him now, its salty jaws just visible in the light; foam-flecked masses of darkness. He pulled back a little. *Dios mío,* he breathed—so close! It was far more threatening than the flights across the mill-pond surface of the Caribbean to the US. He was now a hundred and fifty feet above the waves, well under normal air-traffic radar. But that was not the problem, Sánchez knew. He needed to be invisible to that damn eye in the sky.

Grimly he settled into his frightening task, not even daring to check whether Eddie Montana had followed him all the way down. One tiny mistake in four hours would be fatal. As if in response to his thoughts, a massive swell forged itself into a crest and thundered towards the Gulfstream. Sánchez knew it would pass well beneath him, but was edging the nose up slightly when Pablo Simón awoke in the rear of the aircraft.

His scream of fright was ear-splitting as the mammoth wall of water scraped their wingtips with its smoking mist.

"Ah, Pablo you fly like a *niña,*" Sánchez said, relaxing slightly. "It will be like this until the *Islas Canarias!*"

"*Vete a la mierda!*" swore Pablo Simón, dry-mouthed as he realised how hellish the remainder of the flight would be. Looking out at the silhouettes of his *companeros* in the other Gulfstream, he knew they would be sharing his terror.

* * *

Hog Collins was still at White Storm HQ when the call came in. Stone had left only minutes before. Kane had just arrived at CIA headquarters in Langley.

"This is Jack Mahoney of WorldNet," said the voice.

"Look," growled Collins. "You—"

"Wait!" shouted Mahoney before he was hung up on again. "It's about Kane—off the record, okay! This is personal. I don't know if he's dead or alive—but if he's there, or anywhere, get this message to him. Galena Chagall is—"

"Mahoney, is it?" Collins broke in. "You know I can't."

"Please just fucking listen!" Mahoney interrupted. "The lead item on WorldNet now. Galena Chagall is in trouble in Armestan . . ." His voice trailed off.

"I don't know who the hell you are," he concluded. "I don't even *know* Kane. But from what I've been able to find out from sources at Miami General, there's a chance he wasn't killed like you guys would have us believe. I'm not going to broadcast a fucking word, I promise. There's someone he cares about and I care about who's in deep shit right now—Galena Chagall. If Kane's alive, tell him. Watch our report and watch it soon! If he's dead—whoever this is— you should know that our network is about to show conclusive proof that the Russians are supplying Kalin in Armestan, and that one of our crews has gone missing after shooting it. Got it?"

"Okay," hurried Collins. "Now get off the fucking line."

On the TV monitor in the cramped office, Mahoney watched the opening titles of the bulletin begin. In the adjacent studio, Gerald King and Frank Pluchowski were about to lose their jobs because of him. The world spun slowly around him and he picked up the telephone again.

"*Washington Post,*" said the operator.

"This is Jack Mahoney, WorldNet," he began. "Connect me to the foreign news desk . . ."

"That line is busy, please hold."

* * *

Kane grabbed the phone on the first buzz. He was tired and frustrated.

"What is it, Hog?"

"It's Lena," said Collins quickly. "Turn on WorldNet, call me back."

Shaking his head, Kane replaced the receiver.

"Hey," he shouted around the crowded room. "Where can I see WorldNet?"

The mind-numbing music box tune was still playing through the phone as Mahoney watched Gerald King begin his studio introduction.

"At the top of the bulletin tonight, an exclusive report from Galena Chagall in Armestan, who disappeared shortly after making this transmission. The footage taken by Chagall and her team may explain why, showing Russia's open involvement in the Armestani civil war, a position Moscow has long denied."

Lena's hushed voice came through the speaker.

"Lena," Mahoney breathed.

"John Redmonds, Foreign Editor," a voice suddenly erupted out of the telephone. Mahoney coughed.

"Jack Mahoney, WorldNet," he began.

"Yeah, Jack, I'm watching it," said the other tersely. "Good story. And don't worry, we'll give you guys the credit. That all?"

"Yeah," Jack breathed. He dialled again.

"*New York Times*, editorial."

"This is Galena Chagall in Novominsk, Armestan. This afternoon, at approximately 4:30 P.M., a Russian Air Force transport jet landed here in Novominsk."

For a second Kane was lost in the sound of Lena's scared voice, then the distant speck she was describing on the videotape sparked his mind into action.

"My God," he breathed. *"Haywood!"* he shouted. She appeared before him in seconds.

"WorldNet! Russian jet just landed in Armestan," he muttered, still listening to Lena's commentary.

"Bingo!" smiled Haywood. "I'll get a copy and check that it's our plane, but this feels right. Just down from Volgograd—"

"Yes, yes." Kane motioned her to be silent. Haywood scurried away.

"As of this time the Russian aircraft has not yet taken off, and we . . . *Oh, God!"*

A pit opened within Kane and his mind jangled with anguish. His telephone buzzed, and like a robot he reached for it.

"Hog?"

"That was Galena Chagall reporting from Novominsk, Armestan," Gerald King concluded. "Since filing that report we have had no contact with Chagall or her camera team, and we understand that they have been taken prisoner by, or are hiding from, forces under the control of rebel president Kalin. In other news . . ."

Mahoney slumped. It had been done. The press had the story and would run with it. And at least two men would lose their jobs.

The phone in his small office rang. He picked it up tentatively. It was Lisa Mulcahey.

"Well you sure pulled down the temple," she gasped. "Peterson's just called. He's on his way over, pissed as hell. The idiot hasn't realised that the story came out of Washington or that you're there, but he will once he gets here. I'd let everyone down there know."

"I will," replied Mahoney.

"You had to do it," said Mulcahey. "You had to."

"Yeah," he sighed and hung up.

He stood and walked slowly towards the control room.

"Frank," he said, as he entered.

Pluchowski looked up, smiling. "Great piece, Jack! I—"

"Listen Frank," Mahoney cut him off. "Go home. That piece wasn't supposed to run. I'm gone, and I'll try to take the heat off you and Gerald, but I can't promise—"

"Wasn't supposed to—" the blood drained from Pluchowski's face. "Oh, shit."

Mahoney gripped him by the shoulder. "It was Lena," he began.

"You sonofabitch!" shrieked Pluchowski so loudly that Gerald King heard it in the studio. "You friggin' asshole."

"Frank," Mahoney shook his head.

"It's Peterson—line one," shouted the director's assistant. "He's on his car phone."

Pluchowski turned slowly and stared at the telephone. Mahoney reached for it but the other man snatched it first.

"Mr. Peterson," he shouted. "I didn't—Mahoney lied!" he babbled. "No, Mr. Peterson!"

He let the receiver drop and slumped into a chair. Mahoney picked the phone up.

"Peterson," he said calmly. "This is Mahoney. Right now every metropolitan daily in the country is gearing to run this story tomorrow morning. I've done what I thought I should, and I'm resigning. If you push *anyone* else over this, the papers will have that too—chapter and fucking verse. Now you tell Norton that I did it solo, or else! I mean it, Peterson, you know that."

Mahoney hung up without listening to Peterson's reply and looked at the studio monitor. Gerald King was just reading another introduction.

"How long's this piece coming up?" Mahoney asked the DA.

"Three thirty-two," she snapped back. Mahoney walked quickly through the soundproof door leading to the studio proper. As the taped story ran, Gerald King sat back in his chair.

"What's going on back there, Jack?"

Mahoney told him as the deadline for King's next introduction raced towards them.

"Thirty seconds," came the shout from the control room intercom.

"You did the right thing, Jack." King slapped him on the shoulder. "Now get lost."

"Thanks," gasped Mahoney breathlessly. "Gerald, I'm sorry. You'll be—"

"You forget, white boy," grinned King. "I got a bunch of laws protecting me, and besides which, where's Norton going to find another tame nigger like me?"

King's laughter followed him out, and the anchorman was still smiling as he introduced the bulletin's next item. It was, Mahoney noticed, the piece on Australian toads, resurrected in the chaos following Lena's report.

"The toads live!" he shouted as he walked out into the Washington night.

"She's given us the break," came Hog Collins' excited voice. "That has to be the goddamn Ilyushin!"

"Hog, she could be dead," replied Kane in a monotone, gripping the phone tightly.

"Yeah, I'm sorry, Tom," said Collins quickly.

"I want to talk to the guy who called," said Kane.

"Name was Mahoney, Jack Mahoney," replied Collins. "WorldNet, Washington, he said. Stone's on his—"

"I'm going after Mahoney," said Kane. "Talk later."

"Tom!" but Kane had already hung up. As he strode from the situation room deep inside the CIA's Langley headquarters, he passed Susan Haywood.

"Kane, we're having the picture enhanced," she turned and walked with him. "Where are you—?"

"Back soon, Susan," he replied dully. "Need some air."

He left her in his wake, staring at his back, wondering.

* * *

The sun rose with breathtaking speed. Daylight only made the grey sea look more vicious. Sánchez was a lather of sweat, hunched in his seat, staring like a zombie at the waves ahead of him.

"We are close?" he heard Holtzmann's grumble from behind him.

"*Sí!*" he gasped, not taking his eyes off the sea. It had been that way for nearly four hours. He wondered how Eddie Montana was holding up in the following jet.

"Headwinds at this altitude have slowed us," reported Juan Ruiz, checking the instruments against his charts. "I estimate thirty minutes to Tenerife, perhaps a little more."

Sánchez used a split second to glance at his fuel gauge. At these outer limits of the Gulfstream's range, thirty minutes was a critical amount of time.

"Switch to tank two!" he ordered Ruiz, unwilling to take a hand off his controls to carry out even this simple task himself. It would be very close! During the next twenty minutes he made false promises to a forgotten God.

"Contact Tenerife, Juan!" he whispered finally. "We have to have priority but we can't Mayday or it'll arouse suspicion."

"New call sign is Alpha Foxtrot Hotel," checked Ruiz. Now, however briefly, both aircraft would again be logged into the SatAir computer network. Ruiz was outwardly calm, but hoped fervently that their transitory reappearance on the air-traffic network would pass unnoticed at SatAir headquarters in Brussels. A further change of call signs would occur on their departure from Tenerife.

"Tenerife," he began into the radio. "This is Alpha Foxtrot Hotel and Victor Bravo Tango ex-private airstrip Howard Island, South Atlantic, requesting permission to land."

"Standby, Alpha Foxtrot Hotel and Victor Bravo Tango," came the crackling reply. "We do not have you on radar. What is your altitude?"

"Thirty-one thousand feet, Tenerife," replied Ruiz coolly.

"We diverted to avoid headwinds, you should see us approaching from the west in approximately one zero minutes."

"Do you copy, Victor Bravo Tango?" came the call from Tenerife to the other Gulfstream.

"Roger, Tenerife," came the terse response.

"They're sounding tired," chuckled Ruiz. Beside him, Sánchez nodded. In just over ten minutes the nightmare flight would be over; both jets would climb to thirty-one thousand feet and appear on Tenerife's radar.

"Alpha Foxtrot Hotel, Victor Bravo Tango—is Tenerife your final destination?"

"Negative, Tenerife," replied Ruiz. "Refuelling, transit only."

"Roger, Alpha Foxtrot Hotel, Victor Bravo Tango. We will advise you of landing details when we see you, over."

"Over," Ruiz replied.

"I don't care what you say, Juan," grunted Sánchez. "You doin' some of the fucking flying on the next leg!"

Ruiz noted with amusement how silent the main cabin had been. "Please fasten your seatbelts in preparation for landing," he cracked. "We hope you have had an enjoyable flight."

"You are a funny man, Juan Ruiz," came Holtzmann's growl from behind him.

Mahoney knocked back his fourth whisky as the man entered the bar. It was two A.M. and only a party of five *Washington Post* night-editors at a corner table was keeping the place open. Mahoney gripped his empty glass as he watched the man approach. He was strangely familiar, and as he felt his gaze, Mahoney looked away, racking his brain to place him. Then he heard the voice in his ear.

"You Mahoney?"

He swung around and stared into the icy blue eyes. Then he remembered.

"Kane?" he asked, astonished. "What—"

Kane grasped his shoulder more roughly than he intended, and led Mahoney to a table on the far side of the bar.

"Jesus," Mahoney winced as the steel fingers released him into a chair. "Nice to see you too."

"Mahoney," said Kane in an undertone. "Tell me about Lena."

"Final approach," Ruiz intoned.

"Roger, Alpha Foxtrot Hotel, cleared for landing. Victor Bravo Tango, standby. You will be towed to bays 13 and 14."

"Roger," snapped Ruiz. Sánchez lined the aircraft up with the expanse of tarmac ahead of him. The pressure of having skimmed the Atlantic at over six hundred miles an hour, and the real fear that their fuel was almost out, clashed in his head.

"Diablo!" cried Ruiz as the Gulfstream's nose lifted alarmingly. He took over the controls and Sánchez sank back into his seat.

"*Muchas gracias,* Juan," he gasped as his co-pilot brought the jet into a perfect landing. Spontaneous applause broke out from the cabin, and Pablo Simón whooped with relief.

Then, as the tarmac vehicle approached to two them to the refuelling bay, a tense silence descended on them. Holtzmann grunted as he squeezed himself into a small compartment in the rear of the aircraft, and the *sicarios* hid their weapons. Soon they would know whether the Sobre-cartel had salted the right pockets in this Spanish outpost.

"But there's no way of knowing," Mahoney concluded. "Lena had a portable satellite transponder with her, but from what I saw and heard, if she's not in Kalin's hands, it certainly is. I've got no way of contacting her."

"I'd like a full copy of the tape, Mahoney," said Kane.

Mahoney nodded and reached down into his briefcase. "All yours, Kane," he smiled brokenly, handing it over. "And please tell Caspar Norton where you got it."

"Think he'll still try to arrange a ransom payment?" asked Kane.

"It's all he understands," said Mahoney. "Said he didn't want the 'bimbo' to drag us into Armestan."

Kane's fist tightened. Mahoney looked at him, still unable to conquer the jealousy which gnawed at his soul. But this was a different man to the one he had met in Jerusalem. That Kane had been confident, self-assured. This Kane was trembling, exhausted. And dangerous, thought Mahoney.

"Please, Kane," he asked. "Let me know what you do, what anyone does about her?"

Kane nodded.

"And," Mahoney hesitated. "I should tell you . . . Lena . . . She thinks you're dead."

CHAPTER **FIFTEEN**

Terry!" Lena pointed at the distant clump of houses. Another village to bypass. They were now in the north of Armestan, roughly eighty miles from Novominsk, having driven non-stop for nearly two hours. Terry slowed the van and pulled up.

"Sergei?" Lena asked.

The *danzan* youth peered ahead into the distance, then, as always, behind—even though the dust cloud that had been pursuing them was long gone. "It could be *arabski*," he said in Russian. "It would explain why Rodionov turned back—"

"English!" snapped Terry impatiently. Lena patted his shoulder and translated.

"*If* he's turned back!" said the Australian dubiously. The echoes of the gunfire that had pursued them out of Novominsk still echoed in his brain. They had been lucky. Too lucky, he worried.

"But if the village is *arabski* . . . ?" Sergei trailed off; the *danzan* propaganda about their enemy was eating at him.

"We *have* to get petrol," Terry interrupted. "Lena, we're bloody lucky to have gotten this far. I don't like it, but we've got to give it a shot."

Lena nodded. In the hours that had passed since their mad dash out of Novominsk, her nerves had settled and she was in control. "Yes," she said. Then in Russian, "Sergei, we have to stop here."

The youth shivered, gripping his sides. He did not answer.

"Go ahead, Terry," said Lena.

Terry urged the van forwards. No one spoke. Around them, the land was eerily desolate; no stock animals, no signs of life; a no-man's-land of shifting masters.

"Spooky," said Harry Berg softly as they entered the village. It too appeared deserted. Most of its pathetic houses were shambling ruins and it looked as if it had been fought over recently.

"Looks like Kalin country to me," Terry said nervously.

Lena glanced up at the high hills to their left. "Up there probably isn't," she replied.

They stopped in what had been the town square. There was a stone well and broken flagpole at its centre. Adjacent were the remains of a tiny mosque.

"*Araby . . .*" breathed Sergei, slipping down in his seat.

Terry and Lena got out of the van. Suddenly they heard a sound and swivelled around, startled.

"There!" hissed Terry. The glimpsed the haunted face of a boy staring at them with feral intensity from behind a broken wall.

"*My Amerikantsy!*" shouted Lena. "*My ne danzany!*" But the boy was already scampering away.

"Shit!" swore Terry, bounding off after him. A minute later he dragged the boy, clawing and screaming, back to the van. Lena knelt down and tried to soothe their captive.

"*Ne danzany,*" she looked into his terrified eyes. "Not *danzany,*" she repeated. "American."

The boy shuddered in Terry's grip. His screaming stopped and he began sobbing. He was in terrible physical shape—starving, injured, and very, very scared.

"Let him sit," said Lena. "We are friends," she said to the boy. "Are you from this village?"

The boy shook his head. "No . . ." he choked. "There is no one."

"What happened?" Lena reached forward to hold him.

"I . . ." he sobbed. "Barkusk . . . the *danzany* . . ." His head fell into her chest and he cried.

"Terry," said Lena softly. "Get some of the chocolate from the camera bag."

The cameraman ducked into the vehicle for one of their precious chocolate bars. Lena broke a piece off and held it to the boy's lips. He gulped it greedily and lifted his teary eyes to her.

"Friend?" he asked softly.

"Friend . . ." she smiled and slowly his terror began to subside.

"Let's move it," whispered Terry. "We don't—"

Lena quietened him with a glance. "He was on Mount Barkusk," she said.

Terry's eyes widened and he looked at the boy with pity. "Poor bastard," he sighed.

Lena fed him the chocolate bar while Terry and Harry scoured the village for petrol. Ten minutes later they returned.

"Nothing," muttered Terry. "Not a damn thing." He saw that the boy was calmer and reached forward to pat his head. "Feeling better you little bugger?"

The boy looked up. "His name is Abdur," said Lena.

"Well Abdur," Terry smiled. "I guess you'd better come with us. Not that we're going to get very far."

"*Byinzeen,*" tried Lena. "We need gasoline."

The boy looked at her, then stood and took her hand.

Terry raised his eyebrows.

"Gas," said Lena, turning around and going with the boy. "C'mon."

"Great," replied the Australian.

Abdur led them to a house on the village outskirts. Behind a creaking wall stood a vintage tractor.

Terry quickly checked the gas tank. "Probably diesel," he said. "Still, beggars can't be choosers." He searched the area that had been a garage for the village's most prized possession and came up with a rusty bucket and a length of filthy hose, which he jammed into the tractor's tank. *"Fuck!"* he gasped as he all but swallowed a mouthful of gasoline in his haste to siphon it from the tank. He spat it into the bucket as a thin stream began to flow from the hose.

"Diesel or gas?" chuckled Lena. "What side of the hill?" Their laughter eased the oppressive tension.

"Very fucking funny," said Terry, still spitting the vile taste from his mouth. "We'll soon find out . . ." All of them watched transfixed as the bucket slowly filled.

"About six gallons," guessed Terry as the stream petered out. "Better than nothing."

He pulled the hose from the tractor and handed it to Harry. "Your suck."

"Thanks," the soundman grunted, following Terry as he carried the bucket gingerly back to their van.

Harry managed to transfer the fuel to their van without incident, much to Terry's chagrin. Then they waited nervously as the Australian went to restart the vehicle.

The engine fired. "I guess it's petrol!" he laughed with relief.

"What would have happened if it was diesel?" asked Lena curiously.

"How should I know?" exclaimed Terry. "I'm not a fucking mechanic!"

Lena smiled to herself. That they found humour in such circumstances was amazing.

Kane sat in the CIA car as it sped back to Langley. His mind was a mess.

The car pulled to a halt at the old CIA building at Langley and he strode through the central lobby to the situation room. Passing the familiar etching in the wall—*And ye shall know the truth and the truth shall make you free*—he considered just how far from the truth it was.

"Kane, where the hell?" Haywood's shout jolted him out of his raging thoughts as her head poked into the hallway.

He quickened his pace. Entering the situation room he saw DDO Clark Mitford bent over a computer screen.

Haywood dragged Kane over to it. "Just had the WorldNet tape digitised," she said. "It's our bird alright!"

The man seated at the computer set the digitised video image in motion and Kane watched as the Ilyushin Il–76, enlarged but still so crisp that he could read the call-sign on its tailplane, soared across the screen.

"God knows what was on it," sighed Mitford, his voice twanging with fatigue and concern. "And what it's doing in Armestan of all places."

"What are the Russians saying?" Kane asked.

"Zip!" Haywood said. "Caught between a rock and a hard place. Firyubin won't condemn Kalin, he's only just hanging onto his presidency as it is. And how credible is he going to look if he announces to the world that a renegade germ warfare scientist *may* have stolen the world's largest jet and flown it out of the country unchallenged?"

Kane smiled, despite himself. "A germ warfare scientist in Holtzmann's employ," he corrected her.

"Ruskies don't know that part of the story yet," grunted Haywood.

"Nor will they," said Mitford matter-of-factly.

"Sammy, show the DDO and Kane our sat shot," said Haywood.

The man at the computer flicked onto a new screen.

"Half an hour ago," she remarked as the computer operator zoomed in on the digitised satellite photo. "Shaklin airbase in Novominsk," she added. The Ilyushin was parked near a hangar complex, a convoy of trucks frozen near its loading ramp.

"What other pieces do we have?" asked Kane.

"Nothing," said Haywood.

"Checked with Elazar?" said Kane.

"Oh, shit!" she swore. "We'll do it from the DDO's office."

The threesome hastened towards Mitford's expansive office. Each poured another coffee and sipped silently while the call was placed.

"Colonel Elazar!" Mitford's secretary buzzed them through the intercom. Haywood paced across the room and switched the phone to speaker.

"Sorry, Mordy—" she began.

The Israeli's voice cut her off. "If you're talking about the WorldNet story," he said, "my people in Washington have already gotten it to me. Didn't play on the international bulletin over here—"

"Wasn't supposed to play at all," said Kane abruptly. Mitford and Haywood looked at him curiously and the line to Jerusalem hummed expectantly. Kane quickly described his meeting with Jack Mahoney.

"Norton is a sonofabitch," Mitford reacted—that from a man who seldom swore.

"Sounds like the WorldNet gal has bought the farm," said Haywood. "Can't imagine dear old Kirkland sending the Marines after her!"

Mitford glared at her.

He'll send at least one! Kane swore to himself.

"So I guess," Elazar's voice broke in, "the question is: 'Why Armestan?'"

"Correct," replied Mitford shortly.

"Any ideas, Mordy?" grunted Kane.

"Yes, unfortunately, Tom," said the Israeli, a bitter tone of foreboding in his voice. "Ask yourselves what we really know about Kalin, the 'white' Russian leader."

"Not a helluva lot," admitted Haywood. "Just another psycho-nationalist—"

"A man who hates Jews as much as he hates Muslims," Elazar's voice continued. "But *who* is he?"

Haywood looked at the others, raised her hands and let them drop. "I think the technical term is 'no fucking idea'," she said.

"I'll tell you," muttered the old Israeli. "Kalin is the *nom de guerre* of Alexander Simenovich—" he coughed, "—Kumarov."

Kane lurched towards the telephone. "Mordy?"

"Kalin is Gyorgy Kumarov's elder brother," Elazar concluded.

Kane looked around at Haywood and Mitford. The DDO's face had reddened, Haywood's was ashen.

"This is fast becoming a damn nightmare," exclaimed Mitford. "Elazar, what do you people plan to do?"

"That depends," replied the Israeli immediately, "on what you people plan to do!"

"*Touché,*" said Mitford grimly.

"I'll help you out a little, Mitford," said Elazar. "We'll go in if you go in."

Mitford sighed. "Our president's got a bad habit of involving the UN. And you know we haven't got a chance in hell of convincing the Europeans—let alone Russia—to move against Kalin and risk destabilising Firyubin's position in Moscow. Your people won't go it alone?"

"A straight air strike, possibly," replied Elazar. "But I think it's going to need more than that, somehow. So we'll need you. Armestan is in the centre of Muslim territory— we've got no launchpad for any land-based incursion, however limited. Not enough information about the situation on the ground to risk paratroops. Add to that the problems I face here convincing my government to act unilaterally in what will be seen as support for the Islamic Armestanis.

Realpolitik, Mitford—the art of juggling conflicting insanities."

"I know," said Mitford glumly. "We can forget the Europeans, just like Bosnia. And the President will never authorise an out-and-out US military strike against Kalin. No one wants to risk losing Russia to the hardliners. We have to downscale our thinking—small incursion team, special forces . . ." Mitford paused, then added deliberately. "Though I will have you know that I regard anything short of a pre-emptive military strike as folly. These regional conflicts have proven themselves to be nigh on impenetrable for covert operations. Those in charge think *everyone* is a spy."

"Precisely," snapped Elazar. "A regrettable but accurate assessment."

"But that's what we're going to do," said Kane. "Correct?"

Mitford nodded reluctantly, his eyes not meeting Kane's.

"Yes, Kane," said Elazar. "And given the time frame, I think you need to consider your own role in this."

Kane nodded slowly. "Yeah, I'm it, I suppose."

"Yes, Kane." Mitford looked up at him. "You'll have to go in. That's not to say," he added, "that you won't have support."

Kane grunted, hardly listening. He could not stop thinking about Lena as he considered the mission facing him. The conversation whirled around him for several minutes, Mitford confirming with Elazar what he would put to the President and the National Security Council. Then Kane broke in.

"Susan," he said. "I'll need a briefing on Armestan. Particularly any mercenary outfits they're running. Give me everything: Novominsk, the air-base, Kalin's HQ, and as much as I can get on the sonofabitch himself."

"You got it, Kane!" said Haywood and withdrew quickly.

Mitford stood. "I'm going to push for the use of a

TacForce sub as a base for a joint US-Israeli Special Forces team. Elazar thinks he can sell it as his end."

"Black Sea," mused Kane. "Good idea."

"You get the HUMINT, Tom," Elazar's voice entered the conversation. "We'll come in for them, and you."

"What are the chances of a yea from the President?" Kane asked, his eyes fixed on Mitford.

The career public servant was silent for a minute. "I have to be honest, Kane," he said. "I'm not at all sure of pulling this off. It all sounds so unbelievable . . ." His voice dropped to a whisper. "And do you know why?"

Kane's eyes pierced him as he nodded.

"I do," he said slowly. "Jorge Holtzmann."

The two uniformed *policías* strode towards the pair of Gulf-streams. The jets' refuelling had finished an hour before, but the Tenerife tower had not yet authorised their departure. The tension inside the cabin was at breaking point. Holtzmann had left the cramped sanctuary of the hidden compartment, but as the police approached he hid himself again.

"Ernesto, deal with them," he barked. "Pablo, you deal with Ernesto."

"Okay," replied Cortez, though he had no idea how.

The *policías* had almost reached them.

"Don't try—!" Pablo Simón warned Cortez, slipping his weapon out of sight but within easy reach.

Sweat trickling down their backs, the men inside the aircraft waited.

Cortez ground his teeth as the *policías* stopped. "Diablo," he hissed. "Call them here!"

The pilot nodded, and pushed open his cockpit window. *"Buenos días!"* he shouted.

"Open the cabin door!" snapped the first officer.

"Sure!" replied Sánchez. "What's the trouble?"

"Routine," came the reply.

"Okay, you got it!" said Sánchez. He edged past Cortez towards the rear of the aircraft, shaking, face drawn. "It ain't good, Ernesto!" he grimaced. "This wasn' supposed to happen."

"No," Cortez shook his head. "But no fucking shooting, okay?" He stared at Simón. The *sicario* looked away as a rap sounded at the cabin door.

"Comin'!" shouted Sánchez, disabling and wrenching open the small cabin door. He backed towards the cockpit as the first of the *policías* climbed up the steps.

"*Buenos días,*" the officer said dourly.

"*Buenos días,*" replied Cortez. The officer peered at each of them in turn. Cortez could see Pablo Simón's hands clenching and unclenching. The *policía* looked at his watch. "You going soon?" he said.

"Yes," replied Cortez.

The *policía* stared at him. Then he spoke again. "You have a friend from Madrid," he said slowly. "He wishes you a safe journey." He nodded and climbed from the Gulfstream, joining his colleague to march back across the tarmac to the terminal building.

"Holy Mary!" swore Diablo Sánchez. "Jesus fucking Christ!"

Ten minutes later both aircraft were queued for take-off and Holtzmann rejoined them. Even his impenetrable eyes glistened with relief.

"Poor motherfuckers!" shouted a reinvigorated Sánchez from the cockpit, gesturing to the stained Aeroflot Tupelov clawing its way into the sky ahead of them.

"We may need them, Diablo," Juan Ruiz said next to him, monitoring the radio traffic. Sánchez throttled up.

"Okay!" he yelled. "Let's get the fuck out of here, *amigos!*"

Holtzmann looked out of the window so that no one saw him smiling.

* * *

Kane was slumped over scattered files as Haywood entered the small office.

"Morning, Kane! How's the study?" she grinned, perching herself on the corner of his desk. The dawn sun crept in through a crack in the window.

Kane looked up, eyes red-rimmed. "Morning," he grunted without enthusiasm.

"Update," she said. "The DDO's got the President and the National Security Council in an hour. Stone's flying up for it and Hog Collins is coming here to Langley, to assist us."

Kane nodded. "What else is new?" he asked, struggling to wake up.

"Only a SatAir report that came in a few minutes ago, regular doss-sheet on anomalies in the network," said Haywood. "Two small aircraft, corporate jets by their radar profile, were picked up by a sat for about ten minutes late last night—"

"Where?" interrupted Kane.

"Mid-Atlantic, heading east," replied Haywood. "That's why we got it. Hardly the normal smuggling route. But there aren't that many private travellers that can go trans-Atlantic either. Thought it was worth raising with you. SatAir says the jets failed to respond and their course didn't show up on any logged flight plan."

"SatAir only had them for ten minutes?" queried Kane.

"Yep!" said Haywood. "Which means that wherever they were going they went at close to sea level. Look, Kane, I know it's a wild shot in the dark, but—"

"Yeah, I'm with you," Kane said, getting up. "Got to treat it as Holtzmann. Did SatAir have *any* idea?"

"I'll get back to them," replied Haywood crisply. "This was just a routine report."

Kane looked at a world map on the wall of the office. "If it *is* Holtzmann," he said slowly, "what can we do about it?"

He thought for a minute, then looked down at his desk. "The Armestan air exclusion zone?"

"Didn't stop the Ilyushin," said Haywood curtly.

"Only covers the north," mused Kane. "How are we monitoring?"

"Pretty primitive," Haywood broke in. "And out of our direct control. It's a UN operation, and there's no way the President's gonna authorise telling the world the whole story at this stage."

"Damn," Kane swore softly. "Susan, find out what you can from SatAir now. I'm going to talk to Mordy."

"Yeah—his side has got a healthy disrespect for the rules when push comes to shove." Haywood grinned and turned to leave. "Good luck!"

Kane reached for the telephone and dialled the now-familiar number.

"Elazar," came the immediate reply.

"Mordy," said Kane quickly. "SatAir picked up a couple of aircraft over the Atlantic, heading east. Could be Holtzmann. Like to find out?"

There was a low chuckle from the other end.

"So you want us to do the dirty work again?" said Elazar. "Just in case it turns out to be a couple of millionaires from Florida on joy-flights with their mistresses."

"Yeah," said Kane. "That's about the size of it."

"Leave it with me," replied Elazar. "No promises. It's a long way out of our way, but we can probably at least track them—SatAir is next to useless over Europe. I'll try to get an AWAC up out of Haifa. What's the SatAir reference?"

Kane read from the report.

"Keep me informed," Elazar signed off.

Kane leant back in his chair and sighed. He thought of Mitford and Stone's imminent meeting with the President's National Security Council and knew how difficult it would be to convince the White House of the threat Holtzmann posed. Ever since the US had activated the machinery of war to capture Manuel Noriega in the 1980s, successive administrations had shied away from other such vastly expensive man-hunts. Kane shook his head as he remembered how only a year before, Kirkland had vetoed a recommendation by the NSC to use US forces to take Khun Sa, the warlord who had ruled the Golden Triangle for nearly two decades, and a man personally responsible for nearly two-thirds of the world's supply of heroin.

But no threat had ever come in the shape of Holtzmann, he mulled grimly. Never before had there been an individual better equipped to satisfy his personal vengeance. And Kane agreed with Mordechai Elazar that revenge was his driving force. Holtzmann had the cunning and the will; he had the money; and in post-Soviet Russia he had probably found the means. And yet Kane knew his enemy's greatest ally could yet lie in his being underestimated by a world accustomed to calling him a criminal and not a madman.

As he wondered how Mitford and Stone were faring with Kirkland and the NSC, Kane took some comfort in the thought that Israel was also a player in the game.

"Climb to 30,000 feet, Alpha Foxtrot Hotel, Victor Bravo Tango. Tenerife, over."

"Roger, Tenerife," chuckled Diablo Sánchez. "Next stop, Pakistan, eh Juan?"

Next to him, Juan Ruiz grinned. They were now logged onto SatAir; two corporate jets being delivered to their new owners, a fictional company in Islamabad. There would be no record of them having originated in Colombia, and thus they would raise no suspicion with SatAir in Brussels. But they would still have to deviate from their logged flight plan when they neared Armestan.

"Where's that fuckin' Tupelov, Juan?"

Ruiz shook his head, carefully monitoring the radio traffic and scanning the sky. They had heard the Aeroflot jet earlier announce its destination as Rostov on the Black Sea. It could be their cover.

"There!" exclaimed Ruiz suddenly. There was a glint in the sky some five miles ahead and Sánchez throttled up, dipping his wings to signal the trailing Gulfstream.

"I'm with you, Diablo," its pilot, Eddie Montana, radioed in.

"Give us a piggyback you motherfucker!" cawed Sánchez.

The Tupelov was cruising at thirty-three thousand feet as Sánchez led the two Gulfstreams beneath it and slowed to match the speed of the Aeroflot flight. Now they would be invisible to any SatAir satellite.

"What about ground radar, Diablo?" asked Cortez.

"In this part of the world," chuckled Sánchez confidently, "it's busy as shit. Takeoffs and landings, that's all they care about—otherwise they don't give a damn, they leave it to SatAir. And even if they see us, SatAir won't bother 'cause they don't know we're from Colombia. Relax man, the world is good!"

"That is good, Diablo," muttered Holtzmann, staring out. He was looking at the second Gulfstream, but his eyes were focused far beyond it, towards the dusty grey horizon.

"Our biggest danger," Sánchez went on, pointing to the Tupelov, "is that piece of shit falling out of the sky!"

The men in the main cabin laughed and settled back. Juan Ruiz continued to listen carefully to the babble of radio traffic in his headphones. They would accompany the Tupelov until it reached the Black Sea and turned north for Rostov. Then, if they were lucky, they could hitch beneath another commercial flight heading eastwards over Armestan.

"Relax, man!" repeated Sánchez. Ruiz glanced at his partner; he had rarely seen him so happy.

* * *

"If the Israelis want to use their men," announced President Kirkland, "that's their decision. I don't want *any* of our boys on the ground. The sub will be authorised to use force only if fired upon. Our role in this will *not* be in any way offensive. We'll get the Israelis there and take them home when they're done. Am I understood?" His statement was almost a direct repetition of what Myron Berkeley, his National Security Adviser, had said minutes before to the meeting of the National Security Council.

Clark Mitford looked around—he knew Mordechai Elazar would go ballistic. And why not? he thought glumly. The President's response was the most cautious possible, this side of no response at all. But Mitford was outranked and opposed by everyone at the table except Stone. It was well-known that the only civilian member of the NSC who dared oppose the President and Myron Berkeley—whose views were one and the same—was Vice-President Jeanette Darman, and she was currently on a tour of South America. The Chairman of the Joint Chiefs of Staff, General Mark Westaway, was notoriously antipathetic to Stone. Secretary of State Matthew Porter and CIA Director James Martin were Kirkland appointees, echoing his and Berkeley's line on just about everything.

It was as Mitford had feared it would be. He glanced at Stone.

"With respect Mr. President," Stone said tersely. "The Israelis may not want to go it alone. And we'll have one of our boys on the ground—"

"Kane's deniable," Berkeley broke in, not looking up from his notes. His posture and demeanour suggested that, the decision having been made, the meeting should be wound up as quickly as possible. General Westaway nodded his head.

"We've agreed on Kane," said Kirkland, annoyed. "Let's see what he turns up. But for now we're talking about a possible—and I emphasise *possible*—terrorist threat. If the Israelis want to take it further than that—"

Stone snorted involuntarily and Kirkland's face flushed. "Do you have any idea, General Stone!" he said angrily, "what Congress would do to me if I authorised a military strike—of *any* size—in Armestan? For what? Circumstantial evidence that a damn drug-lord might—*might!*—want to hit a target in Israel? Want me to blow up Syria, Iraq, Iran as well? They want to do the same damn thing! For God's sake, Stone, be reasonable!"

"Yes," muttered Westaway under his breath.

"Sir," Stone forged on. "I think we've heard ample evidence that a weapon of mass destruction has fallen—"

"Enough, Stone!" shouted Westaway, unable to control himself. "Decision's made, understood?"

"Calm down!" added James Martin, rolling his eyes patronisingly. "We provide the machines, Israelis provide the men—simple."

Stone glared at him; the DCIA was a puffy little man whose brashness and tough talk did not extend to his actions.

"We're handing the Israelis the whole damn thing on a plate," Martin continued. "Kane, the TacForce sub, all the damn ELINT we can provide. The works, Stone. And if Kane turns up trumps they hammer the little sonofabitch."

"Which particular sonofabitch?" growled Stone.

"Kasparov, Kalin . . ." stammered Martin. "Holtzmann . . . whoever's in on this thing."

Stone gazed at him, disgusted. "Yeah," he snorted finally. "Got it. Whoever's in on this thing. Maybe Kane could also—"

"He's a fucking agent," said Martin, exasperated. "He'll do what he's told!"

"He's a fucking *Marine!*" swore Stone. "And he's being told to do too much."

Martin shrugged dismissively and looked around the table for support. He caught the eye of the Secretary of State Porter, who came to his aid. "I agree with James," Porter said simply. It was his sole contribution to the entire discussion.

Stone gripped his chair with fury.

President Kirkland coughed and glanced pointedly at his watch. "Right, the Israelis with our support and Kane on the ground. Agreed?" He tried to make it sound like a decision.

The meeting broke up and Stone left with Mitford, still quaking with rage.

"Stone," came a voice behind him. "If you intend working out of Langley on this—" Stone turned to face James Martin, "—you'd best remember whose castle it is."

The big Marine stiffened.

"Keep an eye on him, Mitford," said Martin, striding past.

"Yes, sir," said the other, holding Stone back as Martin disappeared up the corridor.

"I don't believe—" Stone growled.

"Nor do I," muttered Mitford, "but we have to stay in touch with this thing, okay?"

"Yeah," grunted Stone. "And with the paper soldiers!"

Kane took the news coolly. After Mitford had finished, he said, "Why am I not surprised?"

"General Stone, I might say," Mitford added, "was rather more valiant in his defence of you."

Kane looked at his superior.

"Kane," said Stone. "Give me the fucking word and you're off this!"

Kane shook his head, glancing at Hog Collins and Susan Haywood beside him. He walked towards the telephone. "So you heard it all, Mordy?" he said, and an angry answer emanated from the speaker.

There was silence for several minutes, then Kane spoke

again. "Okay," he said slowly. "The way I see it. I go in as a mercenary, join Kalin's International Brigade. Mordy's men on board the USS *South Dakota* will proceed to the Black Sea. They should be able to get within a hundred and fifty miles of Novominsk—we'll assume for now that all the main players are holed up with Kalin in his HQ and not further inland."

"Kane, I want you here to brief my squad," Elazar's voice barked out of the speaker. "If that's okay with your president."

"Right, Mordy," replied Kane. "Now, problem one with what we've been handed: are your men familiar with operating off a TacForce sub, 'cause I sure as hell am not."

"It's okay, Kane," said the Israeli. "Joint manoeuvres last year in the Med."

Kane nodded with relief.

"Alright," said Stone. "Other problems?"

"The main one now," said Kane, "is Cortez. He's a wild-card if he's alive and with Holtzmann. He knows me."

"Not since your plastic surgery," chuckled Collins. "You're no Rembrandt these days, Kane."

Kane grinned. "No," he said. "And there's also the small matter of Cortez's video-testimony. That should guarantee his silence."

Stone nodded dubiously, then Mitford spoke.

"I understand from Susan," he said, "that we are working on the belief that Holtzmann is making for Novominsk—for which we only have the scantest evidence at the moment. I have to say I find it hard to believe that he would jeopardise his security—"

"He's not like the other gangsters in Colombia," Kane broke in. "Whatever else he is, he's not scared of a fight; he's had combat experience with the *Brigada Fascista*."

"And," added Elazar's voice. "I believe it is a question not of machismo, but of ego. Whatever he has commissioned Kumarov to create, and whatever its final purpose is to be, I think that time is nearing and Holtzmann wishes to be there."

"Any sign of the aircraft?" asked Kane quickly.

"None at this end," replied the Israeli.

"Susan?" Kane asked. "Did SatAir—"

"Negative," replied Haywood. "Nothing more. Apart from the fact that if the aircraft continued at their earlier speed they should be somewhere over the Med right now—"

"Well," cracked Elazar. "My boys are somewhere over the Mediterranean as well, and they tell me it's damn busy up there. We're ready, but I don't like our chances."

"No," grunted Kane.

"Okay," said Stone. "So how are you planning to get in to Novominsk, Kane? I thought Kalin had barred all UN flights."

"He's letting in a regular JAT air transport from Belgrade. The Serbs are the only ones actively supporting him. He's even got a pseudo-embassy there. It's where I'll sign on for the International Brigade."

"Tell me more about them," said Stone.

"It's all good news as far as I can see," replied Kane with a grin. "More of a publicity stunt than anything else. Show the West an example of international solidarity in Kalin's struggle against the Muslims. The fact is, from what Susan's been able to dig up, the Brigade consists of scarcely three hundred men, only a few with any military background. Most come from neo-Nazi groups in Europe and Britain. It's an insignificant fraction of Kalin's total force."

"Any Americans?" asked Hog Collins.

Kane nodded his head. "A handful, including two former enlisted men—but all from Armestan originally."

"Why the lack of military?" wondered Stone aloud.

"Kalin's not offering anything apart from the experience," replied Kane.

"So how's he gonna believe you?" asked Haywood. "You

look like you've had all the experience you could do with in one life!"

Kane looked at the group soberly. "I've given that some thought," he said finally. "I'll need a cover, and we don't have much time to get Kalin interested in me. Thought we might try a publicity stunt of our own—leak a story to WorldNet, CNN, whatever shows in Kalin's part of the world."

"And the story is—?" asked Mitford.

"A renegade Marine," replied Kane. "Bad enough to need sanctuary and good enough to make Kalin want to give it to him."

Mitford nodded. "We've done that once before."

"I remember," said Kane. "What Kalin seems to need in his international outfit is a commanding officer. That's the job I'm trying out for."

Stone laughed. "Think you can still remember how?"

"General," smiled Kane. "We've done this age thing before."

"Pax," grinned Stone. "So who is this no-good sonofabitch?"

"John Hawke?" Kane said quietly.

Stone's eyes saddened for a moment. "Yeah," he said. "I guess . . ."

Mitford raised his eyebrows.

"Mutual friend," said Stone. "Delta force with Kane, one of the best. Lived as John Hawke DSC, but that's not what it reads on his death certificate. Lied to his country to die for it. There's a guy called Todd Newman buried at Arlington with his medals. Far as anyone knows, John Hawke still exists somewhere. Wish he did."

"We'll fix it," Mitford said softly. "Susan, pull his file. Fix up some shots of Kane."

The DDO stood up slowly. "So it's done," he sighed, ". . . I don't know what else I can add."

There was nothing more any of them·wanted to say. A tense silence fell on the room.

"Kane," Stone's voice finally broke the tension. "Guess you'd better haul ass to the Holy Land."

"Respect," chuckled Elazar over the line, "it's not what it used to be!"

CHAPTER**SIXTEEN**

The Gulfstreams had left the cover of the Aeroflot Tupelov when it turned north to Rostov and hitched beneath a Japan Airlines flight heading east over the Black Sea. Fifteen minutes later, over northern Turkey, Diablo Sánchez and his partner broke from the JAL flight for their final run to Novominsk. Shuttered in the cabin of their Boeing 747—watching the movie or sleeping—none of the passengers aboard JAL 5 from London saw the pair of smaller jets bank away below. The SatAir satellite registered their exit as an air-traffic anomaly and duly relayed the news to Brussels where it awaited the attentions of a SatAir controller.

But inside an Israeli AWAC early-warning surveillance aircraft, circling above the northern Mediterranean, the sight of the two blips on the screen drew an instantaneous response from its radar crew. Within a minute, a squadron of IDF/AF F–16D Falcons was airborne and streaking north from Haifa.

"Kane!" Elazar's voice rang through the speaker. "The birds have re-appeared. We're chasing them but it's going to be difficult. They're over Armestan, not far from Novominsk. We may not reach them in time—"

"What are you prepared to do?" interrupted Kane.

"There is only one thing we can do," replied Elazar, "and damn the consequences I'm afraid. I just hope we're right."

"Okay," said Kane. "Let me know—"

"Yeah—certainly make our lives a lot easier if he's out of the picture," the old Israeli continued.

"Let me know," Kane repeated, refusing to allow his hopes to be drawn.

"Five minutes," Sánchez announced to relieved groans from his exhausted passengers. He saluted Eddie Montana in the cockpit of the second Gulfstream. They were observing radio silence now; it would not be broken until their final approach into Novominsk.

Juan Ruiz traced his finger across the chart; they were well south of the United Nations air exclusion zone. Sánchez banked his aircraft for their run into Kalin's captial. The city slowly filled the Gulfstream's windscreen and there were more sounds of relief from the main cabin. The sun glinted off Novominsk's broken spires and shattered buildings.

Through his window Holtzmann spied the giant Russian Ilyushin aircraft parked four thousand feet below. He grunted with satisfaction and ran his fingers through his beard.

"Finally, *Señor*," whispered Cortez across the aisle.

"We are here, *niñas*!" Sánchez exclaimed from the cockpit. His co-pilot chuckled as the altimeter spun downwards.

Ruiz glanced down, then flicked the radio on. "Novominsk," he said. "This is Condor One and Condor Two. Permission to land."

A voice answered immediately in broken English.

"Condors, this is Shaklin control. You may land—"

With a broad grin on his face, Diablo Sánchez trimmed the Gulfstream as it started its final approach.

"Hey, Eddie!" he crowed into the radio. "Follow my ass!"

A chuckle from the trailing aircraft crackled over the radio.

"Diablo, I'll wax your ass!"

"In range!" snapped Menachem Dolinsky in the lead Israeli F–16. "Missiles armed."

His two target aircraft floated, helpless as butterflies, in his radar scope. But Dolinsky had no second thoughts as he prepared to loose his two Sidewinder air-to-air missiles; Israel's war was fought against an enemy who used bicycles and shopping bags to disguise their weapons, why not a private jet? He did not know who was aboard the two aircraft he was about to destroy; he did not allow himself to care. He cared only that he was in enemy sky and that he could soon be in the middle of an AA firestorm. His hand tightened on the stick and his heads-up display showed his missiles had locked on.

"Target acquisition," he said coolly.

Sánchez was at five hundred feet, the second Gulfstream circling above, when suddenly the radio cackled with urgent ferocity.

"Hostile aircraft! Alert! Hostile aircraft!"

"What?" Sánchez roared from the cabin. Then he looked up and saw their enemy hurtling towards them.

"No!" he screamed, desperately thrusting the Gulfstream into a steep plunge towards the ground. The sky around them flashed with anti-aircraft fire from Shaklin. Kalin's men were trying to cover their landing. Sánchez twisted his jet in the air—banking and weaving frantically—as the tarmac loomed in his windscreen. His eyes filled with sweat. Two of the fighters thundered past him, the Star of David clearly visible on their tails, their wing cannons blazing at the source of the ground fire. He knew there were more behind him. "Holy Jesus."

"We're fucked!" grunted Juan Ruiz under his breath, holding the flight controls to assist Sánchez if required.

"Get us down!" Holtzmann's sudden shriek tore through the cabin. *"They are Judíos!"*

"Missiles away!" shouted Dolinsky, climbing sharply as his Sidewinders streaked away towards their target.

"Missiles away!" he heard repeated three times as he tore upwards through the flack.

"I'm hit!" he heard the short, dreaded words from one of his squadron. In his peripheral vision he saw a fireball tumble from the sky towards the AA-battery it had been trying to destroy.

"La'azazel!" he swore. "Squadron—come around!"

Kalin burst into the control tower as the Israeli fighter exploded on the tarmac. "AA support!" he screamed. "More fire! Bring them in, *now!*"

"Yes, Kalin!" replied the shell-shocked controller.

"Prepare the emergency trucks!" Kalin ordered. Then he stormed out, trailing Kumarov, and leapt into a waiting Jeep. As they sped across the tarmac to the main anti-aircraft battery, Kalin continued to bellow commands into his walkie-talkie.

For Kumarov it felt like events were being played out in dead silence and slow motion. He stared up with horror, willing the approaching aircraft on with every breath but seeing that in a few seconds it would be over. The Jeep shuddered to a halt and Kalin raised his binoculars to his eyes.

"It is no good!" he exploded. "They are lost."

From the moment the tiny guidance system positioned behind nearly twenty pounds of densely packed high explosive locked onto the circling Gulfstream, its occupants had barely three seconds to live. The Sidewinder's powerful ramjet hurtled it towards its target at supersonic speed. Holtzmann, staring terrified through his window, saw only a white streak against blue. Then, the instant before impact, he saw it; a sleek metallic cylinder. He watched Eddie Montana's jet bank abruptly, desperately stretching for the earth, its undercarriage dropping in anticipation of an emergency landing. *No!* the silent scream echoed inside him. Then the sky exploded and the Gulfstream's disintegrating fuselage spun crazily towards the Shaklin tarmac, spewing flames as it collided with the runway and erupted in front of them. Holtzmann felt their jet touch ground, then, an instant later, as they skewed into the flames ahead, a second Sidewinder missile careened into their tail. There was a massive explosion and inside the aircraft became a maelstrom of smoke and debris. But it was still intact, and Sánchez—shrieking with fear—grounded the craft as heavily as he could and fought frantically to slow it. His steering was lost as, ablaze, they ploughed into the smoke, flames and wreckage of Eddie Montana's aircraft. All on board were wailing in terror. Clutching his seat, his legs barely within the jagged remains of the cabin—Holtzmann looked back and saw the fire begin.

"*Sánchez!*" he howled.

The jet spun crazily on the tarmac. The instant it halted Sánchez bolted from the cockpit, yelling hysterically. With flames shooting into the cabin, and smoke so thick that they were blinded, they clawed their way out of the stricken aircraft. Holtzmann's searching fingers entwined with Sánchez's belt and he was dragged out onto the boiling tarmac. The Gulfstream was almost fully alight, its near-empty wingtanks about to blow as Holtzmann stumbled away. Seconds later he felt the white-hot pain of its explosion and was flattened onto the tarmac, losing consciousness for a moment. Then, feeling like he'd been stabbed a thousand times, he crawled away from the inferno.

Only when he could no longer feel the terrible heat of

the flames behind him did he raise himself on bleeding fingers and look around. Juan Ruiz had not made it out of the plane. Diablo Sánchez had been caught by the billowing fire, his body—that had shielded Holtzmann—now writhing as he was burned to death. The events of the previous few minutes collected in Holtzmann's head, and his face formed an expression of utter, all-encompassing fury. He tottered away, gripped by a rage so blinding he could think only of killing—of condemning someone to death for this travesty.

In the tower, the *danzan* controller was slumped against the window, the unknown pilot's death-scream echoing in his head. From the radio speaker came an ear-splitting hiss of white noise. He gazed at the destroyed aircraft furiously ablaze in the centre of the runway as the survivors of the first jet staggered away.

"Nevelot!" shouted Dolinsky, swooping lower, fingers gripped on his machine-gun control. He waited until he was close enough to see the men on the ground clearly.

Standing beside the Shilka anti-aircraft battery, whose four 30mm cannons were pouring fire towards the Israeli jets, Kalin saw Holtzmann and his men emerge from the smoke.

"Vasily!" he shouted.

His driver snapped to attention amidst the cacophony of the AA-guns and followed the line of Kalin's pointing finger. He nodded, but as he climbed into the jeep he found it impossible to control the shudders of fear racking his body. He glanced up and saw the attacking jets levelling for a strafing run. Stony-faced but knowing he had no option, he jammed his foot to the floor and tore towards the survivors on the runway.

The first Israeli jet came in low with a hellish noise. Machine-gun fire erupted from its wings and exploded along the tarmac hitting two of the stumbling men. Vasily swung the steering wheel desperately to avoid the stream of bullets and, praying aloud, screeched towards the other lone man on the tarmac.

Cortez screamed as the line of fire whipped past him and spun Pablo Simón's body around on the tarmac. In a millisecond Simón's body was unrecognisable, the torrent of lead mincing it and that of his companion *sicario*.

"No!" howled Cortez, watching a second jet come in towards them. Then he saw the Jeep. It was with Holtzmann, about twenty yards away.

"*Señor!*" he shrieked, running towards it. But the Jeep turned and drove away.

"*Señor!*" Cortez screamed again, tears running down his face as he looked up at the jet bearing down on him. A second later machine-gun fire ripped through his legs.

Holtzmann's face twitched.

Judíos! The knowledge ricocheted in his mind. *The Jews!* His fury knew no bounds.

"Coming around!" called in one of the Israeli F–16s.

"Roger," replied Menachem Dolinsky as he lifted the nose of his own fighter to pull clear of the air base. Then he felt the unmistakable thump of a hit. "*Elohim!*" he swore as his aircraft shuddered wildly. The AA round had taken out his engine, at this altitude he had only seconds.

"Hit!" he announced to his wingman in the F–16 above him. "Bailing out!"

He didn't hear the response as his finger jabbed the eject button. His cowling was flung back and he exploded out of his cockpit. Seconds later his parachute billowed and a new fear set in.

He spoke a little Russian and ran the phrases over in his head as the tarmac came up at him. Falling heavily, he twisted or fractured his left leg, he wasn't sure. Hobbling to his feet, he looked around. A Jeep was coming towards him.

The *danzan* driver did not understand the words spewing from Holtzmann's mouth, but his meaning was clear. The Colombian yanked the pistol from the driver's holster as the Jeep pulled up next to the limping figure. Holtzmann climbed out and advanced on the Israeli pilot.

"*Judío!*" he spat the hated word. "*Judío!*"

He held the gun level. Menachem Dolinsky pleaded for his life, but Holtzmann fired the pistol again and again into his face, words of contempt flowing from his foaming lips, his body totally consumed with primal anger.

Finally hurling the gun away, he flung back his head and bayed his revenge to the distant ears of those who had so nearly killed him.

In the Jeep, Vasily Moroz looked on with horrified awe.

Wingman Daniel Bar-Ulan spat a stream of Hebrew profanities as he circled over the AA fire, but their remaining fuel allowed him no choice. Blessing the souls of his commander and the young IDF pilot from Eilat who had been the first killed, Bar-Ulan snapped a command into his radio and reluctantly led the remaining F–16s away to the south.

As he turned back towards the Jeep, still stunned by what had so nearly happened, Holtzmann saw Cortez dragging himself towards them and, further away, another vehicle racing across the tarmac. He recognised Kumarov and a man who could only be his brother.

"Kalin!" said Holtzmann in a daze. "It is the Jews, they know I am here."

Climbing out of the jeep, the air still punctuated by sporadic AA fire, Kalin regarded the body of the dead airman for a moment.

"Come quickly!" he barked and, leaving Cortez to the other Jeep, he took Holtzmann aboard his vehicle and screeched away; through the gates of the Shaklin base, through the cobbled streets of Novominsk, slowing only as they finally approached the Monastery. Inside, Holtzmann said nothing as he was led by Kalin and Kumarov through dim corridors.

"*Señor!*" Kalin said as they entered a large room, ringed with chairs. "We had no more warning than you." He went to embrace Holtzmann but the Colombian shrugged him away. His eyes were glassy.

"Kalin," he said, his voice wavering, his clothes hanging in rags off him. "Our mission is now more urgent than ever. Let us not waste time with pleasantries."

Kalin nodded. "Do you wish to clean up, or eat?" He gestured to the central table, weighed down with food.

Holtzmann paused for an instant, then took a seat. No one spoke as they devoured their meals. The Colombian stared blankly at a point beyond the room, while Kalin observed him silently. At the far end of the table, Kumarov sipped water and watched both men nervously.

"Are you injured?" Kalin asked softly.

"No," muttered Holtzmann, pushing his plate away. "Now we must talk."

"Yes, *Señor,*" answered Kalin.

"We hit them too late," Elazar reported in. "My men reported survivors. Holtzmann may be one of them, Tom, no way of knowing."

Kane sighed deeply.

"And we lost two of ours in the fight," Elazar continued.

"I'm sorry, Mordy," Kane said finally.

"So am I," said Elazar. "But now we have given them warning, regardless of Holtzmann's fate. Perhaps we should reconsider your—?"

"No," said Kane calmly. "I'll be in Israel tomorrow as planned. Let's do this thing."

"Your call, Kane," replied Elazar. "Travel well."

Eighteen hours later, the Tower Air Boeing 747 taxied to a halt at Ben Gurion airport. Kane stood up in the aisle and placed his black hat over his *yamulka*. He was uncomfortably hot in his dark Hasidic garments; the *kapota*, long black coat with the knotted strings of the *tzitzit* dangling from beneath it; his *payot*—forelocks—were slick against his jowls. The disguise was perfect—he was invisible amidst the crowd shuffling off the Tower Air flight and into the spartan terminal building. A sense of urgency stirred his guts.

It had been nearly fifteen years since his first visit to Israel as an adviser to Operation Moses—the largest airlift in modern times. Tens of thousands of *falashas*—Ethiopian Jews—had been saved from the pogroms of dictator Haile Mengistu, ferried from remote desert airstrips in complete secrecy. It was during that audacious Israeli rescue mission he had met Mordechai Elazar; a man who had outlived one intelligence service and was a living legend in two. Fundamental in the formation of the American OSS after World War Two, he had helped transform it into the modern CIA—where he had run field operations in Europe and the Middle East before finally making his *aliya* to Israel. Kane's six months with him at Mossad during Operation Moses had opened his eyes to an unorthodoxy of operation which could only evolve in a country perpetually at war. He had forged a lasting friendship with the old intelligence chief.

Approaching immigration control, he gripped his tattered US passport.

"Jacob Lubetkin?"

He nodded and the Israeli officer asked him quickly what his purpose in visiting Israel was.

"Yom Kippur." He smiled.

"Chag Sameach." The immigration officer grinned and handed back his passport.

"Toda," replied Kane, walking on.

Outside, he blinked furiously as the noon glare exploded in his eyes. He fumbled for his sunglasses and cast his eyes around the chaos. Cab drivers shouted fare prices to the crowd of Israelis, Arabs, and, loudest—he noticed with a grimace—Americans. He heard a soft voice at his side.

"Jacob Lubetkin," it said. He turned and saw a man dressed as he was; a Lubavitcher Jew—though his *kapota* bulged with a weapon.

"Yes," replied Kane.

The man nodded. "Come."

A dark Mercedes limousine pulled up in front of them and the back door swung open. Kane stepped in as four other men drifted out of the crowd and got into two similar cars.

"Welcome back, Tom," Elazar exclaimed as Kane settled beside him. "It has been too long."

"Sure has, Mordy," grinned Kane, shaking his hand warmly as their convoy swung swiftly out of the airport.

The old Mossad man in his rumpled suit was without doubt the most public hero the super-secretive Mossad had ever had. Kane remembered his most recent operation—the rescue of Eli Choransky from the chaos of post-Soviet Astrakhan, where the rabidly nationalist government had been holding the Jewish scientist for 'treason.' The mission had been pure Elazar; meticulously planned and executed with breathtaking speed.

The *Jerusalem Mail* had quoted Choransky's first words the following day and voiced a nation's feelings. *Only you, Elazar!* its tabloid headline had blared in three-inch type.

But Israel had changed, Kane mused as his eyes locked with those of his friend. The valiance of the little country that had won it so much sympathy was now a dream-time, with only a few like Mordy left to give it substance. Now it was tearing itself apart in the effort to re-make itself and make peace with its enemies. *Peace.* Kane rolled the word around in his mind—it was a word which, in his experience, had always masked some measure of deception. He shook his head; he knew Elazar's feelings lay with the dead. Those who had died for what was now being given away; lives he had been responsible for. Kane's eyes watered momentarily as they passed through the airport military checkpoint.

Elazar smiled as he watched Kane's moments of readjustment. Then he spoke.

"Mitford may have his faults," he chuckled. "But he knows how to dress a Lubavitcher."

"Hot as hell, Mordy," complained Kane, pulling his coat and hat off.

"You've got a day and a half of it, my friend," replied Elazar. "Now, business . . ."

They fell to a discussion of the operation; the technical aspects of the mission, its objectives, and the makeup of the Israeli Special Forces unit which would be Kane's primary strike force. The Israeli intelligence chief talked with a vigour belying his years, his eyes keen and his mind as sharp as it had ever been. Before either man had noticed, an hour had passed and they had begun their steep ascent through the Jerusalem hills.

"Kumarov must be captured, Holtzmann *must* be eliminated on the ground, Tom," Elazar concluded. "And if in the process Kalin's dirty war can be dented, so much the better."

"But surely Holtzmann—if we get the chance—" started Kane.

"Tom," said Elazar bluntly. "Kumarov is a spy, and we can deal with those. But Holtzmann? Sooner or later, in this country or yours, he would have to be given a trial. And there can be no trial," he said firmly. "He is a terrorist, an enemy of Israel, and we will deal with him as we deal with

Hamas and Jihad. A trial would make him a martyr to those who share his gutter beliefs. That is my view, and my government's."

Kane nodded, looking at the old Israeli with sympathy. He took the struggle against his country's enemies personally. Sadly his Mossad department was becoming more and more taxed, as the brushfires of fascism were ignited more often. Russia, Serbia, Astrakhan . . . Kane winced as he checked them off in his mind.

Bleached white apartment blocks dotted the hills on the outskirts of Jerusalem. Minutes later the Knesset passed into and out of view and, as if provoked by the sight of his tiny country's seat of government, Elazar spoke again.

"Are you tired?"

Kane shrugged. "What's up first?"

"Your hotel," replied Elazar. "In two hours we have a briefing from my people—biological weapons specialists. Tomorrow you meet the *Sayeret Matkal* squadron who will be on board the *South Dakota*. And in the evening you fly to Belgrade via Cyprus."

Kane nodded.

"Mitford called while you were *en route*," added Elazar. "Your cover story will be leaked today. Hopefully it will have established your bonafides by the time you reach Belgrade."

"Good," said Kane, then retreated into pensive silence.

"And we are here," announced Elazar a few moments later. The three cars came to a halt in front of the foyer of the King David Hotel.

"Freshen up, but stay Lubavitcher, *Jacob*," the Mossad man smiled. "Get something to eat—it'll be a long day and night—and remember to keep kosher. My car will collect you in an hour." With that the convoy roared out of the drive and skirted the walls of the Old City. Kane's eyes followed it until a bellhop swung open the gold and glass doors onto the splendour of the King David.

"Yes, Mr. Lubetkin," the raven-haired receptionist smiled too broadly as she read his reservation slip.

He suddenly remembered the one thing he had against the King David, his well based suspicion that everyone in it worked for Elazar.

"Your room faces the Old City," beamed the receptionist. His room-key dangled at the end of an arm too well muscled for a desk job. "I hope you enjoy your stay, Mr. Lubetkin. Your room has ten channels of satellite television available, and direct-dial . . ."

But he did not wait to hear the rest. He took the offered key, reluctantly tore himself away from her olive eyes, and strode into the gilded labyrinth of the hotel's interior.

How quickly he has worked! Holtzmann thought as Kumarov explained the laboratory and testing facility he had begun to construct. With help from *danzan* troops, Kumarov's men were busily unpacking research equipment from crates outside the central Monastery building, ringed with heavy artillery. The pair walked into the building and down into its cavernous basement. Though Holtzmann's rage had ebbed a little, his cuts and burns bandaged beneath fresh clothes, he still found it a constant effort of will to concentrate.

"The lab itself will be ready by tomorrow," Kumarov was saying. "This is the critical element in the testing facility. The isolation room . . ."

Four of Kumarov's men were engaged in the painstaking task of lining the huge room with specially made sheeting. At one end, they had already begun partitioning off smaller 'rooms' within the main basement.

"Observation rooms," explained Kumarov. "I must know whether there is any evolutionary mutation as the virus enters a human subject. Also, the most efficacious method for its dissemination will be determined by the subjects' reactions."

Holtzmann fingered a portion of the sheeting. It was much thicker than it looked, and heavier.

"Impenetrable," said Kumarov proudly. "And the perimeter will be double-lined. There will be an airlock, of course, and a special ventilation system . . ." Kumarov continued talking and through the aftershock of his escape, Holtzmann finally comprehended the imminence of his revenge. When the explanation was over the Colombian inhaled deeply and with calming satisfaction, and walked from the basement.

In the courtyard of the Monastery, Kalin approached him, followed by a huge man.

"Boris Nikolaevich Rodionov," the *danzan* commander introduced his chief-of-staff. "When you are ready," he continued, "I would like to show you the delivery system for Gyorgy Alexandrovich's little warriors."

"I am ready," said Holtzmann.

Elazar's phrase repeated inside Kane's head as the Mossad car jolted slowly along Ben Yehuda Street; *Holtzmann must be eliminated!* He glanced out through darkened windows. The faces in the pedestrian crowd wore expressions that strained to be normal. In this country, he knew, where cocaine was someone else's problem, and Colombia was simply another country, neither friend nor enemy, the name Holtzmann rang with infamy for only one reason. The father.

The car moved off at a quicker pace and Kane turned his blank stare inward. He had read all the available literature on Elazar's capture of Jurgen Holtzmann in Colombia in 1965, and the transcript of the Jerusalem war-crimes trial. Again he considered the strange irony facing his Israeli colleague.

The car came to a halt outside a nondescript building.

"Jacob," Elazar exclaimed as he entered. "Meet Golda and Benjamin." The two other occupants of the room stood and shook his hand. Kane knew their names were no more real than his.

"Golda's speciality is in the field of biological warfare, primarily in the development of vaccines and antidotes," Elazar explained succinctly. "She has studied all the available material on Kumarov's work for the Soviets. Golda, please."

The well-built woman began to speak in soft, accented English.

"The most dangerous aspect of what I have seen," she said, "is Kumarov's expertise in the field of virology. If he has indeed developed a virological weapon, there is virtually no way of stopping its spread by current medical means, except if we get lucky. Very lucky. As this is the greatest threat, let us deal with it first and I will return to discuss bacteriological weaponry later.

"In both cases, you will be looking for an isolation room. This will most probably be within the most secure and stable structure available. Temperature and humidity must be controlled, so you will see evidence of a sophisticated air filtering system and, I imagine, a back-up generator of some sort.

"Inside the isolation room the actual virus will be contained," she went on. "It may be in fermentation vats or in culture. Until it is to be deployed as a weapon, the virus must be sustained. You will most probably find it in a central position in the isolation room, in containers like this—" She handed Kane some photographs.

"What do I do then?" he asked.

"As collecting samples is, I understand, not a practical option," Golda replied, "you have to destroy the cultures and the viruses with them."

"How?" asked Kane.

"Applying strong direct heat is the best method."

"What are you saying here, Golda?" Elazar interrupted. "Frying it? Grilling?"

"Burning it," she went on. "Burning it, Jacob," she repeated without a trace of a smile.

"I see," said Kane.

"And a napalm attack or such like?" asked Elazar.

"Too risky," replied Golda. "Fire may puncture the containment room without damaging the virus. It is essential that the cultures themselves be purposely destroyed."

Kane nodded. "Got it."

Now Golda moved on to a more detailed description of laboratory equipment and layout—everything he would need to know in order to be familiar with the unfamiliar. Through it all, hour upon hour, he asked questions, took notes, and absorbed.

"And now," she said, "the question of Kumarov's presence in Armestan. If, as Colonel Elazar has said to me, it is not his primary target area, then it can only be a testing ground. It is clear from the available literature I have seen that Kumarov has already carried out tests on human subjects with bacteriological agents during his years with the Biopreparat for the Soviets—anthrax in particular. I see no reason why this will not be the case in Armestan. I would assume he has, as part of his laboratory, specific isolation rooms for infected subjects. I warn you that the effects of these types of diseases are not pleasant. Should you encounter any test victims, there is nothing you can do for them without running the real risk of allowing the virus to escape the isolation area. For, having no idea of the virulence of anything he may have developed, we cannot predict the possible infection rate from an infected individual."

"So any test subjects have to be killed," said Kane matter-of-factly.

"Y . . . yes," Golda stumbled for the first time.

Kane took a deep sigh. "Go on."

"Before I do," said Golda, removing her glasses. "In the event of you yourself becoming infected, you must realise that your infection and its effects are of critical importance to us. Try to detail your infection and its effects. Preparing for the worst, the more information we have the better. The same applies to any and all documentation or computer disks you can bring out."

She coughed and continued.

"In the event that the virus does break out of its containment, or is purposely released into a community in Armestan, you must ensure that strict quarantine regulations are applied."

"So, Golda," Kane said as she concluded the briefing, halfway through the fifth hour. "What's the good news?"

"There is very little, Jacob," she replied. "If Kumarov has developed a bacteriological agent, the news is slightly better than that I have so far described, but only in the hope of a cure for those infected, not in any of the precautions you should take and protocols you should adhere to."

"Can't cure a virus?" he asked.

She shook her head. "Treatments for viruses are hit and miss. Vaccines and cures have been developed for specific viruses but the process is extraordinarily long. It is nearly twenty years after AIDS first became a mass-infection and we are still in a position of treating its symptoms not its root cause—the HIV virus. This is, quite frankly, what scares me about the direction of Kumarov's research."

She had finished, and in a sombre mood the foursome broke for a quick meal. Then it was Benjamin's turn.

"Delivery systems," Elazar explained the second scientist's role. "We have to assume that Kumarov may have progressed as far as this stage. Benjamin?"

"Yes," said the squat Israeli. "As Golda has indicated, the aim of most biological weaponry is the development of an airborne agent. This leads to the belief that an attack by such a biological weapon could be carried out merely by a man with a bottle full of infected air. This, I am pleased to say, is in the realm of science fiction. In reality, as you haveheard, even the hardiest viruses live only as long as twenty-four hours. To be effective therefore, a great quantity of the virus has to be delivered to a dense population centre and once there disseminated as widely as possible. The most practical method for doing this is in the form of an aerosol delivered by aircraft—impossible over Israel, with our air defence system—and difficult at best in Armestan, given that most Armestani population centres are in the north of the country and protected, at least on paper, by the UN's air-exclusion zone. But . . ."

Kane raised his eyebrows as the Israeli continued.

". . . while the UN zone provides sufficient protection against aircraft," he said slowly, "it provides none against missiles. Nor, I am afraid to say, has our country's missile-defence capability shown itself to be adequate. You see, we fear that Kumarov and Holtzmann, through Kalin, may have access to Soviet ICBMs or intermediate-range missiles—probably mobile-based. Your primary task upon reaching Novominsk should be to confirm this. If possible, you—or your support unit—must destroy or disable these missiles as a matter of urgency. They may be SS–20s, which were supposedly phased out after '87 as part of the INF treaty, though we have reason to doubt they were. Or, worst case, Kalin may even have SS–25 "Sickles". Both are mobile-based and both have the range to easily strike targets in Northern Armestan and Israel. Our Patriot Mk III anti-missile systems cannot safely account for either of these missiles. And only one RV—reentry vehicle, or warhead—needs to get through. The SS–20 carries three MIRVs—multiple independently targetable reentry vehicles. The SS–25 can be configured to carry up to ten MIRVs, though its normal payload is one highly sophisticated RV.

"To put this in perspective, let me tell you that if, during the Gulf War, Saddam had chosen to use anthrax in the primitive warheads carried by the Scuds which struck Israel, our estimates put the probable infection rate at close to ninety percent, with a mortality figure only slightly less.

What the world is only starting to realise, Jacob, is that this form of weaponry actually causes greater casualties than nuclear devices. If Kalin does possess ballistic missiles, it bodes very badly . . ."

"What about personal defence against a biological strike?" asked Kane.

"Impractical," replied Benjamin. "Should we consider such an attack is imminent, the only public-defence program we can employ is a mass evacuation."

Kane nodded and listened as Benjamin gathered force; technical details about the SS–20 and 25; the warheads used to disperse biological agents; methods of disarming and destruction; worst-case scenarios. It was ten P.M. before, dog-tired with his mind whirling, Kane thanked Golda and Benjamin and left with Elazar.

"Now," he said to the old Israeli. "I need sleep!"

"The car will be at the King David at eight-thirty," was all Elazar had the energy to say. "Goodnight, Tom."

Kane reached out to grip Elazar's shoulder. "Sounds like you've really gotten Holtzmann angry," he grinned.

"And he, me," replied Elazar slowly. "I first knew his father at Majdanek . . . where I lost my own."

Kane stared into his dark eyes sadly.

Now their gasoline was truly out. With no hope of redemption. The bone-dry desert country stretched out before them in the bright moonlight, with nothing on the horizon to indicate a village or even a lone house.

"Guess that's it," said Terry, kicking the tyre of the van.

In the back of the vehicle, Sergei and Abdur slept, curled into each other for comfort.

Lena stood to one side, gazing at the hills that nudged the dark skyline ahead of them.

"It's eerie," she said. The silence was so complete that the air felt thick with it.

About three hours later they heard the noise—a dull

throb of distant engines. Lena reached into their van for their second rifle, checked its magazine and flicked off the AK47's safety switch.

Whatever was approaching them was doing so solely by the light of the moon. Lena shivered as she, Terry and Harry crouched behind the van, her gun levelled in the direction of the approaching sound. Then suddenly there was a glint of metal on the crest of the closest hill, and they watched dry-mouthed as a convoy of Jeeps moved slowly down the slope towards them. At the head of the convoy they could see a lone rider on a motorcycle. At a distance of about a hundred yards the rider called a halt.

"They're not speaking Russian," Lena whispered as his command echoed to their ears. The man dismounted his motorcycle and, flanked by two others brandishing Kalashnikovs, walked towards them. Lena slid back towards the van's door and pulled a piece of cloth from its interior. Quickly she fastened it over her head as a scarf; if their visitors were Muslim *kadashi* she did not want to provoke them. She trembled as the men stopped a few yards away.

"Easy," she hissed to Terry and Harry as she slowly rose, dropping the gun flat against her side. There was a moment of frightening silence.

"Hello," she called out in English. She did not dare try Russian.

The lead man stared back at her.

"Hello," she croaked again. The man came closer and she could see he was barely thirty.

"Hello," he said in American-accented English. "What the hell are you doing out here?"

"What?" Lena exclaimed stepping forward. "You—"

"Ten years in the States," said the man. "Jersey City. Did high school there, worked at McDonalds, came back to be a warlord compliments of my dad. Sayeed Naderi Massar. But you?"

Lena stared at him in momentary disbelief. Then her tension dissolved and the fear of the last few days bubbled over.

"Steady on, Lena," said Terry, appearing from behind the van. "I'm sorry," he added, grinning crookedly at their visitor. "We're a television crew."

Sayeed Massar peered curiously at him, then at Lena again.

"Who is she?"

"Galena Chagall," replied Terry steadily.

"She a star?" asked Massar.

"No." Lena began laughing again.

"Yeah, I suppose so," said Terry, nudging her with his elbow.

"Galena," said Massar thinking hard. "*Amash!* You do the morning broadcasts on WorldNet right?"

"Evening, where we come from," said Terry. He felt like he was having an out-of-body experience.

Massar turned and walked back towards his convoy, shouting excitedly about the identity of the strange group. Lena again dissolved in barely suppressed hysteria.

"*Lena,*" Terry swore. "Pull yourself to-fucking-gether!"

"I'm sorry—" gasped Lena.

"Wake me up, Harry," Terry muttered to his soundman. "Our girl's gone mad and we've got some renegade hamburglar to deal with."

"An Armestani warlord who lived in Jersey?" Harry replied, genuinely astonished. At this, Terry cracked up as well. It was just too bizarre after all they had been through.

"So you need gas?" Massar returned. "That we got. What else is up?" he asked, clearly enjoying himself. "And how the hell did you get to be out here?"

Terry and Lena both bit their lips viciously. Harry looked at them, and—deciding that neither was capable of rational speech—proffered. "We were in Novominsk. We got video of a Russian aircraft supplying Kalin and we've fled."

The *kadashi* warlord looked Harry Berg up and down.

"You really chose a great spot," he grinned. "There's a regular *danzan* patrol due here in an hour. You would have been in deep shit."

CHAPTER**SEVENTEEN**

Kane lay in his hotel room and stared disconsolately at the ceiling. Holtzmann, Kumarov, Kalin . . . ? What would he find? What were their plans? He rolled onto his side, looking out of the window he had opened to defeat the musty air-conditioning. The night sky shrouded the troubled earth. Tomorrow he would pass through it—to the endgame.

He thought of Lena, then his eyes flickered and closed, driven shut by a compassionate body. But his memories allowed him no respite even in sleep and his dreams were of her.

The buzz of the telephone roused him and freezing air slapped his body as he rolled over to answer it.

"Yes," he gasped into the receiver.

"*Boka tov*, Jacob," came the familiar voice.

"Mordy, what time?" Kane mumbled, rubbing his eyes through their sandpaper lids and realising it was still dark.

"Three-thirty," replied Elazar. "The boat came in early, I'd like you to meet the squad. We're due in Haifa in an hour."

Fifteen minutes later, roughly attired in his Lubavitcher

clothes, Kane walked out of the King David and Elazar pulled up in a three-car Mossad squad.

"You awake yet?"

Kane grunted as he climbed into the car. "There's a helluva difference between being awake and being conscious."

"Your friends took me by surprise too," said Elazar as they pulled away from the hotel. "We had no idea they were so close."

Kane looked out of the window in silence for several minutes. They were nearing the Knesset.

"Closest chopper-pad," said Elazar as they passed through the double steel gates of the Israeli Parliament complex. The car stopped and a *Heyl HA'Avir* officer saluted and stepped forward to lead them under the slowly circling rotor-blades of an Israeli Defence Force Bell 212 Twin Huey. The instant they were buckled in, the chopper lurched into the sky and thundered over early-morning Jerusalem, heading north towards the port city of Haifa. Twenty minutes later they descended into Israel's main naval base on the Mediterranean. As they came down Kane glimpsed the colossal form of an Ohio-class nuclear submarine illuminated by arc lights.

"They still defy my imagination!" shouted Elazar over the din. Kane nodded. It was the USS *South Dakota*, one of the US Navy's 'boomers' reconfigured from its original ballistic missile capability as part of the combined services' TacForce Group. As wars had become smaller and nastier, US military planning had increasingly revolved around small unit, highly mobile "stealth and shock" forces—designed to pinpoint and attack at the heart of regional conflicts. The use of a TacForce sub had underpinned the planning of their operation, both as a communications base, and most importantly, a Black Sea launching point for the Israeli Special Forces squad.

The *South Dakota*'s commander, Captain Brian

Duchesne, frowned as they approached. "Colonel Kane?" he asked tersely, thrown by Kane's appearance.

"Appreciate this, Captain Duchesne," Kane extended his hand.

"Orders," shrugged the tall grey-haired Bostonian, his expression severe as he shook Kane's hand. Then he eyed Elazar and the Israeli introduced himself. Duchesne's eyebrows lifted; he had heard of Mordechai Elazar. "I have been told very little about this operation. I sincerely hope one of you men is going to wise me up real soon. And," his nostrils flared, "that what you tell me will convince me that we're not part of some glorified posse." He fixed Elazar with a withering stare.

Kane glared at the submariner as Elazar replied. "Captain Duchesne, I understand you're limited to surveillance and support for my squadron—and you cannot engage the enemy unless your ship is under threat—"

"Under *direct* threat," Duchesne corrected him with a tight smile. "That right, Colonel Kane?"

Kane nodded reluctantly.

The Israeli glanced at Kane, then returned his attention to Duchesne. "I will of course abide by your operational constraints, Captain," he said steadily. "I will be on board—"

"On board?" reacted Duchesne. "Surely you—"

"Too old?" grinned Elazar. "I *am* the designated commanding officer of the IDF Special Forces unit assigned to this mission. There will of course be a *field* commander as well," he added after a sufficient pause.

"I see," said Captain Duchesne. "Then in that case, Colonel, you and your men had better be ready for boarding by oh-six hundred hours. This facility is unsuitable and vulnerable, we cannot spend the day here. You can brief me once we are under way."

Elazar nodded, his eyes twinkling. "We will be here at oh-six hundred. Thank you, Captain."

"What an asshole!" swore Kane, striding away.

"With what he's got to take care of, Tom, so would I be!" Elazar laughed.

"And your men?" asked Kane.

"They got the same call you did," said the Israeli, gesturing to a low building in front of them. They entered; Elazar's IDF squad was gathered around a single long table. All wore the insignia of Israel's most elite clandestine force, the Mossad's *Sayeret Matkal*. Kane saluted them, and was momentarily surprised at the low chuckle this provoked. Then he remembered how he looked.

"I—" he began, but Elazar's voice overrode his.

"Contrary to appearances, there is a Righteous Gentile among us," said the old Mossad man. This time the laughter was less restrained.

"Colonel Tom Kane," Elazar introduced him. "And I warn you men, he knows your names too. Okay, we haven't got much time. You have covered the overall objectives and strategy of this operation with Colonel Ganor. We will do further work and familiarisation aboard the *South Dakota* but I wanted you to meet Colonel Kane, the man on whom our operation depends."

The men of the *Sayeret Matkal* nodded quietly; those who hadn't known of Kane's Vietnam record had been swiftly educated by their commanding officer.

"Actually," Elazar grinned conspiratorially. "I just wanted to lessen the likelihood of you shooting this sonofabitch the next time you see him!"

Kane joined in as laughter rippled through the crack commando squadron. Then he spoke.

"Men," he began. "All going well, I will be in Novominsk with Kalin by tomorrow, where I'll have the dubious honour of joining his fight. So like Colonel Elazar says—check out the man in the uniform real well before you shoot. Okay?"

The squadron grinned broadly as it faced him.

"Anyway," said Kane. "As you know, I'm the sucker providing your HUMINT for this operation."

The men nodded, faces becoming serious now. They knew the jargon; HUMINT—human intelligence gathering; ELINT—electronic intelligence gathering.

"The USS *South Dakota* will coordinate ELINT from all contributing sources," Kane said. "It is my fervent hope that you will be completing the critical final phase of the operation with as *much* knowledge about the ground situation as it is possible to provide." He paused. "I *know* the danger of ignorance!"

Kane was silent, casting his eyes around the room, then he continued softly. "You will be in the Black Sea in three days. For the sake of your speed of departure, your aircraft for this mission will be those carried by the *South Dakota*— they have been designated as assets of your country. Colonel Elazar has told me that you have worked off a TacForce sub before and that you are familiar with both the AH–64A Apache and the UH–60A Black Hawk. But their weapons systems and personnel configurations are slightly different from your own machines, so be rigorous on yourselves in the pre-op stage. Your US Navy counterparts on the *South Dakota* are there to help you—"

Kane broke off and smiled at Elazar. "That may not always be obvious to you, but it's true, so don't be proud— the last thing we need is another Desert One."

Heads nodded.

"The *South Dakota* will be stationed ten to fifteen miles off the coast. Your mission targets are: one—Gyorgy Kumarov; and two—Jorge Holtzmann. In addition to this, we have to destroy the biological weapons manufacturing facility and any missiles held by Kalin. Kalin himself is not a priority target at this stage, but that may change."

He looked around the room again and his expression became more intense. "I hope we are lucky. We'll need to be. Holtzmann is well advanced in his plans and he knows we know where he is. Remember, he's been hunted all his life. In his mind we're already there, around the next corner, in the next building. He'll be expecting us. We'll have the TacForce sub and more ELINT than we'll need, but in the end, as you well know, it will come down to what happens on the ground."

Kane finished with quiet gravity. "This will not be easy, but we cannot fail. Colonel Elazar caught the father, now we must catch the son. Our mission designation is Operation Pishay-Avot."

Although the Hebrew words came unnaturally from his mouth, the men who faced him all knew the ancient phrase from the Torah, and understood the weight of their responsibility. *Pishay-Avot*—the "sins of the fathers."

One of the *Sayeret Matkal* stood and saluted. He was whippet-thin, taut as a bowstring, and had an accent that was pure Bronx.

"Colonel Kane—we'll nail this sucker's ass to the wall, sir!" The soldier's eyes glittered as his unit thumped the table in agreement.

"Well said, Izzy!" Elazar laughed, and Kane saluted him with a nod and a grin. Fifteen minutes were spent while Kane met the men individually. Then he farewelled the squadron and walked with Elazar to the waiting chopper, to return to Jerusalem, and thence to Ben Gurion—where he was scheduled to board a commercial flight to Cyprus and from there become John Hawke, renegade Marine.

"Good luck, Tom," said Elazar gravely as they parted company on the Haifa pad.

"And to you," Kane replied, wondering how long it would be until they next met, and in what circumstances.

Bumping along behind Sayeed Massar's Jeep convoy, Lena stared out of the window. The land was dusty, the road little more than a track winding up into the hills. She thought of Kane; of her future without him and how she would exist only on the memories of their passion. She was beyond tears. Perhaps grief would come again when she left Armestan. Her cheek was hot against her hand as she closed her eyes for a second and saw his face staring back. The caws of distant carrion birds carried over the rumble of the van's engine. Her eyes opened; rock formations rose out of the hills like frozen lovers entwined and it seemed that the sounds of ancient celebration were swelling from the ground, born again in the afternoon heat. Her gaze fell upon the twisted stone shapes, and memories of passion coursed through her. Kane was a presence within her; the warm breeze brushed his dusty kisses onto her cheek. Her soul throbbed as she lay back on the dark sheets of sleep and prepared to dream. As she fell, reaching for him, she felt awash with joy. She rolled into the cracked vinyl of the seat, gathered her head into her hands and pressed her lips against her palm, kissing him and loving him while the voice of the hot wind whispered that life was no longer the currency.

Terry glanced across at her and smiled at the expression adorning her face in sleep, then he returned his attention to the approaching hill's crest over which Sayeed Massar's convoy had disappeared.

In the everyday telepathy of these things, Kane, aboard an Air Cyprus DC–9, dreamed of Lena. The flight-time for the two hundred mile hop across the Mediterranean was less than an hour, but that had not stopped him falling asleep almost the moment the aircraft had taken off from Ben Gurion. Now Lena's features fogged in his dream.

Twenty minutes later the aircraft hit turbulence on its descent. Kane stirred but did not wake as the face of Holtzmann came to him. The plane lurched across the sky; shadowed eyes pierced him and echoes of screams came on the same winds that tossed the jet like a paper toy. He clawed into the daylight—*away!*—away from the monstrous eyes coming closer.

He awoke with a jolt, shaking. The aircraft bucked and he stared out the window to compose himself. Scrubby clumps of brush and scattered herds of sheep trailed orange dust over the desolate hills. As they descended towards the barren island that served as both a transit point for the Middle East and a staging post for some of the world's most dangerous terrorist groups, he lifted his eyes to the grey mist of the northern horizon. He imagined his quarry somewhere in the darkness beyond. His dream had enhanced the enormity of his mission and his responsibility. He clenched his fist. Fear is normal, knowing the fear is conquering it—the familiar mantra ran through his mind.

Ernesto Cortez lay in his room at the Monastery, his legs swathed with bandages, his mind throbbing with fear. There was nothing he could do. The solitude brought with it the renewed reminder of what he was, a *traidor*. Sooner or later the *yanquis* would act on his information. With the arrest of the first Sobrecartel member in the US would come his own death.

"Damn you, Kane!" he hissed to the emptiness, remembering his tormentor with chilling clarity. To comfort himself he thought of Kane as Angie Furness had last described him, shot-up and barely alive. It didn't help. His imagination taunted him, adding to the physical pain of his injured legs. He listened to the noises outside but it was only the rise and fall of Russian voices. He closed his eyes and longed to be somewhere else; anywhere else. Away from Holtzmann.

Sayeed Massar's northern base at the town of Irtos was nothing more than a rough assortment of tents. He explained to Lena that they were twenty miles from his home city of Tumoakoc, which was currently besieged by *danzan* forces. "And it's likely to stay that way, goddamnit," he said glumly.

Lena sipped her coffee and looked at him; it was hard to get used to this man who looked like a *mudjahadeen* fighter yet spoke like a New Yorker. "Why?" she asked.

"Here in Irtos," he gestured around, "we're still in the mountains. It's hard for Kalin to bother us. But Tumakoc is in the badlands. It's way out in the open."

Lena nodded, her knowledge of Armestan's geography— while far from complete—was good enough to place the besieged city in the vast desert plain north of the Markesh range.

"So what's your fire-power versus Kalin's?" asked Terry, sitting next to Lena.

"Fuckin' nothing," grumbled the *kadashi* warlord. "Russians and Serbs are getting through to him, we have to buy our shit from our 'friends'. But we make do, know what I mean?" Lena looked around at the assortment of weaponry in the camp; Soviet light-tracks, armoured cars and two T–55 tanks, a variety of mobile artillery and a hoard of bazookas, RPGs and even shoulder-launched Stinger missiles.

"Looks impressive to me," she remarked.

"It's all old," Massar replied. "The Stingers we paid a fuckin' fortune for from the Afghanis, and then the UN brings down the air-exclusion zone! Can't fuckin' win." He laughed at his dark joke. "Yeah," he sipped his coffee. "We do alright, for now. Better than in Tumakoc."

Lena glimpsed the sorrow his outward comedy masked. "Can we stay with you?" she asked simply. "I'd like to cover your side of this."

"Sure," shrugged Massar. "Fuckin' crazy if you ask me, but sure, why not? If you need to get your stuff out we can get it to Baku. Same goes for you, when you get sick of it."

"Thanks, Sayeed," she said, turning to Terry and Harry. "You happy to stay?"

"Happy?" replied Terry. "Not quite the word I'd use—But I s'pose we haven't been through this for nothing."

Harry nodded and Lena looked keenly at him, wondering whether Harry Berg had ever disagreed with anyone. Then her eye caught Sergei, standing off at a distance.

"The *danzan* kid," said Massar, nodding towards him. "He can't stay. I'll get him to a UN camp up north, okay?"

"Let me tell him," said Lena. She stood and walked slowly across to Sergei. She owed him and she would not forget it.

"Sergei," she said softly in Russian, putting her arm around his shoulders. "You must go. They will take you to a United Nations refugee camp. You will be safe there and I will try to find you when this is over."

He looked at her through wide eyes and nodded.

"You need not," he said. "I did it for my own self. And for God. Kalin is not the way for our people, you helped show me that. You and . . ." he nodded towards Abdur, who was laughing as one of Massar's men showed him how to break down an AK47.

Lena's eyes filled with tears. She reached forwards and hugged Sergei, then led him across to Massar. The *kadashi* leader stood and, smiling, extended his arms to the young *danzan*.

"May we meet as friends," he said in Russian, also hugging him. "And in peace."

Sergei nodded shyly, then Massar called out to his men. Two disappeared and returned minutes later behind the wheel of a decrepit jeep. As Sergei stepped towards it, Terry stood and gathered him in his brawny arms.

"Take care of yourself, sport!" he said, squeezing him heartily.

Harry's farewell was less vigorous but equally heartfelt. Then Sergei climbed into the Jeep and was gone. The threesome, with Massar between them, watched the dust cloud of the vehicle move towards the horizon.

"Goodbye, Sergei," whispered Lena, tears running down her cheeks.

It was an ugly, grey afternoon as Kane arrived in Belgrade. Even the Danube looked choked and lifeless as it bisected the Serbian capital.

He had stayed in Cyprus only long enough to ditch his Lubavitcher clothes and the identity documents of Jacob Lubetkin. Now, in jeans, sweatshirt, and Cuban-heeled boots, he stood and pulled his rucksack from the locker of the JAT Airbus as John Hawke. His sack contained the basic necessities—army fatigues, boots, and, most importantly, his ComMod ultra-low frequency field communicator, disguised as a multi-band radio receiver.

Outside the terminal building he caught a cab to the Hotel Molda, a cheap hotel in the centre of town where it had been decided he would stay. The pile of backpacks in the tiny lobby confirmed what the CIA had told him about the place. He registered as Derek Jones, though his passport confirmed his identity as John Nathaniel Hawke.

Walking into his musty room, he threw water on his face and grimaced as he caught sight of himself. He had not shaved since leaving the US for Israel, and his appearance—including the ragged remnants of his ear—was as disreputable as it had ever been. He checked his watch, then sat on the bed flicking between the satellite news services on the fuzzy TV. After ten minutes he was rewarded with a WorldNet report. The mug-shots taken at Langley were flashed on-screen as his 'escape,' supposedly during his transit from a US Army prison to Leavenworth Federal Penitentiary in Kansas, was described. After listing his awards for bravery in Vietnam, the report described him as "highly dangerous." Allegedly he'd murdered a fellow officer for informing on an atrocity committed by him during service in Somalia. Kane smiled as he lay back on the bed, hoping irrationally that somewhere, somehow, Lena might see it and know he was still alive.

". . . authorities have now notified Interpol, believing that Colonel Hawke may have already left the US . . ." droned the TV.

When the spot ended, he rose reluctantly, and minutes later walked out into the leaden city and headed towards the Danzanstan Information Bureau, run by Kalin's man in Belgrade, Vladimir Golen. Five blocks later a sullen looking woman scowled as he entered the cramped office.

"I am looking for Vladimir Golen," said Kane.

"Ambassador Golen not here!" she snapped, looking away.

"Where is he?" said Kane through clenched teeth.

The woman looked up again, running her fingers through her sparse hair. "You want . . . International Brigade?" she asked with an expression which could have been a smile or a sneer.

Kane nodded.

"Go to bar. On street, very close." She turned away.

"Thanks," said Kane as he left.

It was easy enough to find Golen's alternative office by the bar's patrons, and the *danzan* "ambassador" himself was instantly recognisable from the CIA shots Kane had seen. Barrel-shaped, with mutton-chop sidelevers, he was holding court with a company of skinheads. The bar was full of them. The International Brigade was their rallying point; a place for neo-Nazi groups to satisfy their racist bloodlust without facing prison terms. Kane shrugged and walked slowly towards the group.

"Vladimir Golen?" he said loudly enough to carry above the din.

Golen looked up through a cloud of cigarette smoke. "Yes?" he rasped. "And you?"

The skinheads rose and surrounded Kane threateningly.

"My name is Hawke," replied Kane steadily. "John Hawke, US Marine Corps."

Golen stared at him through blood-shot eyes. "Hawke?" he rolled the name around his mind. Then it clicked and his eyes flicked up to the television set. "You—?"

Kane nodded.

"I want to talk about a job with your leader," he said. "I want to talk *alone,*" he added, glancing over at the leading skinhead.

"Hawke!" spluttered Golen suddenly, waving his arms. "Yes, yes! Go!" he snapped at the skinheads, who reluctantly withdrew.

"I want refuge," said Kane immediately. "Kalin needs some help with his International Brigade. But I'm not doing it for nothing." His demands stated simply, he sat down.

Golen questioned him for nearly twenty minutes. "You could be helpful to us, Hawke," he said finally. "Or you could be a liability. In any case the judgement is not mine. I can get you to Novominsk, that is all. There you must deal with General Boris Rodionov, Kalin's second-in-command. I will provide you with an introduction. That is all I can promise."

Kane nodded. "Guess that's it then. How do I get there?"

"There is a JAT flight to Novo tomorrow morning at eight," replied Golen. "We have seats on it for diplomatic traffic."

"I'm no diplomat," Kane smiled tightly.

"And these are not ordinary times, Hawke," said Golen. "I hope you understand that."

"Yeah," replied Kane, standing up.

"Stay, Colonel," said the other. "I would be most curious to hear word from the US. How our struggle is being seen there—?"

"Badly," said Kane. "But that's not my business."

Golen shook his head. "I see. You are a soldier—strictly professional, that is good. Where are you staying?"

Kane told him.

"I will meet you there at 6:00 A.M.," said Golen.

"Oh-six-hundred," Kane repeated, and walked out of the bar.

Back at his hotel he removed his radio, thrust it beneath his coat, pushed his passport to the bottom of his rucksack, then left to snatch a late meal. When he returned two hours later, his room, as expected, had been searched. He noted with satisfaction that his passport now lay on the top of his belongings. He'd been checked out, ineptly.

"They're moving the magic dust," said Collins grimly, looking across at Stone. "We can't ignore it."

"No," Stone sighed. The Armestan operation had all but swamped the regular working of Operation White Storm. Now the Sobrecartel was about to distribute the cocaine shipment which had been frozen since the Colombian attack on Holtzmann's headquarters.

"Must've straightened out the kinks," said Collins. "With the boss alive and all. What do we do?"

"We're snookered, Hog," replied Stone slowly. "The President would personally have my nuts if we knowingly let two tons of cocaine go into the system just to protect Cortez."

"And Kane . . ." said Collins.

"Yeah, and Kane," Stone repeated grimly. "All the President's men called him 'deniable'. I'll be damned if I'll let him go in and be denied now. He's coming back."

"Nothing else for it," said Collins after a time. "No dishonour if he comes home."

"There is," growled Stone. "The way Kane sees it . . ." the words died on his lips as he looked up bleakly at Collins. "Damn!"

Kane woke early and swiftly showered. His stubble was fast becoming a beard. He strode down the stairway and through the foyer to the street, in search of a coffee before Golen arrived.

"You, Jones," came the call from the crone sitting in the office. "You, message." She waved a ragged piece of paper in her hand. Nodding his thanks he took it, and walked outside. On it, scrawled in barely legible longhand was the word *bruther*. Kane checked his watch and turned left up the block to where he had seen a public telephone the previous night.

"Hog?" he asked after the connection was made.

"Get Stone for you, Tom," came the reply. Seconds later the General's voice boomed out of the receiver.

"You're coming home, Kane. We have to go with Operation Roundup. Can't have you in Holtzmann's territory when we do that—not with the chance of Cortez being around."

Kane chewed his lip and looked out into the lonely street. "Negative, General," he said. "Past the point of no return here."

"Bullshit, Kane!" Stone exploded through the line. "Haul ass—this is an order! Operation Roundup starts in three hours."

"Sorry, sir," replied Kane quickly. "Remember I'm deniable. This has got to be done and don't let it go bad at your end. Launch the roundup, but—" he spied a figure turn the corner at the far end of the street, "—make sure Elazar makes the fucking boat, sir!" He hung up and reached his hotel just as Golen did.

"Who do you have to kill for a coffee in this town?" he grumbled and Golen laughed, his breath steaming around his face. "We will drink coffee at the airport. Come, I have my car. I have spoken to Novo and General Rodionov is most interested to meet you, Colonel Hawke. You are somewhat of a celebrity." Kane listened with satisfaction as Golen described the WorldNet report almost verbatim.

"Will there be trouble at the airport?" Kane asked gruffly

as they climbed into Golen's car, a gleaming Mercedes. Golen snorted.

"These days in Belgrade," he said, "the simplest tourist is an honoured visitor. And flying to Novo, you are more likely to be congratulated than detained. Feeling here is very strong for Kalin."

Kane nodded. "Did you discuss money?" he asked.

"No," replied the other. "I will leave that to you. But I trust," he smiled, "that when you are situated in Novo, you will treat the matter of payment with the caution it is due. You and I may understand the need, but for Kalin this is not so. His is as much a spiritual war as any other."

What a crock, thought Kane as the airport loomed ahead.

In Nickels, a mouthful of beer caught in Jack Mahoney's throat and he pitched back in his chair when Kane's face appeared on TV.

"Sonofabitch!" he swore. He hoped with every fibre of his body that Kane had gone in after Lena.

"Mahoney, you blinking Irishman!" Craig Massey's plummy voice suddenly split the air in the bar and Mahoney turned from the television as the report ended.

"Massey," he grinned. "Just watching the piece on that runaway Marine—"

"Yes, sounds like a rotter," replied Massey, pulling up a stool. "Listen," he said, abruptly grasping Mahoney's shoulder, "I was sorry to hear about . . . everything. But damned good show in any case."

Mahoney smiled. "Don't worry," he said. "It's done."

"I tell you what," whispered the Englishman loudly. "Buy me a dram and I'll make your night!"

Mahoney laughed and ordered a whisky which Massey gulped thirstily.

"Pay up," chuckled Mahoney.

"It's Peterson," sniggered Massey. "He's been sent to bloody Armestan."

"What?" Mahoney all but shouted.

"*Shh,*" said Massey, holding his finger up for another drink. "Top secret. Norton blew his stack over your little stunt apparently and Peterson was the fall guy. Packed him off to buy back Galena. Can you imagine Peterson in a warzone?" He guffawed and Mahoney didn't know whether to laugh too or cry out in anger.

"It's a crazy fucking world . . ." Mahoney said finally, deciding that joining the Englishman in a whisky was the only response he could make.

Then it hit him.

Peterson knew Kane's face.

BOOK THREE

CHAPTER**EIGHTEEN**

Throughout the United States, in an operation coordinated by the White Storm taskforce—but conducted by the DEA, the Justice Department, the FBI, and a host of State and local law enforcement organisations—couriers, distributors, bankers, and wholesalers for the Sobrecartel were roused from their clubs, their businesses and their beds, and arrested. When it was over, scarcely three hours later, nearly a hundred men and women sat in prison cells across America waiting for their lawyers. And when their lawyers arrived and explained the scale of the operation, those caught in its net rushed to testify against one another, knowing that in a deal with their captors lay their only hope of leniency.

"Rat city," spat Hog Collins during the hurly-burly of the morning after. In all, Operation Roundup would net nearly three tons of cocaine—including the two tons in Louisiana—and behead the Sobrecartel in North America. First reports claimed the authorities had acted on "tip-offs" but analysts pointed to the probable existence of a "super-grass" behind the massive operation. Collins and Stone could not spare a thought for the fate of Ernesto Cortez, though they had, irrevocably, sealed it. Neither could spare a thought for anyone except Kane. And both knew he was not coming home as ordered.

Holtzmann stared in utter disbelief at the pages slipping from the fax machine. Everything had been hit. Accounts frozen. Stockpiles seized.

It was a catastrophe.

"Kumarov," he whispered, crumpling the sheets in his hands.

The Russian looked curiously at him over a steaming cup of tea. "Yes?" he answered.

"Your first subject," said Holtzman, his eyes flashing with wrath as he removed his glasses, "will be Cortez."

Kane shook Golen's hand roughly at the airport and walked onto the waiting bus to join the twenty or so others. Together they constituted the full passenger complement for the flight to Novominsk.

Golen had told him with a wink that the Serbian gesture of solidarity with Kalin was defined not by the number of seats occupied on the flight, but by what the ancient Tupelov carried in its cargo hold. Kane suspected the passengers were merely Kalin's insurance policy. Which was what made the appearance of one—a blue-suited businessman with an expensive briefcase—so striking. The man entered the aircraft first and immediately took a seat in the front row. He looked scared shitless, thought Kane, checking him out as he passed, his curiosity pricked.

Grotesque noises tore from the Tupelov's jets. Kane gripped his seat tightly, knuckles whitening as the fuselage creaked and twisted. Then, once if was obvious that the Tupelov was going to make it, he looked out of the window at Belgrade disappearing below him. He had found the Serbian capital and Serbs he had met to be thoroughly unappealing. It would be so forever, he supposed, a city and a people damned in his memories by the reason for his visit.

Settling back as the aircraft began to cruise, he remembered John Hawke. Kane knew Hawke's war record as well as he knew his own. It *was* almost his own, he thought, as he ran over it in his mind. He closed his eyes and recalled the life his old friend had too briefly enjoyed.

Midway through the flight he checked his watch. Operation Roundup would be well and truly underway. A nudge in his ribs disturbed him and he looked around. A man with bad skin was holding out a bread roll to him and urging him to take it. Kane shook his head and turned back. Beneath him the vastness of the Black Sea stretched into the distance. He felt very alone.

A knock!

Cortez leapt for the door, forgetting his injured legs. It swung open as he tumbled from his bed and Holtzmann stood before him, his face etched with dark fury.

"*Señor!*" Cortez exclaimed, a tremor shaking his body.

"Ernesto, you lied. You have betrayed me," Holtzmann said slowly, an icy waver in his voice. "Soon you will wish you had taken the bullet I offered you in Cartagena. Soon you will envy the dead." His shadowed eyes regarded Cortez's consuming dread.

"What?" shouted Cortez. "What is this, *Señor?*" He felt a tic begin in his cheek. *Calm!* his mind shrieked. He tore his eyes away from Holtzmann and stared behind him, at Kumarov, Kalin, Rodionov and the *danzan* soldiers who had come for him. All wore the same pitiless expression.

"*What?*" repeated Cortez to them, gulping for air.

Kalin and Kumarov said nothing as their pitch-black eyes stared back. Cortez felt sweat running down his back and his eyes filled with tears of fear. His nails dug into his palms as Holtzmann's cold gaze—cruel eyes above a tight smile—kept watching him.

"Come," Holtzmann growled finally and turned.

The *danzan* soldiers, weapons drawn, surrounded Cortez

and he was dragged, legs trailing uselessly, across the central courtyard of the Monastery to the main building. Cortez made mental notes of the security of the complex, his awareness heightened, senses suddenly detached from the uncontrollable anxiety pumping out from his heart. They passed into the dimness of the main building and began down the stairs, past two guards manning a mounted machine-gun. He whispered frantic prayers as he approached a heavy wooden door. A premonition coalesced in his mind and he struggled from the soldiers' grip, collapsing and lying flat against the floor, his breath coming in ragged gasps. The door opened. As he was dragged forwards he heard Kumarov speak. The door started to creak shut and his every sensory organ burned. His eyes darted for one last glimpse outside as the door thudded closed, then he was wrenched to his feet by strong hands and his head was held to prevent him turning away from what he saw.

"*No!*" the word tore from his lips. "*Dios mío—No!*" Four men in isolation suits dragged him through the airlock and strapped him, pleading incoherently, to a chair inside a room with walls of thick, clear plastic.

"*Please, Señor!*" he shrieked over and over.

Holtzmann merely looked on with growing satisfaction as his lieutenant was bound.

"*Mercy of God! Please, Señor!*" Cortez thrashed against his captors but in vain. Finally it was done and he was left alone. He watched as the room was sealed, his mind fixed on the truth of his fate. What Holtzmann had described in Cartagena was now to be used on him.

"*No!*" he wailed. But the sound of the chamber being sealed was all the response he got. Then, eerily distorted through the plastic, he saw them watching him.

"Prepare to die," he heard Holtzmann's voice out of a small intercom set in the ceiling of the room. "Your death will be cruel. Crueller than you can imagine."

"*Please . . .*" Cortez croaked, but all he heard was a

muffled laugh. Then a quiet hiss as a tiny aerosol cloud appeared before his face.

Most of the passengers melted away immediately the aircraft landed at Shaklin, climbing into a variety of rickety vehicles waiting to take them into Novominsk. That had been half an hour ago. Now Kane was one of a group of four sitting on a rough wooden bench inside a corrugated steel shelter. One of the group was the man in the blue suit. He peered at Kane again.

"Do I know you?" he asked finally.

Kane shook his head and turned towards the other two men. They looked more like him.

"International Brigade?" he asked the first. The man looked blankly at him. His partner replied in broken English.

"Yes . . . you know when?"

"No," replied Kane. "We wait."

Nearly an hour later, two surly looking soldiers wearing the distinctive black armband of the International Brigade drove up in a battered Jeep.

"Peterson and Hawke?" said the first brusquely in English. Kane stood, as did the man in the blue suit.

"Come with me," said the soldier. "You . . ." he pointed to the other two. "Wait."

Without looking around, Kane mounted the Jeep and threw his rucksack into the back.

"Do you mind?" said the man in the blue suit, climbing in next to him.

He was terrified, thought Kane again, wondering why the hell such a man would come to Novominsk. He sat in silence and watched the wreckage of the city approach, recognising the Monastery—glowering like a single dark eye in the foothills beyond. He missed nothing as they approached Kalin's HQ, absorbing details he knew the *Sayeret Matkal* would need: guard posts, weaponry, and troop strength. What he saw depressed him. Kalin's men looked well trained, their weaponry well maintained.

They drove through the Monastery's main gates and around to a barracks area in the rear. Then he and the man named Peterson were taken to a small building and each shown to a separate, tiny room. "Wait," was the only instruction given as the door was locked behind him. Kane gave it five minutes, then swiftly removed the ComMod from his rucksack.

Even an electronics specialist would have had difficulty perceiving the communications device hidden within the transistor chips of the multi-band radio. Using a combination of the tuning buttons on the face of the radio, Kane flashed out his first message from Novominsk. The circuitry of the transmitter analysed and compressed his message into a single ultra-low frequency digital pulse that was immediately detected and stored on board one of six geocentric satellites which formed the communications web of America's secret agencies. The satellite relayed the message three times every minute until it received an acknowledgement from its designated receiver, in this case the *South Dakota*.

The job done, Kane sat alone in the small room and listened carefully to the world outside. A single thought entered his head. *Are you out there, Holtzmann?*

The aerial assembly towed behind the USS *South Dakota* received Kane's message almost the second it was sent, and fired back its acknowledgement response.

The eerie twilight inside the submarine had been the same for the past twenty hours that the *South Dakota* had navigated the most critical part of its journey, through the Sea of Marmara, *en route* to the Bosporus—the narrow gateway to the Black Sea. The TacForce sub had to be absolutely invisible; all systems were running on minimum power to thwart surface detection. Though intelligence reports doubted that the Turkish or Ukrainian navies—through whose waters they were travelling—possessed sophisticated submarine tracking systems, it was nevertheless one of the trickiest voyages a submarine could undertake.

And Mordechai Elazar hated every second of it. The gloom, the atmosphere, the confinement.

"Shore com, sir!" Radio Officer Chip MacKenzie rushed up the narrow corridor.

Elazar grunted with relief and followed the gingerhaired seaman to the *South Dakota's* control room. MacKenzie gestured to the LED display and Elazar's eyes flicked over it. Kane was in position.

He scrawled a brief message in response, then turned to MacKenzie.

"Check with Captain Duchesne and include our ETA at the launch site," he said. "I'll be up with the 'copters." His heart beating a little faster than it had been a few minutes before, he walked out through the control room to the forward hangars where his men were training on the *South Dakota's* helicopter fleet.

As the young radio officer began typing the return message, he thought about the man in Novominsk on whom their entire operation depended. MacKenzie had not joined the navy with the thought of combat on his mind, but for the chance to explore technology unavailable to a civilian electronics engineer. As he entered the send code he sighed; while he admired the man for whom the message was intended, he was deeply, deeply glad he was not him.

Lena stared around at the disgustingly cramped refugee camp. It was crammed with the barely living, beyond the reach of the charity organisations that were providing relief elsewhere in this beleaguered land. There was a clinic in Irtos run by the Islamic Red Crescent Society, but it was pitifully small and completely overwhelmed.

She saw a young girl, obviously in the final stages of

death. Lena's compassion, wound so tightly by what she'd been through, sundered. She broke from Sayeed Massar to gather the wretched child in her arms. "Oh baby!" she held her tightly, stroking her hair, seeking to give her an instant of love amidst the hell, and looked up at Terry's lens in exasperation and frustration. He shrugged and turned the camera away. Finally Lena gently laid the girl back onto her filthy blanket and walked on through the crowd. Hands grasped her dress and the camera whirred again. *What else could she do?* the question welled from the misery surrounding her and threatened to engulf her. She looked up from the pleading faces and blinked her wet eyes in the breeze.

"Sayeed," she gulped. "This is . . ." her words evaporated in the hot air. The *kadashi* leader put his arm around her shoulder.

"Kalin won't allow UN convoys through," he said sadly. "We do what we can but it's a fuckin' mess. It's worse in Tumakoc," he added. "Who was it said 'in a war, the Devil just makes Hell bigger'?"

"It's a calamity," she said angrily.

She stayed with Massar as Terry and Harry continued through the refugee settlement. It was the last and most forsaken place they had seen, in a day that had been like a tour of the underworld; a place created by Man where Man's most basic desire—to survive—went unfulfilled. The hapless, helpless, dying victims were everywhere, spread through refugee encampments in the northern Markesh range: families, communities, villages, ravaged by a war the rest of the world had decided to forget. The panorama of poverty and squalor had been relentless: tens of thousands of displaced Armestanis barely alive inside the enclave which Massar and his forces fought so desperately to maintain.

"Why doesn't Kalin just drive through here?" asked Lena, kicking the dirt.

"Can't ensure his supply lines, these mountains are too

fuckin' hard for him," replied Massar. "Besides, why bother? Here, Tumakoc, it's all the damn same. He only needs to starve us out. By winter he'll have beaten the shit out of us without lifting a finger. Before the air-exclusion zone it was even worse. Kalin used to bomb places like this. Soon he'll start again. Fuckin' UN has given up."

Lena looked away. They'd shot nearly ten video cassettes of material. But would it make any difference?

"The tapes?" she asked after a while. "We'll need to . . ."

Massar nodded. "Like I said, I'll get them to Baku, there's got to be someone there who can help you."

"Harry'll have to go," said Lena. "Is it safe?"

"What's safe?" Massar shrugged. "As safe as here. Don't worry."

Lena nodded, and reluctantly turned her frayed mind to the job of composing "stand-ups"—the face-to-camera pieces that would link, and explain, what they had shot. As the sun dipped precariously towards the horizon, she began the first. Staring at the camera, she told an unseen audience of their escape from Novominsk; their meeting with Sayeed Massar, and the misery and deprivation they had witnessed in the *kadashi* mountain enclave. Much later, with the shifting, starving shapes of the refugees surrounding her, Lena finished her last stand-up. She felt completely despairing.

Terry saw her expression through the lens and walked over to hug her softly.

"It's been a long day, Lena," he said gruffly. "Hang in there, okay?"

She dropped her head to his shoulder, her emotions buffeted by exhaustion. Ten minutes later she was asleep as the van pulled away from the refugee camp for Irtos. When they arrived at Massar's base she woke long enough to mumble, "I think I'll turn in," then fell into the rough bedding in her tent and allowed sleep to blot out the horrors; a sleep too deep for dreams. A healing, merciful sleep.

* * *

Boris Rodionov strode in as night fell. Kane had been waiting nearly five hours.

"Colonel Hawke!" boomed the huge man, in passable English. "You have come to join the International Brigade, yes? I am sorry you waited so long. We will eat and discuss this."

Kane shook his hand and followed him outside, across the courtyard and into a mess-hall in the main Monastery building. As they ate, Rodionov quizzed him on his military background, tours of duty and personal details. As he answered, Kane wondered at the accuracy of Rodionov's source. The big *danzan* general appeared happy enough with his answers, though Kane suspected Rodionov's mood was probably partly due to the amount of vodka he'd consumed. Kane poured himself another cup of tea from a samovar, watched another tumbler of vodka being swallowed by his interrogator and waited for the next question. But there were none.

Kalin's chief-of-staff was satisfied, and finally set the terms of his deal with John Hawke. It was four A.M. "You want safety, yes?" said Rodionov.

"I don't want it bad enough not to get paid," replied Kane steadily.

"Ah, yes," chuckled Rodionov. "You will be paid, Colonel. But this will not be American wages! It will be enough for you, and when this war is over there will be richer business to be done here." A conspiratorial grin split his broad face.

"What's the offer, General?" Kane said flatly.

"Ten thousand dollars at the end of six months," replied Rodionov. "It is enough—?"

"No way," said Kane.

Rodionov laughed heartily and swallowed the remains of his glass.

"You will be provided for." He poured another vodka. "And what would you spend the money on here?"

"Let's just say I like to have it," growled Kane. "Okay?"

Rodionov leaned forward, fixing Kane with his brown, bloodshot eyes. "You are a warrior, Hawke," he said. "This I can see. The International Brigade . . . they are hooligans. They just like to kill *araby*. It is a sport for them—a distraction for us. No, I do not need you for this purpose. I need you with me, on field command. Special duties, some extremely unpleasant but necessary. You understand?"

Kane nodded, his expression blank. "I don't give a rat's ass how unpleasant, General. How does it affect the pay packet?"

Chuckling and shaking his head, Rodionov fell back in his chair clutching his glass unsurely. "You are a hard man, Hawke," he grinned. "But I think we are two of a kind. You get two thousand now, two thousand a month until we run out of money. Good?"

He extended his hand over the rough wooden table. Kane regarded it for a second, then lifted his own and grasped Rodionov's. "Deal, General," he smiled. "So when do my Russian lessons start?"

"Colonel Hawke," guffawed the huge officer, slapping his shoulder. "I do not think you will have any trouble being understood!"

"We'll see," Kane said.

"Yes!" chortled Rodionov. "Now, surely, vodka?"

Kane shook his head.

"In that respect, General," he grunted. "I guess I'm the wrong man for your army."

"No," grinned Rodionov. "But I say . . . I find it frightening—this is the right word?"

"Deeds are frightening, General," Kane stared at him. "Words have never scared me too much."

Rodionov returned Kane's stare, then a sudden glint came into his eyes. "Perhaps I can scare you, Colonel," he growled, a mocking grin on his face. "Come!" He tottered to his feet and gestured for Kane to follow him. They wound their way out of the mess-hall and down a long corridor.

Holtzmann was transfixed. It was happening so fast! He had been observing Cortez overnight with hardly a break. Kumarov occasionally joined him to comment on the progress of the disease, then went back to work in his lab and to his own solitary watch on the test subject.

Ernesto Cortez lay on his back in the isolation room, staring directly at them, barely conscious as his immune system lost its fight against the viral invader. His body twitched in delirium and the noises he made were those of an animal dying in pain.

"Incredible!" breathed Holtzmann, his dark eyes shining behind the glasses.

"Yes," murmured Kumarov, who had chosen that moment to rejoin him. "It is exceeding my expectations, *Señor.* Once in the human system it appears to become even more virulent than it was in culture."

"What is happening now?" asked Holtzmann.

Kumarov tore himself from his thoughts to answer him. "As I said, once it was transferred to his bloodstream via his respiratory system, the virus grown in culture began to multiply exponentially—grafting itself onto the subject's red blood—"

"His name is *Cortez,*" growled Holtzmann.

"Grafting itself onto *Cortez's* red blood cells," Kumarov continued. "Transforming them. For these last few hours it has proliferated to the degree that almost his entire blood supply has been altered. His body is quickly running out of oxygen as these mutated blood cells lose their ability to absorb and transport it—the virus has robbed them of that faculty. His blood is literally suffocating him. He would do as well if he had oil in his veins. Yes," he sighed, as the eerie vision of Cortez's torment played before their eyes. "Our virus is destroying its host, who with every breath pollutes the atmosphere with it. The virus will live in the air only a short while, a matter of a few hours at most, but in an urban setting that will be enough to ensure an almost complete infection rate. It will not be a matter of isolating victims, but sheltering the few who are *not* infected. I—"

Suddenly the huge oak door into the lab burst open, Rodionov and Kane all but falling inwards.

Kane glanced up and his eyes locked with Holtzmann's. It was as if an icicle had been hammered into his spine. He could not look away.

"Hawke!" boomed Rodionov, waving towards Cortez. "Now are you so—"

"What?" Holtzmann's roar cut him off.

"Rodionov!" Kumarov strode towards the huge man, his voice shrill and equally enraged as Holtzmann. "Get out! Get out!"

Rodionov laughed, gripping Kane's shoulder and straightening himself.

"Kalin will be told!" shrieked Kumarov. "There are to be no outsiders!"

Rodionov glowered at him, but even in his drunkenness he realised his mistake. "Come Hawke!" he muttered. "We will leave the comrade-doctors—"

But before they could move, an abrupt and soul-chilling scream tore through the room. It was Cortez. He was upright, straining against his bonds one last desperate time. His face was swollen grotesquely, no longer human, and within it his dying eyes burned with anguish.

And with recognition.

"Ka—!" he began to squeal.

Cortez lost his breath, staring wildly but mutely at Kane. In the confusion of the moment, Holtzmann's gaze whirled towards his former lieutenant, then slowly back to Kane.

"He seems to know you?" he said in a curious undertone.

"No," Kane gasped, meeting Holtzmann's eyes again.

Never had he felt a presence like the Colombian's. "Sorry, it's just so fucking horr—"

"*Señor!*" Kumarov's shout interrupted him. "Cortez, he is—!"

Holtzmann turned again, as all in the room watched the man behind the plastic sheeting begin his final struggle with death.

"*Adiós*, Ernesto!" hissed Holtzmann. "Go to hell!"

Then there was silence.

CHAPTER NINETEEN

Lena awoke, blinking the grit of an overnight dust storm from her eyes. She rolled out of her bedding and peered through the flap of the tent. It was very early morning, still dark, and the camp was quiet. The shadow-shapes of guards slouched past in the distance, then she saw Sayeed Massar, sitting cross-legged in front of his tent, smoking. She buckled her sandals and walked over to him.

"You didn't sleep?" he asked.

"Slept fine," she smiled. "Had a few hours on everyone else. And you?"

"Never do, much," he tugged at his cigarette. "Besides, it's the only time this fuckin' place looks beautiful," he said. "When you can't see it."

"Rather be in Jersey?" asked Lena.

Massar chuckled. "It hasn't got that bad yet. Come on, let me show you something."

He led her to his motorcycle and she climbed on behind him. They chugged away from the camp, waved on by the weary guards and followed a rocky mountain track along the top of a ridge, heading beyond the refugee camps they had visited the previous day. Looking around, Lena could see what Massar meant. In the purple mist of the pre-dawn, the land and the shacks of its inhabitants were painted in soft watercolours.

They rode north through the mountains until finally, with the sun beginning to spill across the dry saucer of the desert plain below, the *kadashi* leader pulled up at the edge of a high cliff. Without speaking he handed her a pair of binoculars and pointed towards the city far below. Its ragged shapes were caught in the rising sun like broken glass and, destroyed though it was, Lena could sense it had once been a majestic place.

Massar turned off his motorbike and inhaled deeply in the silence. He looked out, following her gaze.

"Tumakoc," he said simply, then closed his eyes. "My family still lives there . . . I hope."

The sunlight flowed over the city like molten amber and now Lena spied Massar's enemy. Dark camouflage webs, stubbornly unreflective in the gathering dawn, were slung over the *danzan* fortifications, artillery emplacements and tank groups which ringed the city. From where she stood, Lena thought sadly, the besieged city looked like a jewel set in a tarnished brooch.

"What did he say to you?" growled Holtzmann, advancing on Kane. Rodionov was leaning against the door, either too drunk or too sober to speak.

Kane stood his ground. "No fucking idea," he replied steadily. "Who are you?"

Holtzmann ignored his question. "I knew that man. And he knew you. *What did he say?*"

Kane did not avert his eyes from the Colombian, who was now almost upon him. Behind the dark-tinted glasses, Kane glimpsed a ferocity he had seen in men's eyes as they killed; in Holtzmann's it was burning constantly.

"General Rodionov," he tried. "Who is this man?" But Rodionov was dangerously silent. Kane breathed deeply. His mouth was dry. Rodionov's blundering had thrown him into the worst possible situation and his mind screamed with the urgency of acting. Holtzmann's face was now inches from his own and his eyes had not deviated from him. The drug-lord spoke again, his eyes flashing.

"Do you want to join him?" he said, gesturing towards Cortez's body.

Kane shook his head. "I am Colonel John Hawke," he said gruffly, his tongue working hard between arid lips. "US Marine Corps . . . formerly."

The answer jolted Holtzmann. "Marines?" His eyes flicked across to Rodionov. "What is this?"

"Deserter," explained the big *danzan* commander, blinking with the effort of speaking coherently. "Wants to join us."

Kane was aware of the man who could only be Kumarov standing behind Holtzmann. "I don't know what he fucking said," he said again. "First time I saw him."

"I am not so sure, *yanqui*," replied Holtzmann. His eyes looked beyond Kane to Kalin, who had just entered the room.

"*Señor?*" said the *danzan* leader. "What is the disturbance?"

"An unwanted guest, Kalin," growled Holtzmann. "Very unwanted!"

Kalin followed Holtzmann's gaze to Rodionov, who began speaking rapid-fire Russian.

"Fool!" swore Kalin when he had listened to enough. He spat an order and Rodionov withdrew from the room. As Kane turned to do likewise he felt Holtzmann's glowering eyes follow him out, burning into his back.

"Get rid of him!" Holtzmann demanded.

Kalin shook his head. "It is not that simple," he said tersely. "Beyond our project I must think of the future of my struggle. Men like him are necessary . . . and rare."

"He is a *yanqui*! And he has seen—" Holtzmann gestured to the isolation room and Cortez's body.

"He will be watched," promised Kalin.

Holtzmann stared at him angrily for a second. "I do not like it," he muttered finally. "But let it be. Shall we examine the delivery system? Time is our enemy, with or without another *yanqui*."

Kalin said nothing, turning on his heels to leave the room. Holtzmann stomped after him with Kumarov trailing behind, shivering at the first sign of conflict between the two men. They stepped into the pale dawn and waited as Kalin's vehicle was made ready to take them to Shaklin. In that moment, looking around at the Monastery's defences—frail and ethereal in the thin light—Kumarov had a chilling sensation of how tenuous their ambition was. A premonition flashed through him of how simply their failure could be brought about. His brother and Holtzmann—lesser beings together than when apart. Wills too identical to admit the existence of the other.

And to further dishearten him, the first tentacles of the *manari*—the infamous wind that blew from the eastern desert—wrapped around him and promised that today, like yesterday, it would blow at full force. Impossible conditions for effective dispersal of the virus.

Kalin's vehicles roared up and Kumarov dutifully took his seat, a glum expression on his face.

"Sleep . . ." muttered Rodionov as they reached Kane's quarters. The *danzan* commander shuffled down the corridor and Kane closed his door softly. Through his tiny window he watched the dawn, and saw Kalin's convoy leave the Monastery. He shook his head, delayed shock coursing through his body. Cortez had recognised him, Holtzmann was suspicious. "Damn!" he whispered to the air. Then he shuddered as he recalled Cortez's death. Walking slowly to the door, he chocked it with a chair. Taking the ComMod from his rucksack, he typed a brief message. He had found Kumarov's laboratory, but he knew he would not be allowed so close again. Sighing, he fell wearily onto his bed and, though the morning hubbub of men and machines grew outside, he was soon unaware of it as sleep took him prisoner.

Elazar's eyes, sunken in flesh that felt spongy from its exposure to the sub's close atmosphere, flicked across the screen as he read Kane's message and he frowned.

"Acknowledge receipt," he said grimly to Chip Mac-Kenzie.

"Bad news, sir?" the radio officer could not help but ask.

"The worst," grunted the old Israeli. "The very worst."

"I'm sorry, sir," replied MacKenzie unsurely, but Elazar had turned and walked away.

MacKenzie swiftly flashed the acknowledgement to Kane's ComMod. That done, he resumed his monitoring of the passing sea traffic.

The *South Dakota* was pushing towards the eastern shore of the Black Sea, as invisible as the water itself with its stealth technology and a stream of satellite information augmenting its on-board enemy detection systems. They had completed the most difficult part of their journey, through the narrow channel of the Bosporus, without incident. In twelve hours they would be in their desired position off the Armestan coast.

MacKenzie listened idly to a conversation between a cargo ship and port control at Odessa, sharpening his Russian and laughing quietly at what he understood of the feisty banter.

It was almost noon when Harry Berg finally farewelled Lena and Terry. His Jeep became a dusty plume as his *kadashi* driver sped him south-east to Baku in Azerbaijan. With him were their precious videotapes and a rough script that Lena had written and recorded that morning.

There was an uncommon chill in the teeth of the *manari*.

The wind had been gathering force all morning and now blustered in great gusts through Massar's camp. Harry would be back in two days, Lena reminded herself, but for now the absence of the solid soundman pushed her a little more into the arms of unreality.

"What's happening?" she broke from her thoughts as she saw Terry and Abdur approaching. The Australian had his camera to his eye and the *kadashi* youth was waving a microphone at the end of a fishpole extender in a manner that suggested more a weapon than a recording device.

"Steady," barked Terry. "Give us a level. Talk for us, Lena." She chuckled and obliged, telling Abdur in Russian the dangers of being Terry's soundman. But the boy showed no sign of listening to anything other than the volume of her voice in his headphones as he struggled to keep the microphone out of Terry's shot.

"Not bad, you little bugger," laughed Terry finally, as Lena's impromptu patter dried up. "Like I said, any idiot can be a soundman!"

Lena translated. "He says you are doing well, Abdur."

"So what are we up to today?" asked Terry, dropping his camera to his side. "Sayeed's staying put here for a while, right?"

Lena nodded. "He took me to look at Tumakoc this morning," she said. "The second biggest city still under *kadashi* control. Kalin's got it surrounded. Thought we might get some shots of it."

"Sure," replied Terry. "Haven't got the long lens anymore, but we'll give it a go. Right then, I'll have a word to Sayeed and rustle up a guide. C'mon Abdur!"

The boy followed him happily and Lena watched the strange pair. A gust of wind whipped through the camp and she felt like flying with it, away.

Mikhail Shevchuk looked across at Kalin. ". . . the Sickles are ready," he finished simply. "All that remains is for me to program the coordinates for the targets, particularly the MIRV—that will take time."

The toe of Kalin's heavy boot set up a drumbeat of satisfaction as he stared at the three sleek missiles before him. The SS–25s had been relocated to their camouflaged launching site high on Mount Barkusk. "The two single warheads will be Tumakoc and Kirkusk," he said after a time. "Tumakoc first."

The *danzan* weapons engineer shrugged. "Where will the RVs be loaded?"

"They will need to be taken to the Monastery, to the isolation chamber," said Kumarov, standing behind Kalin with Holtzmann. "The first will be ready by tomorrow morning. After the success of the test I estimate we can produce approximately a kilo of the virus per day." His hands fidgeted nervously. More than his brother and possibly even Holtzmann, he felt the pressure of time.

"It is far beyond our needs," he added. "Even for targets as large as those we plan to strike. For Tumakoc tomorrow, this infernal wind is our danger."

"The wind is the wind," said Shevchuk. "We can only be ready. The virus will be under pressure in the RV?"

"Yes," Kumarov replied. "You will set the program to discharge the warheads at an altitude of five hundred metres. The virus will be released in aerosol form."

"And what of my men, holding the city?" asked Kalin.

"As discussed," replied Kumarov. "They must withdraw to the windward side of the city, which I will assume to be the east if the *manari* prevails. They must not come within five kilometres of the western perimeter of the city in the first six hours after discharge. The priority is not their proximity to the city but their ability to maintain a strict quarantine. No one must be permitted to escape."

"No one has," chuckled Kalin.

"And how long before we can inspect it?" asked Holtzmann impatiently.

"After six hours any free virus in the air will have died," replied Kumarov. "But we will go in after eight to be certain. The danger will only be the localised spread of the disease from infected subjects. Unless we are in the immediate proximity of a living, infected subject, we will be safe."

"You are sure?" asked Kalin.

Kumarov nodded. "The test on Cortez confirmed it."

"So we strike tomorrow, Kalin?" snapped Holtzmann.

Kalin glanced at him, his eyes burning. "Misha?" he turned to Shevchuk. "You are happy?"

The weapons engineer nodded. "We will need to check local conditions at Tumakoc," he said. "But if we fire before oh-eight-hundred we should avoid the wind."

"Good!" grunted Holtzmann, turning away.

"Yes, yes," stuttered Kumarov. "And now Sasha, we must return. I have to prepare—!"

"Wait!" snapped Kalin, annoyed at the haste and Holtzmann's pressure.

"Misha," he said again, with deliberate slowness. "There is no danger of our losing the missile? If you need more time, speak now."

Shevchuk stared at him. "With these birds," he shrugged, "there is always risk. But it is made no greater by our firing it tomorrow, Kalin."

The *danzan* leader kicked the ground. "So we will do it," he said curtly, and strode out, Holtzmann following.

"I will bring the warhead at oh-six-hundred," said Kumarov to the weapons engineer. "Enough time?"

"More than enough," replied Shevchuk, dropping his head and tapping at the launcher's computer terminal.

Kumarov stared at him, his hands trembling and sweating. "oh-six-hundred," he whispered, as if to himself. Then he too walked slowly out.

* * *

Kane came to with a throbbing headache and anxiety churning his stomach. He checked his ComMod and saw the acknowledgement from Elazar. Then he pulled on his army boots and walked gingerly into the corridor. His door was not guarded, but his eyes met those of the *danzan* soldier standing by the next doorway and he guessed it was the room in which the man Peterson had been put. In response to the soldier's curious glance, Kane made an eating motion, received a nod from the other and walked by.

He was midway through a bowl of scalding thick soup and a stale bread roll when Rodionov's bellow rang across the mess-hall. He strode towards Kane, showing no signs of fatigue or a hangover, with his air of authority fully restored.

"Eat up," he roared. "We must go and earn our money. Kalin is not happy with either of us today!"

Kane plunged his spoon into the soup. "What's the plan?" he asked through a mouthful.

"Special duties," laughed Rodionov. "You and I are going north, to a position near Tumakoc—an *arabski* city we have surrounded."

Kane shrugged and wolfed down the remainder of his meal, running over in his mind what he knew of the siege of Tumakoc.

"Got a cigarette?" he asked, feeling a sudden need for one. Rodionov pulled a packet from his tunic. Kane gagged as he drew back on the rank tobacco and the *danzan* commander laughed. "Not Marlboro, eh!"

Kane coughed again and shook his head, swathed with smoke.

"Get your kit," said Rodionov as they left the mess-hall. "Weapons issue is there." He pointed to a doorway in a small building abutting the Monastery's central courtyard. Kane nodded and jogged towards it.

Returning to his room he secreted the ComMod beneath his combat fatigues, now hung with hand grenades, and ammunition for his newly issued AK74. As he was leaving he heard shouting from the next room. His eyes met those of the *danzan* guard who shook his head and muttered something disgustedly in Russian. Peterson banged on his door; the guard rolled his eyes and endured the din stoically. Kane flashed him an understanding grin and left.

"Who is the other American?" he asked Rodionov an hour later as they sat in a *danzan* army transport, rumbling through the foothills of the Markesh mountains.

"A fool," laughed Rodionov.

Kane shrugged, returning his attention to the road ahead and the spectacularly bleak mountains rising before them.

"Bloody quiet," remarked Terry, looking up from his eyepiece. "Most genteel siege I've ever come across in this part of the world. Normally the bastards can't resist lobbing shells all day!"

"Yes," replied Lena. It had been a wasted trip to the lookout point over Tumakoc, but she knew Terry did not begrudge the time.

"I've done what I can with it," he said. "Without action it doesn't really say much."

"I know," replied Lena. "Got to keep busy though."

"Yeah," he smiled. "You know, if we're not doing anything tomorrow I might see if we can't get a bit closer—"

"Let's see what Massar says about that," said Lena. "Mahoney's told me about how close you like to get!"

"Bloody Jack," grumbled Terry good-naturedly as he packed his gear into the Jeep. "C'mon Abdur—what do you reckon? We find something a bit more taxing to do tomorrow?"

The *kadashi* boy nodded eagerly and Lena smiled. The pair had developed a telepathy that obviated the need for a common language.

"Wheels up!" shouted Terry from the Jeep and together they began the hour-long journey back to Irtos.

* * *

Through the long afternoon and well into the night, Kumarov toiled feverishly. The virus was reproducing itself at an astonishing rate in the lab's five fermentation vats, but not fast enough to deliver the promised amount by morning. Now he and his team were assembling a sixth vat and the requisite cultures to begin the reproduction process. From time to time Holtzmann wandered into the lab and watched the activity through the clear plastic. But he did not speak, nor did Kumarov.

The labour went on until well into the early hours of the morning, then, finally, face streaked with sweat behind the mask of his isolation suit—in which he had been encased for nearly eighteen hours—Kumarov knew he had succeeded. The missile's reentry vehicle was winched from the crate it had been transported in from Mount Barkusk, and Kumarov watched, anxiety clawing at his throat, the delicate process of transferring the virus to its pressurised container inside the warhead.

He breathed with relief as the job was completed. Then the warhead's exterior was carefully washed and wheeled out through the air-lock.

Kumarov had stripped out of his isolation suit and ordered his men to shut down the lab for the night when he saw Holtzmann, sitting silently in the far corner of the room, observing him.

"It is done?" his voice came from the depths of his throat.

"It is done," replied Kumarov. "Soon we shall know."

"Yes," breathed Holtzmann.

CHAPTER**TWENTY**

The sun had no idea what it was rising to, thought Holtzmann, as the truck carrying him and Kalin rumbled through the dawn towards Mount Barkusk. He could not deny or disguise his nervousness, nor could Kalin, seated next to him. Neither man spoke as Novominsk fell behind them and they drew nearer to the mountaintop missile launch site.

Alighting from the vehicle, both men hurried towards the entrance to the natural cave which had been converted first into a *danzan* fortress and now a heavily defended storage site for Kalin's prize. The three SS–25 mobile launchers were well inside the mountain; hulking shapes in the shadowy light. Well out of aerial view, they could be rolled into their launch positions in minutes.

"*Señor!* Sasha!" shouted Kumarov as they entered. They joined him at the first mobile launcher.

Shevchuk was checking the flight trajectory coordinates he had entered into the missile's stellar-inertial guidance system. "We are ready," he said finally.

Kalin nodded. "Begin," he ordered. The throb of the mobile launcher's tow vehicle reverberated through the cavern and the SS–25 inched its way out. When it was in position on the concrete-laid launch pad outside the cavern, hydraulics raised the giant missile to its firing attitude. It was the most powerful weapon of war ever created by the Soviet Union.

Holtzmann was spellbound as his eyes traced the missile's imagined trajectory in the sky. Shevchuk ran final checks, then, with a glance and a nod towards Kalin, he initiated the firing sequence. The men fell back and watched.

Seconds passed before the air was torn by a sudden crescendo of noise. For a moment, the SS–25 struggled with the shackles of the launcher, then it ripped free and began its ascent; at first impossibly slowly, like a child's toy, then with greater and greater acceleration. The gleaming missile became a dart in the sky, then a glittering pinprick trailing its white exhaust into the lower reaches of space.

"Magnificent!" breathed Holtzmann in a daze. Then the three walked to the armoured convoy that would transport them to Kalin's northern base outside Tumakoc.

Shevchuk ambled back into the control room inside the cavern. Two minutes later, the missile's guidance system flashed an order through its circuitry and, shedding its solid-fuel stage, the SS–25's warhead dipped its nose and began to plummet earthwards.

"Missile up!" shouted radar officer Marco Vasta aboard the *South Dakota*. His warning rang over the intercom and brought Elazar scurrying to the sub's control room. Captain Duchesne stared over the shoulder of his radar officer.

"Type?" he asked gruffly.

"SS–24 or 25," snapped back the answer. "I'd guess a 25. Incredibly steep trajectory, though." Vasta's eyes were glued to the console.

Seconds later, when the United Nations air-exclusion zone over northern Armestan was breached by the missile,

Chip MacKenzie picked up the shocked and confused reaction from UNHQ.

"Where is it?" asked Elazar breathlessly.

"Target?" broke in Captain Duchesne.

"Can't say yet," replied Vasta, doing some swift calculations. "Not going far—looks like Tumakoc in the northeast, it's the only city in the trajectory area."

Elazar felt suddenly faint and fell backwards.

"Colonel?" asked Captain Duchesne sharply.

"The missile—" breathed Elazar in sudden realisation. "Kumarov—the virus, they're using it. So soon!"

"Damn!" Duchesne swore, staring at the other, his face drawn.

"Comin' down," announced his radar officer.

"No," muttered Elazar.

Duchesne dropped his head.

"Twenty seconds till impact, sir!" said Vasta crisply.

"No!" Elazar repeated, closing his eyes and feeling time run out.

Lena stirred the ashes of the fire with a stick and sipped her tea as the first shockwave split the sky. She jerked her head up but could see only an exhaust trail, then the second *boom* cracked around her as, far above, the missile thundered towards Tumakoc.

"Could be UN fighters," said Sayeed Massar. "Sounds too big though." Together they stared curiously at the white line in the sky.

Thirty miles north, Kane swallowed the dregs of his coffee from a tin mug and shivered in the morning chill. He had not slept on the overnight journey to the *danzan* position outside Tumakoc, and he stared dully out at the desert landscape with disinterest.

"Here!" Rodionov flopped beside him and spread a map

on the ground. "Your unit will position itself on the main road," the big man's finger jabbed at the point.

Kane nodded. "What are the orders?"

"We are hitting Tumakoc with . . ." Rodionov paused and looked into Kane's eyes. "With what you saw at the Monastery. A biological weapon."

Kane's mind reeled. "Special duties, General?" he answered, struggling with his shock. "You didn't mention fucking *germ* warfare."

"I—" started Rodionov, then stopped and shrugged. "It is no matter. It is so. There *will* be an attempt by the *araby* to break out of Tumakoc. You are to stop them at all costs."

"How many men on our side?" Kane asked through clenched teeth.

"There will be nearly a thousand covering the road, as well as artillery in the hills," said Rodionov. "But yours will be the critical unit. Fifty men for close-quarter combat if required."

Kane now realised why he had been drafted into the fight so soon after his arrival in Novominsk. The frontline against any breakout from Tumakoc had to be expendable in case they themselves were infected.

"What's the risk to me and my men?"

Rodionov nodded, expecting the question. "A great risk," he said staring steadily at Kane, "if you allow the enemy to come too close—"

"Details, General!" Kane snapped. "How's it being dropped, what's the agent, how long before it disperses?"

Rodionov chuckled, then answered. "SS–25 missile from Novo. I do not know the agent, but you saw its effect. It will disappear from the air after six hours, but the population will still be infectious." He paused. "You are not afraid, are you, Colonel Hawke?"

Kane shook his head. "Just like to know what I'm up against, General." Then he stood, gripping the butt of his AK74 tightly.

Just then there was a single explosion in the sky above Tumakoc.

"It's blown," Marco Vasta reported crisply.

Captain Duchesne's eyes tore away from the console and onto Elazar. "Colonel?" he said glumly. "I think we should talk to Washington."

"Stone!" Susan Haywood shouted as she reached his temporary office at Langley. "The DDO's on line with the *South Dakota.*"

Stone propelled himself from his chair and started down the corridor towards Clark Mitford's office.

"It's Elazar," whispered Haywood as Stone sat next to her.

Mitford's answers were terse, the conversation lasting little more than three minutes. When it was over, the DDO's face was ashen. "A ballistic missile went up out of Novominsk," he said slowly. "SS–25 we think. Single RV. Target was Tumakoc in northern Armestan. Elazar is certain it was carrying whatever Kumarov has concocted. Wants me to get authority for a remote reconnaissance of the city. I think we should . . . we'll need it for proof if, and when, we go in."

"Jesus," gasped Stone, horrified.

His men were well-trained, Kane saw, and ferociously disciplined. Their convoy, flanked by four Jeeps, ground to a halt about seven miles from Tumakoc on its northern side. The main road to the city was pockmarked but still passable. Kane chose a site where high ground on either side allowed the maximum fire zone.

"Dig in," he ordered. The adjutant Rodionov had paired him with a translator and the men fanned out, setting machine-gun nests and artillery pieces into the slopes leading up from the road. Kane stared into the distance, to the skyline of Tumakoc, imagining what was happening inside the doomed city.

The men dug in expertly. Now it was simply a matter of waiting for their enemy to come to them, funnelled out of the city by their terror.

It appeared as a fine white mist; tiny aerosol particles teeming with Kumarov's virus, billions upon billions of ultra-microscopic organisms drifting over the city through air only slightly ruffled by wind. The cloud spread widely, over an area of perhaps ten square miles.

Millions of the droplets fell harmlessly upon the dry shattered stone, concrete and earth of the city. But of the kilogram of culture that had been contained in Kumarov's warhead, scarcely ten grams was required to infect every human inhabitant of Tumakoc; children playing in the rubble, women bartering food for the day, men carrying the night's dead towards the graveyard.

And so, as a droplet was caught in the gulp of a baby pausing for breath at its mother's breast, a million copies of Kumarov's virus were inhaled. And, as a young girl yawned in her bed in another part of the city, roused by her mother's call, the virus entered her. Two lovers rolled on stained sheets and gasped as ecstasy gripped their bodies. Tossed in their heaving lungs the virus began to replicate itself. A father staring out of his glassless window; a woman hurrying to the water pump; an old man drawing on a morning cigarette, one of the two he rationed for himself each day. The virus passed into them all and became a part of them; deadly, malignant, and rapacious.

In the hour it took the mist to disperse through the city, hundreds, then thousands, then tens of thousands of men, women, and children unknowingly invited death into their bodies along with the air they needed for life.

And for the first few hours life went on as usual. Life as

it was in a city under siege; a sullen, reluctant existence defined as life only by having death as its alternative.

The beginning of the end for Tumakoc was heralded by choking noises which erupted from the chest of two-year old Salim Abu-Toama, whose family lived in a small apartment in the city's north. Her father, Khaled, bent down to comfort her as she struggled to breathe. She coughed again and the virus entered his nasal passages and shortly afterwards, his red blood cells. Soon, reproducing at an exponential rate, the virus was streaming through his veins. Half an hour later, when his pregnant wife awoke, he spoke to her about their daughter's worsening affliction, and in so doing passed the virus on to her. And so it went in homes, hospitals, playgrounds and workplaces across the city. That Salim Abu-Toama would be the first to die meant nothing. The Holtzmann Plague had begun. Tumakoc was its first killing ground.

The day dragged on listlessly. Lena had spent the morning at the Red Crescent clinic, helping tend to the refugees. Now she was back at Irtos, at Massar's base. Massar was meeting other *kadashi* warlords in the camp's huge central tent.

Lena handed Terry a cup of tea as a Jeep tore up to the camp and two *kadashi* fighters leapt out shouting.

"Looks important," said Terry, as, still yelling, the two pushed their way past Massar's guard and disrupted his meeting.

"Yes," replied Lena. "I—" but she did not finish. The warlords, with Massar at their head, shot out.

"Get the camera," she called, jogging towards Massar.

"What's happened?" she asked him quickly.

"Tumakoc!" he answered through tight lips, staring straight ahead. "Something . . . we don't know. Sounds like a fuckin' gas attack by Kalin."

In the scant time it took Terry to organise his camera

gear, Massar's convoy had formed up and was driving out of the camp.

"Come on!" shouted Lena, pointing to their van.

"Hope it's been fuelled up," swore Terry as he started it. Lena clambered in, quickly followed by Abdur who had been alerted by the sudden activity. They roared off in pursuit of the convoy.

"Poison gas?" mused Lena.

"Saddam and the Kurds, remember?" replied Terry, his hands sweating on the wheel as he kept the van on the narrow rocky road.

She nodded, recalling the scenes of streets jammed with the swollen blue forms of people who had died where they stood; an obscene man-made Pompeii.

"There's no limit to what we'll fucking do to one another!" Terry echoed her thoughts.

Forty minutes later the convoy halted at the lookout point above Tumakoc. Both the city and its attackers were eerily quiet.

Massar strode towards their van. "We got a radio report," he said, his voice broken by grief or rage, Lena could not tell. "It's fuckin' hell!"

The authorisation for reconnaissance of Tumakoc took five hours to wring out of the White House but the instant it was received by the *South Dakota,* Captain Duchesne issued the order.

In one of the submarine's former nuclear missile tubes a computer-directed procedure began, arming what appeared to be a stocky missile. In fact, collapsed within its casing was one of the new generation Stealth Remote Reconnaissance Aircraft. Its makers—Lockheed—had given it the designation SRR–1 Skyeye, a pilotless aircraft with a wing-span of ten feet, constructed with the latest anti-radar technology. A miniature version of its larger brother, the F–117A stealth fighter—the Skyeye was designed to remain invisible to air-to-air and surface-to-air radar as it carried out its remote-controlled reconnaissance mission.

As soon as pre-launch checks were completed, the Skyeye missile was hurled from its tube by a burst of high-pressure air. Ninety feet from the surface its rocket booster ignited to propel the missile through the water and into the air. A hundred feet above the Black Sea the Skyeye shed its silver casing and—like a high-tech butterfly emerging from its cocoon—unfolded its wings, fired up its tiny jet and silently cruised towards the Armestan coast. The missile casing sank to one hundred feet and was kept at that depth by its buoyant collar as the *South Dakota* turned towards it for pick-up.

Elazar clenched his fists as he heard the dull sound of the Skyeye's launch.

The sleek spy-plane attained and maintained an altitude of thirty-five thousand feet for most of its half-hour journey north, dropping to five thousand feet as it closed on Tumakoc and began transmitting pictures through its on-board cameras. The first scenes that flickered onto the screen inside the *South Dakota*'s control room were impossibly wide, showing large expanses of the city but very little detail. Then the Skyeye neared the city's centre, its images tightening considerably as its cameras were remotely manoeuvred by the *South Dakota*'s SRR–1 'pilot,' Lieutenant Ned Beattie. The Skyeye required a specially trained controller like Beattie to guide it to its target, though it also used the latest NavTech inertial guidance system, which—in the unlikely event of contact being lost—would bring the aircraft back to its launch site. Now Lieutenant Beattie fine-tuned the three cameras on the SRR–1 to sharpen focus.

As the tiny reconnaissance craft throttled down and began a long slow circuit around Tumakoc, Elazar breathed deeply. On the video panel he could clearly see people filling the streets—every street in every section of the city. Some of the mobs were milling, some were gathered around a central point. Now Beattie switched to the camera set for extreme close-up, and they saw the first bodies. The Skyeye's camera-eye showed a street where the dead were laid out in rows, but in others they were piled atop each other. As Beattie became accustomed to the city's geography, the view from the Skyeye became more and more horrific, and the scale of the mass-murder more apparent.

"This can't be a biological agent," muttered Duchesne. "It's happening too quickly."

Elazar shook his head. "I do not know . . ." he shuddered.

"Keep recording, Captain?" asked Beattie.

"Yes," replied the submariner. "God knows what our masters will do with this."

"Proof beyond propaganda is what they wanted," growled Elazar. "They must act against Kalin now, there is no excuse."

"You and me both know there's always an excuse," said Duchesne with a hint of bitterness. "MacKenzie," he snapped without turning from the screen. "Any news?"

"Just babble mainly, sir!" responded the radio officer. Over the past hours he had been monitoring various HAM radio operators broadcasting from Tumakoc. "They're still calling it poison gas," he continued, his face mirroring the distress of those he was listening to. "Sounds like a real mess, sir."

"It is . . ." Elazar said softly as he watched the returning pictures from the Skyeye.

"Look!" exclaimed Duchesne, and Ned Beattie guided his remote charge along the main north-south road bisecting Tumakoc. It was jammed with people and vehicles; people being carried, dragged or dragging themselves out of their homes and into trucks, trailers and cars.

"Coming around," said Beattie and the scene momentarily disappeared. Then the Skyeye again dived towards the disorganised cavalcade.

"They're going to try to break through," Elazar said in a monotone.

"Poor devils," breathed Duchesne.

"Can we check Kalin's positions?" asked Elazar. Duchesne nodded to Beattie and the Skyeye wheeled into a wider circuit.

"They're locked in," grunted Elazar as he viewed the *danzan* forces ringing the city.

"Poor devils," Duchesne repeated.

Kane knew he had to get a message to Elazar, knew equally it was impossible. Bunkered in his command foxhole, with his adjutant next to him manning the radio, he was trapped by his assumed responsibility. He surveyed the horizon through his binoculars and grimaced. He knew that once the exodus from Tumakoc began, his force—and the other *danzan* units surrounding the city—would not be fighting, but massacring. He glanced at his watch.

"Gorda!" he hissed to his adjutant. "Any news from any other sectors?"

The young man shook his head. Kane sighed and settled back against the dirt.

They gathered outside the central mosque in Tumakoc, the *Al Um'far*. The crowd was growing by the second; the desperate and the dying; jostling, crushing, falling underfoot. Assisted by such concentration, the virus was spreading quickly to those not infected. It was also growing more virulent as it mutated within the bodies of its hosts before being passed on. As its genetic code became more focused on its task, so the virus was becoming deadlier—adapting to the local climatic conditions, blood groups of its hosts and air quality. Those infected with the new viral mutations were succumbing even more swiftly than those infected by the original culture from the missile. Children—who in Tumakoc were largely malnourished, their immune systems at a low ebb—were dying at a dramatic rate. The death toll was already in the thousands, but tens of thousands more were showing symptoms.

Now, inside and outside the *Al Um'far,* working side by side with the firebrands and agitators urging people to join the convoy north out of the city, Tumakoc's few doctors battled the virus at first without knowing what they were fighting. Their means were rudimentary, their supplies almost non-existent, as more and more people poured towards the *Al Um'far.* Every few minutes another victim went into respiratory distress, and another death wail added to the cacophony.

Dr. Ibrahim Abu-Ramadan looked around the throng with despair and horror. *"Go!"* he wanted to scream to them. *"Go with the convoy!"* He too felt the hysteria which gripped the mob, driven by the fear of what was happening and the greater fear that it would happen to them. Tumakoc's order, its social structure, the sense of community-in-adversity that had sustained it for months under the almost daily barrage of *danzan* guns, had broken down utterly within the space of hours. Dr. Abu-Ramadan felt a shuddering begin beneath his hands and looked down with pity as his patient of the moment—a boy no more than three years old—looked up at him in terror. Then the child joined his sisters and brothers who had already died.

Abu-Ramadan, a tall aristocratic *kadashi* man in his late fifties, ran a trembling hand through his shock of grey hair and felt as if he might faint with anguish and sorrow. Then he realised that he too was infected—the first prickling sensation that his body was not receiving enough oxygen. "Oh merciful Allah," he whispered in the din. How could the gas still be lingering? he wondered, but he would be dead before he knew the answer, the virus seeking out his body's disk-shaped red blood cells, erythrocytes, to transform into metabolic extensions of itself. His lungs would soon become useless balloons, filling and re-filling but with no effect, the air exhaled exactly as it had been inhaled, the faculty of respiration irretrievably lost as more and more erythrocytes were altered by the virus. His fear was sliced through by the clashing sound of vehicles starting up to join the convoy. In a split-second he decided to join the mob and escape Tumakoc, whatever the cost. He did not understand what had happened to his city, and for a man such as himself that was more terrifying than the thought of death in the face of *danzan* guns. He could feel the icy finger of *Shaitan* crooked around his heart and his soul reached out for Allah as he slung himself aboard the last of the trucks revving away from the *Al Um'far*.

"Allah be merciful," he crouched in the jolting truck, praying, head gripped in his hands. He did not notice when they left the outskirts of the city and passed into no-man's-land.

"We'll go down," swore Massar, tearing the binoculars from his eyes. "We fuckin' have to!" From the field radio beside him came jabbering noises of chaos and panic. When the voices were coherent they spoke only of poison gas and mass death. Massar had heard enough; enough to know that whatever was going on in Tumakoc, it was facing its worst hour.

He gave the signal and his *kadashi* force began along the treacherous cliff-top until the sheer drop eased. Then they turned onto a precipitous stony track which zig-zagged three thousand feet down to the desert floor.

"Jesus Christ," muttered Terry, gripping the steering wheel of their van grimly. Lena was silent, as was Abdur, their eyes flared with fear, both at the descent and what lay at the bottom.

"Steady, steady!" muttered the Australian to himself as the van skidded dangerously close to the edge. Rocks bounced wildly down the slope.

"Bloody hell," he gasped as the tyres regained their purchase on the road. "This is fucking madness!"

"Yes," whispered Lena. Then there was a tremendous thump and the van came to a sudden halt.

"Great!" shouted Terry in disgust, leaping out to inspect the damage. "Rock's gone through the fucking sump!" Helplessly they watched the rest of the convoy disappear ahead of them, Lena kicking the ground in frustration.

"Oh well," muttered Terry, pointing down towards Tumakoc. "At least we're closer than we were."

"Colonel!" exclaimed Kane's adjutant, ripping off his headphones. "They are coming, the *araby*!"

Kane looked at him for a second. "How many?"

The *danzan* soldier spoke crisply into the radio. "Two or three thousand," he reported seconds later. "They are in trucks and civilian vehicles. Only two tanks escorting."

Kane looked away, revolted by what he had to do. "Battle positions," he grunted. "Fire at will." There were no further commands he could, or needed to, issue in such a cruel and single-minded venture. It would only be a question of his side having enough bullets and shells to do the job. He scrambled to the top of his foxhole and took up a firing position. On either side of him, *danzan* soldiers smiled, fingers gripping triggers expectantly. *This was a good war for men who liked to kill,* Kane thought disgustedly. Then the first faint rumble came from the city outskirts and suddenly the air around him filled with gunfire.

"Eight hours," muttered Kumarov, pacing inside the tent in a state of high anxiety.

"Patience," said Kalin. Of the three, he was the most at ease.

Holtzmann had spoken little since their arrival at Kalin's northern base, twenty miles south of Tumakoc, and then only to ask what could not yet be answered: How successful had the virus been?

"You realise, Zhora," Kalin went on, "your weapon *must* have worked, otherwise the *araby* would not be fool enough to risk this breakout."

"Nevertheless—" began Kumarov in response, but he was interrupted by the sudden crackle of the radio. It was Rodionov again.

"Revised estimate for main *arabski* group is five thousand," he informed them calmly. "Well within our planning. Smaller groups have been stopped by artillery before clearing the city. It will take an hour or two to repulse the main group. Radio traffic we are monitoring here indicates widespread confusion in the city and massive casualties."

The transmission ended and Kumarov looked up. "We should go—" he began.

"Patience, *bratishka*," Kalin laughed again. "It is the first lesson of command that one always know the outcome of the battle before one takes the field."

At this even Holtzmann snorted with mirth.

"Assuming all is well with Tumakoc," he said, "I will require my missile to be fired within forty-eight hours, understood, Kalin?"

The *danzan* leader nodded. He was feeling expansive— certain that the strike on Tumakoc had been a success. Like Holtzmann, he now wanted to move quickly, before the international community realised what had happened. Before his few allies, like Russia's President Firyubin, were forced to act.

"*Señor.*" He smiled. "If my brother can oblige, I would hope to achieve our final aim even earlier than forty-eight hours. Perhaps even tomorrow. I have political considerations that will not be served by delay."

Holtzmann nodded gratefully but did not answer, gripping his hands tightly with the force of his welling anticipation.

* * *

"My God," croaked Lena. "They're driving straight into the guns!"

"We have to get this," said Terry, racing to the van. "C'mon, we'll head down on foot."

They swiftly split up a basic camera kit and set off, Abdur proving an expert guide down the remaining portion of the cliff. They reached its base in time to see the first vehicles fleeing Tumakoc chewn up by the *danzan* guns.

"What a bloodbath," whispered Terry, as he carefully focused his camera and began shooting. Abdur gestured that he was going to check the track ahead.

"Fine mate," muttered the Australian. "I'll use the camera-mike."

Lena stared in silence for several minutes as the carnage continued in earnest. "What are they running from?" she wondered aloud.

Suddenly there was a rustle and Abdur returned.

"We can get closer," he whispered in hurried Russian. "It is safe—" Lena translated for Terry.

"If it was a gas attack," said Lena as they moved forward again, "we *have* to get the proof!"

"Just how fucking close are you planning to go?" asked Terry as a low branch slapped his face. "Let's keep our heads on."

Unable to answer because she did not know the limits of her fear, Lena gritted her teeth and pushed on in the stooping jog they had instinctively adopted.

Inside the *South Dakota* all eyes were fixed to the video panel with horrified fascination as the Skyeye beamed back the slaughter of those pouring from the city in the doomed convoy. The pictures it had already recorded would be ample to convince Washington and the UN that Kalin was using a weapon of mass-destruction. The current atrocity would give them even greater reason to act, thought Elazar.

Tumakoc was dying, its blood the haphazard caravan of trucks and other vehicles pouring north into the ambush Kalin had set. Elazar shook his head, unable to accept what he was witnessing. Unable to accept that he could do nothing about it.

"Sons of bitches!" growled Duchesne behind him. The warning light showed on the Skyeye screen.

"Bring it in," he ordered reluctantly.

"Washington must surely act," Elazar muttered as the picture faded. He was rocking backwards and forwards on the balls of his feet. "Surely!"

CHAPTER**TWENTY-ONE**

Present in the Oval Office was the same group as had gathered before: the President; National Security Adviser, Myron Berkeley; CIA Director, James Martin; Secretary of State, Matthew Porter; and Chairman of the Joint Chiefs of Staff, General Mark Westaway. Though the Skyeye tape, satellited directly from the *South Dakota,* was gruesomely hypnotic, both Stone and Clark Mitford kept an eye on the faces of the men who comprised the National Security Council.

As the videotape ended, the President turned in his chair. "What do you say, Myron?" he asked soberly, obviously deeply shocked.

Berkeley held his counsel for a moment. Then, with a glance towards Martin and Porter, he began. "Mr. President," he said, "this is a grave matter, and yet I see a danger in making our decision purely on the basis of these pictures—"

"And the radio reports from Tumakoc!" Stone cut in.

"Yes, yes," Berkeley said. "Nevertheless, we must know what we are dealing with here. We have to formulate a course of action in tandem with the Russians, we cannot leave them out in the cold."

Mitford coughed. "I have to state quite clearly Mr Berkeley, that based on our available knowledge, we do not have the luxury of time at our disposal. Our satellite information suggests only one or two locations where Kalin's remaining missiles could be—"

"Let the man finish, Mitford," growled James Martin.

The CIA director nodded towards Berkeley, who glared at Mitford and continued. "Mr. President, the international implications of a US pre-emptive strike against Kalin are massive," he paused. "We need time to seek a UN and NATO response and while we are doing that, this video must not be released to the media—or the Israelis—other than those on the *South Dakota*."

"All the same, Myron," drawled the President, "Kalin's shown he can do it and is prepared to do it, and I can't help but feel that we should plaster him."

Berkeley nodded as if in agreement. "We could," he stared back, then turned towards Porter. "Matthew, what do you think? Particularly about the Russian response?"

The Secretary of State straightened in his chair and coughed. "We would put Firyubin in an impossible position, Mr. President," he said, sounding as if the words had been written for him.

Stone hissed. "I think we're more goddamn afraid of Russian now than—"

"Enough Stone!" snapped General Westaway. "I will have attack plans drawn up for Kalin's possible missile sites in Novominsk, Mr. President. An air-strike, pending UN Security Council approval, how does that sound?"

"Better, General," said Kirkland. "Any objections, Myron?"

The National Security Adviser shook his head. "Could I also suggest, Mr. President," he said, "that given the broadening implications of this thing, we also hold back the Israelis on the *South Dakota*. We don't want to show our hand to Kalin, and this is no longer just a manhunt."

"It never was!" growled Stone.

"That would be—" began Mitford.

"Militarily correct!" Westaway interrupted.

Stone looked at him in shock. "God damn! I don't believe I'm hearing you!" he said. "Chances are that Holtzmann's going to do to Jerusalem or Tel Aviv what he did to Tumakoc and not only is our response limited to asking the UN for help, but we're going to stop an operation we have already approved and set in place—?"

"Approval is withdrawn until further notice," snapped Kirkland, standing abruptly and being joined by everyone except Stone and Mitford. They had walked into the room expecting to leave it with a full-scale commitment to end the threat posed by Kalin and his biological weapon, and had instead seen their operation put on ice.

"What about Kane?" spluttered Stone.

"As I said, he's deniable," retorted Berkeley angrily.

Kirkland strode over to Stone. "This won't take long, General," he said in an undertone. "I want to see the end of Kalin and his nasty little weapon just as much as you do, but I have to take everything into consideration. The days of the US leaping onto a white charger like the Lone Ranger are over. Sometimes you men have trouble coming to terms with that!"

He spun away and Stone strode out angrily with Mitford. In the limo back to Langley he sat stock-still, his face drawn tight by fury.

"You going to tell Elazar, or will I?" Mitford asked eventually, but Stone couldn't even muster a snort of disgust, so profoundly was he in its grip.

"Sons-of-bitches! *Sons-of-fucking-bitches!*" Elazar stormed out of the control room when he heard the NSC decision.

Finally—burnt out by its own intensity—his tirade waned and he collapsed despondently onto his narrow bunk. The scenes from Tumakoc, scenes the men who had just handcuffed his operation had also seen, flashed in his mind.

"How could you?" he whispered to the cold steel ceiling of his cabin.

Within the writhing mass of humanity, Dr. Abu-Ramadan looked wildly around. The air was filled with smoke, the stench of burning flesh and the shrieks of the dying. Trucks were exploding and yet more came on, roaring up and around him. Next to him, also sheltering behind the smouldering ruin of their vehicle, was a young woman, catatonic with fear. He looked at her and her eyes responded. There was nothing left. The air was riddled with automatic fire as he grasped her hand and ran away from the hell into salvation and paradise. Hand in hand they burst from the smoke and as they faced the guns their chests swelled, and they reached out towards their murderers.

"*Allah akbar!*" Abu-Ramadan screamed and heard his companion do likewise.

Kane watched through narrowed eyes as the pair ran out of the fire zone. Their clothes were ablaze, their hands outstretched. Next to him the machine-gun chattered, swinging around to pick them off. Then he fired, a second late, a foot high. Never in his life had he hated Man as badly as he did those surrounding him—and those who were their masters.

The chaotic mass of vehicles and humanity were herded by the guns like a mob of cattle. A few shots emanated from the *kadashi* side but they were not a fighting force. That they had advanced at all towards the *danzan* frontline was testament only to the momentum of the convoy backed up behind them. Vehicles ploughed into those in front, or careered around them, trying to run the gauntlet of the *danzan* guns. None made it. Soon, spreading out from the road was almost half a mile of destroyed vehicles and their occupants cowering behind, or running out into premeditated death. Yet still the convoy crushed forwards.

For an hour it went on and the killing was relentless. Then, finally, during a lull in the artillery and machine-gun fire there was silence from the *kadashi* side. All were either dead or had fled back into the city they had risked their lives trying to escape. Through his binoculars Kane saw a long line of *kadashi* survivors marching through no-man's-land. His eyes watered with pity.

Rodionov strode up. "Well done, Hawke!" he beamed, slapping Kane's shoulder and those of the men around him. "None of the *araby* escaped. It is good!"

Kane nodded numbly, his face streaked with grime and his hands aching from firing his weapon. He doubted he had hit any of the enemy but it gave him little solace.

"What now?" he grunted.

"We wait," said Rodionov, checking his watch. "Kalin is coming."

Kane's eyes glinted. "Cigarette?"

"Bastards," growled Terry as his eye finally lifted from the camera. "Fucking animals!"

Abdur too, shook with fear and anger as he continued to hold the microphone towards the ebbing noises of the massacre below.

"Get this stand-up," muttered Lena. Moving forwards, she crouched in front of the camera and began to speak.

"We are on the hills overlooking the city of Tumakoc, Armestan, from which this morning came reports of a poison gas attack by forces under the command of rebel president Kalin. So far we have been unable to get close enough to the city to confirm that, but radio operators in contact with the ethnic Armestani forces outside Tumakoc report deaths numbering in the thousands and also said that some inhabitants of the city had heard an explosion, possibly a bomb or missile, at around 8:00 A.M. We have just seen what appeared to be an attempt by around five thousand of Tumakoc's inhabitants to escape the city. Their convoy was attacked and wiped out by Kalin's forces. There is only one word to describe what is going on here and that word is 'unspeakable.' If the West can see the horror we have just witnessed and continue to witness, it must surely act. We are going to try to get closer to Tumakoc and report further from there . . . Galena Chagall, WorldNet."

"We're going to try to get closer?" echoed Terry in disbelief. "Lena?"

She stared at him. "We have to try."

"You're stark raving fucking mad," he gasped. "And I thought I was supposed to be the lunatic!"

The distant dust of Sayeed Massar's column was just visible to the north-west of the city, skirting the *danzan* line.

"We'll go around," said Lena. "Follow them."

"That's ten miles at least," Terry replied. "And we're walking—"

"Any better suggestion?" she interrupted.

"Yeah," he replied. "Go back!"

"And do what?" she said, her temper suddenly flaring. "Wait for more nickel and dime action? Something *safer*? We've got to find out if this was a gas attack, Terry, and if it was—"

"Look, Lena," he said bluntly, holding her by the shoulders. "We're both fucking scared, right?"

Lena nodded, anger in her eyes.

"And right now we've got enough material to send back, somehow, to New York, right?" he continued.

Lena nodded again.

"If we head into it," Terry finished, "we could come back with nothing, zip, zero! And I mean it!"

"Terry," Lena exhaled. "We have to—"

"Fuck it," hissed Terry. He knew she was right. "Okay,"

he said finally. "I'll give it a try. But remember, Lena, I didn't even do *basic* training."

"Thanks, Terry," she grinned brokenly. "We'll be okay . . ." her voice trailed off unsurely.

"What about the little bloke?" asked Terry.

Lena swiftly explained to Abdur and entreated him to stay behind. "After that?" he said incredulously, gesturing towards Tumakoc.

Lena looked into his young-old eyes and understood. "Come then," she said, and wearily the threesome began to pick their way over the rocks, working their way north along the slopes surrounding the city, trying to control their fear.

Sayeed Massar let the binoculars fall. The *danzan* soldiers below had their guns aimed at Tumakoc's West Gate. With grim resolution, he signalled to his men and they moved forward silently. Massar had chosen his entry point well. He looked behind, staring into the low sun, then once more at the city where he'd been born, where his family still was. *I am coming,* he swore. Then he dropped his hand.

They scrambled down the slope with no more noise than the wind and swiftly overran the *danzan* position. The only threat, a heavy machine-gun, was used too late. By the time it was swung around, Massar's men were well into butchering their enemy. Thirty *danzany* died, versus two of Massar's men. The engines of the convoy started up again with a brutal roar. The *kadashi* fighters had opened a chink in the siege-line, and through it they now poured, men hanging from vehicles, firing their guns at an enemy real and imagined during their mad dash to the city.

Then as they passed beneath Tumakoc's ancient stone gate, there was, all too briefly, the joy of sanctuary; the pleasure of not having died, not yet anyway.

"*Keff!*" Massar's booming command halted the convoy. He leapt down from the cabin of the truck and stared ahead into the eerie desolation. Something—an instinct born of having witnessed Kalin's methods of war—jagged inside him. He broke his squadron into two groups; one to stay at the West Gate, the other to proceed with him into the city proper. With fear gnawing at his guts he gave the order to move ahead.

For half a mile there was nothing, no sign of life, or death. Then there was the realisation of what they had come to.

They had broken into Hell.

It was all about them; in the streets, in the squares, and the rubble-strewn remnants of buildings. Omnipresent death.

In shock, Massar slowed the convoy and led a foot patrol in advance of it. His boots struck the cobbled streets as he advanced towards a man attempting to organise a small group of nurses on the fringes of one of the larger groups of victims.

"What's happened?" Massar asked. "Are you a doctor?"

"Dr. Ali Mustapha," the man said, barely stopping. "And you?"

"Sayeed Massar," he replied.

At this the doctor turned around. "Massar? Have you come with many? Can you get us out?"

Massar shook his head sadly. "No, we're as trapped as you. But what's happened here?"

"I do not know," Mustapha said. "At first I believed it to be gas, but now?" he shook his head in confusion. "The deaths go on, and it is more a sickness that is killing them. Some show only the symptoms for a matter of minutes, then they die, but others? No one will remain inside, they think whatever it is has gone into the buildings and that is why it is still killing. But I do not know."

He pointed towards an old woman lying on the ground, choking.

"She has been like that for three hours," he explained.

"But some who seem healthy, they will—" He dropped his head. "So what can you do?" he asked.

"I'm not sure," stumbled Massar. "Are there any authorities left?"

"If there are," replied the doctor, "they will be at the *Al Um'far.*"

Massar grasped his shoulder "Allah be with you," he said and turned to leave, picking his way past the dying mass of humanity stretched across the road.

He signalled his men to proceed, which they did with gut-wrenching slowness, past streets that were covered with the dying and the dead. In the mile drive to the central square and the *Al Um'far,* Massar saw thousands of casualties. But it was nothing next to the sight which met him and his men in what had, in peaceful times, been called The Square of God. Massar stared disbelievingly. Now it had been given over to Satan.

Unable to control himself, he retched violently over the side of his truck.

It was early evening as Kalin's heavily armed convoy rolled up to Rodionov's field HQ just outside Tumakoc.

"Boris Nikolaevich!" the *danzan* leader shouted as he alighted, followed by Holtzmann and Kumarov.

Rodionov saluted and stepped forward. "A total success, Kalin!" he said boastfully. "The enemy has been kept in. Our line was breached only once."

"Breached?" Kumarov's voice was shrill with worry.

"Do not be worried," soothed Rodionov, his eyes glinting. "The *araby* were incoming, not outgoing!" He laughed, and as the others grasped his meaning so did they.

"Nevertheless," ordered Kalin. "Ensure we have men in position to deal with attack from any other force that may try to relieve the city."

"It is done," reported Rodionov. "I have Colonel Volka in

the south, and the American, Hawke, on the northern perimeter."

"How did he perform?" asked Kalin curiously, unable to stop himself glancing wickedly at Holtzmann.

"Well, Kalin!" replied Rodionov briskly. "He is a warrior, without doubt."

"When can we inspect the city?" Holtzmann barked.

Rodionov looked at Kalin. "I will send a unit under Hawke to clear the way, we will follow an hour later. I do not expect any resistance, but we must be sure. And what of the virus—?"

"It will be safe," interrupted Kumarov. "Your men must avoid coming in direct proximity with any of the city's inhabitants, local infection is still possible."

"How close?" asked Rodionov dubiously.

"Close enough to smell their breath, General," smirked Kumarov.

Rodionov stared at him for a second, his deep-set eyes flashing angrily. "Very well, *comrade-doctor,*" he growled. "I will order our advance party into the city." He snatched his walkie-talkie from his belt.

"Hawke, form up," he snapped. "Mark your route carefully and have it report back at regular intervals. We will be coming in behind you."

"Roger," came the terse reply. "Moving out."

A low rumble began in the distance.

"So Kumarov," exclaimed Holtzmann suddenly. "Are you ready to see what you have done?"

Kumarov looked at him. "Yes, *Señor.*"

"Look!" Lena pointed to the armoured column moving out from the *danzan* lines.

"Going in for the kill," remarked Terry. "Lena, we—!" He was interrupted by Abdur's return.

"There is a way into the city," the boy gasped in Russian.

"There is a *danzan* position down the hill but they are all dead. I think Sayeed Massar—"

Lena nodded quickly. "No sign of any others?"

Abdur shook his head. "It is in a gully, I could not see. We must be careful."

Lena translated for Terry, who rolled his eyes to the sky. "Remind me," he whispered as they began to crawl forward on their stomachs, "to get myself off Jack Mahoney's list—" but his voice shook and his words were formed in a mouth dry with fear.

Slithering across the ground, Lena felt a dreadful mix of apprehension and responsibility. They were inviting death, and if Terry and Abdur were killed it would be squarely her fault. But something greater than fear was driving her, something she could not have described even if she had tried. Lena watched Abdur's back, ready to pull up the instant he did. To her it seemed they were making a frightful din, until the abrupt sound of a bird cawing nearby showed her what noise really was.

They passed the *danzan* machine-gun nest that Massar and his men had overrun. Lena gasped. The bodies were not scattered as they should have been in the aftermath of battle, but neatly stacked. She wanted to warn Abdur but he was too far ahead. She froze and felt Terry bump into her. His eyes followed her finger to the bodies. His jaw tightened as he saw them. Lena nodded ahead—turning back could be as dangerous as continuing—and began to drag herself forwards again, heart thumping, eyes darting frantically, sweeping the ground for any sign of Kalin's men. Now they were beyond the gully; before them lay a vast open area of scree, dotted with occasional mud brick huts, long deserted. Tumakoc was still over five miles away. They paused in a small clump of scrubby bushes.

"Don't seem to be any of them out there," Lena mouthed into Terry's ear. He shook his head. Abdur motioned for them to go on, but Lena held up her hand. Looking around she pointed to one of the mud-brick shelters about two hundred yards from their position. Terry and Abdur nodded, and they scampered out into the clear ground.

With a bag of batteries and videotapes bumping against her back, Lena made no attempt to stay low. There was no cover, so speed was their only choice. Her breath came in sharp gulps and she ignored the pain of her feet striking rocks as they propelled her towards their target. They had covered half the distance to the hut when the shots rang out.

"Oh shit!" she heard Terry cry out, and turning, saw him stumble, a red stain billowing out from his shoulder.

"Terry!" she screamed and raced to him just ahead of Abdur. The boy took the camera. Lena grasped Terry under his arms and held him tightly as they lurched frantically towards the hut. The shots became a fusillade now, ricocheting around them, zinging off stones. *"Ah!"* Lena felt a white-hot pain in her leg but did not look down. Her eyes screwed up as she saw Abdur reach the hut.

"Come on!" she shouted, as much to herself as Terry and in a final anguished burst they scrabbled across the broken earth exploding with the impact of bullets and dived towards the hut. Abdur ducked out and helped them inside to safety. For several minutes Lena could not talk, her body pumped with the rhythm of her racing heart. The bullets did not let up.

"Terry?" she gasped, rolling over in the dirt. He was panting, his face pinched with pain. His shirt was torn around the wound, which was high in his shoulder. The bullet's exit had punctured his upper arm, but cleanly.

"It's gone through," muttered Lena.

"Don't think anything's broken," he grunted with pain. "Just sore. But I think we've had it anyway."

Lena turned from him and quickly checked her own injury. It was a flesh wound, already congealing. She pushed her eye to a crack in the wall. They'd been lucky, the *danzan* soldiers were just above the position where their dead comrades lay, standing and pointing towards them. Lena quickly surveyed the distance they had to cover to reach Tumakoc then looked back at the soldiers. A small squad was now crawling towards the hut, rifles thrust in front of them.

"Abdur!" she hissed, flicking her head towards the city. He nodded.

"Terry!" she said urgently. "They're coming, we've got to keep going. We'll take all the gear, how are you?"

"Fine," he lied.

"Go Abdur!" she ordered and the boy sped off across the wasteland towards the next hut, about five hundred yards away. "Go Terry!" she pushed him and he followed Abdur, stumbling with pain. She raced to join him, wrapping her arm around him.

"C'mon Terry!" she pleaded, as again the air was split by gunfire. Then they were running and shouting with fear. Lena cried out wildly and her heart pounded with a greater ferocity than it seemed her body could bear. She dug her shoulder into Terry and virtually lifted him from the ground as she ploughed on through air thick with the sounds of her coming death. She was blind with fear and exhaustion, and it was only with Abdur's reappearance—again helping her with Terry over the final yards and into the hut—that she knew she had cheated the *danzan* bullets. She threw herself to the earth and grasped clods of it in her hands.

"Oh God," she repeated again and again, tears flowing freely down her cheeks.

"Lena," Abdur prodded her. She nodded and pulled herself slowly to her feet. Terry winced as together they supported him and set off to the next distant hut. Again the bullets chased them, and though she knew they must be almost out of range, the terror of their pursuit was no less real.

Finally, about two-thirds of the way across the no-man's-

land to Tumakoc they felt secure enough to rest, their bodies burning with fatigue and the pain of their injuries.
Abdur had now been winged by a shot too, but Terry's
wound was by far the most serious. Lena set to work to
staunch the blood still pumping from his shoulder, bandag-
ing it tightly with cloth torn from his shirt.

"Okay?" she asked, pushing his hair from his face and
staring at him.

"In point of fact I'm fucked," he said brokenly. "But no
point in discussing that here."

"Terry, I'm sorry—" she began.

"We'll be right," he grunted, closing his eyes. Then, a few
minutes later, he pushed himself up.

"It's not going to get any better, I guess," he sighed and,
less urgently now, they walked the remaining distance to
the city. Lena wondered what they would see, finding
strange comfort in the thought that there was at least a little
light left in the day to shoot by.

Kane surveyed the block ahead as he advanced slowly with
his *danzan* unit. Each step brought the promise of the crack
of a sniper's rifle or the thud of a mortar shell.

But none came, and they moved carefully to the next
block. They were nearly through the outskirts of Tumakoc.
His men spread out at each building, some checking inside,
others covering them. Most of the buildings had been recently deserted, and it was not until they were half a mile
into the city that they saw the first of the victims. A shout
came from his unit's forward scout.

"Araby!"

The unit instinctively flattened themselves against walls
and in doorways, then crept ahead cautiously. Kane joined
the scout behind a pile of rubble and scoured the street
with his eyes. At the far end there was what, at first glance,
appeared to be three large groups of people seated in a

semi-circle. Kane lifted the binoculars, knowing what he would see.

"Dead," he grunted the confirmation to his adjutant. Kane felt nauseous as he walked on. Stricken families who had come out to the streets hoping the air would cleanse them littered the ground. In the first group, all but an old woman were dead, draped over one another in the order in which they had succumbed to the disease. The old woman sat cross-legged, looking at what must have been her entire family, singing in an undertone punctuated by a gasping, wheezing cough. She looked blankly at the approaching troops and kept up her singing. She had no fear left, and made no protest as one of Kane's men raised his rifle and shot her through the head.

"No!" shouted Kane, his voice echoing down the desolate street. "They want to see exactly what has happened." His adjutant translated Rodionov's order. The *danzan* fighter shrugged, lowered his gun and continued marching slowly forwards. The second and third groups in the street were all dead.

The clusters of bodies became more commonplace, crammed outside the huge apartment blocks which ringed the city. They did not find anyone else left alive, and Kane guessed that those still able had sought help, or died elsewhere. There was a rumble of vehicles ahead and he watched as, in the distance, two trucks lurched towards the centre of town. He shuddered to think what lay further into the city. He looked around. He had only two hundred men, and even though they were supported by five tanks, he decided they had gone far enough for now. He gestured for the radio and called Rodionov.

"Do you want us to take this city or do you just want to see what has happened?" he asked.

"How far in are you?" replied Rodionov.

"About two miles," replied Kane. "All's quiet but I'd say

there's action ahead. If you want us to go any further we'll need reinforcements."

There was a pause, then Rodionov came back on.

"The dead, how effective was the weapon?"

"Almost a hundred percent as far as we've seen," reported Kane.

Another pause, then—"Stay where you are," said Rodionov. "We will be joining you."

"Roger," Kane clicked off the radio and handed it to the adjutant. "Secure the area. Kalin is coming."

He forced his eyes away from the sight of a young girl's body lying on the road ahead. She was wearing a pink dress that lay crumpled in perfect symmetry around her. Her eyes were glassy and bulging, her frozen expression one of astonishment. Death had found her before she had time to live and something in Kane's heart tightened a notch or two.

Massar was doing what he could but the task was worse than hopeless. His men were keeping the roads clear to and from the square outside the *Al Um'far* so that those piling in for the little help available did not die in the crush. His trucks ferried bodies from the area to outlying parts of the city, but there was no question of burial; the casualties were unbelievable. As he walked among the melee, Massar saw those tending to the victims become victims themselves; some clutching their throats and dying within minutes, others collapsing to the ground and writhing for much longer as they were strangled from within.

Dr. Ali Mustapha joined him. "This is not consistent with a poison gas. Not at all. This is biological—bacterial or viral!"

"You're sure?" asked Massar abruptly.

"Never completely sure of anything!" Mustapha's eyes drilled into him. "But it has all the signs of being an outbreak of some sort, the symptoms are not those of a poison."

"Kalin attacked us with a disease?" Massar shook his head in horror and disbelief.

"Germ warfare," said the doctor matter-of-factly.

"Anything—?" began Massar, crushed by the enormity of it.

"I've been trying!" snapped the doctor. "Antibiotics are having no effect at all. Nothing else we can do except treat the symptoms, and they don't last long. We must try to quarantine the infected, but I don't think there's much hope without outside help. Excuse me—" The doctor moved briskly away through the crowd, and Sayeed Massar asked himself the same dreadful question that was being asked by every living inhabitant of Tumakoc.

Numbly he called for his field radio.

"West Gate," came the crackling response.

They were on the western side of the city, Lena realised. The sun was dipping low as they passed beneath a stone gate destroyed by the civil war.

"*Mahallak Keff!*" the call rang out across the rubble-strewn street ahead. Lena froze.

"Sayeed Massar?" she shouted back.

A tall thin *kadashi* fighter appeared from behind a ruined building. As he came closer, Lena recognised him as one of the warlords who had been at Irtos.

"Where is Sayeed?" she asked in Russian. The man gestured towards the centre of the city. Lena nodded.

"He says Kalin has attacked with a disease, not gas," said the *kadashi* chieftain.

"Disease?" Lena looked blankly at him for a moment, her mind grinding slowly.

"What?" asked Terry weakly.

"Kalin's used a biological weapon," she replied grimly.

"So what do we—?" began Terry.

"Softly softly, Terry," she said. "Cover our faces and stay clear of the living."

Her cameraman nodded, his face etched with the pain of his injury.

"We go," she said to the *kadashi* commander. He shrugged. "And you?" asked Lena.

"We wait for Massar," he replied and turned away to rejoin his men.

"C'mon," muttered Lena. They tore strips of cloth from their clothes and wrapped them around their faces. Then they started forward.

Like Massar before them, they were not long in the city before the magnitude of the death toll became obvious. Jagged by the pain of his wound, Terry perched his camera awkwardly on his left shoulder. A deep ache was spreading out from his right side, but the occasional tremble in his shots was due to what was unfolding as he walked the streets of Tumakoc. In a life which had included most warzones of the late twentieth century, he had never seen anything as horrible.

Ahead of him, Lena stumbled forwards. She was in a daze, her soul throbbing with disbelief as she gazed around and ahead. No one was alive. From the hands of one man she pulled a scrap of paper. On it he had written four words in Russian: "It was the *danzany*." A pathetic last whisper he had hoped would travel to the rest of the world.

"What have they done?" her cry was muffled by cloth.

Not a murmur broke the deathly stillness.

Street after street, block after block, building after building. They came across a small square in which the victims numbered over a thousand. Terry raised his camera for the shot but the effort was too great. Lena heard him shout and swung around in time to see Abdur juggling the camera and the Australian sprawled on the ground. She ran across to him, leaping over the bodies in her way.

"Terry!" she knelt beside him. His wound had begun to bleed again, and he looked shocking.

He tried to speak. "Got to pull the plug, Lena," he muttered through his mask. "I've had it."

She nodded, and opened his shirt to re-bandage the wound.

"We've got enough," he continued through chattering teeth. "I've never seen anything . . ."

"No," replied Lena in a low voice.

He sat up slowly and looked around. "We've got to get away."

"Abdur!" she called softly and the boy joined them, his face torn by confusion. Then, suddenly, the roar of an engine shattered the brooding twilight.

Though Massar had been infected less than two hours, already the effort of sucking air into his lungs was becoming noticeable as the pestilence bloomed within him.

"Muhammad," he said softly to his closest lieutenant, Muhammad Nusur. "I have the fuckin' illness."

His comrade's eyes flared, shot through with foreboding. "Are we . . . ?" he asked, gazing with horror at the endless stream of bodies being moved out of the square.

"Maybe . . . maybe not," Massar whispered. Both men were passing through dimensions of fear and their words were loaded.

"My family," Massar said in a stronger voice. "My family is among them somewhere." He gestured at the corpses littered about, awaiting collection, his mind clashing. "The *danzany* surround us," he barked. His eyes flashed rebelliously against a quiet death. "What else is there to do but die for Allah?" He smiled inside at the thought of how much his father would have loved to hear those words. Then one of his men informed him that a *danzan* force containing several senior officers had been spotted moving into the city.

"Come Muhammad," he exclaimed, all trace of fear driven out by his conviction. "Let's do it one last fuckin' time!"

His lieutenant, whose faith had always been closer to the surface than Massar's, gathered his leader's intent. He needed only an instant to decide. "One last time!" he stiffened, then slapped Massar's shoulder. *"Allah akbar!"*

Massar rallied his *kadashi* fighters. They listened to him stoicly, then, after a moment's contemplation of their fate, raised their weapons and shouted for vengeance in death against the *danzany*. Muhammad Nusur watched as his leader climbed into one of the convoy's jeeps.

"Wait for me, Muhammad," he said.

Abdur uttered a strangled sound as he saw the approaching vehicle, a black shape against the coming night.

"It's Sayeed Massar!" he went to dash forward.

"No, Abdur," gasped Lena, grabbing him. Beside her Terry swore softly as he dealt with the increasing pain throbbing through his body.

Massar pulled up about twenty yards from them.

"Go back!" he shouted urgently. "Kalin's used a germ weapon. Go back to the West Gate!"

Lena stood and, with Abdur, helped Terry to his feet. Massar tore past them in the jeep.

Fifteen minutes later they reached the city perimeter and saw Massar standing at a distance from the *kadashi* chieftain they'd spoken to earlier.

"You have pictures of—?" shouted Massar as he saw them.

"Yes," replied Lena.

"Good," said Massar. "This is Hamed Abu-Tumeh. He's going to try to break out. You have to tell the world about this, Lena."

She nodded. "Sayeed—?"

"I gotta stay," he snapped. "I've got the damn thing."

"No—!" cried Lena.

"Tell the fuckin' world, Lena," Massar repeated sadly. "Goodbye." Then he climbed back into his Jeep and was gone.

"My God," she sighed hopelessly, tears running down her cheeks. She stared at Abu-Tumeh.

"Sayeed Massar," he murmured, gazing intently back at the city. "Allah be with you." He looked down at her.

"Come," he said gruffly. "Night is here."

"But the *danzany*?" she shook herself suddenly. "We cannot go back. They are there."

"The position is manned again?" asked Abu-Tumeh. She nodded and described the location of the *danzan* gun emplacement.

"We must try," muttered the rangy *kadashi* warrior, looking into the gloom ahead. "I will send men as a diversion, and try to drive the main column to the north of them. It is our only chance."

He issued a sharp command and his men obeyed silently.

In the gathering darkness, Massar re-joined Muhammad Nusur, and briefed his men for their final battle.

"Abu-Tumeh?" asked Nasur.

"He's with the American journalist—they have pictures of this. He has to get her out," replied Massar.

"He will, Sayeed," said Nasur, looking with sudden yearning at the western horizon, fighting back the terror within him. Then Massar grasped his shoulder.

"Let's go, Muhammad. It's time."

Kane stubbed his cigarette and alighted from his Jeep as Kalin's vehicle approached. In its lights he saw Rodionov lift his huge bulk out first, followed by Kalin. A second vehicle disgorged Kumarov and Holtzmann, and they walked across the square towards him: Kalin, pale and gaunt, gesticulating to Rodionov; Kumarov, nervously looking ahead—a thin little man in crumpled clothes with lank hair and hunched shoulders. And Holtzmann? He appeared strangely unmoved, arms folded beneath his unkempt beard. He seemed smaller than he had in the laboratory beneath the Monastery, and yet, even from where Kane stood, his presence, his malice, was palpable.

They stopped at the first pile of bodies, Kumarov leaning down and speaking excitedly to Kalin and Holtzmann while Rodionov walked on. Kane strained his ears but could hear nothing. He gripped his gun. The urge to open up on the three men huddled around the bodies gripped him fiercely, but he would be killed and Kumarov's deadly creation would remain—to be used again, either in this criminal war or another.

He could not do it. He stayed at his forward post, one eye on his unit. They were barely visible in the darkness as they patrolled the streets and lanes leading into the square.

"Hawke?" Rodionov asked as he walked up. "Well done. Any still alive?" Kane tossed his head towards a building two blocks further up the street.

"There were some. Want me to secure it?"

"The good doctor wants to talk to some live ones," said Rodionov.

Kane nodded, gave a shout to his men, and moved towards the building at a jog.

Kumarov scowled as he reached Rodionov. "They must be interrogated. We have to—"

"It is safe?" Kalin broke in.

"Colonel Hawke is making it so, against my better judgement," muttered Rodionov.

"A good *danzan*," Kalin chuckled, watching Kane leading the men further up the street.

Holtzmann grunted, turning to Kumarov. "It is very, very good . . ." he said in a low even voice. "It seems your virus kills even faster than you had imagined."

"Yes!" Kumarov agreed. "It has obviously mutated further *in situ*. But we must find survivors. They must be kept for observation in strict quarantine."

"*Bratishka,*" Kalin laughed. "We have little time for niceties such as this. We have only one more strike and then it will be over. We will forget the manner of our victory and so will the world."

"But!" protested Kumarov, knowing the reality of what his brother was saying, but unwilling to break with his creation. "Surely there will be other—?"

"No," said Kalin firmly. "The *araby* will make the claim to the West and the West will find it difficult to believe. And even if one day it chooses to, we will be the legitimate power in Danzanstan."

Kumarov was suddenly sullen and silent, which amused Holtzmann. "Do not worry," he growled. "You will not be without work. I have much for you to do when this is over."

Kumarov looked away into the distance. The truth was that this glimpse of what his virus could accomplish had emboldened his recurring apocalyptic dream. He saw the American soldier waving at them in the dimness.

"Sasha," he nudged his brother.

Kalin looked up. "Let us go," he said, and strode towards Kane. Seconds later, they were standing before a stricken group of *kadashi*, kept at a safe distance by the guns of Kane's men, eyes averted from the torches shining on them.

"Isolation suits!" ordered Kumarov. Rodionov barked a command into his walkie-talkie and within moments the suits were brought. Swiftly Kumarov directed Rodionov, Kalin, Holtzmann, and Kane to don them and, pulling his own on, advanced on the *kadashi* group.

"We have come to help you," he lied through the perspex mask.

The eldest of them, a woman, looked up at him. "The breathing," she croaked in Russian. "It is so difficult."

Behind his mask Kumarov smiled and began questioning her. The more she volunteered of her condition, the more pleasantly surprised he was. "When did you fall ill?" he asked.

"Around midday," replied the woman earnestly, labouring under the delusion that he was a doctor.

Rodionov and Kane watched the pathetic exchange, uncomfortable within the confines of their glittering isolation suits. "And how did the first—!" Kumarov began to ask, then a sudden clatter of gunfire rent the air and he dropped immediately to the ground.

"Hawke!" shouted Rodionov urgently, sheltering Kalin with his body. From the darkness somewhere above them the shots continued to ring out. In the street ahead, one of Kane's men was already dead, another soon would be, clutching a grievous neck wound. Rodionov grabbed Kalin and stormed through the nearest doorway, followed by Kumarov and Holtzmann.

Kane flattened himself against a building and waved his men towards the source of the sniper fire.

"How—?" Kalin gasped as they reached cover. "I thought this was secure!"

Rodionov started to bluster an answer but was cut off.

"Just get us out of here," shouted Holtzmann. *"Get us out!"*

The diversion was working and Massar, hearing the confusion outside, led his men forward from their lookout position. His being was still flooded with adrenaline and disbelief that Kalin himself was part of the *danzan* incursion unit they had come for.

Painstakingly, he and his men crawled along the charred roof-beams of the apartment block towards their trapped enemy. Through a crack in the roof Massar watched with satisfaction as the supreme *danzan* leader and his party tried to exit the building, only to be forced back by another burst of sniper fire. He gestured to his men, and suppressed a cough. Only a few more minutes, he swore, feeling for his gun as he crept, flattened against the rafters, closer and closer to his target.

Their attacker's strategy was clear and the darkness their ally, Kane realised as he saw Rodionov's failed attempt to break from the building with Kalin. It was not sniper fire ricocheting through the streets now, but covering fire. Covering who and where? Though his peripheral vision was obscured by his mask, his eyes flashed from building to building. His men were already climbing towards the probable source of the fire. Within minutes the snipers would either be dead or forced to withdraw. His eyes narrowed on Kalin's current refuge, then flicked up. There was a glint of metal, a movement in the gap between the two buildings. For a second he stood conflicted by his duelling responsibilities. If Kalin and the others were killed by the *kadashi* it would save him the job and still leave him free to take out the lab.

A bullet thudded into the wall above his head. Rodionov gestured urgently to him. Then he saw the big *danzan* general look up. *Damn!* Kane swore, Rodionov had heard the *kadashi* in the roof and was now spraying the rafters with automatic fire.

One of Massar's men screamed as he took Rodionov's shots in the leg, and peering into the blackness, Massar fired his own weapon downwards at the four glittering shapes.

"Kalin!" he yelled to his men. "He must not escape."

In that instant Rodionov knew that, whatever the dangers in the street outside, it was suicide to remain.

"Out!" he bellowed, emptying his magazine and—in the confusion and darkness—snatching up Kumarov as he bolted from the building. A second later he realised his terrible mistake and stopped as Kumarov and Holtzmann stumbled on in their suits to safety.

"Kalin!" he shouted, as he rolled desperately to avoid the hail of bullets. He heard Kalin scream. Then he looked up and saw Kane.

With Kumarov and Holtzmann's escape, the decision was made for him and in an explosion of madness, Kane spun into the street, feeling bullets sear the air around him.

Running as fast as his isolation suit would allow, he passed Rodionov and tumbled the final yards into the doorway. Now he was operating on pure instinct; no reason, no thought. It was him and those who wanted to kill him. There was nothing else.

In his agony Massar lost his grip. Rodionov's final burst had torn through his stomach. He hit the ground hard and, as he rolled over, heard his men landing around him. He looked up, ghastly pain scorching his body.

There, trapped by a ring of guns held by his men, was Kalin, staring out in horror from behind his mask.

"You are dead," croaked Massar, blood spilling from his lips.

"No!" shrieked the danzan leader.

"Let me see him as he dies," Massar gasped, smiling at the sweetness of his vengeance as he watched his men slash the gleaming material with their knives and jerk the headpiece off. As he was unmasked, Kalin's expression was of pure terror.

"Kill him," Massar barked. Then something jagged his dying mind, enough to keep his eyes from their final closing—another silver figure advancing towards him in the gloom, firing a weapon. He saw his men fall, saw Kalin clutch his head between his knees, blubbering but still alive. Massar's eyes rolled as he fought to delay his death long enough to comprehend what had happened.

* * *

Kane faced the *kadashi* warrior in the sudden lull. He raised his gun but could not fire. Massar looked up at him and understood. For a moment his eyes yearned for escape, for life.

"*No!*" he screamed. "*Allah akbar!*" and before Kane could react, with his final mortal effort Massar launched himself at his enemy, attacking Kalin like a mad dog, tearing at him with his hands, clawing at his eyes, chewing at his face with his teeth, now fixing his lips over Kalin's mouth and biting deep into his profane flesh. Kalin's scream was lost inside Massar's gripping teeth and together they rolled in the dust, the *danzan* leader clawing at the head affixed to his. With a silent prayer for the brave, doomed *kadashi* and for his own stained soul, Kane withdrew his knife. Kalin was still screaming as Kane raised the blade and plunged it into the back of his attacker. There was a sudden deep grunt, an exhalation of death into Kalin's throat as Massar felt the steel penetrate between his ribs and into his heart. He fell from Kalin, blood gurgling from his mouth.

"I too have killed you, *Shaitan!*" he cried out, then his eyes closed and his face relaxed. His task had been done. As his life was eclipsed he heard his father's voice whispering inside; *to paradise, Sayeed Massar.*

Kane trembled as he felt Kalin's stare upon him, but his eyes were fixed on Massar. *What have I done?* came the shriek within. His gun clattered to the floor.

"Help me," croaked Kalin.

In a daze, Kane dropped his arm and helped the *danzan* leader to his feet. He had deep bites and claw marks across his face. He wiped himself with his sleeve and then, grabbing a rifle from one of the *kadashi* fighters killed by Kane, he pounded its butt methodically into Massar's head. Then he spat on the corpse and, extending his hand to Kane, walked into the street.

A horde of *danzan* troops surrounded them and hustled Kalin away for medical treatment.

The sniper fire had stopped. There was an eerie peace. But so profound was Kane's self-torment that he was aware of nothing. Not Rodionov's congratulations. Not the fact that Kumarov and Holtzmann had also survived. He was falling through an abyss of his own creation and he was as immobile as those who had died by his hands.

He stood staring out through the dull perspex of his mask and it was only when Rodionov embraced him in a bear hug that Kane's taunting spirit returned him to the world. The world as it now was.

"You have done well, Colonel!" boomed Rodionov again. "You have done very well! Kalin is in your debt. Now, let us leave this shithole and get back to Novominsk. Perhaps I can yet teach you to drink."

Kane looked at him. He had never felt so desolate. He watched the three he longed to kill climb into their jeeps, then realised numbly that he no longer had his gun, and slowly pulled off his isolation suit.

Forgive me, the plea rang in his mind for the unknown man, as he joined Rodionov and drove out of Tumakoc. He cast a backward glance towards the city but there was no forgiveness there.

CHAPTER **TWENTY-TWO**

I t was well into the night before Abu-Tumeh ordered his men out. Lena watched him as he circulated amongst his men. Those who would make the diversionary assault on the *danzan* position had no illusions about their chances of living but nor had there been any shortage of volunteers. Lena watched the man Abu-Tumeh had chosen to lead the assault prepare for battle and suddenly realised the hand-grenades he was strapping to his body were never meant to be removed. Her eyes flared in horror as he stood and made ready to leave. Five minutes later the doomed squadron left through the portal of the West Gate. She heard a gruff whisper beside her and turned to see Abu-Tumeh stiffly farewelling his men and muttering a prayer for their souls.

The hour that they waited for the assault team to reach its position ticked by like torture. Then finally it was time. Terry had packed his camera equipment into the back of the truck that he and Abdur would ride in.

"How'd you pick which one?" Lena asked him, standing at the tailgate, her voice shaking.

"Eeny, meeny . . ." replied Terry in the gloom, just as nervously. He handed her a videocassette. "We've got two tapes," he said, tapping his shirt. "Carry one each, okay?"

"Okay," breathed Lena, staring at him. "We're really not cut out for this are we?"

"I dunno," he grinned brokenly. "You'd never want to *not* be scared, would you?"

She shook her head. "Good luck," she whispered and leant forward to hug him.

His arms tightened around her. "G'luck, Lena," he said hoarsely. "Take care—" A sob caught in his throat and he held her even tighter.

"And you," she said, closing her eyes, not wanting to let him go. Then the first shots rang out in the distance.

"Lena, go!" he hissed, and she pulled away.

As she clambered into the cabin of her truck, the reports of two explosions swamped the noise of revving engines. She thought of the martyred men and hoped they had found their heaven. Then the convoy was off, rumbling and grinding into the night. Lena was braced with her head on her knees, jaws clenched in fear, hoping none of them would die.

Kane feigned sleep during the drive back to Novominsk, haunted by the face of the *kadashi* fighter. But his waking nightmare during the rough journey brought a meaning beyond its torment.

He knew why the man had chosen death.

The landmines could have been laid by either side in the war, at any time in its history. In such wars they are the first weapons deployed and the last discovered, often by the innocent. The first of them lifted Abu-Tumeh's lead truck into the air in a fireball, instantly killing all its occupants. The second truck was no luckier. The third, running through the cratered tracks of its companions, careened into the burning wreckage and overturned. But it did not explode.

As she lurched forward, Lena had no idea what was

happening. She was thrown clear. Still alive, she lifted her head in time to see Terry's truck swerve crazily to the left, spilling people from its rear before it, too, detonated a mine. There were shouts in Russian from behind her and Lena realised they were *danzan* soldiers. She stumbled away, scrambling desperately up a slope, grasping rocks, bushes, anything. Around her she saw forms in the darkness, heard gunfire and screams but she kept on, half-running half-dragging herself.

Then a chatter of machine-gun fire erupted over her head and she heard the grunts of men dying and the agonised sounds of those who had been hit but not killed. She flattened to the ground and looked up. In the moonlight she saw a squad of *danzan* troops approaching, methodically killing all who lay before them. An injured man next to her stood and tried to run but he was mown down.

Crying with fear, her hands clawing at the earth in anticipation of her death she yelled out. *"Nyet! Ya Amerikanka! Telereporter!"* She wept, and gulped air that was half dirt, so hard was her faced pressed into the ground. She repeated her desperate shriek, again and again. *"Nyet! Ya Amerikanka! Telereporter!"*

She heard them approach, heard their weapons clank, heard their muttered discussion in Russian as they stared down. They were going to kill her.

"No!" she screamed and rolled over to face them. Three rifle muzzles were pointed at her. Her stomach exploded with terror as she tossed her head and pleaded for her life.

Abdur nursed Terry in his lap trying to staunch the flow of blood from his shoulder as their truck accelerated away, pitching violently as it strove to escape the ambush.

"Give up," shouted the older fighter who had helped Abdur drag him into the truck. "He is dead."

"No," swore the boy, and tore his shirt to re-bandage the wound. As he grappled in the dark he felt and withdrew a videocassette from Terry's clothing. Dropping it to his feet, he felt the cameraman's body shudder in his lap. "He is alive!" he yelled.

The older man chewed his lip and looked away.

They dragged Lena to her feet, covered with dirt and vomit.

"Shall we fuck her?" exclaimed the first of her captors.

"Grigor, you fucking worm! I wouldn't fuck her with yours!" said the second.

"Fuck her then kill her," came a third voice. "You two hold her down!"

"No!" she screamed as she felt rough hands begin ripping at her clothes. The videotape beneath her shirt fell to the ground and one of the soldiers smashed it with his heel as he continued pawing at her.

"Stop! Get away from her!" came a sterner voice out of the darkness. "American?"

Lena nodded, shuddering with fear. "Yes," she replied through jittering teeth. "American television . . ."

"You were with the *araby*!" the voice accused, and glancing up she saw that it belonged to a pock-marked *danzan* officer who was standing some yards from her.

"I was . . . in Tumakoc," she answered slowly.

"Then you must die," he replied, stepping back. He turned to his men. "Kill her then report to quarantine, *immediately!* Understood?"

"Understood!" snapped his three subordinates as he strode away.

"No!" wept Lena, and her mind grasped one final straw. "Kalin! *Kalin knows about us!*" she screamed in Russian.

"Stop!" came the instantaneous shout from the darkness and the *danzan* officer was before her again.

"If you are lying," he said cruelly, "your death will be much less pleasant than it could have been here."

Uncaring, eyes streaming with tears, she nodded.

"Just," she stammered, "just tell Kalin." Then she sank to the ground, falling, half-undressed, between her captors.

The *danzan* officer stared at her thoughtfully.

"Dress her, I will have to inform Novo," he ordered briskly. "Take her to quarantine, and stay there. You're probably fucking infected yourselves!" With a grunt of annoyance, he spun away.

For the final hour of the journey, through a night thickened by dust and low cloud, Kane's mind flew like a predator around a single question. It was Holtzmann's weapon, when would *he* use it? Holtzmann would not risk waiting, he had no reason to, given the events at Tumakoc. He felt for his ComMod, still safe within the thick padding of his combat jacket. He knew he probably had only the night, or what remained of it, in which to act. His mission was three-fold: destroying or disabling the remaining missiles, whose location and state of readiness he did not know; destroying the manufacturing lab; and capturing or killing Kumarov and Holtzmann. If he failed to achieve any one, he had failed completely. And he knew the odds he faced were immense.

The *Sayaret Maktal* aboard the *South Dakota* could conceivably take out the missiles but they alone could not storm Kalin's heavily defended base for the lab and their two human targets. He considered an Israeli airstrike, but that would have no guarantee of success, even if he knew where to direct it. It was impossible, no matter how much his mind scoured for an answer.

Then he seized upon it. His only chance.

An alliance.

He stared at the nearing lights of Novominsk, desperate determination fusing within him.

At last their convoy pulled up inside the Monastery. Kane saw Kalin ushered away by a junior officer. He watched, wondering what demanded Kalin's immediate attention. Then he felt Rodionov's massive hand on his shoulder.

"Come!" exclaimed the big *danzan* general. Kane followed him into the war-room. Even Holtzmann did not object as he entered; his rescue of Kalin had assured him a place within the inner circle. They gathered around a samovar and discussed what they had witnessed at Tumakoc. A junior officer appeared abruptly at the door.

"General Rodionov," he said, snapping to attention. "Kalin requires you."

Kalin was wheezing as Rodionov entered the communications hut.

"Some news, Boris Nikolaevich," he said looking up. "They have caught the American journalist in Tumakoc."

As Kalin spoke, Rodionov observed his leader carefully, his eyes measuring the distance between them. The *danzan* leader was racked by a cough, and Rodionov realised what had befallen him. *Mother of God!*

"I must sleep," choked Kalin. "Tomorrow is a day of destiny."

"Yes, Kalin," Rodionov responded, backing out.

Kalin gazed at him.

"Boris Nikolaevich," he said softly. "I do not feel well."

Rodionov dropped his eyes. "You are tired, Kalin," he breathed.

From behind his desk, Kalin tried to stand, then fell back into his chair, exhausted by the effort.

"It can not be . . ." he whispered, then stared at Rodionov again. His eyes were flared with terror. "Send my brother to me, *immediately*!"

"Yes, Kalin, I—" began Rodionov. Then he stopped.

His leader had passed out.

It was unearthly to be in such proximity to Holtzmann. He had removed his glasses and his eyes flashed constantly. His presence was like a disturbance in the air, a power removed from humanity. Kane sipped tea and seethed with hatred.

Rodionov had still not returned when the weapons engineer, Mikhail Shevchuk, entered the war room.

"It is done," he said wearily to Kumarov. "Kirkusk, and the MIRV for Israel—all have been programmed."

Holtzmann nodded as Kumarov translated.

"Two of the warheads for Jerusalem?" the Colombian asked sharply.

Shevchuk looked annoyed. "Do I look like a fool?" he grumbled to Kumarov in Russian before giving his answer, deliberately spelling it out.

"The MIRV contains six reentry vehicles," Kumarov translated. "Two targeted for Jerusalem, one each for Tel Aviv, Haifa, Eilat, and Galilee."

"As he ordered a hundred times," added Shevchuk in Russian, but Kumarov ignored that.

"Excellent," said Holtzmann. "And are you ready, Kumarov?"

"Yes," replied Kumarov. "By tomorrow evening—there will be enough of the virus then and I will prepare the warheads—"

"No sooner?" barked Holtzmann.

Kumarov shook his head.

Kane listened, his ears prickling.

"And the coordinates? Is your man sure?" Holtzmann fixed his eyes on Shevchuk. Kumarov repeated the question in Russian and Shevchuk shook his head, muttering angrily.

"He says he will re-check them tomorrow," Kumarov translated. "But in any case, with this agent there is some room for error."

"There will be no error," growled Holtzmann. "As it is, we do not know how effective the Jews' anti-missile capabilities are."

Kumarov spoke again in Russian, this time provoking laughter from Shevchuk.

"*What?*" shouted Holtzmann, clenching and unclenching his hands.

Kane watched him curiously. Gone was the self-assurance of the past few hours. Holtzmann was growing extremely nervous as his hour approached.

"He says not to worry," said Kumarov. "The Israeli Patriots can scarcely cope with Scuds, which are World War Two technology. It is impossible that they will be able to stop modern reentry vehicles from an SS–25."

Holtzmann nodded brusquely and Kane shuddered that such a discussion was taking place. He needed to concentrate—to plan.

"You are *sure* there will be a sufficient quantity of the virus?" Holtzmann again asked Kumarov.

The Russian scientist nodded. "Yes, I am certain."

Holtzmann could not stand still. He paced the room, Kane's eyes following him. He whirled around. "You, *yanqui,*" he said in his guttural voice. "Do you think the Israelis have the capability to stop such a missile?"

"SS–25, multiple warheads?" Kane replied. "No. Not unless they get lucky."

The minutes ticked by, marking Rodionov's absence. Then the *danzan* general returned, his face drawn. Shevchuk swiftly gave his report in Russian, drained his tea, and left. *Where to?* Kane wondered desperately.

Rodionov poured himself a vodka, then spoke.

"They have caught an American who was in Tumakoc," he said blankly.

An electric chill sliced through Kane's heart.

"Who are we discussing?" came the dark undertone of Holtzmann's voice.

"Television reporter," replied Rodionov, turning slowly towards him. "Galena Chagall. She gave us trouble. We were going to dispose of her when she eluded us. Now she has been found. Kalin has ordered her brought here for questioning."

"An American?" Kumarov gasped. "From Tumakoc? She will be infected. This is good! Ensure strict quarantine is observed."

Rodionov turned to Kane. "Colonel Hawke?"

Kane barely heard him. A hurt greater than any he had ever felt rebounded through his body. If he moved a muscle he was sure he would break down.

"I will be in the laboratory," said Kumarov, standing.

Rodionov watched him leave. "Hawke?" he repeated.

Lena was dragged, terrified, along a rough track and thrown into a hut. The door was slammed. Minutes later it opened again and something was tossed in.

"Put it on," shouted the officer who had captured her. She stared at the object on the floor. Seconds passed before she realised what it was. An isolation suit. Trembling with fear, she pulled it over her torn clothes.

"It seems you are known to Kalin," said the officer, entering the half-light of the *danzan* quarantine hut.

Behind the smeared mask of the suit, Lena choked back her tears and forced herself to look at him.

"You will leave for Novo immediately," he added and continued to stare at her. "You are as much our enemy as the *araby,* so do not expect to be well treated." A strange smile played on his face. "Do not remove the suit or you will be shot."

She turned from him and walked towards a waiting jeep. Three soldiers pulled her into the rear of the vehicle. Then they backed up and roared into the night. As they drove, Lena shivered inside the suit although it was impossibly hot. The nightmare was continuing and she knew, however long the trip was, she would have no respite from it. Closing her eyes brought only images from Tumakoc.

They thought she was infected; the thought haunted her, along with the fear that it may be true.

For the first hour she stared into the gloom, hoping that the Jeep would be attacked by the *kadashi*, but the hope faded with every *danzan* checkpoint they passed. They were on the desert lowlands and when the moon caught the peaks of the Markesh range to her left, she realised they were securely within Kalin's territory. She closed her eyes and in the muffled atmosphere of the suit ignored the jibes thrown at her by the soldiers. She tried to sleep but sleep would not come. Finally she began composing poetry in her head, words that would never be written down, drawn from the regrets and pleasures of her life. She remembered her childhood, her parents, friends, and lovers.

And she remembered Kane. While the dislocated verse circulated in her head, she prepared for the end. Crazy thoughts plagued her: unpaid bills, apologies unmade, chances not taken. Of her time in Armestan she thought nothing; it was a dark, unapproachable morass. She thought of Terry and he too joined the swirling ache. Had he lived or died? The world had become insane, a madness of which she was only the most insignificant speck; nothing she had done counted, nothing existed outside the madness, she had been simply washed with it and now it was ending.

After a while her fear peaked and she stared into the black distance, trying not to think at all.

"Colonel Hawke," said Rodionov for a third time.

Kane raised his head.

"Let us eat," Rodionov continued, his expression dark. "You will join me in the mess?"

Kane looked at him curiously, then nodded.

"Goodnight, *Señor*," said the *danzan* general as he left, but Holtzmann did not answer.

* * *

"Where are you, Kane?" growled Elazar, rubbing his raw eyes and staring vainly at the radio console.

Chip MacKenzie turned around wearily in his chair. Neither man had slept. They had formed a bond of sorts, the old man whose wishes were not being answered and the young man whose job it was to listen to the silence. The confinement of the submarine was working like poison on Elazar; he knew his men felt the same way. He was helpless, bound not only by the order from Washington but by Kane's muteness.

He tramped towards his cabin, as much to give MacKenzie a rest from his constant presence as to try to sleep. He felt old, far too old, and as he lay on the bunk he could not help but feel that the world and his method of dealing with it had passed him by.

"What is it, General?" asked Kane as they emerged into the courtyard.

Rodionov kept his silence until they were well away from the surrounding buildings. Then he stopped and grasped Kane's shoulder.

"It is Kalin," he whispered urgently. "He is infected."

Kane stared at him and nodded. "I guessed."

"*Bozhe!*" swore Rodionov. "I do not know—"

"Is there an antidote?" asked Kane quickly.

"No," Rodionov said, his hands clenching and unclenching.

"What have you done?" asked Kane carefully. "He will surely die by tomorrow." He watched the changing expressions on the other's face.

"He is unconscious," Rodionov muttered. "Come!" He grabbed Kane's jacket roughly and led him to the far side of the courtyard. Without a word they strode through the dark corridor and into Rodionov's spartan living quarters. He gestured Kane to one of two simple chairs in the room and closed the heavy door.

"It is difficult," he said tersely.

Kane nodded.

"He will blame us," breathed Rodionov. Kane could see that he was failing to deal with the situation. They sat in silence for several minutes.

"Will you succeed him?" Kane asked simply, looking directly into the big man's eyes.

"There is only me," Rodionov said finally.

Kane watched Rodionov's hands as their movements became less frantic. Logic was working its way through the thick folds of the Red Army veteran's brain.

"There is only me," Rodionov repeated slowly. "But when he knows?"

"What will he do?" asked Kane.

"I do not know, Hawke," muttered Rodionov. "He is . . . unpredictable."

"Then you must assume command now," said Kane.

"Hawke," the *danzan* general sighed finally, "I have set a guard on his quarters, but this is not something I can decide now. It will be morning in a few hours, we will see how he is—"

"He will be dead, General," said Kane softly.

"Da," whispered Rodionov. "Then the decision will have been made . . ." He looked at Kane with a crooked grin on his face. "Hawke, you will stay?"

"Yes, General," said Kane steadily, meeting his eyes. "I will stay."

Rodionov nodded and waved him out.

As he traversed the courtyard, Kane's mind was working feverishly. His alliance had been forged, but time was running out. Entering his room, he pulled the ComMod from his jacket.

Alone in Kalin's bunker, Holtzmann's eyes stared into the past. He remembered the moment his vengeance was created. He remembered the boy staring at the flickering village television set. Remembered the last moments he ever saw his father's face. And his final words. The words that became his own life's work. *And death will find all of you—as one.*

He shifted in his chair, more at peace than he had been for forty years. His dream had only hours left to run. There was nothing beyond it, nothing he cared about. It was the point he had fought the world to reach.

And now he would. He closed his eyes, made sightless by his exhilaration, and let it reverberate through him. Then, after a time, he stood, his face set with determination, and walked down the stairway to the laboratory.

On the brink of involuntary sleep, Kumarov watched his men at work inside the sealed section of the lab; eerie shapes in the bright neon, walking before him in their glittering isolation suits. Then he heard the main door open.

"You will be ready?"

It was Holtzmann.

Kumarov ground his teeth. *"Yes, we will be ready,"* he muttered. "In eighteen hours—"

"It still gives our enemies a full day," said Holtzmann hoarsely.

"Who?" rasped Kumarov, agitated. "And how will they know?"

"They will find out," Holtzmann grunted, "The *yanquis,* the *Judíos.* They know we are here, they attacked the airport. They may—"

"Señor," interrupted Kumarov. "In that case, allow me to finish here—there is much to be done. You should rest."

For some time Holtzmann did not respond, then finally he turned and left the room. "Ensure you are ready," he said from the doorway. *"Nothing* can be allowed to stop this."

* * *

"Colonel Elazar!" the excited shout rang down the narrow passageway. Elazar was on his feet in an instant.

"Lieutenant MacKenzie has a message," stuttered the ensign, "from Novo!"

Elazar was already past him, staggering towards the control room like a drunk, befuddled by weariness and shaking his head to clear it. "MacKenzie!" he gasped as he entered.

"Shorecom, sir," grinned the Texan. "It's him." He pressed a button on the console. The decoded transmission came up on the computer screen and a hard copy slid out of the adjacent printer. Elazar's eyes flicked across the screen, his face hardening.

Captain Duchesne, who had also been roused from his bunk, entered the control room.

"At least two missiles—SS–25s. One with MIRV, target Israel," Elazar read grimly. "Jerusalem, Tel Aviv, Eilat, Haifa, Galilee, and Kirkusk in Armestan. Missiles to be launched tomorrow evening, Novo time. Exact launch time unknown. Launch location unknown." He finished and turned to Duchesne.

"My God," breathed the sub's commander.

"I have to inform my government," said Elazar quietly. "They must be allowed to make their own decision, regardless of our situation here."

"You know I have to get clearance—" Duchesne began.

"Then please get it, Captain!" Elazar snapped, his eyes reddened with fatigue. "Please! Surely they cannot refuse us."

"I wouldn't have thought so, Colonel," replied the sub's commander steadily but his voice admitted the alternative possibility. "I'll do what I can. MacKenzie!"

"Yes sir!" replied the radio officer, already making the connection to Washington.

The hurriedly convened National Security Council again sat in the Oval Office. It was late afternoon, Washington time.

The President had cancelled a meeting with the Japanese Prime Minister and his mood was foul.

"Goddamnit, Myron," he was shouting. "Let the damn Israelis go!"

"Mr. President," replied Berkely steadily. "We have our proposal before the UN Security Council—it is meeting as we speak. If we act unilaterally and pass on the information, we leave ourselves open to—"

"I don't give a shit," swore Kirkland. "If this thing escalates any more we're going to have to go in ourselves. Let the Israelis deal with it!"

The National Security Adviser looked around the room for allies but for once had none. Matthew Porter and James Martin were silent; General Westaway was staring at the floor. Behind them, Mitford and Stone were immobile.

"They got twelve batteries of Patriots from us, Mr. President," Berkeley continued. "They—"

"Don't work," Stone cut in.

Berkeley glared at him, then looked to Westaway. The Chairman of the Joint Chiefs nodded reluctantly.

"If the Israelis go in and screw it up," Berkeley strained under what he considered to be his duty, "our hand is blown. Even if they don't screw it up our hand is blown. If it's got to be done, it's got to be done right. We need to know what we're going in against. Kane's information is incomplete. We don't know for sure how many missiles Kalin still has. We don't even know for sure what kinds of missiles he has, apart from the two SS–25s. And in any scenario he will still have the biological agent, and if we warn him—?"

The President gripped his desk and gazed out over the White House lawn. Angry as he was, he knew Berkeley had a point.

"Mr. President," countered Clark Mitford. "I strongly urge that we both inform the Israeli Government and allow the Mossad squadron aboard the *South Dakota* freedom to operate."

"What would that solve?" snapped Kirkland.

"The commandos could take out the manufacturing lab in the Monastery," Stone replied for Mitford. "At least we know *its* location. If necessary they can bring Kane out at the same time. If what he says about Kalin's infection is true, there'll be a level of confusion within the command structure we can exploit—"

"And the missiles?" General Westaway interrupted.

Stone shrugged. "Seems to me a matter of priorities. The missiles are set to fly whether or not we act. This way we can at least take out the means of production, along with Kumarov."

Kirkland nodded and Stone looked relieved. The decision might be late, but it was coming. Then the President's intercom buzzed.

"Mr. President, Ambassador Fitzpatrick for you or the Secretary of State . . ."

Growling with displeasure the President put the call on speaker and answered. A second later the normally smooth voice of the United States Ambassador to the United Nations came on line.

"Mr. President," he sounded harried. "Security Council's just heard from Firyubin. He's offered to personally mediate with Kalin; cease-fire, peace talks, the whole box and dice. It's going to be difficult to oppose—"

Stone's angry sigh broke the sudden silence.

Kirkland glared at him and looked around the room. "Michael," he said. "I'm with the NSC now. The situation has magnified. I'd call it critical. How do we know Firyubin can deliver?"

"We don't," came the swift reply. "But he's in the picture and I don't think we can ignore that. If we do, Russia will veto."

"Damn," swore the President. *"Damn!"* Again he sur-

veyed the faces in the room. No one spoke, not even Berkeley. "Your thoughts, Myron?" snapped Kirkland.

"I . . ." began Berkeley, "that is . . ." He coughed as
he gathered his thoughts, then continued in a more controlled voice. "In normal circumstances I would advise that
you speak to Firyubin directly."

Kirkland rolled his eyes. Russia's latest president was as
notoriously unreliable as his predecessor, Yeltsin, and for
the same reason.

"Damn drunken promises," he growled, then his frustration boiled over. "Why in hell is everyone so damned concerned about this shitheap of a country? Jesus Christ!"

There was absolute silence as Kirkland strode around his
desk.

"Okay," he said finally. "Michael, let the Security Council know that I'm going to talk to Firyubin."

"Yes, Mr. President," said Fitzpatrick. "I'll set it up."

"And for our ears only," Kirkland continued. "I'll give
the sonofabitch until noon Moscow time to respond, with a
confirmation from Kalin of a cease-fire."

"I understand," came the response from New York. "I'll
keep you advised."

"Do that, Michael," barked Kirkland. "And make that a
written confirmation!" He turned to those assembled before
him. "Well gentlemen," he said angrily. "What a class-A
screw-up this has turned out to be."

Lena watched the dawn break over Novominsk. She was
sweating profusely within the isolation suit as the Jeep began its long descent down Mount Barkusk. She shuddered
as she glanced down its slopes, wondering at how much
more awful the war had become.

The taunting from her *danzan* captors had long since
stopped. All they wanted now was hot food and a bed. She
was just a job to be completed. Inexplicably, a tune erupted
in her head and she found herself humming it under her

breath. She smiled brokenly as she remembered she had made love to it with Kane. Then the memory became too painful and other stray, wasted thoughts skulked through her mind.

She began thinking about the devotion of Sayeed Massar's men; the thin man with the grenades strapped to his body and his faith in his God. She wished for the security of her long-lapsed faith, the fantasy of passing on, not dying, of meeting her father again, of meeting Kane. But it would not come. The dawn and the ugliness of the world around her snatched whatever vestiges of faith she had and left her empty, hopeless and condemned.

She listened as one of the *danzan* soldiers radioed news of their approach. "Oh God." Fear steamed from her lips and fogged her mask.

Kane checked his watch, keeping lookout on the courtyard below, scouring it for a sign of activity, some reason he could use to escape his quarters. He stared at the ComMod in exasperation. Where was Elazar? Chewing his lip he quickly typed out a further message and resumed his post by the window.

It was five A.M.

On the *South Dakota,* there was an air of stultifying purgatory as Elazar awaited news from Washington. It was six hours until the President's deadline expired.

Kane heard the jeep long before it reached the gates of the Monastery, a lone sound in the early morning stillness. He launched himself into the corridor, surprising the bleary-eyed guard outside the adjacent room, and jogged out into the courtyard, crossing quickly towards the main gate. Then a shout rang out.

"Colonel!"

It was Rodionov.

Kane stopped and turned reluctantly towards him.

Lena entered the compound and was driven directly to the main building, where the Jeep was surrounded by more *danzan* soldiers. They bundled her inside and down a flight of steps. Reaching a door, they banged on it loudly. After a few seconds a figure dressed in a suit identical to hers opened it.

"What?" came his muffled voice. He peered at her, then his eyes flared behind the mask. "Yes! Leave her!"

The man was joined by others who led her towards what looked to be an array of plastic curtains. Opening the first, they pushed her in, and then further through until she found herself in a laboratory. She struggled but was gripped by strong hands and shoved roughly through another opening in the plastic.

Then one of her captors spoke in Russian.

"The suit," he ordered. "Remove it!" She froze and the man shouted again, beginning to unfasten it. She stepped from it into what she now realised was a sealed chamber. The man withdrew, taking her suit and leaving her staring through the thick plastic, terrified.

At his bench, Kumarov grunted with annoyance. He had no time to spare for her interrogation. He did not even wonder why—so many hours after her infection—the woman was still alive.

Lena could not stand still. Her body shook with fear and apprehension. She held her arms tightly to her sides, gripping herself, senses straining for any sign of the illness, but her body ached and her fatigue was so total that she could not tell. She finally sat on the bed in the chamber and closed her eyes tightly, desperate to shut out the clinical nightmare that now surrounded her.

* * *

"Kalin is still alive. But it is horrible . . ." Rodionov's voice trailed off and his brown eyes bored into Kane's face. "I have assumed control," he said simply. "There is no other way."

"But what of the other two?" asked Kane. "His brother and Holtzmann?"

"They are of no importance in this," grunted Rodionov. "They will be gone soon. But I will need you—these next days will be difficult."

Kane looked at him, knowing that he was a far different creature to Kalin. With different priorities, he hoped. "I gave you my word," he affirmed. He thought carefully before speaking again.

"The missiles," he said slowly. "The ones they were talking about last night. Will you still fire them today?"

"I—?" Rodionov shook his head distractedly. It was not a matter that he had considered. "Why?" he asked.

"Why target Israel?" asked Kane. "It'll bring a response— a massive response. Is it worth the risk to us? Especially now? The *araby* are one thing, but the Israelis?"

Rodionov grunted. "It was Kalin's arrangement. In return for the weapon."

"*Kalin's* arrangement?" said Kane pointedly.

The big *danzan* fighter stared at him. "It is difficult," he said in a conspiratorial voice. "It is Kalin's affair, I do not know all of it—"

"Surely you will be informed?" Kane broke in, needling him.

"I . . . *blyad!*" Rodionov spat. "What you say about the Israelis is correct, but we have made a *deal!*"

"This is war, General," said Kane. "I have to advise you of the lack of military wisdom in this—"

"I know!" snapped Rodionov. He held his head in his huge hands and tried to think.

"Rodionov!" came the sudden shout. It was Holtzmann, striding swiftly across from the other side of the courtyard.

"I must see Kalin," stormed the Colombian as he reached them. "Who has set the guard, they——"

"*Señor!*" Rodionov cut him off. "Kalin is dying. He is under quarantine. I have taken his place as commander."

Holtzmann's eyes flashed from him to Kane, then abruptly he spun away.

"He is now *your* problem," said Kane as he watched Holtzmann disappear into the main building.

"*Acht!*" swore Rodionov in response.

"Kumarov!" Holtzmann's shout penetrated the door of the laboratory.

"*Chort vazmee,*" swore Kumarov inside his suit. He walked out through the airlock and admitted Holtzmann. The Colombian grabbed him urgently.

"Kumarov! Kalin has been infected. His quarters are surrounded by guards and Rodionov is——"

"*What?*" gasped Kumarov. "No!"

He sank to his knees.

"*No!*" The force of his scream drove Holtzmann back. "*No, Sasha!*"

"Nothing," breathed the Colombian. "Nothing can interfere!"

"Holtzmann," shrilled Kumarov, weeping, "he is my *brother!*" Suddenly he dashed into the airlock and through to the sealed section of the lab. Reaching it, he realised his folly and it settled on him like a terrible weight. He looked out at Holtzmann, knowing the only course of action available to him.

"Sasha . . ." he wept as he made the preparations. His brother had been his father, his saviour.

Now he would be the cause of his brother's death.

Holtzmann stared impatiently at Kumarov as he worked, a curse on his lips as he re-appeared through the airlock and pulled off his isolation suit.

"I warn you, Kumarov—" he began.

"We must go to Rodionov!" shouted Kumarov. "He must let me see Sasha!"

"Rodionov?" mused Holtzmann, glaring at him. "Oh yes. He will let you through . . ." Then he guffawed. "Rodionov remains very much in my debt!"

The slighter man stared at him, swamped by grief, not understanding Holtzmann's words, or caring to.

"We will go to see your brother now," said Holtzmann coolly. "And then we will fulfil my objective."

"I must see Sasha," muttered Kumarov tonelessly. "He is—"

"I am sorry," grunted Holtzmann. "But in every war there are casualties, I am sure Kalin realises this better than you. That missile must be fired from Barkusk tomorrow."

They turned to go, then Kumarov stopped. "Wait!" He depressed the button of the intercom to the sealed section of the lab and stammered an order in Russian. As one of his men stepped into the airlock carrying isolation suits, Holtzmann wandered to the far side of the room, to the chamber which had, so briefly, housed Cortez.

"This is the *yanqui* woman?" he asked.

There was no answer from Kumarov as Holtzmann walked close to the clear plastic and stared into Lena's terrified eyes. Gathering spit in his mouth, he hacked at her, laughing as he did. She looked away and he depressed the intercom on his side of the plastic wall.

"It is a most terrible death," he chuckled. "I have seen it."

Then he laughed again and they left her.

Lena watched the pair leave the room beyond, her sanity fast disintegrating. Light sparkled off the plastic and she could see her dull reflection in it. She stared at it until sheer exhaustion dragged her into a merciful, deathly sleep.

CHAPTER TWENTY-THREE

Terry, no!" shouted Harry Berg as his partner was carried from the tattered remnants of the *kadashi* convoy to the tiny Red Crescent clinic, with Abdur trailing behind.

Harry—who had returned to Irtos only hours before from Baku—gripped the boy's hand and waited outside, praying in his own fashion.

Finally the young Pakistani doctor whose thankless lot it was to operate the clinic walked out. "I have done what I can for your friend," he said in very Oxford English. "His injuries are not so bad, but he had lost a tremendous amount of blood. I gave him plasma—it is all we have here—but he needs whole blood. You must take him back to Baku."

"Fine," replied Harry, gesturing to his *kadashi* driver. "We have to take Terry to Baku, ask the boy what he wants to do."

The driver put the question to Abdur.

"He says he must stay to fight the *danzan*."

"Okay," Harry patted Abdur's shoulder. "We'll go now."

Terry's stretcher was securely fastened in the rear of the Jeep, then the doctor checked the plasma drip hanging above him.

"Be careful," he said, then handed Harry a foam container. "More plasma," he explained.

"Thanks," replied Berg. He reached down to shake Abdur's hand but the boy embraced him.

"He . . . okay?" he asked.

"Okay I hope," Harry replied, looking to the heavens.

The boy smiled and tears ran down his cheeks. Then he held up his hand and dashed away. Harry watched curiously as he scrabbled in the rear of one of the trucks and returned holding a single videocassette in his outstretched hand. "Tumakoc," he said.

Harry nodded and took it from him. "Goodbye," he said and climbed into the jeep.

"Allah be with you, Terry," Abdur whispered brokenly in *kadashi* as they sped away.

Holtzmann was hard-pressed to keep up with Kumarov's stumbling jog towards Kalin's quarters. From a window overlooking the courtyard, Rodionov and Kane saw them.

"Battle stations," said Kane, looking at the isolation suits Kumarov carried. "They want to see him." Kalin had regained consciousness and Kane's stomach gnawed at him as he watched the pair approach.

"Yes," grunted the *danzan* general.

"What is this?" Kumarov shrilled when he saw them.

"You know," said Kane sharply.

"Silence, *yanqui*!" snapped Holtzmann.

"He is my brother, Rodionov," shouted Kumarov. "I demand to see him!"

"No," replied Rodionov sternly. "He is dying, we must leave him in peace."

There was a terrible coughing from behind the door, and a strangled shout. *"Bratishka!"*

Kumarov glared at Rodionov. "You will let me in!"

"What can you do?" asked the bigger man.

Kumarov looked around. "I . . ." he stammered. "I can help him." His black eyes pleaded with Rodionov.

The *danzan* general was silent, unsure.

"General?" muttered Kane, sensing Kumarov's purpose. "It would be humane."

Rodionov glanced at him. "Is it an antidote?" he asked curiously.

Kumarov dropped his head. *"Nyet,"* he said barely audibly. "It . . . it will hasten his death. But please," he implored Rodionov. "Let him think it is . . ."

Rodionov nodded. Quickly they donned the isolation suits Kumarov had brought, then Rodionov barked an order to the guards. Like four alien beings, they entered the room. Kumarov cried out behind his mask as he saw Kalin, phlegm covering his face and bedclothes. The *danzan* leader's eyes widened as he saw them staring at him through the perspex of their masks. He wheezed horribly and was possessed by a dreadful coughing fit. His terror, which he had so far kept at bay, broke through to his soul. *"No!"* he shrieked. *"No!"*

Kane, Rodionov and Holtzmann stood back as Kumarov knelt beside his brother and, with violently shaking hands, withdrew a syringe from his case.

Kalin's eyes fixed on it and he began to laugh. "You see! You see!" He forced himself up and crowed at the other three, hacking up another gobbet of phlegm as he did. "Zhora, it is a cure?"

"Sasha—" began Kumarov, then he nodded slowly.

"Rodionov!" Kalin spat as Kumarov held his arm in preparation. "When I am—!" The threat hung in mid-sentence as Kumarov jabbed the needle into his forearm and depressed the plunger.

"You will—" croaked Kalin. His face screwed with fury, then with a sudden instant of horror, then shock. He stared at Kumarov. "No . . . *bratish*—" he began clawing at his brother, then collapsed forward.

Kumarov slumped over him and wept uncontrollably, his body bucking with the force of his grief. Rodionov gestured to Kane and Holtzmann to withdraw and they did so, pulling off their suits as soon as the door was closed.

"Now Rodionov," said Holtzmann, as soon as he was clear of his suit. "Let us make the final arrangements for *my* missile." His eyes—unmoved by what they had just witnessed—bored into the new *danzan* leader.

"Holtzmann . . ." Rodionov sighed, looking more at Kane than the Colombian. "I am afraid I cannot—"

"Before you go on, *General!*" spat Holtzmann, "ask yourself if you know the full terms of my contract with Kalin, and now, with you?"

"The missile for Kumarov's weapon?" Rodionov countered.

Kane stepped forward as Holtzmann spoke again.

"A little more than that!" Holtzmann replied, a malicious glint in his eyes. "There was one other favour I performed for Kalin. The transfer of Armestan's cash and gold reserves from the United States!"

Rodionov grunted. He guessed what was coming next.

"They are assets I *still* control!" Holtzmann barked. "My insurance policy, Rodionov. Do you understand?"

The big *danzan* fighter dropped his head.

"How do I know," he muttered, looking up at Holtzmann, "that if the missile is fired you will honour your side—?"

"The *arrangement* was that the relevant documents would be received by Vladimir Golen in Belgrade before I left Novominsk. These papers will now be made out to you—as commander of course," replied Holtzmann. "Is that acceptable?"

"I have no choice," Rodionov said finally. "We will proceed."

Kane shuddered as he heard the words.

"Come, Hawke—" growled Rodionov, turning away.

Kane shot a hateful glance at Holtzmann as he left and glimpsed the evil fire burning behind his enemy's eyes.

The sound of Kumarov's weeping, high and guttural, accompanied them out.

"Hawke?" said Rodionov. "What do you think?"

"I think there are other means," muttered Kane, knowing the delicate territory he was treading.

"What other means?" snapped Rodionov.

"The West," replied Kane, "or Russia. They would be interested in what Kumarov has developed and in the man himself. You could barter." Kane stopped and looked at Rodionov keenly, judging his next words with care. "And Holtzmann . . ." he began. "I—"

"What?" asked Rodionov.

Kane swallowed. "I was attached to an American operation for a short time, hunting Holtzmann. My guess is that if you could deliver him to the Americans, your assets would be found and freed . . ." His words trailed off as he awaited the *danzan* general's response.

Rodionov rubbed his chin thoughtfully. "Why did you not mention this before?"

Kane shrugged, his heart thumping. "You know Holtzmann," he said. "He would think I was a spy."

Rodionov nodded; within the renegade Marine's admission was also his innocence of the charge. "So?" he asked. "You think I should deal with the Americans. But if you are wrong, our fight will be bankrupted."

"General!" Kane said urgently. "*If* you fire that damn missile at Israel they'll carpark you!"

Rodionov nodded again. "But if I give up the weapon, then *we* lose it too."

Kane looked at him. "Your call," he said. "How big is your own target?"

"Kirkusk," Rodionov grunted. "Two million—"

"*Two million!*" Kane reacted. "Jesus Christ, General, you

think we can keep two million people penned into a city? The damn disease will get out for sure. Fire the missile and you stand the chance of not only wiping out the *araby* but the whole fucking country."

Kane trembled. He knew he was pressing Rodionov hard but had no alternative. It was the only way.

"Perhaps—?" rumbled the big man.

"Do you want to die like Kalin?" asked Kane sharply. "I sure as hell don't!"

Rodionov's eyes drilled into him, tension gripping his huge frame. "No," he said. "But the missiles are going to be fired this evening. There is not enough time to make the contact with America and receive the guarantee about our assets."

"Delay Holtzmann," replied Kane.

Rodionov shook his head. "As you said, Hawke, I know Holtzmann. He will not be delayed, and if America chooses not to deal, then I will have lost on both fronts." He was teetering on the brink of a decision.

"There *is* still time," insisted Kane, his mind searching frantically for the answer that would satisfy Rodionov. "Golen? He could make the approach."

"There is no US embassy in Belgrade," muttered Rodionov.

Kane thought wildly. "The woman. The American journalist. She could—"

"No, she is locked in the lab. She is infected," said Rodionov, and paused. Then, abruptly, an idea came to him. "But there is someone else—the man who was with you on the Belgrade flight. He is from her company—he came to secure her release. Yes!"

"The man?" Kane recalled the businessman now. "Peterson?" A warning instinct stirred in him but it was swamped by the necessity of the moment. Rodionov wanted to deal, that was all that mattered.

"You are right," said the big general as they strode towards Peterson's quarters. "We will win this war without their weapon, Hawke!"

"Exactly," said Kane, but his unease was increasing by the second. The man's name ricocheted through his brain. *Peterson?* They reached the room. Rodionov snapped an order to the guard and the door opened.

Just as it did, Kane remembered.

"*General . . .*" he began, but was interrupted by Peterson's squeal.

"Kane!" he shouted, launching himself towards them, a broad grin on his fleshy face. "*Goddamn!* I've been sitting here for these past days with nothing to do except think about where it is I know your damn face from. *Kane!* Right? The anti-drugs hero!"

Kane stood rigid, in complete shock.

Peterson grabbed his hand and addressed Rodionov. "So our side's helping you guys?" he said proudly. "Well seems you've gotten the right man. Kane's a big name back home. So big we can't even frigging mention it!" He laughed uproariously at his own joke, unaware of the sudden, terrible expression forming on Rodionov's face.

Rodionov turned slowly towards Kane. "What is this?" he said in a low, menacing voice.

"General, I don't know who this motherfucker is," said Kane steadily, eyes flashing.

The bigger man returned his gaze. Then his face reddened and his body began to shake. "*Kane?*"

"Yeah, Kane!" chortled Peterson, still immune to what was happening.

"Hawke," Rodionov bellowed. "You are a—!"

Kane's mind whirled with rage and disbelief. Rodionov swung at him in fury but in one lightning movement Kane cracked his elbow into the larger man's temple. Spinning around, he saw the guard—taken by surprise at the speed of what was unfolding—raising his gun to shoot. Kane's foot shot out and struck his chin, snapping his head back and dropping him to the floor. Kane snatched his rifle and brought it up as Rodionov scrabbled for his own weapon.

"General!" screamed Kane. Rodionov's hand froze as he stared down the barrel of Kane's rifle.

"Slow and easy, Rodionov," growled Kane, picking up Rodionov's pistol. "Get up."

"Kane," spluttered Peterson. "What—?" he did not finish, as the butt of Kane's rifle smashed into his head.

"Now, Rodionov," Kane hissed, shouldering the rifle and gripping the pistol tightly. "We're going to the laboratory—as buddies—got it?"

"You will die, Hawke," Rodionov gasped.

"Then," Kane replied through tight lips as he shoved the pistol under Rodionov's tunic, "so will you, General."

The warheads had been primed, returned to their crates and were now aboard the lorry that would transport them to the launch site. Kumarov and Holtzmann were about to climb into the cabin as Kane and Rodionov entered the courtyard on the far side, walking closely together, in deep conversation.

Holtzmann looked across at the distant pair curiously, then turned away in annoyance and lifted himself into the truck. He did not trust Rodionov and had never trusted the *yanqui*. But now it did not matter—the deal was intact, nothing could change that.

The engine roared and the truck moved towards the Monastery perimeter. As it waited for clearance at the main gate, Kumarov also saw Kane and Rodionov. A dull alarm bell rang in his mind as he watched them disappear inside the main building.

"They are going to the lab—?" he murmured.

Holtzmann did not reply, staring outwards with fierce preoccupation. Kumarov—still awash with grief at his brother's death—turned back numbly and settled into his seat.

* * *

Kane paused at the top of the stairs, knowing there was a guard-post on the first landing.

"Rodionov," he said, gripping the *danzan* commander viciously by the arm. "My orders are to burn the lab, got it? If you give me away you'll fucking burn with it—do you understand?"

Rodionov nodded, but his eyes sparked rebellion. Kane knew his anger would overcome his fear very soon. He twisted the pistol against Rodionov's skin, jamming its barrel into his ribs. "Let's go," he growled, pushing the *danzan* general in front of him. As they rounded on the guards, Kane draped his free arm around Rodionov's shoulders and again began talking boisterously in English. He nodded to the guards. They stiffened to attention; the *yanki* colonel was already a respected figure in the Monastery. With ten more steps they entered the laboratory.

"Rodionov," Kane said, as he secured the heavy door. "The lab, the missiles and our two 'friends'—they're my mission objectives. You want to deal?"

"Hawke," Rodionov spat. "I do not trust you or America! You think I am scared of you?" his eyes narrowed. "I say it again—you are dead!"

Kane shrugged. "So what." Training his gun on the *danzan* commander, he searched the lab quickly. He found tape and electrical flex. Binding and gagging Rodionov, he moved to the plastic wall dividing the lab. Behind it, four figures in isolation suits stared out dumbly. Kane moved along the plastic, to the chamber where Cortez had died.

Then he saw Lena, prone on the floor.

"*Lena!*" he shouted and pressed his face against the plastic in shock. Her eyes fluttered open.

"Kane?" she said weakly as she struggled into awareness. "*Kane?* They told me you were dead."

"Lena," he breathed, then spoke more loudly, "Tell them to get you out of there!"

"But Kane," she moaned, holding her palms up to the plastic. "I'm infected—"

"Get out of there!" he roared.

She stared at him then backed away from the plastic. He heard her shout in Russian, and he aimed his rifle towards the lab-workers. One of them swiftly passed through the airlock into Lena's cell and dressed her in an isolation suit. Then he led her slowly out from the main chamber, the seal hissing as it opened.

"Back." Kane gestured the man with his gun and he scuttled back into the isolation section.

"Lena," he breathed.

Behind the mask she smiled and reached out for him. They embraced, then Kane pulled away.

"When did you get to Tumakoc, how long after?" he asked urgently.

Lena looked puzzled. "Eight, nine hours, I guess."

"Any direct contact with any living—?"

"No," she replied.

"Get the suit off," he said.

She shook her head. "I have the—" he heard her muffled voice begin.

"Lena," he said slowly. "Take the suit off—*you're okay!*" She looked at him, then her eyes dropped and she unfastened the suit.

"Kane, they're sure—" she whispered again as her mask came off. He stared at her, intoxicated by her presence. Head spinning he held her and kissed her deeply. Then he heard a sound from behind. It was Rodionov, slamming his fist against the floor, his eyes fixed on Lena, terrified.

Kane looked at him, an idea flashing into his mind.

"What's happening, Kane?" Lena gasped. She was shuddering, tears flowing down her cheeks. Kane held her tightly and did not speak. Slowly her shivering ebbed as she pressed against him.

"You have to help me," said Kane eventually. "We've got

to destroy this place. Get back into the suit and take the rifle. You still remember how to use it? The place has got to be torched. Find petrol, kerosene, anything."

"Sir." She leaned forwards and kissed him again, then replaced the mask over her head, took his rifle and walked back through the airlock into the isolation room. Seconds later he heard her muffled commands in Russian and saw the men behind the plastic obey.

Kane withdrew his ComMod from his jacket and tapped a message to Elazar. He doubted whether the signal would penetrate the basement, but knew if it failed to make contact with the orbiting satellite it would automatically resend until it received acknowledgement from the *South Dakota*. That done, he crouched next to Rodionov who struggled and turned his head away.

"Rodionov," he said. "Terrible thought isn't it—going the way of Kalin?"

The *danzan* general grunted.

"But she's not infected, Rodionov," Kane said after a time. "It's been too long."

Rodionov rolled his head towards Kane.

"It's the truth, General," said Kane. Rodionov had to want to live, badly. Kane's eyes broke from his captive and watched Lena behind the plastic wall. She gave him the thumbs-up; one of Kumarov's men was holding two jerry-cans. Kane motioned her to the plastic.

"Get me two suits and come out," he said. She nodded and appeared through the airlock a minute later.

Kane spoke to her quickly as he pulled on his isolation suit. "This is all Holtzmann's work, Lena," he said. "They've got more missiles, SS–25s, like Tumakoc—"

"Kane, I know!" exclaimed Lena as she dragged off her mask. "Somewhere on Mount Barkusk. They were talking about it."

"Good—and I'm sure when we get there we'll know exactly where to go. Right, *General*?" Kane fastened his own mask. "Cover him," he said to Lena, then, gripping his pistol, walked into the isolation room. Its four occupants looked through their masks at him with frightened expressions. Kane pointed to the jerrycans.

"*Kyiraseen!*" said one of the men. Kane's eyes flashed around the lab, recalling what Elazar's Mossad expert, Golda, had told him. Swiftly he identified the critical areas and moved through the lab, dousing fermentation vats, cultures and benches with the kerosene. He saw two gas cylinders in the corner of the lab, checked their markings and opened their taps. Then he motioned the men out of the lab with his pistol and, snatching an item from one of the lab's shelves, withdrew from the room, trailing the last of the kerosene up to the airlock.

Rodionov's eyes narrowed as Kane approached him.

"Done?" asked Lena.

Kane nodded, thinking hard. "Almost. The other suit is for Rodionov," he said. "Keep him covered." Bending down, he untied Rodionov. "Up," he snapped. "Get into the suit."

Rodionov complied sullenly. As he pulled the mask over his head, Kane stopped him.

"No," he said. The *danzan* general looked at him as Kane held up a small, sealed glass phial.

"The virus, Rodionov!" he snapped. Rodionov's eyes bulged in horror, fixed on the phial. Kane spoke again. "The gag comes off. Follow every instruction completely or you'll join Kalin. Understand?"

The *danzan* general nodded quickly. Then Kane taped the phial to the inside of his suit, behind his neck. From Rodionov's throat came a low guttural noise of horror.

"Anything goes wrong," said Kane as he lifted the mask and tore the tape from Rodionov's lips, "and I break the glass. Say 'yes I understand'."

Rodionov gazed at him, partly in shock, partly in rage.

"Say it, General," said Kane.

"Yes," Rodionov muttered. "Yes, I understand."

"Good," replied Kane, then continued in a chilling monotone. "General, you will tell your men that there has been a leak, the lab is contaminated and must remain sealed. Tell them we may have been infected and that we're proceeding to Shaklin to fly to Belgrade for treatment. Get us transport and order this building be completely evacuated." Then he lifted the mask and sealed it over Rodionov's head.

Kane stepped back. "Lena, explain to these men very carefully that we will be leaving the Monastery and that if they want to stay alive they'll leave without protest and not try to remove their suits. Then kit up yourself."

Lena nodded and began translating.

"Good," said Kane as she finished and donned her mask. "Almost there." He looked at Rodionov through the perspex of his mask. All traces of self-assurance had gone from the big man's eyes, because they were eyes that had seen Kalin's death.

"Wait and cover," he ordered Lena, then—pushing Rodionov in front of him—walked back through the airlock into the isolation room. He moved through the lab, applying a match to the viral cultures and fermentation vats. They waited until the flames had risen, then left, Kane shoving Rodionov ahead. Once through the airlock, Kane swapped his pistol for Lena's rifle.

"Keep it hidden," he warned, moving towards the airlock and unsealing it. Then he strode to the main door. "Lena," he said. "My guess is we've got about twenty minutes before the gas in that room blows, so let's move. And I want to know everything Rodionov says in Russian."

Lena looked scared, but that was fine. She should be.

The flames licked against the plastic sheeting as Kane grasped the wooden door and swung it open. With his rifle slung over his shoulder and his hand pressed against the phial in Rodionov's suit, he pushed the *danzan* general out first.

"Close the door," Kane ordered Lena at the rear.

They made their way up the stairs. Again the guards manning their posts stood to attention, but this time General Rodionov and the *yanki* colonel stopped. Rodionov spoke in rapid-fire Russian, and Kane watched the men's expressions carefully, not daring to glance around at Lena. Unconsciously he pushed the phial harder into Rodionov's neck. The guards saluted hurriedly, then bounded up the stairs in front of them.

"Okay?" asked Kane as he saw them disappear outside.

"Okay," she replied. Slowly they made their own way up the stairs and into the courtyard.

Inside his jacket the ComMod again tried to send the earlier message. This time the orbiting satellite beamed back its acknowledgement.

"Yes!" yelled Mordechai Elazar as the communications console suddenly lit up with Kane's transmission. His eyes locked onto the words. "The launch site is on Mount Barkusk. Coordinates coming soon." He glanced at Duchesne. "Kane is destroying the lab, wants us to take the missiles out."

"Prepare your men," said the sub's commander. "We still have an hour to wait. I'll push Washington hard, see if we can't at least use the Tomahawks now."

Elazar's frustration boiled inside him but he knew Duchesne's hands were tied.

"Do what you can, Captain, I will be with my men."

Duchesne watched him go, his own anger mounting by the second. "Acknowledge Kane's message," he ordered. "Tell him we're standing by. And tell him—" he glared at the ceiling. "Tell him we might have to take this thing to the deadline. Then get me Washington!"

"Yes, sir," snapped the radio-officer.

"Bring her up, fifty feet," Duchesne continued crisply. "Ready the Tomahawks. Surface condition check."

"Sir!" came the response.

They walked as a tight group towards the centre of the courtyard.

"If the lab blows," growled Kane to Rodionov, "you talk us out!"

The two guards drove up in jeeps, Kane gestured them out. "General," he nudged Rodionov behind the steering wheel of the first and sat next to him. Then he brusquely motioned two of Kumarov's men to join them, and for their colleagues to take the second vehicle with Lena. She climbed in behind them and Kane waved them forwards.

As they passed through the main gate of the Monastery complex, Kane saluted the guards. Then they were out, seven silvery figures amidst the dust thrown up by their Jeeps.

"Rodionov!" shouted Kane once they were well clear of the Monastery. "The missiles—Mount Barkusk." Behind his mask, Rodionov nodded and turned the Jeep north along the Barkusk road.

Holtzmann and Kumarov leapt from the lorry as it ground to a halt outside the cavern. The truck was immediately surrounded by the heavily armed *danzan* squadron guarding the position.

Mikhail Shevchuk greeted them, standing beside the two SS–25s on their mobile launchers. "Where is Kalin?" he asked, suspiciously.

"Dead," replied Kumarov through trembling lips.

The *danzan* weapons engineer took the news impassively. "Rodionov is in charge?"

Kumarov nodded.

"Let us begin!" spluttered Holtzmann, not following the

conversation. "How long to load the warheads into the missiles?"

"Twenty minutes," said Shevchuk, turning to begin.

Holtzmann walked to the far side of the chamber, his boots rapping on the concrete floor, gripped his hands together, his soul ready to detonate. He cast his eyes about the cavern; heavily defended, with entrenched artillery pieces and machine-gun nests. He stared out over the grim mountain. "You have communications with the Monastery?" he asked finally.

Shevchuk did not even look up as Kumarov translated. "Of course."

"It's time," said Stone, sitting with Mitford outside the Oval Office. Two minutes later they were ushered in to join the President and his National Security Council.

"Firyubin can't be found," said the President in a monotone. "We tell the Israelis." Myron Berkeley was downcast as Kirkland continued. "We let the Mossad squad operate off the *South Dakota*. They've requested Tomahawks but I cannot agree to any direct offensive involvement on our part— you have to understand, Stone."

He turned to his speaker-phone. "Michael?"

The Ambassador's voice came on line from the UN building in New York. "Yes, Mr. President?"

"You'll have to stall the Security Council," said Kirkland. "Tell 'em we're still trying to track down Firyubin. Even the Russians will believe that."

There was a pause as Michael Fitzpatrick digested this.

"When it comes time," continued the President, "we'll deal with our explanation as we see fit. All going well, the Israelis will take the heat."

Stone glared at him. *The Israelis will take the heat?*

"Yes, Mr. President," Fitzpatrick could not keep the dubiousness from his voice, but Kirkland ignored it.

"A surgical strike is all it'll be, Michael," he concluded.

"Otherwise the Congress will have my head. I'll advise you of the outcome."

He turned to the gathering. "That's it!" he said simply, in the tone of a man who has made an immutable decision. "Mitford and Stone, you will continue to liaise with the *South Dakota* and keep James and Myron informed. Tell the Israelis it's in and out—or we leave 'em there."

Stone nodded.

"My God, I hope we're doing the right thing," sighed Kirkland as the men filed out of his office.

As he felt the submarine rise through the water, Elazar's mind spun around its new central point. *Would they be in time?*

"Surface!" came the call.

Ten miles off the Armestan coast a patch of sea suddenly split into foam as the huge vessel broke the surface. As big as a World War Two heavy cruiser, the *South Dakota* wallowed in the swell, dark grey in the murky green ocean as massive hydraulics drove the extended flaps outwards from the flight deck. Hatches opened and men poured from them onto the flat expanse of the staging and take-off area. Two stood apart.

"It is good, Ari," the first shouted above the rasp of the waves washing against steel.

"Yes, it is good, Colonel Ganor," said the other. "We will fly."

"Colonel Elazar!" Colonel Ishmael Ganor reported over the intercom. "We can go with Pishay-Avot."

Then both men descended into the hangar area and climbed into their respective Apache helicopter gunships.

"Launch Operation Pishay-Avot," Elazar's voice rang through the control room. Captain Duchesne saw the fire in his eyes.

"Launch Operation Pishay-Avot," repeated *South*

Dakota's commander. The rumbling of the hangar doors opening sounded and he turned towards Elazar again.

But he was gone.

The Jeeps were passing through the scree-ridden desolate slopes of lower Barkusk when Kane ordered a halt. Jumping from the vehicle, and gesturing Rodionov and Kumarov's men out, he led them to the other Jeep.

"Out of the suits," he said. "But not you Rodionov." He and Lena stripped the isolation suits off, and Kane methodically slashed the tyres of the second vehicle.

"Lena—tell them they stay here, for their own sakes," he said. Lena quickly translated, then she, Kane and Rodionov remounted their Jeep and set off again up the slopes of the mountain.

Twenty minutes later, they again jerked to a stop.

"Where, Rodionov?" asked Kane.

Reluctantly the *danzan* general raised a hand and pointed to a barely visible overhang of rock about half a mile further up the mountain.

Kane studied it carefully in the late afternoon light. Even from a distance, he could see it was an easily defendable position, with only one access road. He frowned, then withdrew the ComMod from his jacket, reading Elazar's earlier message grimly. The *Sayeret Matkal* were at least forty minutes away, he realised, even if they'd been airborne the instant the deadline expired. "Damn!" he muttered, then flashed a message back to the *South Dakota*. The coordinates for their position would automatically be discerned by its inbuilt Global Positioning System, but he added a physical description of the missile launch site.

"What?" asked Lena, observing him. His eyes flashed to her, then Rodionov.

"The cavalry," he said grimly. "I hope."

"What now?" she replied.

Kane's eyes scanned the slope ahead. "There—" He indicated a circle of boulders fifty yards to the west, and they idled towards it. From the cover the huge stones provided, Kane had a clearer view of the site. He chewed his lip as he weighed up the situation.

"I've got to go up, Lena," he said. "With Rodionov."

She nodded, scared. "Kane—"

"It's okay," he said, even though it wasn't. "What defences up there, Rodionov?"

The *danzan* general's eyes were red with rage, his lips white. "Two companies. AA, artillery and machine-guns," he said gazing at Kane with pure hatred.

Then hatred turned to desperation, and with a sudden movement born of fury and hopelessness the *danzan* commander snatched at Kane's rifle and whipped him across the temple with its barrel.

"Now!" he spat, his finger tightening on the trigger.

The first helicopter rose on its elevator-pad to the broad surface of the *South Dakota*'s flight-deck. Swiftly its rotor unfurled, its rear assembly swinging around and locking into place. The whir of its motor was already beginning as it was rolled to its take-off position, making way for the second Apache rising from the hangar area.

"Apache One away," Captain Duchesne heard the report in the control room.

"Apache Two away!" Duchesne looked around. Where was Elazar? he wondered.

"Apache Three away!"

Shevchuk looked around at Holtzmann. "They are loaded," he said. Kumarov's translation carried from the metal desk where he was sitting, head in hands.

"Excellent," breathed Holtzmann.

"Now we wait," said the *danzan* weapons engineer.

"We wait?" Holtzmann growled when he understood. *"We wait?"*

"Señor," muttered Kumarov, trudging across the cavern to him. "Shevchuk says he must wait for Rodionov's authority to fire, he will try to contact him at the Monastery but—"

Holtzmann stiffened. "We will not wait!" he shouted. "That missile is *mine!*"

Shevchuk turned to Kumarov.

"Nyet," he said after a second and, meeting the Colombian's baleful stare, shouted an order which echoed through the chamber.

Holtzmann brought his fists up in fury, his eyes flashing wildly. He saw the *danzan* guards approaching, guns levelled. "You will be sorry!" he shouted, pushing roughly past the troops to the outside of the cavern.

Shevchuk watched him, then turned to Kumarov.

"He is mad," he said simply.

"Yes," answered the other.

Holtzmann stared out, his body shuddering with anxiety, his mind eroding under the stress of being held back from his revenge. Then he saw a glint of silver on the slope below.

"Kumarov!" he shrieked a second later.

Lena did not stop to think as she slammed her fist against Rodionov's neck and felt the phial smash under the blow.

Kane felt Rodionov's body slacken for an instant. With all the force he could muster he slammed his shoulder into the bigger man, propelling them both out of the Jeep. As they fell, Kane saw Rodionov's split-second expression of horror behind his mask.

Rodionov hit the ground hard, his body thumping against the rocks. He felt his chest heave, felt himself gasp against his will, felt the fetid air inside his isolation suit enter his lungs. There was a second of overwhelming shock. His hand felt for the phial, its broken shards in his neck.

Then he screamed, wailing like a child, rocking on his knees, hands tearing at his mask.

"Lena!" shouted Kane, rolling away from him and grabbing the rifle from the ground.

Lena was still in the Jeep, transfixed by Rodionov's terrible sound of fear, as Kane scrambled behind the wheel. He started the vehicle and pulled away, slinging the rifle back to her.

"Keep down!" he yelled.

Then the first rattle of machine-gun fire sounded from the cavern above.

"It is the *yanqui!*" Holtzmann roared above the din as the *danzan* troops opened up on the fleeing jeep. "And the woman—the infected woman!"

Shevchuk, binoculars to his eyes, watched as Rodionov threw the mask away and stumbled up the slope towards them. His commander's unearthly shriek carried to his ears.

"Cover him!" he shouted. A squadron of troops rushed from the cavern and started down towards Rodionov.

As Holtzmann watched, fear descended upon him. Fear of what the unfolding events meant.

"You will *not* stop me!" he swore aloud.

A few minutes later, surrounded by his men, Rodionov fell into the cavern. *"No!"* he howled again and again. His eyes rolled in his head, and he spun around.

"Hawke you will die!" he bawled. Then he collapsed at their feet.

The bullets exploded around them and Lena cried out as a round grazed her head. Blood clouded her vision and Kane desperately skewed the jeep to avoid the fire.

"Kane, I'm hit!" Lena yelled, but he did not answer.

He had no time to.

CHAPTER **TWENTY-FOUR**

Eight minutes into the launch of Operation Pishay-Avot, all five of the AH–64A Apache gunships had lifted off the *South Dakota*'s flight deck. They circled the massive submarine awaiting their charges; two UH–60A Black Hawks carrying the *Sayeret Matkal* squadron.

"Hawk One, away!" the flight deck officer reported.

Elazar stood beside him, watching as the desert-camouflaged chopper lifted from the *South Dakota*. The second Black Hawk rolled off the elevator pad to its take-off position. Elazar nodded to the officer beside him and, stooping as he approached it, took his place among his men. Looking out at the gently pitching flight-deck, he listened as the all-clear was given and the Black Hawk hovered clear of the sub.

"Let's go, Ari!" Elazar heard the *Sayeret Maktal*'s field commander over the headset from the lead Apache.

"Affirmative!" whooped the other. The air-cavalry unit wheeled through the sky and swooped towards Armestan, the Black Hawks surrounded by the Apaches—deadly wasps around their queens.

"Colonel Elazar," the pilot's voice crackled through his headset over the din of rotors.

"Yes?" Elazar shouted into his mouthpiece.

"The *South Dakota*, sir," came the response. "Captain Duchesne—"

"Sonofabitch, he's gone with them!" Duchesne gasped as he confirmed Elazar was on board the chopper. He turned from the communications desk. "The man must be seventy!"

MacKenzie looked up at his commander.

"If we all had such endurance," Duchesne shook his head in disbelief. Then, smiling despite himself, he issued another order.

"Missile room," he barked. "Are the Tomahawks ready?"

"Aye, aye, sir," came the curt response.

"Lieutenant MacKenzie," said Duchesne. "Get me Washington again."

The jeep screeched to a stop as soon as they were out of range of the *danzan* guns.

"I'm sorry," sobbed Lena. "I should have shot—"

Kane examined her head wound, then held her to him. "You did fine, Lena." He tore a strip of cloth from her shirt and roughly bandaged her injury.

"Will they get here—?" she asked.

"God knows," whispered Kane, his eyes fixed on the western horizon. "Mordy!"

Lena pulled back from him and stared at his etched face. Bullets *pock-pocked* behind them. They were together, and alone, in enemy territory.

"Kane . . . will we make it?" she breathed.

Rodionov was silent, shivering with fear and rage as he watched the disappearing dot of the Jeep. He sensed Holtzmann at his side but did not avert his eyes from the target of his fury.

"General," growled the voice next to him. "Who is he?"

"His name is *Kane!*" replied Rodionov through clenched teeth.

A coldness washed through Holtzmann.

"Shevchuk," shouted Rodionov, whirling around. "The missiles—?"

"They are armed and ready," Shevchuk replied. "Kirkusk and Israel."

"Damn Kirkusk! Damn Israel!" Rodionov swore in a chilling undertone, thinking only of revenge. His mind was a chaos of deathly images; of Tumakoc, of Kane. And of Kalin's death.

"Damn the *Amerikantsy!*" he shouted finally. He grasped Shevchuk by the shoulders.

"The SS–25," he rasped. "It can reach America?"

Holtzmann looked quickly at Kumarov, who whispered the translation.

"General," the Colombian stepped forward suddenly. "You cannot—"

"Silence!" roared Rodionov, then brought his face close to Holtzmann's. "You will *not* order me."

Holtzmann fixed him with narrowed eyes.

"I too will have my vengeance," the *danzan* commander went on. "Kane has infected me!"

Holtzmann stumbled back. "No!"

"Yes!" hissed Rodionov. "Inside the isolation suit. He put the virus inside the suit!"

"Rodionov," barked Holtzmann, his mind under siege and more calculating for it. "If you die, what use is Kirkusk? And if he was bluffing, what is your war without the funds I hold?"

Rodionov stared at him.

"Fire *your* missile not at Kirkusk but Washington!" Holtzmann's voice rang out. "Mine *must* go as planned, *do you understand?*"

With Holtzmann's logic penetrating the fog of his terror and rage, Rodionov found himself nodding.

"Can it be done, Shevchuk?" he whispered, not taking his eyes off Holtzmann.

"I will see," said the weapons engineer, scuttling to his desk. A moment later his calculation was done.

"Range to Washington is 9,250 kilometres," he said. "The SS–25 has an outer range of 10,500. It is possible. Will I reprogram—?"

"*Yes!*" swore Rodionov.

Shevchuk nodded and turned away.

"*Immediately!*" Holtzmann's voice echoed.

"And now," said Rodionov, his eyes glittering. "I will find Kane!"

"The *South Dakota!*"

Stone strode to the console. They were in the White House situation room, the central communications base for US military operations. Beside Stone were Mitford and General Westaway.

"Washington, Captain Duchesne—*South Dakota,*" came the Bostonian accent. "Request again, permission to use Tomahawks on enemy missile position."

Stone glanced at Westaway. The Chairman of the Joint Chiefs of Staff rolled his eyes.

"*South Dakota*—ETA for the Israelis?" he snapped.

"Twenty—repeat two zero minutes, Washington," came the crisp reply.

Westaway rubbed his furrowed brow. "I don't know," he said to Stone and Mitford.

"*South Dakota,*" snapped Stone. "Standby."

"Washington," Duchesne's voice sounded more urgent. "Kane believes the missile firing is imminent."

"*Believes?*" Westaway repeated. "It's not enough, Stone. The President's not going to launch us into this—"

"General," growled Stone. "Go to the President again. Give him the damn option!"

Westaway looked at him furiously, shook his head and left.

"*South Dakota,*" said Stone urgently. "Permission being sought. Tell Kane to get closer!"

"Roger, Washington," Duchesne replied tersely. "Out."

"Get fucking closer," Stone hissed to himself. "But stay alive!"

The ComMod was on open connection to the *South Dakota,* and Kane received the message almost the instant it was sent from the submarine. He drew breath as he read the words.

"Kane—look!" Lena exclaimed. He lifted his eyes and saw three jeeps leave the cavern, loaded with *danzan* troops.

"Rodionov," he breathed, as the vehicles began to ascend the mountain. "Got to check their readiness," he said, looking around. He had no choice. "Lena, you've got to come with me."

"Kumarov," said Holtzmann, unable to contain his foreboding and his memory of the Israeli air strike on Shaklin.

The Russian looked at him.

"If it is Kane," Holtzmann continued, "he will not be alone. They may attack us here."

Kumarov stared into the pits of Holtzmann's dark eyes.

"Do you want your creation to be destroyed, Kumarov?" barked Holtzmann. *"Do you?"*

Kumarov shook his head. "No . . . I—"

"Then tell *him,*" Holtzmann jerked his head towards Shevchuk. "Tell him to fire the missiles, now!" Holtzmann pushed Kumarov towards the launchers, still lowered in their transport position.

Shevchuk looked around as they came up. Kumarov blurted out Holtzmann's suspicions in Russian. The weapons engineer glanced nervously out of the cavern.

"The second missile is now ready," he said quickly.

"Can they be fired together?" asked Holtzmann.

"No," Kumarov translated. "Each must be clear of the other."

"Then let us do it!" the Colombian all but shrieked.

Shevchuk nodded and issued a single command to the men gathered around the launchers.

Within seconds, the transports chugged into life and the massive launch assemblies were towed to their firing position outside the cavern. Shevchuk yelled another command. Engines were cut. He walked to the control panel on the first launcher, checked the flight coordinates one last time and then flicked a switch. Hydraulics groaned as, almost imperceptibly, the first SS–25 was raised.

Holtzmann's eyes gleamed as they followed its progress. "Death will find you!" he whispered.

"No!" gasped Kane as he saw the launchers roll out of the cavern. They were a thousand yards from the launch site, and he could hear the sound of Rodionov's squadron closing on them. He checked his army belt. He had two handgrenades, his standard kit. That was all. He scrabbled for Lena's forgotten pistol on the floor of the Jeep.

"Keep going," he shouted, dropping his rifle next to her and pulling himself from behind the wheel. "Keep going north." He looked at her for a second. "Get away from here."

"Kane—" she started but he had spun away from the jeep and was racing down the mountain in a stooped sprint.

"No, Kane," she croaked.

Then she heard the roar of Rodionov's patrol behind her.

"Oh, God," she screamed as she gripped the wheel and the Jeep once again revved into life.

* * *

Kane paused momentarily. Behind him, Rodionov's squadron halted and there was distant shouting. He had been spotted. Below, the first launcher slowly raised its SS–25 into firing position.

Groaning in fear and frustration, he pulled the ComMod from his jacket and flashed a message to the *South Dakota*. Then, with the first of his pursuer's bullets cracking over his head, he set off again.

"Blyad!" Rodionov yelled, his eyes following Kane's hunched figure zig-zagging between boulders. "Go! Go!" he bellowed, driving his men on, his desire to kill Kane possessing him totally.

Kane glanced back as he ran and saw them coming. Saw also the dust cloud of Lena's jeep tearing north. The missile was now in its final position. He was almost close enough. He saw Shevchuk approach the first launcher.

No! his mind shrieked. In that instant he tripped on the loose surface and tumbled out of control down the rocky slope, striking a boulder with brutal force. He tried to move but a broken rib jagged his flesh from within. He looked helplessly on, then pulled himself into a crawling position and inched closer to the cavern. He screamed aloud in pain as he dragged himself to the top of a small hillock overlooking the cavern entrance. With difficulty he unclipped a hand-grenade from his belt, armed it and threw it.

A jolt of agony ripped though his body. Muscles had been torn by his effort, yet the hand-grenade rolled uselessly down the slope and exploded well away from the missile. He ground his teeth against the ricocheting pain and armed his remaining hand-grenade. In a supreme effort of will he tottered to his feet and flung the grenade towards the launcher. Then he fell heavily to the ground, battling the fog threatening to envelop him. He reached for his pistol. It was gone.

* * *

"No!" Lena shrieked as she saw him fall. She pulled the Jeep behind a natural rock wall. Her face set in an expression of grim determination, she wedged the rifle next to her, and started back.

"The *South Dakota*!" came the urgent shout.

"Go ahead—*South Dakota*!" snapped Stone.

"Kane reports one missile in firing position," replied Duchesne.

"Goddamn!" hissed Stone.

"Roger, *South Dakota*. Standby," he said, snatching the telephone handset that would connect him to the President, wherever in the White House he was.

"Mr President, this is General Stone," he exclaimed a second later as Kirkland answered. "At least one missile is about to be fired. Request authority for the *South Dakota* to use its cruise missiles."

There was a pause. Mitford looked at Stone from the far side of the situation room—saw his features tighten.

"But Mr. Pres—!" the big general reacted. He was stock-still as he replaced the handset. *"South Dakota,"* he intoned mechanically. "Negative."

"Roger, Washington," came the curt reply. "Out."

Stone stared at Mitford. No words were necessary.

"Mr. President, it would have drawn us into a situation we could not have afforded to be in when the dust from this thing settles," Myron Berkeley reassured Kirkland as he replaced the phone. The National Security Adviser was standing behind his chair, holding it tightly. "General Westaway, don't you agree?"

"What I said," Westaway replied nervously as he watched President Kirkland's inner tension escalate. "Tomahawk is subsonic—wouldn't reach the target that much before the Israelis—"

"This feels wrong," his commander-in-chief broke in. "We're standing by and . . ." his voice trailed off. He struggled to compose himself.

"I'm going to the situation room, Myron," he said. "You start advising our friends on the Hill about this. If the Israelis need help—if this thing winds up one more notch—I'm goddamned going to give 'em everything we can muster. And General—you make sure Jerusalem is aware of every last piece of intelligence."

With that he strode from the room. Westaway looked at Berkeley.

"What do you think?" he asked lamely.

"I think we have no friends on the Hill," replied Berkeley.

Flying close over the terrain at nearly two hundred miles per hour, the five Apaches and two Black Hawks thundered towards their target. Elazar chewed his lip as the seconds eked by. He saw nothing, heard nothing—his mind was devoured by anxiety.

"Pishay-Avot leader!" Duchesne's voice squawked in his headset. "*South Dakota*—Kane reports one missile in firing position. Washington negative on Tomahawks."

Now Elazar's rheumy eyes came into focus.

"Roger," he replied, staring ferociously ahead. "Out."

Holtzmann stood watching the final moments of the prelaunch process. He had seen it before, during the strike on Tumakoc; he knew how close his vengeance was. He did not see Kane's grenade bounce off the lip of the cavern and down.

Suddenly there was an explosion and Shevchuk was tossed backwards from his position at the missile. Holtzmann raced to him, his mind reeling. The Russian groaned feebly, a shard of metal protruding from his forehead, a deep gash in his neck. Uncaring of his injury and his pain, Holtzmann grabbed his shoulders and dragged him back towards the launcher.

"Fire it!" he screamed at the near-unconscious man. *"Fire!"* Pulling him upright, Holtzmann slapped his face again and again until Shevchuk's arm finally reached out and one by painful one, he depressed the final buttons in the launch sequence. After his finger had fallen for the last time, his head lolled back. Holtzmann dragged him from the launcher and waited.

Seconds later a low rumble began deep within the casing of the SS–25. Holtzmann dropped to his knees, entranced. The main rocket detonated, the missile trembled with its thrust, and slowly rose.

"Father!" hissed Holtzmann. "Father . . ."

Kane shuddered as he heard the unmistakable sound. Scrabbling desperately for his ComMod, fighting unconsciousness, he tapped out a desperate two word message. *Missile away.*

Then he blacked out from the pain.

•

"My God . . ." muttered Duchesne as the message was received by the *South Dakota*.

"Missile away," shouted MacKenzie.

"Target two miles!" shouted Ari Mosher in the lead Apache. They were twenty seconds from the launch site.

"Missile away."

"There!" shouted his co-pilot Gideon Arendt, pointing. Like a surreal picture they saw the missile rising slowly from the earth, angled towards them, accelerating with every second. Mosher jabbed his finger onto his weapons console. Immediately, two Sidewinder AA missiles fired beneath his chopper.

"Too close," shouted Arendt behind him. The Sidewinders would not have time to lock onto their target. The massive enemy missile filled their windscreen as the Sidewinders tore uselessly by it. The SS–25 was now no more than an eyeblink away, but it was enough time for both men to understand what had to be done. Two pairs of hands tightened on controls.

"Jerusalem, Ari!" screamed Gideon Arendt.

"To Jerusalem!" came his pilot's last words as with a whip of his hand he spun his Apache directly into the accelerating missile. The first explosion occurred within microseconds as the SS–25 plunged into the chopper. But still the missile charged skywards, through the incinerated Apache and the remains of its crew. It was almost clear of the suspended fireball when a second explosion erupted around it; the Apache's own weapons—missiles and cannon shells—going up. For a splitsecond it seemed to those watching, horrified, from the remaining choppers that their comrades' deaths had been in vain, but then, in a searing flash, the SS–25's casing split apart and its solid fuel stage detonated, hurling its multiple warheads airwards.

"To Jerusalem," prayed Elazar for the two brave men.

As she struggled to control the jeep, Lena saw the explosion, glimpsed the specks of warheads tumble through the sky and flash soundlessly above Novominsk as they detonated. Then she heard the shots below.

Kane was surrounded.

She kicked the Jeep's accelerator to the floor. "No!" she yelled as she hurtled towards him.

"Kane!" shouted Rodionov, raging at his enemy's unconsciousness. He smashed a backhanded fist into his face. Kane grunted and slowly his eyes opened. *"The virus!"* he screamed. "Was it in the bottle?"

Kane looked up, blood gushing from his mouth. All he could think about was the missile.

"Stop the others," he grunted.

Rodionov hit him again, pulping his nose. "Tell me!" he bellowed. *"Tell me!"*

Kane's eyes glinted with a confidence only the certainty of death can bring. "Stop the missiles, Rodionov—" he croaked through broken lips. "Kumarov . . ." his words trailed off as he struggled to stay conscious.

Rodionov's face drained of blood, his eyes flared with hatred. He reached across to one of his men.

"A gun," he growled. "Give me your gun."

Lena did not think, did not give herself time to.

"Kane," she screamed, driving headlong down the mountain. The Jeep careened over the loose rocks, threatening to overturn. She saw Kane's tormentor hit him again. Her hands tightened on the wheel; every muscle in her body was dedicated to steering the vehicle.

"Kane!"

"General!" came the urgent shout, startling Rodionov as he raised the gun. Kane threw his arms up with all his remaining strength and gripped the barrel. Rodionov fired once, and the bullet exploded into the dirt next to Kane's head. He rolled over, still hanging on, bucking beneath the muzzle's wavering death. Bullets spewed into the ground as Rodionov's finger locked around the trigger and Kane knew that at any second one could intersect with his head, knew there was no hope, but his being refused to succumb and within the hell-fire surrounding him he fought desperately to live.

Ducking the first stream of bullets, Lena spun the Jeep towards the largest group of Rodionov's men, feeling the vehicle plough into them, jolt, then break free of the collision. Looking up, turning the wheel wildly to maintain control, she screamed as a bullet caught her high in the shoulder. With one arm she turned the Jeep in a skidding arc back towards the *danzan* soldiers. She knew she could not last much longer, and, gritting her teeth in a fury beyond fear, her eyes locked onto the struggling figures at the centre of the group.

It was Rodionov's massive bulk that saved Kane. As Lena's Jeep hit the huge fighter it jagged him and skewed away from the point of impact. Kane lay on his side, not understanding what had happened, just watching blankly as Rodionov's life was ground out of him between the Jeep and the cruel rocky surface.

Only then did he see Lena fall from the Jeep and lie still on the ground.

The smoke from the massive explosion still hung before the cavern. Holtzmann could see nothing and, what was worse, did not know for certain which missile had been fired and destroyed. His body quaking with rage, he dragged Shevchuk towards the second launcher.

"Kumarov," he howled. "Help me!"

But in his bewilderment, the Russian stood still. Holtzmann pulled Shevchuk upright. Though he was dying, the agony of his injury was bringing the *danzan* weapons engineer out of his stupor.

"It was destroyed," Holtzmann screamed into his ear. "The first missile was destroyed! *What was its target?*"

Shevchuk didn't answer. Like an automaton, he flicked the switch to raise the second missile to its firing position. His fingers dropped to the control panel but he could not bring the screen into focus. He felt the keyboard beneath his fingers, closed his eyes and saw the console in his mind's eye. With three agonising keystrokes he began the launch procedure.

"This is to Jerusalem?" Holtzmann bellowed—in his hysteria caring only about the city in which his father had died. But still Shevchuk did not answer.

"Helicopters!" came Kumarov's shriek.

"No!" roared Holtzmann, whirling around.

Shevchuk opened his eyes. Grinding his teeth against the pain of his coming death, his blurred gaze searched for a switch. Found.

Another? Found.

He depressed the firing button. The final sequence had begun.

"To Jerusalem?" Shevchuk heard Holtzmann shriek.

"Attacking!" shouted Manny Eliav. His Apache now flew in the lead position and the Hellfire air-to-ground missiles he had just fired streaked towards the cavern.

"Roger. Attacking." He heard his wingman's voice on his headset.

Seconds later the first Hellfire struck, exploding in the mouth of the cavern and obliterating the view.

"Down! Down!" he heard the order to the Black Hawk pilots as he wheeled around for another attack.

The four Hellfires failed to hit the launchers but they destroyed the cavern almost totally. Those inside were caught in a red hot blast that threw them further inwards, killing many of them as it did. Standing outside in the lull, unharmed, Holtzmann's gaze was blind, staring into the dark abyss of his soul; to the yearning he so willed to be satiated. Then he looked around through the smoke and fire, the rocks, debris, and destruction, and saw the missile, untouched, still aiming towards the sky. He felt its dull rumble begin. The roar grew louder and louder. He saw Kumarov, thrown clear, bleeding from his head, lying as if dead.

Holtzmann scrambled towards the launcher, stumbling over the low walls of stone that had been thrown up by the explosions. Now he stood by the quaking SS–25. His hope; his last reason for existence. He saw that it was going to be.

He saw Shevchuk had been thrown directly beneath the rocket of the missile by the blasts of the attacking helicopters, his legs mangled.

Holtzmann slammed his fists into the steel of the launcher as the rumble grew louder and louder. Every skerrick of his being willed it to fire.

"Jerusalem!" he screamed in triumph as the noise grew louder and drowned the racket of the attacking helicopters and the din of his soul. There was another explosion, but again the missile escaped.

"Jerusalem!" he wailed again as he watched the looming shapes of the helicopters swoop towards him.

Then Shevchuk—his expression twisted, his life measured in seconds—jerked his head up and spoke. "*Nyet . . .*"

Holtzmann dropped down beside the dying man. His hands wrapped around his throat, trying to throttle the lie that burned into his brain. "No," he croaked, his hands tightening around Shevchuk's neck. "*Jerusalem!*"

In the final ghastly moment before the rocket detonated and his body was lost in a gush of flames, Shevchuk stared back. And shook his head.

Then he exploded in the thundering ignition of the missile's firing. Thrown back but uncaring, Holtzmann's howl began, rising above the turbulent sounds of the missile beginning to lift off. He fell to the floor, clawing at it, maddened by the last words he had heard.

Then the missile was gone.

"*No!*" shouted Elazar as he clambered to the cavern with his men. The SS–25 was ten feet above the earth now, moving unstoppably skyward. The launcher was falling back when the soldier who had so long ago assured Kane he would whip Holtzmann's ass, raised the tube of a B–300 anti-tank rocket to his shoulder and fired. The rocket glanced off the missile, which shuddered from the impact. But as the anti-tank round detonated against the cavern wall, it was as if it had only served to speed its intended target's ascent towards the heavens.

"Inform base!" snapped Elazar. Then, silently, he watched the missile fly, soaring past the still-circling Apaches, into the azure sky. He watched until the flames were distant and its trail of smoke the only signs of its flight. He watched and prayed for his country.

Crawling towards Lena with Rodionov's gun in his hand, Kane was kept conscious only by the thought of her. Death had lost its bite. He heard the dull roar of the missile firing but he no longer cared. There was Lena and that was all. He looked ahead, face smeared and bleeding, fingers pulling him automatically along the ground. He had almost reached her when he saw the *danzan* soldiers; Rodionov's squad had reformed. Six men crested the ridge. And now they saw him.

"No," croaked Kane. Lena was stirring, writhing gently with pain as she came to. He struggled the final few yards to where she lay, held her and pushed them both towards the wrecked jeep until they were wedged beneath it; wedged against the unrecognisable mass of torn flesh that had been Rodionov. Kane braced his rifle between his knees and stared along its sights as the six men raised their own guns.

"Kane," whimpered Lena. But he did not have the strength to answer as his finger grabbed the trigger and he fired a burst towards the oncoming troops. He missed, and the thud of returning fire began around them.

"Kane!" her cry was part-pain, part-fear. Again his finger jerked the trigger and again he missed. Now the men were scarcely a hundred feet away. Kane ground his teeth, firing sporadic bursts. But although his gaze was fixed on their attackers, he was thinking solely of Lena. The *danzan* troops were only fifty feet from them. Without looking at her, he made his decision.

"I love you," he said, rolling away from the Jeep, firing indiscriminately, trying to draw their attackers' fire as he tumbled down the slope.

Lena's scream was constant as she reached out for him, then she could watch no more and scrambled further beneath the Jeep, oblivious to the fact that now she was all but cloaked by Rodionov's entrails.

The NSA satellite in geocentric orbit over the Mediterranean was the first link in the early-warning system to detect the missile. It was the first to report that the SS–25 was not targeted on Israel. The news flashed to Washington, thence to Israeli Air Defence HQ and the *South Dakota*.

Lieutenant MacKenzie passed it immediately to Elazar's squadron.

Holtzmann wept. His body shuddered as hideous uncertainty gripped it. Unthinking, uncaring, he crawled towards the cavern's opening and watched the trace of the distant missile in the sky. He opened his mouth to cry out but nothing came forth.

Because he heard the voice.

"Jorge Holtzmann—my name is Mordechai Elazar!"

Elazar stood just beyond the cavern, surrounded by the *Sayeret Maktal* squadron.

"Holtzmann!" he shouted again. "Jorge Holtzmann. My name is Mordechai Elazar."

He and his men stepped back at the sudden sound which issued from the cavern. A singular noise of hatred and rage the like of which they had never heard before—a thin strangled shriek, magnified by malignity.

Elazar shuddered, then spoke again. "Holtzmann—we

are tracking the missile. It will not hit Israel. *What is its target?*"

Holtzmann reeled, clutching what had become the remnant of his dream. He staggered at first towards the name so hated, then away, the world spinning him, disassembled, into insanity.

Kumarov, ebbing into consciousness, was the only witness to Holtzmann's torment. Like a maddened beast, still shrieking, he scrambled into the cavern's depths, then stood stock-still and looked out.

"My will!" he howled. "My will is the greater!"

Then he turned and ran.

"Manny!" shouted the co-pilot urgently. He signalled to the port side. "Could be Kane!"

Flight Lieutenant Manny Eliav spun the chopper into almost a full roll. The Apache's chain cannon was already clattering as he came around against the squadron attacking the lone man on the ground. In a second of murderous fire it was over. He spun the chopper slowly in the air on full hover, looking for other targets and saw a woman break from behind a Jeep and stumble towards the man lying face-up on the ground.

"Wounded!" snapped Eliav into the headset. "Fifty yards north-east of target, get up here—could be Kane."

Elazar heard the report flash through on his walkie-talkie as Holtzmann turned and fled.

"Colonel Ganor, your squadron after him!" he shouted, then turned and sprinted like a man of twenty out of the cavern, his unit behind him.

"Danny," he yelled into the walkie-talkie. Their medic was with the Black Hawks. "Get airborne. Wounded to evacuate. Eliav has the position."

"You don't get to die twice, Kane!" he swore with fierce determination.

Lena was oblivious to everything except Kane's body lying flat across her lap. His eyes were open, and he seemed strangely calm. That was what frightened her so much.

"Oh, Kane," she pleaded. "Please don't die!"

The Black Hawk lifted quickly and took only a minute to cover the ground to the hovering Apache. Daniel Goldbaum leapt from the chopper with his medical kit as Elazar and his men arrived.

"Is it Kane?" the medic asked Lena. She looked at him, and at Elazar standing behind. Then her head fell to Kane's chest and she heard the thump of his heart.

"Yes, it's Kane," she choked.

"Mr. President," Myron Berkeley's voice rang out across the situation room.

Kirkland turned around. All eyes were on the electronic screen marking the missile's trajectory. Soon it would reach its apogee and begin to descend. Then its precise target would be known.

"The Hill wants to hear from you now, sir!" Berkeley continued. "They're not happy. Coates and Johnson are in the Oval Office. And the UN, the Russians—"

"Not now, Myron," Kirkland broke in, his eyes fixed on the path of the missile. The speaker squawked again.

"*South Dakota*—Washington."

Stone replied to Duchesne's transmission. "Go ahead, *South Dakota.*"

"Colonel Elazar reports no other missiles at launch site. Kumarov captured. Kane wounded and being evacuated."

"Thanks, Captain," Stone responded, his gaze also locked on the missile-tracking screen. He went to speak again, but another voice swamped his.

"Now we get the hell out of there." It was Berkeley, striding forwards. Stone whirled around.

"*South Dakota*—repeat, Washington?" Duchesne could not keep the disbelief out of his voice. "The operation is proceed—"

"Listen, goddamnit," Berkeley exclaimed. "The Hill's in an uproar, the Russians have heard about it—they're threatening to launch an air assault in support of Kalin."

"Washington," Duchesne's voice snapped back. "Kalin is confirmed dead. The operation is incomplete. Colonel Elazar must confirm the destruction of the manufacturing facility—"

"Kane already reported it destroyed," yelled Berkeley. "Bring the Israelis in. This was a surgical strike, not a goddamn war!"

In the control room of the *South Dakota,* Captain Duchesne's blood suddenly boiled. "Listen, Washington," he fumed. "I'm duty bound to patch you through to Colonel Elazar directly. This operation is Israeli, we're only their goddamn bus ride!"

"What—?" began the voice from Washington but Duchesne paid it no heed.

"Lieutenant MacKenzie, patch this asshole through to Colonel Elazar!" he ordered through gritted teeth.

Stone was grey-faced and rigid as he listened to Berkeley. The President was also listening, but his greater concern was what was happening on the screen before him. The missile was about to turn back towards earth. Any minute now they would know.

"What is it, *South Dakota*?" Stone heard Elazar's unmistakable voice come on, followed by that of the submarine's commander.

"I'm not sure I can tell you that, Colonel," Duchesne said tersely. "We're on line with Washington."

"Yes?" snapped Elazar.

"Colonel Elazar," Berkeley began. "Bring your men back—all hell is breaking loose—"

Stone clenched his teeth.

"Negative," Elazar broke in, not caring to hear any more. "Apart from anything else, one of the missiles appears to have struck Novominsk itself. This place is going to be a disaster area in a matter of hours. You get the—"

"Don't you give me any goddamn orders," shouted Berkeley, recovering from the momentary bewilderment of being countermanded. "You get the hell—!"

"Listen, you sonofabitch!" Elazar roared. "We have an American journalist on the ground here. She's seen it all. This is no longer a clean in and out! Got it? Added to that, we have a possible virus outbreak looming in a city of over three hundred thousand people. You find the means of dealing with it and get them here within the next few hours or, like I said, you're dealing with a tragedy for which I'll make sure you're held personally responsible!" Elazar disconnected and Stone whooped inside.

Berkeley looked around but did not attempt to answer. White fury enveloped his features.

Kirkland turned to him. "He's right, Myron."

"Mr. President . . ." his National Security Adviser began, but then Clark Mitford—who had been so silent as to almost have been invisible—spoke.

"Look," he pointed to one of a bank of TV monitors on the far side of the situation room.

"WorldNet, Mr. President," he said. "It's out."

"Hey y'all—shut the fuck up!" The bellow jolted him out of his daze. Jack Mahoney glanced down the bar in its direction.

"Holy shit, will you look at that!" there was another shout. Mahoney focused through the day's intake of beer at the television blaring above the pool table. At first all he saw were bodies, hundreds of bodies. Then he saw Lena.

"Evidence of a weapon of mass destruction," she was saying. "We have seen thousands of dead this afternoon and have no doubt that tens of thousands more have been killed in this devastated city. This is Galena Chagall in Novominsk, Armestan."

Mahoney went to shout but his emotions gagged him. He stood still, gazing at the television, wrestling with his conflicting passion. "Lena!" her name finally tore from his lips.

"Shut up, bud," came the response from up the bar.

"We will continue feeding this material shot two days ago in the city of Tumakoc," intoned the local WorldNet anchor. "Apparently what we are seeing is a chemical or biological attack on the Muslim enclave in the north-east of Armestan. As we told you, this is a WorldNet special broadcast. We are feeding live from a transmission point in Baku, Azerbaijan where sound-recordist Harry Berg is on line. We have not previewed this material and strongly advise parents to keep children from watching. Now, Harry Berg in Azerbaijan, could you explain for us when and how this material was shot, and where you believe correspondent Galena Chagall is right now?"

Mahoney looked away, knocking over his glass and gripping the bar to quieten his trembling hands. He did not want to hear any more. Partly-joyous, partly-drunk, he stumbled out into the New York day. Outside he stared at the sun, feeling it permeate his stupor, ignoring the stares of passers-by as his instinct soothed him.

She was alive.

As the sun warmed his face, Jack Mahoney was as happy as he could ever remember being.

They landed heavily on the pitching deck of the *South Dakota*. Lena watched Kane being carried out, then climbed after him. As he disappeared under the urgent carriage of the submarine's medical staff, she stood and stared across the Black Sea.

"Don't make this a habit, Kane," she whispered out to the brooding coastline of Armestan.

Terry stirred awake.

"Harry," he groaned. "So this is heaven . . ."

Berg smiled at him. "Baku, Terry—you're in hospital, you're going to make it."

The Australian grimaced. "The tape?" he asked. Berg held it up and the cameraman sighed with relief through clenched teeth.

"Do us a favour, Harry?" he croaked. "Satellite the fucking thing to whoever wants it . . . there must be a ground station here somewhere."

"It's done, Terry," Berg's eyes moistened. "The whole fucking world has seen it."

As Terry smiled and closed his eyes, the realisation washed through his mind that it was the only time he had ever heard Harry Berg swear.

"Good on you, Harry," he muttered before falling asleep again.

"Alert! Alert!" screamed the intercom inside Israeli Air Defence HQ, deep beneath Jerusalem.

The SS–25 had raked through inner-space without a murmur in its circuitry. Shedding its solid fuel stage, its warhead began the long arc earthwards. Twelve batteries of Patriot Mark III anti-missile systems swung into firing positions as Israeli radar began to track the ICBM.

"Nathan," shouted the chief radar officer. His finger jabbed as the trajectory of the re-entry vehicle became clear. The men's mouths dried, both in relief and shock. A few seconds' calculation confirmed the NSA report; Israel was not the target.

"Standby," came the cry again. "Midcourse, single RV, appears to be set for . . ."

"DEW reports midcourse phase. Single RV inbound to the continental United States. Tracking now!"

"Oh, Holy Lord," breathed the President.

There was stunned silence in the room.

"What's the target?" said Kirkland through clenched teeth.

"Standby," came the response. "RV five minutes from terminal phase. Target—Washington, DC."

Holtzmann fled back through the cavern blindly, dashing against objects without caring, ricocheting further and further into the depths of Mount Barkusk until he was finally disgorged from a small tunnel onto the mountainside. Blinking wildly in the sudden glare, he heard his pursuers.

"No!" he screamed, stumbling down the rocky slope.

As Colonel Ishmael Ganor and his unit reached daylight, Holtzmann was well down the mountain; now running, now rolling; picking himself up to gesticulate madly at them, then fleeing anew.

"Ten minutes to impact . . ."

Kirkland was frozen with shock. Time compressed, the lives of those walking the streets of his city possessed him. Lives he had betrayed. In ten minutes, he knew, nearly a million Americans were going to fall victim to something he could have saved them from. He had once had weeks, now he had minutes. When he closed his eyes his mind played the images he had seen from Tumakoc, when he opened them the images were playing on the flickering TV above his head.

"Five minutes to impact. RV in terminal phase," the voice droned above the chaos of radio traffic and communications between the various arms of America's military establishment reporting their so-far uncoordinated attempts to deal with the imminent threat. They had been taken completely by surprise.

In the corner of the room, Myron Berkeley was slumped in a chair, watching the pandemonium blankly.

Over the east coast of the United States, fighter squadrons took off in waves, armed with the latest air-to-air weapons systems. Patriot Mk III batteries readied to lock onto the incoming SS–25 warhead.

All in vain.

The truth was that the United States did not possess an anti-missile defence system. It had not since 1976, when the Anti-Ballistic Missile Treaty led to the deactivation of all ballistic missile interceptor systems. President Reagan's "Star Wars" dream had never been more than that. The capital city of the world's most powerful nation was now just a huge target for the SS–25.

And the President of the world's most powerful nation could do nothing more than watch the dreadful descent of Holtzmann's final weapon.

The warhead was now unpowered. Grasped by gravity, it hurtled earthwards along its pre-ordained ballistic trajectory. Its velocity made it difficult to see, let alone provide a fix—visual or radar—for the weaponry which faced it. Shedding chaff to further confound any attempts to zero in on it, the warhead seared into the lower atmosphere untouched. It broke through ten thousand feet, within range of the Patriot anti-missile batteries. The sleek missiles were fired from their multiple launchers. Thirty-six Patriots tried and failed to lock onto the warhead. The countdown in the White House situation room was like a doomsday clock.

"Impact fifteen seconds," came the voice through the speaker. Myron Berkeley let out a choking sound.

"Passing through five thousand feet," said the voice. Glances were exchanged between those in the room.

There was cloud cover at fifteen hundred feet over

Washington DC—the altitude at which the sensor in the SS–25's reentry vehicle was primed to detonate a small charge and disperse the virus culture as an aerosol cloud.

At a thousand feet the warhead burst through the cloud.

Intact.

"RV failure," the speaker voice intoned.

In the scant seconds that remained only Stone realised what had to be done.

"Fix the point of impact!" he shouted. "Evacuate the area immediately. Mr. President—" he whirled on Kirkland. "We'll need executive authorisation to mobilise everything in the impact zone."

Kirkland nodded.

"Communications!" Stone commanded. "Army, airforce, navy, National Guard, city and county police, fire department—we need everything around that impact point as soon as possible. Find any service or agency with biological defence units and or isolation equipment and get 'em—"

A chilling voice interrupted him. "Five, four, three—"

With its supersonic thunderclap preceding it, the eight-foot long SS–25 warhead passed over the White House at barely five hundred feet. Over West Potomac Park at three hundred feet. The Potomac River at two hundred, where it was glimpsed by commuters on the Arlington Memorial Bridge. Over the John F. Kennedy Gravesite at fifty feet.

"Two, one. Impact," came the voice.

"Jesus Christ, where is it?" screamed President Kirkland.

There was a massive explosion of earth as the warhead plunged into the soft turf of Arlington National Cemetery at two thousand miles per hour, drilling nearly thirty feet into the ground. When the first members of the cemetery ground staff reached the crater, they heard a hissing sound. Five men peered with astonished expressions into the pit at the crater's centre, trying to determine what had struck the earth with such impact. Three breathed the first wisps of the virus as it spiralled invisibly into the atmosphere.

"Impact point—Arlington National Cemetery," reported the voice.

"Stone," yelled Kirkland. "Get going—I want you on this." He snatched for his private line. "Get me Arlington Cemetery—make damn sure they know it's me!" he ordered. Then seconds later. "This is President Kirkland. A missile has just come down there. It contains a germ warfare agent. Every military, federal, state, county and city agency you can think of is getting to you. Get the area evacuated immediately and seal it—you got me?"

He replaced the phone, biting his lip, then turned to his Secret Service shadow. "I'm going over there," he said. As he turned to leave the situation room he noticed his National Security Adviser, head in hands, on the far side of the room.

"Myron," growled Kirkland. "Consider it your last act with this administration to get Colonel Elazar whatever he needs to deal with the situation in Novominsk."

Myron Berkeley looked up and nodded slowly.

Jorge Holtzmann reached the Monastery as darkness fell. It was there, in a scuffle with a fleeing *danzan* soldier outside the main gate, that the virus entered his lungs.

Inside the complex he saw that anarchy reigned. The main building which had housed Kumarov's lab was a smouldering ruin. In the courtyard, men were screaming, shooting wildly into the air, and a solid line of army vehicles jammed the road to Novominsk. Holtzmann did not understand the babbled Russian, but he understood what he saw, and seeing it, slunk away. At some point on his slow trek to Novominsk, knowing that there lay his only hope of shelter from his enemies, he stumbled upon a knife and used it to cut the beard from his face.

When the quarantine was declared at midnight, and the first NATO-assigned Starlifters began shuttling troops and medical personnel into Shaklin from Turkey, Holtzmann was trapped in Novominsk along with the three hundred and fifty thousand other unfortunates who were beginning to feel the bite of his creation. He was just one more, and a stranger; shunned by those who were also infected, those who did not care to help him, and those who simply did not understand his manic pleas.

As Novominsk—like Tumakoc before it—descended into chaos and hell, as the virus spread and the people poured into the streets, Holtzmann found a place from which he dared run no further. The virus was beginning to choke the last scraps of life from him as he crawled to a shattered window in a ruined building and stared out. He saw the desperate milling that would soon stop, heard the cries of children and wails of their parents that would also soon stop. Every sob surrendered by his disease-racked body reminded him that it was not the Jews, but he who was soon to die. He felt death's cold-steel claws tear his lungs. Dying was a sensation more terrible than even he had imagined it could be. His teeth chattered with terror and pain.

Then his death began in earnest, the final minutes. Wisps of oxygen circulated in his blood vainly, rigormortis set in while he was still alive. Fingers, hands, toes, feet—his death crept inwards, advancing; row after row of barbed icicles marching a slow paralysis towards his heart. And though he was scarcely still living, what remained alive remained aware. He still felt pain and he was still able to remember. He remembered Cortez's death and its progression. Dreadful hacking coughs seized him. He remembered Kalin's death. And that was worse—that as he died he knew he was surely going to and how. It gave substance to the hideous phantasms haunting him, flitting around his eyes, dancing in the dead air he exhaled, laughing at the pleas which flew piteously from his mouth along with the phlegm and bile from his body. Barely breathing now, every breath a choice between the pain of it and death, choosing only at the last moment to draw upon his scant remaining life to breathe and feel the air settle like acid in his lungs.

Now seeing all the more clearly what lay ahead of him and crying as he saw that the ghost of his father was not among those who beckoned with rotting fingers. Death punched through his thin ragged raw lungs with one final cold punch and he died horribly, twisted more cruelly than pain alone could cause, a final hellish expression set on his face.

EPILOGUE

A week after his evacuation—"more bandages than body"—Kane returned to Armestan with Lena.

With Mordechai Elazar at their side—they gazed out over the sea of tents and flags of the various governmental and charity groups that had been brought to Novominsk for the grisly task of coping with the plague. Two distinct rings of canvas roofs circled the city.

"Inner group is the frontline," Elazar explained, exhaustion dogging his words. "Victims are still coming in from Novo and surrounds. All we can do is give them morphine and help them die. We're trying to treat them, trying to find a vaccine or cure in case this hell is visited elsewhere, as Kumarov is still claiming it will be."

"You believe him?" Kane turned to the old Israeli.

"He is a psychopath," hissed Elazar. "He *wants* it to break out again."

"What's the count in Washington?" asked Kane after a time.

"Twenty-five," Elazar said with a bitter laugh. "Next to this . . ." He paused and sighed. Then he pointed to the outer circle of tents, denser and thicker than the inner group. "The morgues," he said simply.

The three of them climbed into Elazar's Jeep, and drove

slowly towards the inner ring of tents. Before reaching them, they passed huge, freshly-dug trenches.

"Mass graves," said Elazar. "It's what we've been forced to do. We have the bodies out for identification, but within another day . . ." his voice trailed off and he turned the Jeep slowly down a corridor between the morgue tents, pulling up beside one. "C'mon," he grunted, leading them in through its open sides.

"This is the foreigner's section," he said as he walked slowly in front of them. "International Brigade and such like—" Then he stopped.

"Oh, my God!" Lena reacted first.

Kane looked down and his eyes narrowed.

"Holtzmann!" he whispered, transfixed by the withered corpse and the frightful expression on its face. His head throbbed as he stared at the man who had desired such evil. Disgust erupted inside him. Lena screamed. She had wandered a few yards away and was now standing rigidly before another corpse.

"Peterson?" she gasped in shock, shaking her head as she gazed through wide eyes at the body.

"Yeah," muttered Kane. "He came to get you."

Lena started to cry. "You idiot," she said softly, turning and walking slowly away. Kane watched her, then joined Elazar who was still standing before Holtzmann's body.

"He is gone," said the Israeli in an undertone. "An anonymous death, as he deserved." Then he gripped Kane's shoulder. "Thank you."

Kane nodded.

"Come," he said softly, and together they left Holtzmann to eternity.

They were silent as they drove on through the aftermath of a war defeated by a tragedy. Each of them was possessed by their own thoughts, until finally Elazar pulled up again.

"Kumarov," he said as he alighted. "Here." He gestured into the rear of the jeep and they saw the isolation suits.

"Never wanted to get into another one of those in my life," Lena said brokenly.

"They're the fashion in the wasteland," replied Elazar grimly as they pulled the suits over their clothes. Once clad, they strode the twenty yards to the inner circle of tents around Novominsk, towards a large, pre-fabricated structure.

They walked in silently. Kane and Lena looked around. Six survivors were lying on their backs, wheezing horribly, close to death.

Elazar left them for a few minutes, then returned with three other men, also in isolation suits. Two were guards. The third was Gyorgy Kumarov.

Kane walked towards him, passing the barely mortal human beings on either side. The two guards obeyed Elazar's gesture to leave immediately.

As the soft *whoosh* of the door sealed them in, Elazar spoke.

"Look at them," he said, leading Kumarov to the first survivor. It was a young woman, her face a mask of anguish despite the painkiller dripping into her arm. Kumarov's eyes glittered behind his perspex mask.

"What do you think of your work, Kumarov?" asked Kane.

The Russian looked into his eyes. "It is magnificent!"

"We want a treatment," Elazar said steadily.

"No!" spat the Russian. Then he smiled. "Your governments will deal with me regardless of this. Regardless of any treatment. These people are not their concern—"

Elazar and Kane gazed at him helplessly—they were beyond rage, revenge or hatred. A sad expression settled on Lena's face as she regarded Kumarov. *What had Man become?* she wondered.

Kane uttered one word. "Please!"

But Kumarov shook his head. "No," he repeated. "I will deal with your superiors regarding my future."

Kane knew what he said was true; his government would buy Kumarov, keep him and his dread science for their own. Suddenly, in a movement too quick for Elazar to react to, even had he wanted, Kane's hand flashed out. In it was a knife. Staring at it, realisation came slowly to Kumarov. He saw Kane's eyes on his suit and followed them down, to the slit that had been opened in the gleaming material. Then he felt the hot air from the room assail his nostrils.

"No!" he screamed in horror. Kane waved to the laboratory equipment set up in the room.

"Cure yourself," he said slowly, then turned away, holding Lena for support as he did. With a glance at Kumarov, Elazar followed.

"No one in and *no one out!*" he said to the guards. Kane saw they were *Sayeret Matkal*.

Kumarov slumped to the floor, his head falling into his hands at the battle within him. The fear of death closed around him. He rocked on his knees before the laboratory bench. He did not want to die. He did not want to suffer. But he could not destroy what he had spent a lifetime creating. The unthinkable dilemma whirled around him and his genuflections became more and more frantic. The shriek which finally issued from his lips began deep within his soul.

But there was no one to hear him.

And there would be no one to watch him die.

It had been two months. Something propelled Mordechai Elazar from his desk in his Jerusalem office and he limped to his window, staring across the deepening glow which lit the old city. The spindly shadows of the trees on the Mount of Olives were like long black tendrils draped over the hill-

side. The spire of the Russian Orthodox church gleamed, as
did the golden orb of the Dome of the Rock. Beneath it the
Western Wall was cloaked in shadow.

It was a city he was now too old to defend, the reluctant
admission forced itself into his mind.

He thought of Kane, and Lena Chagall. He remembered
their farewell to him.

"Will you tell me the things no one else will about him,
Mordy?" she had asked half-seriously.

"If I did . . ." he had laughed. "The world would be a
rather too obvious place, wouldn't you agree?"

The memory brought a smile to the old man's lips as he
closed his office door and made his slow way home. As the
sun dipped low, he raised his hand in salute to the west. *To
the lovers!* he chuckled at the passing illicitness of his
thought, meeting the curious stare of a hawker trudging up
his street.

Then he paused at his door and looked behind him, to
the hills surrounding the city he loved, the city whose in-
spiration would doubtless house his soul in time. Towards
the memorial garden of Yad Vashem, where he had stooped
before four saplings and brushed the dirt from their plant-
ing off their brass plaques. His smile faded as he remembered the men he had lost. *True believers,* came the whisper
inside.

Then he turned and left his city and all it meant, behind
his closed door.

The nightmare again. The living envy the dead.

Their whispers fill his mind. Friends or enemies, it no
longer matters, there is no way of telling one from the
other. He walks between them. They rest mercifully in their
piles and mounds, in death uncaring of the decay and their
incompleteness, eaten by vermin already so diseased they
are immune. He wishes he could join them. He holds his
hands out but no one comes. Envy is his alone. But he

knows he must die, and the whispers tell him of the agonising path he must tread. The mounds give way to a vast sea of acid and he begins to walk towards it. Such a painful ocean! His body shudders at the certain knowledge of death and what lies between it and him. He turns back and sees the hornet swarm gathering, roaming from body to body, foraging for life. There is no escape from it as it inevitably senses him and spirals into the sky above.

He smiles with pity at himself, and at the majesty of the Armageddon which Man has wrought. Man's final step over the line, and he did not see it coming. A backdoor apocalypse, this devilish chameleon germ which ushered Man towards the warehouse of extinction, to become another curiosity among the many.

"The smell is what hits you isn't it?" he hears her voice in the muted chatter. He clambers desperately upon the rotting mounds searching for her but cannot find her, for faces have melted under the glare of the disease. The stench and the confusion cocoon him for a moment from his fate—but soon he knows he must emerge, a metamorphosis into another dimension which surely cannot be more cruel than the present. Now he sees a face, pressing against the thin wall of his cocoon. Who? A face so innocent and yet so diabolical. Oh yes! He who chose himself to be the lone horseman of this apocalypse. The face observes him not with pity but curiosity. The piper of Hamelin returning to find one left in the daylight.

The face draws even closer now, pushing through the mass of the dead, dripping with the ragged pieces of their bodies. An innocent face made more evil by the knowledge within. Evil eyes floating on such a virginal countenance. The face smiles and the obsidian eyes which once glittered with foul ambition glitter again with the malevolence of certainty. The face disappears for a moment and he hears it laugh before he sees it again, emerging from the gloom with a soft sucking noise. How quickly the dead have rotted!

Those who stood in line, hope searing them at every moment when all they wished for was an earlier place in the queue for death.

"And you?" whispers the face. "You are consigned to the living. You will be the envious."

"But there are no others," he replies, his answer magnified by the silence around it.

"That makes it worse," giggles the face and recedes. Oh, the horrible cackle which fills the air as the acid mists rise from the sea and the hornet swarm shrieks above.

"No!" Kane shouts aloud, bucking into consciousness; the electricity of his body has gathered enough force to wake him. A spark of hope, or of desperation? He gasps and looks at Lena, then arises silently and faces the mirror, skin slick with sweat and tears in the midnight gleam. The nightmare lingers, its shock wearing off too slowly.

He shakes himself as he turns from the mirror in the half-light. He cannot return to sleep, he knows that. He trudges towards the lounge room. The nightmare will not leave him. It is like an infection, and he knows it has taken hold. "Oh, God!" he sighs as he falls back into the armchair, still unable to avoid the grim slideshow in his head which plays on and on.

"Kane?" Lena appears before him. His tears dampen her neck.

"I love you!" he whispers, and holds her to him.

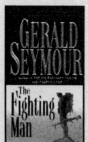

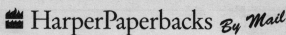

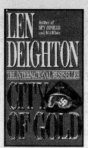

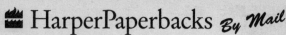